1997

1. Michael R. Pitts. *Western Movies*
2. William C. Cline. *In the Nick of Time*
3. Bill Warren. *Keep Watching the Skies!*
4. Mark McGee. *Roger Corman*
5. R. M. Hayes. *Trick Cinematography*
6. David J. Hogan. *Dark Romance*
7. Spencer Selby. *Dark City: The Film Noir*
8. David K. Frasier. *Russ Meyer—The Life and Films*
9. Ted Holland. *B Western Actors Encyclopedia*
10. Franklin Jarlett. *Robert Ryan*

1998

11. Ted Okuda *with* Edward Watz. *The Columbia Comedy Shorts*
12. R. M. Hayes. *3-D Movies*
13. Steve Archer. *Willis O'Brien: Special Effects Genius*
14. Richard West. *Television Westerns*

1999

15. Jon Tuska. *The Vanishing Legion: A History of Mascot Pictures*
16. Ted Okuda. *The Monogram Checklist*
17. Roy Kinnard. *Horror in Silent Films*
18. Richard D. McGhee. *John Wayne: Actor, Artist, Hero*
19. William Darby *and* Jack Du Bois. *American Film Music*
20. Martin Tropp. *Images of Fear*
21. Tom Weaver. *Return of the B Science Fiction and Horror Heroes*
22. Tom Weaver. *Poverty Row HORRORS!*
23. Ona L. Hill. *Raymond Burr*

ALSO BY ROY KINNARD

"The Lost World" of Willis O'Brien
(McFarland, 1993)

HORROR IN SILENT FILMS

A Filmography, 1896–1929

by Roy Kinnard

McFarland & Company, Inc., Publishers
Jefferson, North Carolina, and London

The present work is a reprint of the library bound edition of Horror in Silent Films: A Filmography, 1896–1929, first published in 1995. *McFarland Classics* is an imprint of McFarland & Company, Inc., Publishers, Jefferson, North Carolina, who also published the original edition.

Front cover: Lon Chaney in *The Phantom of the Opera* (1925)

Library of Congress Cataloguing-in-Publication Data

Kinnard, Roy, 1952–
    Horror in silent films : a filmography, 1896–1929 / by Roy Kinnard.
    p. cm.
    Includes bibliographical references and index.

    ISBN-13: 978-0-7864-0751-4
    (softcover : 50# alkaline paper) ∞

    1. Horror films—Catalogs. 2. Silent films—Catalogs. I. Title.
PN1995.9.H6K46 1999
016.79143'616—dc20   95-6727 CIP

British Library Cataloguing-in-Publication data are available

©1995 Roy Kinnard. All rights reserved

No part of this book may be reproduced or transmitted in any form or by any means, electronic or mechanical, including photocopying or recording, or by any information storage and retrieval system, without permission in writing from the publisher.

Manufactured in the United States of America

McFarland & Company, Inc., Publishers
  Box 611, Jefferson, North Carolina 28640
    www.mcfarlandpub.com

TABLE OF CONTENTS

Introduction 1
Abbreviation Key 6

The Filmography

1896	 8	**1913**	 52
1897	 10	**1914**	 60
1898	 11	**1915**	 69
1899	 12	**1916**	 80
1900	 13	**1917**	 88
1901	 13	**1918**	 95
1902	 14	**1919**	 97
1903	 16	**1920**	 108
1904	 18	**1921**	 123
1905	 19	**1922**	 128
1906	 20	**1923**	 144
1907	 21	**1924**	 159
1908	 23	**1925**	 168
1909	 27	**1926**	 182
1910	 33	**1927**	 199
1911	 40	**1928**	 212
1912	 45	**1929**	 224

Epilogue 231
Bibliography 233
Index 235

INTRODUCTION

The horror film as a genre was officially born in the early sound era, on November 16, 1931. On that date, Universal Pictures released their now-classic production of *Frankenstein*, directed by James Whale and featuring Boris Karloff as the artificially created monster. This film was Universal's carefully made follow-up to *Dracula*, released by the studio earlier that same year to resounding box office success, and *Frankenstein* was, in turn, such an unqualified hit that it literally created a new type of movie — the horror film — and was the first picture to be referred to as such.

Before *Frankenstein*, in the silent era, there were no horror movies as the public thinks of them today, although there were certainly many films containing terrifying scenes and horrific plot elements. Classic movies like *Nosferatu* (1922), *The Hunchback of Notre Dame* (1923) and *The Phantom of the Opera* (1925) spring to mind, yet these pictures were not made or promoted as "horror" films. For the most part, films of this sort were marketed as colorful, offbeat melodramas (*The Phantom of the Opera*) or, as with Germany's *Nosferatu* and other foreign imports, presented as special "art" films. Even Lon Chaney, the silent screen's celebrated "Man of a Thousand Faces," renowned for his portrayals of grotesque characters, did not limit himself exclusively to this type of role. Chaney's portrayals of "normal" characters in straight dramas (*Tell It to the Marines*, for example) far outnumber his celluloid monstrosities, and he was certainly not a "horror star" as Boris Karloff and Bela Lugosi would later be considered, regardless of how he may be classified in retrospect today.

But even though the horror film was born in the sound era with *Frankenstein*, the sound films drew heavily on *silent* films of the horrific and fantastic as a basis for their visual design and thematic development. *Frankenstein* looks the way it does because director James Whale screened *The Cabinet of Dr. Caligari* (1919) and modified that expressionistic German classic's exaggerated visuals,

Introduction

while adapting pictorial and thematic elements from other silents like *The Golem* (1920) and *The Magician* (1926) as well. Whale, it should be noted, was secure enough in his own unique talents to even publicly admit his celluloid "borrowing" in published interviews. To further illustrate this point, *King Kong* (1933) used *The Lost World* (1925) as a sort of unofficial blueprint, and the seminal German vampire film *Nosferatu* (1922) inspired, at least in terms of structure, the opening portion of Universal's *Dracula* (1931).

With the release of director Tod Browning's *Dracula* in February of 1931, Universal Pictures altered the cinematic interpretation of horror forever. Before *Dracula*, horror films tended to veer away from the supernatural and offered "logical" explanations for their fantastic onscreen events, as in Browning's own 1927 film *London After Midnight*, in which the monstrous "vampire" of the story (Lon Chaney) is revealed to be a fake. With *Dracula*, though, Browning and Universal tapped into a much deeper psychic realm — Lugosi's vampire was *real*, and the supernatural events depicted *did* occur, within the context of the film. This was underscored by an epilogue speech delivered by Edward Van Sloan (as Dracula's nemesis Professor Van Helsing), shown in the original release prints, in which Van Helsing reminded the theater audience that vampires *did* exist.

As mentioned previously, Universal solidified this approach with *Frankenstein* later in 1931, and continued on in this vein until the horror cycle faded in 1936, producing a series of unequalled horror classics, including *Murders in the Rue Morgue* (1932), *The Mummy* (1932), *The Old Dark House* (1932), *The Invisible Man* (1933), *The Black Cat* (1934), *Bride of Frankenstein* (1935) and *Dracula's Daughter* (1936). All of these films, in one way or another, owed something to their predecessors of the silent era.

The second American horror film cycle began in 1939 with the release of Universal's *Son of Frankenstein*, and continued until 1946, resulting in a string of enjoyable grade "B" pictures that were much more quickly paced and more modern in style than — but noticeably inferior to — the studio's 1930s classics. Aside from the lavish *Son of Frankenstein* and *The Wolf Man* (1941) — one of the best horror films ever made — Universal released nothing in this period to equal the consistent artistic quality of their 1930s output, and in the 1940s the "B" picture unit at RKO under the guidance of producer Val Lewton filmed the only noteworthy horror movies of the decade. Shot on low budgets using studio contract talent, the Lewton films took a more intellectual approach than Universal did during the same period. While Universal, in desperation, costarred their tired, overly familiar monster menagerie in films like *Frankenstein Meets the Wolf Man* (1943) and *House of Frankenstein* (1944), Lewton was producing films like *The Cat People* (1942) and *I Walked with a Zombie* (1943), which, although saddled with ludicrous titles by crass studio executives, remain unsurpassed in their restrained atmosphere, sensitive characterizations and intelligent direction, the best of them helmed by Jacques Tourneur.

In 1956, director Terrence Fisher's Eastmancolor opus *The Curse of Frankenstein*, produced by Hammer Films in England, initiated the modern era of explicit horror gore that, intensified even more, is still with us today. It was in 1958, though, that director Jacques Tourneur made what is probably the last truly great horror film, *Night of the Demon*, retitled *Curse of the Demon* for American release. Its sophisticated restraint and brooding atmosphere recall Tourneur's work for Lewton in the '40s, and its stark black-and-white visuals echo not the lurid color excesses of its own time, but the evocative pictorial technique of the best silents like *Nosferatu*.

Nearly every horror movie classic made between 1931 and 1945 (before the screen's monsters were "modernized" in the atomic age) was influenced to some degree by an earlier silent film, or, at the very least, by the silent screen's pictorial style, yet, in most published studies of horror films, little is written about the *silent* "horror" film, or to use this book's title, *Horror in Silent Films*. Often the silents are mentioned only briefly, as a required prelude to the sound movies, and the main cause of this neglect has probably been the difficulty in obtaining and screening prints of acceptable quality.

Many silent movies have been lost due to chemical deterioration resulting from the unstable nitrate-based stock they were originally filmed on, and those that *do* survive are often no more than scratchy, faded copies, printed not from the original negatives, but cheaply duplicated from existing prints that are usually in worn condition, and projected at the wrong speed, so that the action looks frantic and comedic. Originally, silent movies were as bright and as sharply defined as any modern film, and they were full of color as well, enhanced with tints and tones (such as blue for night scenes and amber for sunlit scenes) that heightened their emotional impact, and were often accompanied by full orchestras playing carefully arranged music scores.

Movies are (or at least were originally intended to be) the most democratic of art forms, and while it is all well and good that many early films are preserved in archives, this means little when access is restricted to a privileged few. With the arrival of the video age, though, at least the most famous silent movies—the ones that still have some commercial appeal—are no longer the exclusive property of archives and private collectors, and, if they are not exactly *widely* available, they are, at least, a good deal more accessible than they ever were before, and in versions with excellent print quality and appropriate music scores at that. Thanks to mass-market videocassettes and laser discs, it is now possible for *anyone* interested in landmark films like *Nosferatu* and *The Cabinet of Dr. Caligari* to view them in at least an approximation of their original form. Most of these films were, and those that survive remain, popular entertainment containing varying degrees of artistry. A few, like *The Cabinet of Dr. Caligari*, are genuine works of art, still analyzed, studied and emulated by filmmakers today.

In selecting the films included herein, the question arises: What exactly defines a silent "horror" film? There are moments of pure terror in director G. W. Pabst's German classic *Pandora's Box* (1928) as gut-wrenching and as intense as anything to be found in *any* horror film, past or present, yet *Pandora's Box* is not considered to be a horror film. Nevertheless, it *is* included here, on the basis of its few horrific passages, as is the Lon Chaney melodrama *West of Zanzibar* (1928). This is such a macabre tale, and its already dark, oppressive atmosphere is influenced so heavily by Chaney's malevolent performance, that it merits inclusion, even though the film contains no "monsters" or other standard horror movie trappings, so atmosphere alone, then, can define a film as "horrific."

This book, literally a catalogue of silent screen horrors ranging from 1896 to 1929, is an attempt to document exactly how indebted the horror films of the sound era are to their voiceless celluloid forebears. The embryonic basis for every horror movie convention and cliche, as well as the very first screen versions of many a later sound classic, are to be found in these pages. To be included in this catalogue, a film must be essentially "horrific" in nature, containing one or more of the stock horror movie elements—haunted houses, ghosts, witches, skeletons, monsters, hypnotism, the occult, etc.—

Introduction 5

or else present an overwhelmingly horrific atmosphere. And since horror *comedies* also contain these elements (and since the line between horror and comedy has always been very fine), they also have been included.

For each release year examined herein, the films are listed alphabetically, with cast and credit information, and, in the case of foreign films, original foreign title and country of origin when known. Foreign films known only or primarily by their foreign titles are listed alphabetically under their *foreign* titles. Cross references in the main part of the book and the index of course will permit access to any film listing by a variety of means.

Contemporary review excerpts have also been included, even when the opinions are extreme or contradictory, as an indication of how these films were originally received by both the industry and general press. The dates of reviews for imported films are sometimes much later than the release dates for those movies.

Running times are also listed; the reader is advised that exact running times are difficult to ascertain with silent films, since original projection speeds were often variable from theater to theater, and in many cases the films were later abridged for reissue, with only the shortened versions surviving today. The running times listed here, in either minutes, number of 35mm reels (each reel equal to 10 to 13 minutes, depending on the original silent projection speed), or exact footage, are culled from a variety of reference sources, and in most cases indicate the original *theatrical* running times.

ABBREVIATION KEY

The following abbreviations are used for production companies:

    AM&B   American Mutoscope and Biograph
    C&M   Cricks and Martin
    WB&E   Williams, Brown and Earle

THE FILMOGRAPHY

1896

1 Conjuring a Lady at Robert Houdin's (Star Film, 1896). [*Escamotage d'une Dame Chez Robert-Houdin*] France. 2 minutes.
Production: Georges Méliès.
Notes: By means of a simple "jump cut," a woman is transformed into a skeleton.

In the first years of motion pictures, the creative impetus came not from America, but from Europe, with France and Italy leading the world in cinematic innovation, until the rise of D. W. Griffith in America during the teens and the establishment of the Hollywood studios after World War I. The earliest films were "documentary" in nature, crude, static visual records of street scenes, trains arriving at stations, and so on. When the public tired of these mundane celluloid novelties, filmmakers turned to literature and the stage for inspiration in developing first, tableau-like scenes, and later, more complicated and detailed plots for the new medium.

In France, Georges Méliès (1861-1938), a former stage magician, saw the camera from a unique perspective—as an extension and elaboration of his theatrical illusions. For over 15 years (from 1896 to 1912—his first film was *Playing Cards* [*Partie des Cartes*] in 1896) Méliès produced, directed, designed and sometimes performed in hundreds of short "trick" films, calculated to both thrill and amaze early moviegoers. Méliès was not sophisticated in his grasp of the screen's narrative aspects—his brief movies ran anywhere from two minutes to a half hour in length, and were short on plot as well as characterization, the stagebound camera simply recording the action as it moved from left to right with only minimal editing. Méliès' sole purpose, though, was that of any good magician—to mystify and hold his audience in an entertaining manner, and in this he succeeded thoroughly.

Méliès' special effects were simple, but artfully and entertainingly designed. With his technical associate Eugene Calmels, Méliès constructed his own production studio (Star Films) installing, with the assistance of photographic expert Lucien Reulos, a moving camera mounted on rails, which allowed a smooth "dolly" approach to the photographed subject. In this manner, a person or object could be made to seemingly "enlarge" onscreen when photographed by the approaching camera and then double-exposed onto stationary scenery. Imaginatively rendered painted backdrops were raised and lowered in and out of camera range as needed. The release prints of Méliès' films were often painstakingly hand-colored for richer visual effect and greater impact, with a effect and greater impact, with a variety of colors laboriously added frame by frame.

Méliès' peak years were 1901 to 1904; he managed his own movie theatre (the Théâtre Robert Houdin) in Paris, and his brother Gaston opened a branch of Star Films in New York. Méliès' subjects naturally tended to be fantastic—at times even horrific—in nature, and when contemporary audiences saw them, they were thrilled by these charming films. If they were terrified at all when viewing the more macabre entries, where the basic figures of Halloween (the skeleton, witch and devil) held sway, it was with the benign, delightful shudder produced by a well-told ghost story, with the audience secure in the knowledge—and constantly reminded by the painted backdrops—that none of this was, after all, "real."

Of the 498 shorts produced by Méliès from 1886 to 1912, 137 exist today. Watching Méliès' surviving films now, it is important to remember that audiences of the period did not interpret these special effects as "reality," but responded to them as they would any magician's trick—with amusement and appreciation for the conjurer's expertise, wit and style. Because Méliès was so honest about what he was doing, these early films retain their charm (if not all their original impact) for the modern viewer, and any history of the horror film must begin in late nineteenth-century France with Méliès and his innovative celluloid excursions into the fantastic.

Escamotage d'une Dame Chez Robert-Houdin *see Conjuring a Lady at Robert Houdin's*

2 ***The Haunted Castle*** (Star Film, 1896). [*Le Manoir du Diable*] France. 2 minutes.
Alternate titles: The Manor of the Devil; The Devil's Manor.
Director/Producer/Screenplay: Georges Méliès.
Cast: Georges Méliès.
Notes: This brief film, probably the first horror movie, featured a living skeleton, witches, and the titular devil, played by none other than Méliès himself.

Manoir du Diable, Le *see **The Haunted Castle***

Nuit Terrible, Une *see **A Terrible Night***

3 ***A Terrible Night*** (Star Film, 1896). [*Une Nuit Terrible*] France. 1 minute.
Production: Georges Méliès.
Notes: A man is understandably alarmed by the appearance of a giant beetle. With this film Méliès unwittingly anticipated the "giant insect" films of the 1950s.

1897

4 The Alchemist's Hallucination (Star Film, 1897). [*L'Hallucination de l'Alchimiste*] France.
Production: Georges Méliès.
Notes: A star with five female heads and a giant face emitting people from its mouth are featured in this short film, which was hand-colored frame by frame.

Auberge Ensorcelée, L' *see The Bewitched Inn*

5 The Bewitched Inn (Star Film, 1897). [*L'Auberge Ensorcelée*] France. 3 minutes.
Production: Georges Méliès.
Notes: An unfortunate vacationer is frightened when, preparing to bed down for the night, he disrobes and his clothing suddenly comes to life, with a chair moving under its own power, and so on.

Hallucination de l'Alchimiste, L' *see The Alchemist's Hallucination*

6 The Haunted Castle (G.A.S. Films, 1897). Great Britain. 50 feet.
Director: George Albert Smith.
Notes: Only 1897 and already Méliès had imitators. Like Méliès, George Albert Smith was a former stage magician.

7 The Hypnotist at Work (Star Film, 1897). France.
Production: Georges Méliès.
Notes: A girl is put into a trance, and then magically (but tastefully) unclothed.

8 The Laboratory of Mephistopheles (Star Film, 1897). France.
Production: Georges Méliès.
Notes: Satan's disembodied head floats across the screen. Filmed using the same sets from Méliès' 1896 release *The Haunted Castle* (*q.v.*).

9 The X-Ray Fiend (G.A.S. Films, 1897). Great Britain. 54 feet.
Alternate Title: X-Rays.
Cast: Tom Green (Professor).
Notes: The skeletons of embracing lovers are revealed by a professor's X-ray machine.

1898

10 ***The Accursed Cavern*** (Star Film, 1898). [*La Caverne Maudite*] France.
Director/Producer: Georges Méliès.
Notes: Ghosts are featured in this short film.

11 ***The Astronomer's Dream*** (Star Film, 1898). [*Le Rêve d'un Astronome*] France. 3 minutes.
Alternate titles: La Lune à un Mètre; L'Homme dans la Lune.
Production: Georges Méliès.
Notes: An astronomer dreams that he ascends to the moon via a rope ladder; an omnivorous moon swallows a telescope. This film was hand-colored. American producer Sigmund Lubin imported *The Astronomer's Dream* in 1899 and retitled it *A Trip to the Moon* (no relation to the later 1902 Méliès production of the same title).

12 ***The Cavalier's Dream*** (Edison, 1898). 1 minute.
Director: Edwin S. Porter.
Notes: The Devil is seen in a dream.

Caverne Maudite, La *see* ***The Accursed Cavern***

13 ***The Corsican Brothers*** (G.A.S. Films, 1898). Great Britain.
Notes: A ghost appears in this famous tale.

14 ***Ella Lola, à la Trilby*** (Edison, 1898).
Notes: Based on *Trilby*, by George Du Maurier. This is the earliest known adaptation of Du Maurier's story featuring the diabolical mesmerist Svengali.

15 ***Faust and Mephistopheles*** (G.A.S. Films, 1898). Great Britain. 75 feet.
Notes: Adapted from Goethe.

16 ***A Novice at X-Rays*** (Star Film, 1898). [*Les Rayons Roentgen*].
Production: Georges Méliès.
Notes: This film depicts a scientist using his X-ray machine to extract a living skeleton from an otherwise unharmed patient's body.

17 ***Photographing a Ghost*** (G.A.S. Films, 1898). Great Britain. 76 feet.
Notes: A ghost is released from a box (labeled "ghost") and a photographer attempts to take its picture.

Rayons Roentgen, Les *see* ***A Novice at X-Rays***

Rêve d'un Astronome, Le *see* ***The Astronomer's Dream***

1899

18 Beauty and the Beast (Pathé, 1899). France.
Notes: Based on the fairy tale by Gabrielle Suzanne.

Bon Lit, Un *see* **A Midnight Episode**

19 Cleopatra (Star Film, 1899). [*Cléopâtre*] France.
Alternate title: Cleopatra's Tomb.
Production: Georges Méliès.
Notes: In this Méliès effort the celebrated Queen of the Nile is resurrected from death. Cleopatra was retitled *Cleopatra's Tomb* by Charles Urban, an American based in London who was Méliès', as well as George Albert Smith's, distributor.

Cléopâtre *see* **Cleopatra**

Colonne de Feu, La *see* **The Column of Fire**

20 The Column of Fire (Star Film, 1899). [*La Colonne de Feu*] France. 1 minute.
Production: Georges Méliès.
Notes: This brief film was based on the concluding scene from H. Rider Haggard's adventure novel *She*, in which the queen of a lost kingdom gains immortality from a magical column of fire.

21 The Devil in a Convent (Star Film, 1899). [*La Diable au Convent*] France.
Production: Georges Méliès.
Notes: Satan cavorts through this Méliès release, which was inexplicably retitled *The Sign of the Cross*, by Charles Urban.

Diable au Convent, La *see* **The Devil in a Convent**

Évocation Spirite *see* **Raising Spirits**

22 The Haunted House (Lubin, 1899).

23 A Midnight Episode (Star Film, 1899). [*Un Bon Lit*] France. 1 minute.
Production: Georges Méliès.
Notes: A giant insect attacks a camper.

24 The Miser's Doom (Paul, 1899). Great Britain. 220 Feet.
Director: Walter R. Booth.
Notes: The title miscreant suffers a fatal heart attack after confrontation with a girl's spirit. Like Méliès, director Walter R. Booth was a former magician.

25 Raising Spirits (Star Film, 1899). [*Évocation Spirite*] France.
Production: Georges Méliès.
Notes: Ghosts are depicted in this Méliès production.

1900

26 *Chinese Magic* (Paul, 1900). Great Britain. 2 minutes. 100 feet.
Alternate title: Yellow Peril.
Director: Walter R. Booth.
Notes: A Chinese conjurer is transformed into a huge bat.

27 *The Clown and the Alchemist* (Edison, 1900).
Notes: Strange apparitions are depicted.

28 *Faust and Marguerite* (Edison, 1900).
Director: Edwin S. Porter.
Notes: Edwin S. Porter — still three years away from his groundbreaking cinematic milestone, *The Great Train Robbery* — shot this film using incidental stop-motion animation, a technique that would later be used more extensively by the Edison studios in filming a series of animated dinosaur comedies produced by special effects technician Willis H. O'Brien (1886-1962), who would then go on to provide the similar but much more advanced effects for *The Lost World* (1925) and *King Kong* (1933). The Devil and a skeleton are depicted in *Faust and Marguerite*, based on Goethe.

28a *The Mystic Swing* (Edison, 1900). 1 minute.
Director: Edwin S. Porter.
Notes: A woman and a skeleton are made to appear and disappear by a magician.

29 *Uncle Josh in a Spooky Hotel* (Edison, 1900). 1 minute.
Notes: Ghosts are depicted.

30 *Uncle Josh's Nightmare* (Edison, 1900). 2 minutes.
Notes: A ghost appears and disappears.

1901

31 *The Haunted Curiosity Shop* (Paul, 1901). Great Britain. 140 feet.
Director: Walter R. Booth.
Notes: A mummy comes to life and then promptly dissolves, with only a skeleton remaining. This film was produced by Robert Paul (1869-1943), the pioneer inventor of the British movie camera. Paul's

studio was meticulously copied from Méliès' facility, duplicating Méliès' production techniques.

32 Little Red Riding Hood (Star Film, 1901). [*Le Petit Chaperon Rouge*]. France.
Notes: Based on the children's tale, depicting Red Riding Hood's encounter with a monstrous wolf.

33 The Magic Sword (Paul, 1901). Great Britain. 180 feet.
Notes: This features a ghost, witch, ogre, good fairy and a magic cauldron.

Petit Chaperon Rouge, Le *see* Little Red Riding Hood

34 Scrooge (Paul, 1901). Great Britain.
Director: Walter R. Booth.
Notes: Based on *A Christmas Carol*, by Charles Dickens.

Sept Châteaux du Diable, Les *see* The 7 Castles of the Devil

35 The 7 Castles of the Devil (1901). [*Les Sept Châteaux du Diable*]. France.
Director: Ferdinand Zecca.

36 Undressing Extraordinary (Paul, 1901). Great Britain. 200 feet.
Director: Walter R. Booth.
Notes: A living skeleton is featured.

1902

Belle au Bois Dormant, La *see* Sleeping Beauty

37 The Enchanted Cup (Paul, 1902). Great Britain. 300 feet.
Director: Walter R. Booth.
Notes: Using a magic cup and a gorgon's severed head, a peasant rescues his sweetheart from dwarves.

38 Jack and the Beanstalk (Edison, 1902). 10 minutes.
Director: Edwin S. Porter.
Notes: The popular fairy tale, featuring a giant.

39 The Prince of Darkness (AM&B, 1902).
Notes: The Grim Reaper frightens a man to death.

40 Satan's Treasure (Star Film, 1902). [*Le Trésor de Satan*]. France.
Production: Georges Méliès.
Notes: A thief who opens Satan's treasure chest is pursued by emerging specters.

41 Sleeping Beauty (Pathé, 1902). [*La Belle au Bois Dormant*]. France.

A Trip to the Moon (1902).

Director: Ferdinand Zecca.
Notes: Based on the fairy tale. This film was pirated by Sigmund Lubin in 1903.

Trésor de Satan, Le see *Satan's Treasure*

42 *A Trip to the Moon* (Star Film, 1902). [*Le Voyage dans la Lune*]. France. 15 minutes.
Director/Producer/Screenplay: Georges Méliès.
Photography: Lucien Tainguy.
Cast: Georges Méliès (Expedition Leader), Bluette Bernon (Lady in the Moon), Victor Andre, Delpierre and Farjaux Kelm-Brunnet, and ballet girls of the Théâtre du Châtelet.

Notes: A Trip to the Moon is undoubtedly Méliès' best-known and most frequently screened production. Loosely adapted from the writings of Jules Verne (*From the Earth to the Moon*) and H. G. Wells (*First Men in the Moon*), this one-reel fantasy depicts a lunar voyage by a group of scientists (dressed in formal attire) who encounter a race of crustaceous lobster-men, and the adventurers' subsequent return to Earth. Like most of Méliès' films, *A Trip to the Moon* was conceived with a healthy dose of tongue-in-cheek wit (the lunar rocket, fired like an artillery shell out of a cannon à la Verne, is prepared for launching by a group of leggy chorus girls), and illustrates both Méliès' strength and his weakness.

Méliès' sense of perspective did not allow him to take either his own considerable talents or his work too seriously, and this attitude imparted a farcical, buoyant quality to his films that made them all the more appealing. On the other hand, Méliès failed to recognize the immense potential of film as a dramatic narrative medium, and so never advanced his directorial vocabulary. Though entertaining, *A Trip to the Moon* looks exactly the same as Méliès' first efforts of six years before, with the action still moving from camera-left to camera-right like a ping-pong game. The next year (1903) Edwin S. Porter's *The Great Train Robbery* would explode the "fourth wall" between screen and viewer when a cowboy, in close-up, pointed his gun straight into the camera lens and fired — startling audiences of the time and altering the creative direction of cinema in one electrifying instant. Méliès, though, continued with his same overly familiar techniques. *A Trip to the Moon* contained hand-colored sequences in the original release prints. Sigmund Lubin pirated *A Trip to the Moon* in America, retitling the film *A Trip to Mars*.

43 ***The Troublesome Fly*** (Biograph, 1902). 1 minute.
Notes: A man is bitten by a giant fly.

Voyage dans la Lune, Le *see A Trip to the Moon*

1903

44 ***The Apparition*** (Star Film, 1903). [*Le Revenant*]. France. *Production:* Georges Méliès.

Notes: A hotel guest is annoyed by mysteriously animated candles and furniture.

45 Beelzebub's Daughters (Star Film, 1903). [*Les Filles du Diable*]. France.
Production: Georges Méliès.

Boîte à Malice, La *see* **The Trick Box**

Cake-Walk Infernal, Le *see* **The Infernal Cake-Walk**

Chauldron Infernal, Le *see* **The Infernal Cauldron and the Phantasmal Vapors**

46 The Damnation of Faust (Star Film, 1903). France.
Production: Georges Méliès.
Notes: Based on Goethe. Faust is haunted by monstrous visions of Satan and demons.

47 Davy Jones' Locker (AM&B, 1903).
Notes: A puppet skeleton appears.

Faust aux Enfers *see* **Faust in Hell**

48 Faust in Hell (Star Film, 1903). [*Faust aux Enfers*]. France. 4 minutes.
Production: Georges Méliès.

Filles du Diable, Les *see* **Beelzebub's Daughters**

49 The Infernal Cake-Walk (Star Film, 1903). [*Le Cake-Walk Infernal*]. France. 5 minutes.
Production: Georges Méliès.
Notes: Horned demons and magical balls of fire appear inside Satan's cave.

50 The Infernal Cauldron and the Phantasmal Vapors (Star Film, 1903). [*Le Chauldron Infernal*]. France. 2 minutes.
Production: Georges Méliès.
Notes: The Devil boils three women in his cauldron, transforming them into flying spirits, and then into flames.

51 Jack and the Beanstalk (Lubin, 1903).
Notes: Based on the fairy tale.

52 The Monster (Star Film, 1903). [*Le Monstre*]. France.
Production: Georges Méliès.
Notes: A living skeleton is depicted.

Monstre, Le *see* **The Monster**

Oracle de Delphes, L' *see* **The Oracle of Delphi**

53 The Oracle of Delphi (Star Film, 1903). [*L'Oracle de Delphes*]. France.
Production: Georges Méliès.
Notes: A living sphinx avenges the desecration of a tomb.

Portrait Spirite, La *see* **A Spiritualist Photographer**

Revenant, Le *see* **The Apparition**

54 Sherlock Holmes Baffled (AM&B, 1903).
Notes: Based on Sir Arthur Conan Doyle's famous character. A man disappears magically.

55 Snow White (Lubin, 1903).
Notes: Based on the fairy tale.

Sorcier, Le see **The Witch's Revenge**

56 *A Spiritualist Photographer* (Star Film, 1903). [*La Portrait Spirite*]. France. *Production:* Georges Méliès.

57 *The Trick Box* (Star Film, 1903). [*La Boîte à Malice*]. France. 1 minute.

Production: Georges Méliès.
Notes: A girl vanishes from a scientist's magic box. Georges Méliès appears on-screen.

58 *The Witch's Revenge* (Star Film, 1903). [*Le Sorcier*]. France.
Production: Georges Méliès.

1904

59 *The Bewitched Traveller* (AM&B, 1904). Great Britain.
Producer: Cecil Hepworth.
Notes: A guest at an inn is mystified by disappearing objects.

Bourreau Turc, Le see **The Terrible Turkish Executioner**

60 *The Cook in Trouble* (Star Film, 1904). [*Sorcellerie Culinaire*]. France. 7 minutes.
Production: Georges Méliès.
Notes: A sorcerer uses demons and devils to torment a cook, who is roasted in a stewpot.

61 *Faust* (Star Film, 1904). France.
Production: Georges Méliès.

62 *Faust and Marguerite* (Star Film, 1904). France.

Production: Georges Méliès.
Notes: Faust's deal with the Devil, from the original material by Goethe.

63 *An Impossible Voyage* (Star Film, 1904). France.
Production: Georges Méliès.
Notes: Galactic explorers battle a giant octopus. The original release prints were hand-colored.

64 *The Mistletoe Bough* (Clarendon, 1904). Great Britain. 500 feet.
Director: Percy Stow.
Notes: A bride vanishes at her wedding; 30 years later the groom, prompted by a vision, opens a chest and discovers her skeleton. Based on a poem by E. T. Bayley.

Sorcellerie Culinaire see **The Cook in Trouble**

65 The Terrible Turkish Executioner (Star Film, 1904). [*Le Bourreau Turc*]. France.
Production: Georges Méliès.
Notes: An executioner zealously beheads numerous victims.

1905

66 Beauty and the Beast (Clarendon, 1905). Great Britain. 11 minutes.
Director: Percy Stow.
Notes: Based on the fairy tale.

67 The Black Imp (Star Film, 1905). [*Le Diable Noir*]. France. 6 minutes.
Production: Georges Méliès.
Notes: An impish demon torments a guest at an inn by multiplying the number of chairs in the room, setting the bed afire, and so on.

68 The Conscience (Pathé Frères/Hubsch, 1905). France. 9 minutes.
Notes: A murderer is haunted by a black-clad vision of Death and an apparition of his victim.

69 D.T.'s or the Effects of Drink (Gaumont, 1905). Great Britain. 4 minutes.
Notes: An unfortunate drunk is haunted by visions of demons and monsters.

Diable Noir, Le *see* **The Black Imp**

70 The Electric Goose (Gaumont, 1905).
Director: Alf Collins.
Notes: A cooked goose is restored to life by electricity.

71 The Fairy of the Black Rocks (Paul, 1905). Great Britain.
Notes: A group of skeletons are seen cavorting in a graveyard.

72 The Freak Barber (Paul, 1905). Great Britain. 3 minutes. 168 feet.
Director: J. H. Martin.
Notes: A barber cuts his customers' heads off, and is then dismembered himself.

73 The Palace of the Arabian Nights (Star Film, 1905). [*Le Palais des Mille et Une Nuits*]. France.
Production: Georges Méliès.
Notes: A sorcerer, genie, dragon, ghosts, stone monsters and an enchanted sword are depicted, as well as a battle between living skeletons and swordsmen.

Palais des Mille et Une Nuits,

Le see *The Palace of the Arabian Nights*

74 *The Thirteen Club* (AM&B, 1905).
Notes: Members of the title club mock superstitions and die, their bodies replaced by skeletons.

75 *Trip to the Center of the Moon* (1905). [*Viaggo al Centro della Luna*]. Italy.
Cast: Mario Caserini.

Ulysse et le Géant Polyphème see *Ulysses and the Giant Polyphemus*

76 *Ulysses and the Giant Polyphemus* (Star Film, 1905). [*Ulysse et le Géant Polyphème*]. France.
Production: Georges Méliès.

Viaggo al Centro della Luna see *Trip to the Center of the Moon*

1906

77 *Aladdin and the Wonderful Lamp* (Pathé, 1906). 15 minutes.
Notes: Vases are transformed into grotesque human faces; a magician, gnome and giant are depicted.

78 *The Convict Guardian's Nightmare* (Pathé, 1906). France. 8 minutes.
Notes: In a dream sequence, a convict is transformed into a skeleton.

79 *Esmeralda* (Gaumont, 1906). France. 10 minutes.
Directors: Alice Guy Blanche, Victorin Jasset.
Cast: Henri Vorins (Quasimodo, the Hunchback), Denise Becker (Esmeralda).

Notes: Based on Victor Hugo's 1831 novel *Notre Dame de Paris*, this was the first screen version of *The Hunchback of Notre Dame*.

Fée Carabosse, La; *ou*, Poignard Fatal, Le see *The Witch*

80 *Mephisto's Son* (Pathé, 1906). France. 19 minutes.
Notes: The Devil's son is driven away by a crucifix.

81 *The Merry Frolics of Satan* (Star Film, 1906). [*Les Quatre Cents Farces du Diable*]. France. 18 minutes.
Alternate Titles: The 400 Tricks of the Devil; The Frolics of Satan.
Production: Georges Méliès.

Notes: In Satan's laboratory, a woman is transformed into a monster, a man is roasted on a spit; a skeletal, apocalyptic horse is also shown.

82 The Mysterious Retort (Star Film, 1906). France. 3 minutes.
Production: Georges Méliès.
Notes: In a dream sequence, the Devil's messenger, a monstrous reptile with a crocodile's head, and a grimacing face in a spider web are seen.

Quatre Cents Farces du Diable, Les *see* **The Merry Frolics of Satan**

83 The Rajah's Casket (Pathé, 1906). France. 9 minutes.
Notes: A rajah's casket is carried off on a dragon. Originally hand-colored.

84 A Spiritualistic Meeting (Star Film, 1906). France. 4 minutes.
Production: Georges Méliès.
Notes: A séance and ghosts are shown.

85 The Witch (Star Film, 1906). [*La Fée Carabosse;* ou, *Le Poignard Fatal*]. France.
Production: Georges Méliès.
Notes: A witch curses a troubadour, who is frightened by ghosts and various monsters, including a giant frog, a giant owl, a winged serpent and horned wormlike creatures.

86 The Witch's Cave (Pathé, 1906). France. 6 minutes.
Notes: A skeleton and appearing/disappearing figures are depicted in a dream.

1907

87 Babes in the Woods (Miles Bros., 1907).
Notes: In a fairy-tale type of story, Mrs. Bear attempts to roast two children and eat them for dinner.

88 The Bewildering Cabinet (1907).
Notes: Two girls are turned into hideous ogres by a magic cabinet.

89 The Clock-Maker's Secret (Pathé, 1907). 15 minutes.
Notes: When the Devil attempts to claim a clock-maker's soul, his daughter saves him by driving the Devil away with a cross.

90 The Doll's Revenge (WB&E, 1907).
Notes: When a cruel boy destroys

his sister's doll, the dismembered parts reassemble and the doll grows to enormous size; another huge doll then appears, and the two dolls tear the boy asunder in revenge.

91 ***Faust*** (1907). France.

92 ***Flower of Youth*** (Pathé, 1907). France.
Notes: A demon, fairy and ghosts are depicted.

93 ***The Ghost Holiday*** (WB&E, 1907).
Notes: Ghosts and skeletons leave a graveyard in celebration.

94 ***The Ghost Story*** (Vitagraph, 1907).
Director/Producer: J. Stuart Blackton.

95 ***The Golden Beetle*** (Pathé, 1907). France. 3 minutes.
Notes: At the command of the "Golden Beetle," a magician is burned alive.

96 ***The Haunted Bedroom*** (Urban-Eclipse, 1907). France. 5 minutes.

97 ***The Haunted Hotel*** (Vitagraph, 1907). 8 minutes.

98 ***The Haunted House*** (1907). [*La Maison Hantée*]. France.
Director: Segundo de Chomon.

99 ***A Knight Errant*** (Paul, 1907). Great Britain. 8 minutes.
Director: J. H. Martin.

Screenplay: Langford Reed.
Cast: Langford Reed.
Notes: An ogre, witch, dwarf and fairy appear in this film.

100 ***Legend of a Ghost*** (Pathé, 1907). [*La Légende du Fantôme*]. France. 17 minutes.
Notes: A woman fights demons, dragons and a vampire in hell; a ghost's voice is heard from a grave.

Légende du Fantôme, La *see* **Legend of a Ghost**

101 ***Little Red Riding Hood*** (Pathé, 1907). France. 5 minutes.

Maison Hantee, La *see* **The Haunted House**

102 ***Nature Fakirs*** (Kalem, 1907). 8 minutes.
Notes: A "Dingbat" (a huge chicken-like beast) attacks a professor and his assistant.

103 ***Oh That Molar!*** (Alpha, 1907). Great Britain. 215 feet.
Director: Arthur Cooper.
Notes: A man suffering from a toothache dreams of demonic animated teeth dancing in his head.

104 ***The £1,000 Spook*** (1907). Great Britain.
Director: Walter R. Booth.
Notes: A ghost materializes from vapor.

105 ***The Pearl Fisher*** (Pathé, 1907). 9 minutes.

Notes: A fisherman, lured by a vision of the "Queen of the Deep," swims through the depths of the ocean encountering grotesque underwater monsters and emerges in an undersea structure containing various plants and strange animals.

106 *The Pied Piper* (Clarendon, 1907). Great Britain. 755 feet.
Director: Percy Stow.
Screenplay: Langford Reed.
Notes: A piper lures children when payment is refused for luring rats; based on the poem by Robert Browning.

107 *The Professor and His Waxworks* (WB&E, 1907). 11 minutes.
Notes: Wax sculptures are endowed with life.

108 *The Witch Kiss* (Pathé, 1907). France. 6 minutes.
Notes: This film was hand-colored.

1908

109 *Aunt Eliza Recovers Her Pet* (1908). France. 7 minutes.
Notes: After stealing a pet bird, cooking it and eating it, a thief is sawed in half, and the bird, miraculously alive, is freed.

110 *Beauty and the Beast* (Pathé, 1908). [*La Belle et la Bette*]. France. 11 minutes.
Notes: Based on the fairy tale by Madame Leprince de Beaumont.

111 *The Beauty of the Sleeping Woods* (Pathé Frères, 1908). [*La Belle au Bois Dormant*]. France. 15 minutes.
Director: Segundo de Chomon.
Notes: Based on *Sleeping Beauty* by Charles Perrault.

112 *The Bee and the Rose* (Pathé, 1908).
Notes: The "Queen of the Bees" is captured by a spider.

Belle au Bois Dormant, La *see* *The Beauty of the Sleeping Woods*

Belle et la Bette, La *see* *Beauty and the Beast*

113 *The Bloodstone* (Lubin, 1908).
Notes: A cursed ring spreads violence and death in its wake.

114 *The Castle Ghosts* (Aquila, 1908).
Notes: A man impersonates a ghost.

115 The Cat's Revenge (Lux, 1908). 4 minutes.
Notes: A man is haunted by the ghost of a cat.

Cauchemar du Fantoche, Le *see Fantoche's Nightmare*

116 A Christmas Carol (Essanay, 1908).
Notes: Based on the story by Charles Dickens. Scrooge is haunted by ghosts.

117 The Devil (Edison, 1908). 17 minutes.
Notes: A woman is frightened when the Devil appears before her.

118 The Devil and the Gambler (Vitagraph, 1908). 8 minutes.
Notes: A man gambles with Satan to save a woman's life.

119 The Devil's Three Sins (1908).
Notes: In a dream sequence a knight sees visions of Satan.

120 Dr. Jekyll and Mr. Hyde (Selig Polyscope Co., 1908). 13 minutes.
Re-issue Title: The Modern Dr. Jekyll.
Notes: Robert Louis Stevenson's 1885 novel *The Strange Case of Dr. Jekyll and Mr. Hyde* had been adapted for the London stage by Thomas Russell Sullivan in 1887 and had starred Richard Mansfield. Mansfield's acting was reportedly magnificent and electrified audiences of the period, but performances of the play were suspended, in the interest of good taste, when Mansfield was upstaged by a real-life monster—Jack the Ripper—who was busy terrorizing Londoners at the same time.
Sullivan's play was simplified for an American tour by adaptors Luella Forepaugh and George Fish in 1897, and it was this streamlined version that served as the basis for Selig Polyscope's film production, whose leading man remained anonymous. This 1908 production of *Dr. Jekyll and Mr. Hyde* was the first film adaptation of Stevenson's novel, and it was the first American horror film. Like the play, this film was divided into four acts.
Review: "The successful reproduction of this well-known drama has surpassed our expectations...."—*The Motion Picture World.*

121 The Doctor's Experiment (1908). France.
Notes: People acquire the characteristics of monkeys after receiving glandular injections.

122 The Dream of an Opium Fiend (Star Film, 1908). France.
Production: Georges Méliès.
Notes: A girl is transformed into an old hag in a dream sequence.

123 The Fairy's Sword (Hepworth, 1908). Great Britain. 775 feet.
Director: Lewin Fitzhamon.
Notes: An ogre and a magic sword are shown.

124 *A Faithless Friend* (Hepworth, 1908). Great Britain. 500 feet.
Director: Lewin Fitzhamon.
Notes: A skeleton comes to life in a dream sequence.

125 *Fantoche's Nightmare* (Gaumont, 1908). [*Le Cauchemar du Fantoche*]. France.
Alternate Title: The Puppet's Nightmare.
Director: Emile Cohl.
Notes: Strange monsters are depicted in this animated short.

126 *Fun with the Bridal Party* (Star Film, 1908). France.
Production: Georges Méliès.
Notes: A ghost is featured.

127 *The Hanging Lamp* (Pathé, 1908). France. 5 minutes.
Notes: A wolf-like demon is shown.

128 *The Haunted Castle* (Pathé, 1908). France. 12 minutes.
Notes: A witch and ghosts appear in this film.

129 *In the Bogie Man's Cave* (Star Film, 1908). France.
Production: Georges Méliès.
Notes: A fairy and gnomes appear in this film in which the Bogie Man fries a boy for dinner.

130 *Incident from Don Quixote* (Star Film, 1908). France.
Production: Georges Méliès.
Notes: A suit of armor is transformed into a giant spider.

131 *The Legend of Sleepy Hollow* (Kalem, 1908). 14 minutes.
Notes: Based on the story by Washington Irving.

132 *The Leprechaun* (Edison, 1908).
Notes: A leprechaun and a witch are depicted.

133 *Lord Feathertop* (Edison, 1908).
Notes: Based on the story by Nathaniel Hawthorne. A witch endows a scarecrow with life.

134 *The Magic Garden* (Paul, 1908). Great Britain.
Notes: A drunken gardener sees a giant frog and a giant snake.

135 *The Magic Mirror* (Pathé, 1908). France. 8 minutes.
Director: Ferdinand Zecca.
Notes: An inventor applies a magical fluid to a mirror and the man's double emerges.

136 *The Man and His Bottle* (Hepworth, 1908). Great Britain. 350 feet.
Director: Lewin Fitzhamon.
Cast: Thurston Harris.
Notes: A drunk is tormented by demons and monsters who then imprison him in a whiskey bottle.

137 *The Monkey Man* (1908).
Notes: A monkey's brain is transplanted into a human being.

138 *The Nusemaid's Dream* (Hepworth, 1908). Great Britain. 8 minutes.

Director: Lewin Fitzhamon.
Cast: Gertie Potter.
Notes: A baby is chased by giants in a dream sequence.

139 Oriental Black Art (Star Film, 1908). France.
Production: Georges Méliès.
Notes: Spirits leave and reenter a woman's body.

140 Prehistoric Man (Urban-Eclipse, 1908).
Notes: Pictures of a prehistoric man and a monster come to life.

141 The Princess in the Vase (AM&B, 1908).
Cast: D. W. Griffith.
Notes: In a dream sequence a cremated Egyptian princess is reincarnated from her own ashes.

142 The Professor's Secret (Gaumont, 1908). France. 10 minutes.
Notes: A drug devolves people into monkeys.

143 The Saloon-Keeper's Nightmare (Gaumont, 1908). France. 7 minutes.
Notes: A man is tormented by Satan.

144 Satan's Smithy (Pathé, 1908). France. 8 minutes.
Notes: Satan lures a blacksmith into hell.

145 She (Edison, 1908). 17 minutes.
Notes: Based on the adventure-fantasy novel by H. Rider Haggard. The queen of a lost tribe is immortalized by a magical flame.

146 Sherlock Holmes in the Great Murder Mystery (Crescent, 1908). Denmark.
Notes: Sherlock Holmes discovers that a murderer is really a gorilla. Based on Sir Arthur Conan Doyle's character and Edgar Allan Poe's story *Murders in the Rue Morgue*.

147 Slumberland (Vitagraph, 1908).
Notes: Gnomes appear in a dream sequence.

148 The Snowman (AM&B, 1908).
Notes: A snowman comes to life and frightens a man.

149 The Specter (Pathé, 1908). France. 8 minutes.
Notes: A cobbler is haunted by the accusing spirit of a man he murdered.

150 Spiritualistic Séance (Pathé, 1908). France. 5 minutes.
Notes: Spirits and a supernatural manifestation at a séance are depicted.

151 Spooks Do the Moving (Pathé, 1908). France.
Notes: Students masquerade as ghosts in order to steal an elderly couple's furniture.

152 The Thieving Hand (Vitagraph, 1908). 5 minutes.

Notes: An artificial hand develops a will of its own.

153 Too Much Champagne (Vitagraph, 1908).
Notes: In a dream sequence a man is abducted by Satan, and scenes from Dante's *Inferno* are depicted.

154 Toula's Dream (Pathé, 1908). France.
Notes: In a dream sequence a monstrous head appears in a pan and frightens a cook.

155 Trick Film [title unknown] (Pathé, 1908). France. 15 minutes.
Notes: Two men undress and are revealed to be living skeletons; a flower girl is transformed into a goblin.

156 Trilby (Nordisk, 1908). Denmark.
Director: A. R. Nielsen.
Photography: Ole Olsen.
Notes: Based on George Du Maurier's book.

157 Wages of Sin (Vitagraph, 1908). Italy.
Notes: A cholera victim comes back to life inside a tomb.

158 Wave of Spooks (Pathé, 1908). France.
Notes: Ghosts are transformed into skeletons, and visions of hell are depicted.

159 Wedding Feast and Ghosts (Cines, 1908). Italy. 7 minutes.
Notes: Newlyweds are chased by ghostly figures.

160 The Witch's Donkey (Pathé, 1908). France. 8 minutes.
Notes: A witch casts a spell on a donkey.

161 The Wonderful Charm (Star Film, 1908). France.
Production: Georges Méliès.
Notes: A man is torn asunder by a wicked spirit and is then reassembled in exchange for his soul.

1909

162 The Ancient Roman (Cines, 1909). Italy. 11 minutes.
Notes: Three professors discover a Roman gladiator alive in an ancient tomb.

163 An Apish Trick (Pathé, 1909). 9 minutes.
Notes: A man exhibits simian traits when his wife injects him with a serum derived from monkeys.

164 *The Ballad of a Witch*
(Ambrosio/Warwick, 1909).
[*La Ballata di una Strega*].
Italy.
Alternate title: The Witch's Ballad.
Photography: Giovanni Vitrotti.
Notes: A witch compels a fisherman to drown himself.

Ballata di una Strega, La *see The Ballad of a Witch*

165 *The Bewitched Manor House* (Pathé, 1909). France. 7 minutes.
Notes: A haunted castle, monstrous beasts and Satan are depicted.

166 *The Bogey Woman* (Pathé, 1909). France. 7 minutes.
Notes: Children are turned into vegetables by the Bogey Woman.

167 *The Butcher's Dream* (Lux, 1909). 9 minutes.
Notes: In a dream a butcher imagines that he is being butchered by animals.

168 *Capturing the North Pole* (Urban-Eclipse, 1909). Great Britain. 7 minutes.
Notes: In this fantasy-adventure featuring Baron Munchausen, the "Spirit of the North" is depicted.

169 *The Cat That Was Changed into a Woman* (Pathé, 1909). [*La Chatte Métamorphosee en Femme*]. France. 12 minutes.
Director: Louis Feuillade.
Notes: The gods transform a cat into a woman.

Chatte Métamorphosée en Femme, La *see The Cat That Was Changed Into a Woman*

170 *The Dance of Fire* (Pathé, 1909). 3 minutes.
Notes: A dancer arises from a crevice in the earth and dances until a giant spider forces her back into the ground.

171 *Dante's Inferno* (Milano, 1909). [*L'Infèrno*]. Italy. 59 minutes.
Director: Giuseppe de Liguoro.
Photography: Emilio Proncarolo.
Art Direction: F. Bertollini, A. Fadovan.
Cast: Salvatore Papa, A. Milta.
Notes: Based on Dante; visions of hell are shown.

Défaite de Satan, La *see The Defeat of Satan*

172 *The Defeat of Satan* (Pathé, 1909). [*La Défaite de Satan*]. France. 14 minutes.
Notes: Satan masquerades as a sorcerer.

173 *The Devil* (Edison, 1909).
Notes: An adaptation of the then successful play of the same title starring George Arliss; introduced the now-familiar idea of Satan appearing as a contemporary urban sophisticate.

174 *The Diabolical Tenant* (Star Film, 1909). [*Le Locataire Diabolique*]. France. 7 minutes.

Alternate title: Diabolical Lodger.
Production: Georges Méliès.
Notes: A strange tenant arrives in his new dwelling with a trunk and valise containing numerous pieces of furniture, which he unpacks one item at a time. The objects—pictures, chairs, a piano, and so on—dance and move about the room, frightening the landlord. This film was hand-colored.

175 Dr. Jekyll and Mr. Hyde (Nordisk, 1909). Denmark. 17 minutes.
Director/Screenplay: August Blom.
Cast: Alwin Neuss (Dr. Jekyll/Mr. Hyde), Oda Alstrup.
Notes: Based on the Stevenson novel. This film was released in the United States under the title *Jekyll and Hyde* in 1910. The story here concluded weakly with a happy "dream" ending.

176 The Doctor's Secret (Star Film, 1909). [*Hydrothérapie Fantastique*]. France. 13 minutes.
Production: Georges Méliès.
Notes: A patient is blown apart and then reassembled by doctors.

177 Doomed (Pathé, 1909). France. 14 minutes.
Notes: A man possesses satanic hypnotic powers.

178 The Egyptian Mystery (Edison, 1909). 9 minutes.
Notes: A pendant from an Egyptian tomb makes any object touched by the wearer disappear.

179 Electric Transformations (Clarendon, 1909). Great Britain. 7 minutes.
Director: Percy Stow.
Notes: A professor's invention melts metal—and people's faces.

180 The Evil Philter (Pathé, 1909).
Notes: A man is haunted by demons after a hag gives him a love potion.

181 Faust (Edison, 1909). 17 minutes.
Notes: Based on Goethe.

182 The Ferryman's Sweetheart (Gaumont, 1909). 14 minutes.
Notes: A ferryman dies after seeing visions of his lost sweetheart.

183 The Forbidden Fruit (Pathé, 1909). 12 minutes.
Notes: A magical castle is created for a peasant couple by a magician who warns them not to look under the cover of a large dish stored in one of the rooms. The wife ignores this warning, and an enormous frog emerges from the dish, chasing the couple from the castle.

184 Fortune Favors the Brave (Star Film, 1909).
Production: Georges Méliès.
Notes: A genie and a fight with a dragon are depicted.

185 Gertie the Dinosaur (1909).
Notes: In this animated short (the first popular cartoon) animator

Winsor McKay brings Gertie, a comical brontosaurus, to life, as well as a pterodactyl and a mammoth. Cleverly drawn, this cartoon was intended to be exhibited in tandem with a live performer who would interact by tossing Gertie a ball, and so forth.

186 Goddess of the Sea (Le Lion, 1909). 14 minutes.
Notes: A shepherd drowns while trying to escape from a goddess.

Graa Dame, Den *see* **The Grey Lady**

187 The Grey Lady (Nordisk, 1909). [*Den Graa Dame*]. Denmark. 14 minutes.
Alternate title: The Grey Dame.
Director/Screenplay: Viggo Larsen.
Producer: Ole Olsen.
Photography: Axel Sorensen.
Cast: Viggo Larsen (Sherlock Holmes), Forest Holger-Madsen, Gustav Lund, Elith Pio.
Notes: Based on Sir Arthur Conan Doyle's character. Holmes must solve the riddle of a ghostly woman in grey who is seen by murder victims just before they die. The offending spirit is unmasked by Holmes and revealed to be an all-too-human schemer. This film was the sixth in a Sherlock Holmes series released by Nordisk and the last with Larsen, who was subsequently replaced by Otto Lagoni, Alwin Neuss and Holger Rasmussen, in that order.

188 Hansel and Gretel (Edison, 1909).
Notes: A witch is depicted from the fairy tale.

189 The Haunted Castle (Pathé, 1909). France.
Notes: A ghost guards a girl from prospective suitors.

190 The Haunted Man (Duskes, 1909). Germany.
Notes: This film introduced the good/evil twin "doppelgänger" premise later exploited so effectively in the German screen adaptations of *The Student of Prague,* among other films.

191 Her Dolly's Revenge (Lux, 1909). 5 minutes.
Notes: In a dream sequence a little girl is stabbed to death by her own doll.

Homme Qui Rit, L' *see* **The Man Who Laughs**

192 The Hunchback (Vitagraph, 1909).
Notes: Based on Victor Hugo's *Notre Dame de Paris,* this film was an unauthorized remake of the 1906 French film *Esmeralda* (*q.v.*).

Hydrothérapie Fantastique *see* **The Doctor's Secret**

193 The Hypnotic Wife (Pathé, 1909).
Notes: A wife casts a hypnotic spell on her husband.

194 The Imp of the Bottle (Edison, 1909). 12 minutes.
Notes: Based on the story *The Imp in the Bottle,* by Robert Louis

Stevenson. The title imp grants wishes, but those who die with the bottle in their possession are damned.

Infèrno, L' see *Dante's Inferno*

195 ***The Invisible Thief*** (Pathé, 1909). France. 6 minutes.
Director: Ferdinand Zecca.
Notes: Based on H. G. Wells' novel *The Invisible Man,* this is the first screen incarnation of that story.

196 ***The Last Look*** (Pathé, 1909). 10 minutes.
Notes: The (fictional) premise that a dead man's eyes retain an image of the last sight he saw holds the solution to a murder mystery.

Locataire Diabolique, Le see *The Diabolical Tenant*

197 ***Lunatics in Power*** (Edison, 1909).
Notes: Based on Edgar Allan Poe's story *The System of Dr. Tarr and Professor Fether* in which a mental hospital is overrun and controlled by the inmates. This production eliminated all horrific elements from the source material, though, and instead played the tale for broad laughs. Three years later, this same plot was filmed "straight" by Éclair in France as *The System of Dr. Tarr and Professor Fether* (*q.v.*).

198 ***The Man Monkey*** (Pathé, 1909). France. 7 minutes.
Notes: A hypnotist exchanges a man's brain with a monkey's.

199 ***The Man Who Laughs*** (1909). [*L'Homme Qui Rit*]. France.
Notes: Based on the novel by Victor Hugo about a hideously deformed man who wears an eternal grin.

200 ***The Marvelous Pearl*** (Cines, 1909). Italy. 12 minutes.
Notes: A pearl casts a spell on a man who wanders into the sea and drowns.

201 ***Mephisto and the Maiden*** (Selig Polyscope Co., 1909). 15 minutes.
Notes: A lustful friar trades his soul to Satan in exchange for two hours with a girl.

202 ***The Mirror of Life*** (Pathé, 1909). France. 5 minutes.
Notes: A young couple gazing into an enchanted mirror see themselves grow old.

203 ***Miss Faust*** (Pathé, 1909). France. 10 minutes.
Notes: A distaff adaptation of the Faust legend. Miss Faust trades her soul for youth and beauty. Originally hand-colored.

Momie du Roi, La see *The Mummy of the King of Ramses*

204 ***The Moonstone*** (Selig Polyscope Co., 1909). 17 minutes.
Notes: Based on the novel by Wilkie Collins. A hypnotic trance is depicted.

205 *Moonstruck* (Pathé, 1909). France. 12 minutes.
Notes: Moonmen are seen in a dream.

206 *Mother Goose* (Edison, 1909). 5 minutes.
Notes: Based on the nursery rhyme. A spider frightens Miss Muffet and abducts a young boy.

207 *The Mummy of the King of Ramses* (Lux, 1909). [*La Momie du Roi*]. France. 10 minutes.
Director: Gerard Bourgeois.
Notes: The mummy of Ramses is brought back to life by a professor.

208 *The Mystery of the Lama Convent* (Great Northern, 1909). Denmark.
Alternate title: Dr. Nicola in Tibet.
Notes: Monks restore life to the dead.

209 *The New Jonah* (Pathé, 1909). 7 minutes.
Notes: A huge, scaly, web-footed monster is shown.

210 *The Nymphs' Bath* (Gaumont, 1909). France. 6 minutes.
Notes: Ghosts are depicted.

211 *The Old Shoemaker* (Gaumont, 1909). France. 14 minutes.
Notes: A murderer is driven mad by visions of his victim.

212 *The Oriental Mystic* (Vitagraph, 1909). 6 minutes.
Notes: A woman is frightened when a Turkish mystic appears and disappears in mirrors.

213 *Papa Gaspard; or, The Ghost of the Rocks* (Le Lion/Brockliss, 1909). 12 minutes.
Notes: A miser masquerades as a ghost in order to guard a fortune stashed in a cave.

214 *Phaedra* (Pathé, 1909). France. 15 minutes.
Notes: A sea monster is depicted.

215 *The Phantom Sirens* (Urban-Eclipse/Kleine, 1909).
Notes: Fishermen are lured to their doom by sirens.

216 *The Princess and the Fisherman* (Gaumont, 1909). France. 15 minutes.
Notes: A witch gives a fisherman a castle and a beautiful princess on the condition that he must return to the witch whenever he hears the sound of a bugle. He fails to respond and the castle sinks into the ocean, drowning him and the princess.

217 *The Revenge of the Ghosts* (1909). France.
Director: Emil Cohl.
Notes: An animated cartoon depicting ghosts.

218 *Shooting in the Haunted Woods* (Gaumont, 1909). France.

219 ***The Spirit*** (Gaumont, 1909). France. 9 minutes.
Notes: A medium and spiritualism are the subjects.

220 ***The Spirit of the Lake*** (Cines, 1909). Italy. 10 minutes.
Notes: Sea nymphs, an apparition and a bewitched knight are shown.

221 ***The Suicide Club*** (AM&B, 1909). 5 minutes.

222 ***The Sword and the King*** (Vitagraph, 1909). 17 minutes.
Notes: A ghost haunts a king after he is cursed by an old hag.

223 ***Talked to Death*** (Lubin, 1909).
Notes: A woman literally talks people to death.

224 ***'Tis Now the Very Witching Time of Night*** (Edison, 1909). 8 minutes.
Notes: Sleeping in a haunted house on a bet, a man is frightened by bats, witches and skeletons.

225 ***The Ugliest Queen on Earth*** (Gaumont, 1909). France. 12 minutes.
Notes: An ugly queen abolishes all mirrors in her kingdom; she then sees her reflection in an executioner's axe and dies.

226 ***The Wild Ass's Skin*** (Pathé, 1909). France. 16 minutes.
Notes: Based on Balzac's *The Wild Ass's Skin*. The title hide contains magic powers granting wishes at the expense of the owner's soul.

227 ***The Witch*** (Le Lion, 1909). 10 minutes.
Notes: A witch imprisons a girl's soul in a dummy; imps, phantoms and a hunchback are also shown.

228 ***The Witch's Cavern*** (Selig Polyscope Co., 1909).
Notes: A man who is half monster is believed to be a witch's son.

1910

229 ***The American Suicide Club*** (Lux, 1910). 10 minutes.

230 ***Another's Ghost*** (Pathé, 1910).
Notes: An innkeeper who supposedly killed a variety artist is haunted by a ghost.

231 ***Back to Life After 2,000 Years*** (Pathé, 1910). France. 13 minutes.

Notes: An ancient Roman emerges from his tomb and sees modern-day Rome. This film was retitled *The Roman's Awakening* in England.

232 The Beechwood Ghost (Powers, 1910).
Notes: A fake ghost appears.

233 The Bewitched Messenger (Bat/Brockliss, 1910). 12 minutes.
Notes: A witch is depicted.

234 The Bride of the Haunted Castle (Artistic/Pathé, 1910). 15 minutes.
Notes: A living skeleton confronts a bride trapped in a castle.

235 The Budda's Curse (Lux, 1910).
Notes: A magical Indian priest curses a household.

236 Cagliostro (Pathé Frères, 1910). France. 20 minutes.
Cast: Helene du Montel.
Notes: A girl is under the mesmerist Cagliostro's hypnotic spell.

237 The Castle Ghost (Pathé, 1910). 9 minutes.
Notes: A man in a haunted house shoots a ghost, but the apparition turns out to be a girl.

238 A Christmas Carol (Edison, 1910). 17 minutes.
Notes: Adapted from Dickens.

239 Countess Ankarstrom (Deutsche Bioscop, 1910). Germany. 20 minutes.
Notes: When a gypsy predicts that the first hand a duke shakes will cause his death, the prophecy comes true.

240 The Demon of Dunkirque (Warwick/Ambrosio, 1910). 14 minutes.
Notes: A devilish creature imprisoned in a bottle inside an alchemist's laboratory grants wishes to the man who frees him.

241 The Detachable Man (Pathé, 1910). 7 minutes.
Notes: A man has the ability to detach his limbs.

242 The Devil (Powers, 1910). 8 minutes.
Notes: People are frightened by a man costumed as Mephistopheles.

243 The Devil's Mother-in-Law (1910). 14 minutes.
Notes: The Devil marries a girl and imprisons her mother in hell.

244 Dr. Mesner's Fatal Prescription (Warwick, 1910). 12 minutes.
Notes: A husband hynotizes his wife and orders her to commit suicide.

245 The Dream of Old Scrooge (Cines, 1910). 11 minutes.
Notes: Adapted from Dickens' *A Christmas Carol*.

246 The Duality of Man (Wrench, 1910). Great Britain. 580 feet.

Notes: Based on Stevenson's *The Strange Case of Dr. Jekyll and Mr. Hyde.*

247 The Electric Vitalizer (Kineto, 1910). Great Britain. 9 minutes.
Director: Walter R. Booth.
Notes: The title device revives historical figures.

248 The Enchanted Wreath (Warwick, 1910). 8 minutes.
Notes: An imp makes a girl disappear; she is brought back by a witch.

249 The Fairy Bookseller (Pathé, 1910). 13 minutes.
Notes: "Beauty and the Beast," "Puss 'n' Boots," "Bluebeard" and an ogre are seen in a dream.

250 The Fairy Jewel (Milano, 1910). 7 minutes.
Notes: A fairy drowns a hunter who is after a gem.

251 Faust (Éclair, 1910). France.
Notes: Based on Goethe.

252 Faust (Pathé, 1910). France. 35 minutes.
Notes: Based on Goethe. This film was hand-colored.

253 Faust (Cines, 1910). Italy. 16 minutes.
Cast: Fernanda Negri-Pouget.
Notes: Based on Goethe.

254 The Fiendish Tenant (Gaumont, 1910). 7 minutes.
Notes: A man renting an apartment removes all of his furniture and several human beings as well from a single bag. When he departs, he leaves behind a cabinet that explodes when the landlord strikes it.

255 Frankenstein (Edison, 1910). 16 minutes.
Director: J. Searle Dawley. Edison production #6604.
Cast: Charles Ogle (the Monster), Augustus Philips (Dr. Frankenstein), Mary Fuller (Frankenstein's fiancée).
Notes: This adaptation of Mary W. Shelley's 1816 novel *Frankenstein* preceded the famous Boris Karloff sound version by more than 20 years. In advance publicity distributed to exhibitors, the producers were characteristically timid about their offering, commenting: "In making the film the Edison Company has carefully tried to eliminate all the actually repulsive situations, and to concentrate its endeavors upon the mystic and psychological problems that are to be found in this weird tale."

Nevertheless, Charles Ogle's disheveled, grimacing monster is one of the most grotesque Frankenstein monsters of all, and the filmmakers managed at least one effect that was particularly grisly for that time—raw meat appearing over the bones of a skeleton as the monster is created in Frankenstein's laboratory. The film's resolution is unexpectedly poetic with Ogle's monster, horrified by his own appearance after gazing into a mirror, dissolving away into nothingness. Although not commonly available, prints of this film do exist, and clips have been shown on television.

256 *The Freak of Ferndale Forest* (Warwick, 1910). 9 minutes.
Notes: A child is transformed into a hideous beast by a beggar.

257 *The Ghost of Mudtown* (Pathé, 1910). 9 minutes.
Notes: A village is terrorized by a ghost.

258 *The Golden Supper* (Biograph, 1910).
Cast: Dorothy West, Edwin August, Charles H. West.
Notes: A girl, Camilla is prematurely buried in a comatose state.

259 *Haunted by Conscience* (Kalem, 1910). 17 minutes.
Notes: A ghost is depicted.

260 *Hop Frog* (Continental/Warwick, 1910). France.
Alternate title: Hop Frog, The Jester.
Director: Henri Desfontaines.
Notes: Based on the story by Edgar Allan Poe. A jester, tormented by men in monkey costumes, douses them with oil and sets them afire.

261 *House of the Seven Gables* (Edison, 1910).
Notes: A house is cursed. Based on the book by Nathaniel Hawthorne.

262 *Hugo the Hunchback* (Selig Polyscope Co., 1910).
Notes: An unauthorized remake of the 1906 French film *Esmeralda* (*q.v.*).

263 *Hypnotism* (Lux, 1910). 11 minutes.
Notes: Under a hypnotist's influence, a girl commits a robbery.

264 *A Japanese Peach Boy* (Edison, 1910). 15 minutes.
Notes: A boy and his mother are captured by ogres in a cavern; a huge snake is turned into a magic wand.

265 *The Jealous Professors* (Lux, 1910). 7 minutes.
Notes: Two professors turn each other into a monkey and a toad with potions.

266 *The Key of Life* (Edison, 1910). 16 minutes.
Notes: Hindu charms transform a kitten into a murderous cat-woman.

267 *The Legend of the Undines* (Pathé, 1910). [*La Légende des Ondines*]. France. 8 minutes.
Notes: A knight is lured into the sea by a beckoning siren.

Légende des Ondines, La *see* The Legend of the Undines

268 *Little Snow White* (Pathé, 1910). France. 18 minutes.
Alternate title: Little Snowdrop.

Frankenstein (1910): Charles Ogle as the monster.

Notes: Adapted from *Snow White,* by the Brothers Grimm.

269 ***A Lively Skeleton*** (London Cinematograph Co., 1910). Great Britain. 270 feet.

Notes: A girl's suitor uses a skeleton to scare her physician father's patients.

270 ***The Lobster Nightmare*** (Walturdaw, 1910). Great Britain. 495 feet.

Notes: In a dream a man is tortured by imps and a giant lobster.

271 ***The Love of a Hunchback*** (Empire/Butcher, 1910). Great Britain. 540 feet.

Notes: An unofficial remake of the 1906 French film *Esmeralda* (*q.v.*).

272 Lured by a Phantom (Gaumont, 1910). [*Le Roi de Thule*]. France. 12 minutes.
Alternate title: The King of Thule.
Notes: A king drowns after following visions of his dead wife into the sea.

Max Hypnotize *see* **Max Hypnotized**

273 Max Hypnotized (1910). [*Max Hypnotize*]. France. 9 minutes.
Cast: Max Linder.
Notes: Two servants hypnotize their master and order him to commit a murder.

274 The Minotaur (Vitagraph, 1910). 16 minutes.
Notes: The legend of Theseus and the Minotaur is depicted.

275 Museum Spooks; or Dreams in a Picture Gallery (Walturdaw, 1910). Great Britain. 6 minutes.
Notes: Figures step out of paintings and dance around a man who is asleep in an art gallery.

276 The Mystery of Temple Court (Vitagraph, 1910). 15 minutes.
Notes: The spirit of a murdered woman appears to a man in a dream and, pointing to a closet, reveals where her body is hidden.

277 Necklace of the Dead (Nordisk, 1910). Denmark. 17 minutes.
Notes: A girl is nearly buried alive.

278 Oh, You Skeleton (Selig Polyscope Co., 1910).
Notes: Skeletons chase a maid.

279 Old Scrooge (Cines, 1910). Italy. 12 minutes.
Notes: Based on Dickens' *A Christmas Carol*.

280 The Phantom (Pathé, 1910). France. 12 minutes.
Notes: A girl is transformed into an old witch by the God of Phantoms; she then throws a curse on a student.

281 The Pit and the Pendulum (Warwick, 1910). [*Le Puits et le Pendule*]. France. 11 minutes.
Director: Henri Desfontaines.
Notes: Based on the story by Edgar Allan Poe. A tribunal orders a man to undergo torture in the Chamber of Horrors.

Puits et le Pendule, Le *see* **The Pit and the Pendulum**

282 The Queen of Spades (Deutsche Bioscop, 1910). Germany. 15 minutes.
Notes: A gambler desperate to learn the secret of winning frightens a countess to death and then learns the secret from her ghost. Based on the story by Pushkin.

283 The Queen of Spades (1910). Russia.
Director: Gontcharov.

Notes: Based on the story by Pushkin.

Rival de Satan *see A Rival to Satan*

284 *A Rival to Satan* (Pathé, 1910). [*Rival de Satan*]. France. *Director:* Gerard Bourgeois. *Notes:* Satan, disguised as a Hindu priest, lusts after a woman.

285 *Robert, the Devil;* **or,** *Freed from Satan's Power* (Gaumont-Lux, 1910). France. 17 minutes. *Notes:* Satan and evil spirits are shown.

Roi de Thule, Le *see Lured by a Phantom*

286 *The Romance of the Mummy* (Pathé, 1910). France. 14 minutes. *Notes:* Based on the book by Theophile Gautier. Lord Evandale falls asleep before the mummy of an Egyptian queen and dreams that he is in ancient Egypt and romantically involved with the queen; he then awakens and meets a beautiful girl who looks exactly like the dead queen.

287 *St. George and the Dragon* (Edison, 1910). *Notes:* Based on the legend—St. George battles the dragon.

Séance de Spiritisme *see A Spiritualistic Séance*

288 *The Secret of the Hand* (Lux, 1910). 17 minutes. *Notes:* A sinister Chinese cult amputates a man's hand and sends it to his friends.

Séance de Spiritisme *see A Spiritualistic Séance*

289 *The Skeleton* (Vitagraph, 1910). 7 minutes. *Notes:* A skeleton performs stunts and frightens policemen.

290 *The Snake Man* (Lux, 1910). France. *Alternate title:* The Serpent Man. *Notes:* A man has the ability to change into a snake.

291 *The Soap Bubbles of Truth* (Pathé, 1910). 7 minutes. *Notes:* Bubbles rising from the bottom of a well predict that a thief will kill a miser.

292 *Sorceress of the Strand* (Éclair, 1910). France. 11 minutes. *Notes:* A fisherman cursed by a witch disguised as a maiden drowns.

293 *The Spectre* (Pathé, 1910). France. 15 minutes. *Notes:* An innkeeper is tormented by the spirit of a man he killed.

294 *The Spirit of the Sword* (Pathé, 1910). France. 8 minutes. *Notes:* A soldier's magic sword frightens a servant ordered to fetch it.

295 *A Spiritualistic Séance* (Gaumont, 1910). [*Séance de Spiritisme*]. France. 7 minutes.
Notes: A man hiding under a table convinces people at a séance that spirits are present.

296 *Testing a Soldier's Courage* (Gaumont, 1910). France. 8 minutes.
Notes: A lieutenant shoots at a ghost haunting his room.

297 *A Trip to Davy Jones' Locker* (Pathé, 1910). France. 11 minutes.
Notes: A specter, spirits and a demon are shown.

298 *A Trip to Mars* (Edison, 1910). 5 minutes.
Notes: Defying the law of gravity with a chemical mixture, a professor floats to Mars where he meets a half human creature and tree monsters.

299 *Vengeance of the Dead* (Pathé, 1910). France. 11 minutes.
Notes: The portrait of a woman murdered by a girl comes to life, points an accusing finger at the murderess, and steps out of the picture frame.

300 *Wanted—A Mummy* (C&M, 1910). Great Britain. 9 minutes.
Notes: A man pretends to be a mummy.

301 *Wedded Beneath the Waves* (Gaumont, 1910). France. 8 minutes.
Notes: A man and a girl are swallowed by a giant fish.

302 *The Witch of the Glen* (Warwick, 1910). Great Britain. 9 minutes.
Notes: Men are frightened by a witch who commands two spirits.

303 *The Witch of the Ruins* (Pathé, 1910). France.
Notes: A witch beats a man unconscious with a stick.

304 *The Witches' Spell* (Urban, 1910).
Notes: A peasant captured at a witches' revel is cursed and transformed into a beast.

1911

305 *The Baby's Ghost* (Lux, 1911). 7 minutes.
Notes: Burglars are frightened by a ghost.

306 *Baron Munchausen* (Star Film, 1911). France.
Production: Georges Méliès.
Notes: From stories by Rudolph E. Raspe.

307 ***Baron Munchausen's Dream*** (Pathé, 1911). [*Les Hallucinations du Baron de Munchausen*]. France.
Notes: From stories by Rudolph E. Raspe. Dragons are shown in a dream sequence.

308 ***Beneath the Tower Ruins*** (Urban/Eclipse, 1911). Great Britain. 14 minutes.
Notes: A ghost is shown.

309 ***The Bewitched Window*** (Pathé, 1911). 12 minutes.
Notes: A painter is haunted by a spirit and a devil.

310 ***Bill Bumper's Bargain*** (Essanay, 1911). 18 minutes.
Cast: Francis X. Bushman (Mephistopheles).
Notes: This was a burlesque of the opera *Faust,* by Gounod.

311 ***Bill Taken for a Ghost*** (Lux, 1911). 8 minutes.
Notes: The title prankster masquerades as a ghost in the Chateau of Spookeybrook.

312 ***Blood Vengeance*** (Ambrosio, 1911).
Notes: Based on a play by D'Annuncio. The ghost of a girl's mother orders her to kill her murderess with a bag of asps.

313 ***By the House That Jack Built*** (Imp, 1911).
Notes: Under the influence of a witch's potion, a girl's soul leaves her body; the heart of a prince is stolen by a wicked queen.

314 ***The Curse of the Wandering Minstrel*** (Walturdaw, 1911). 10 minutes.
Notes: After a minstrel curses a castle, the castle is invaded and the lord crushed to death under a gateway.

315 ***Dandy Dick of Bishopgate*** (1911). Great Britain. 11 minutes.
Director: Theo Bouwmeester.
Notes: After locking his dead fiancée's room for 40 years, an insane man dies after seeing a vision of her.

316 ***Death*** (Biorama, 1911). 5 minutes.
Notes: The Grim Reaper is depicted wandering the streets of a city.

317 ***The Demon*** (Ambrosio, 1911). Italy. 17 minutes.
Cast: Mme. Cemesnova, M. Navatzi.
Notes: Based on a poem by Lermontof. A woman is tempted by Satan.

318 ***The Devil as Lawyer*** (Messter, 1911). 10 minutes.
Notes: Satan disguises himself as an attorney.

319 ***The Devil's Sonata*** (1911). 14 minutes.
Notes: A strange violinist exerts a hypnotic influence over a girl.

320 ***Dr. Charlie Is a Great Surgeon*** (Éclair, 1911). 7 minutes.

Notes: When a surgeon replaces a man's stomach with a monkey's, the patient begins acting like an ape.

321 *Dr. Jekyll and Mr. Hyde* (Thanhouser, 1911). 15 minutes.
Director: Lucius Henderson.
Cast: James Cruze (Dr. Jekyll/Mr. Hyde), Marguerite Snow (the Minister's Daughter), Harry Benham (the Minister).
Notes: This was a simple and unimaginative adaptation of the Stevenson novel, with Hyde committing suicide by drinking poison at the conclusion. Contemporary publicity maintained that James Cruze played both Jekyll and Hyde, but decades later actor Harry Benham (who plays the minister) claimed that it was he, wearing monster makeup, who had portrayed Jekyll's bestial alter ego, though Benham's contention has never been proven. A close examination of the film seems to indicate that it is, in fact, Cruze playing both halves of Jekyll's personality. This is the earliest screen version of *Dr. Jekyll and Mr. Hyde* still in existence, and the film is available (on the same cassette with John Barrymore's 1920 version) from Kino International Video.

322 *The Electric Villa* (Pathé, 1911). 7 minutes.
Notes: A roasted chicken comes back to life.

323 *An Evil Power* (Selig Polyscope Co., 1911). 17 minutes.
Notes: A girl falls under the influence of a hypnotist.

324 *Faust* (Hepworth, 1911). Great Britain.
Director: Cecil M. Hepworth.
Cast: Hay Plumb, Claire Pridella, Jack Hulcup (Mephistopheles).
Notes: From the opera by Gounod; this film was synchronized with a sound disk.

325 *Faust and Marguerite* (Gaumont, 1911). France.
Director: Jean Durand.

326 *The Fisherman's Nightmare* (Pathé, 1911). 10 minutes.
Notes: Water nymphs condemn a fisherman to be burned alive.

327 *From Death to Life* (Rex, 1911).
Notes: A chemist/necromancer accidentally turns his wife to stone.

328 *The Ghost's Warning* (Edison, 1911). 17 minutes.
Notes: A castle is haunted by a girl's spirit.

329 *The Golden Beetle* (Cines/Kleine, 1911). Italy. 60 minutes.
Notes: A murderer with a dual personality is depicted.

Hallucinations du Baron de Munchausen, Les *see Baron Munchausen's Dream*

330 *Haunted Cafe* (Messter, 1911). Germany. 7 minutes.
Notes: When a man in a restaurant falls asleep, he dreams of supernatural events occurring around him; a waiter vanishes then reappears, a girl materializes from nowhere, the furniture moves under its own power, and so on.

331 *The Haunted House* (Gaumont, 1911). 13 minutes.
Notes: A haunted house is really the headquarters of a criminal gang.

332 *The Haunted House* (Imp, 1911). 17 minutes.
Notes: A man convinces villagers that a house is haunted.

333 *If One Could See into the Future* (Ambrosio, 1911). Italy.
Notes: The Grim Reaper is depicted.

334 *The Inner Mind* (Selig-Polyscope Co., 1911). 17 minutes.
Notes: A hypnotist-detective is featured.

335 *Jones' Nightmare;* **or,** *The Lobster Still Pursued Him* (Acme, 1911).
Notes: A man is pursued by a giant lobster in a dream sequence.

336 *Kitty in Dreamland* (Klein/Urban, 1911). Great Britain. 9 minutes.
Notes: Witches and an ogre appear in a dream.

337 *The Legend of the Lake* (Cines, 1911). 10 minutes.
Notes: A legendary fairy exacts vengeance on murderers.

338 *Little Red Riding Hood* (C&M, 1911). Great Britain. 8 minutes.

339 *Little Red Riding Hood* (Essanay, 1911). 11 minutes.
Cast: Eva Prout.

340 *Little Red Riding Hood* (Majestic, 1911).
Cast: Mary Pickford (Little Red Riding Hood).

341 *The Living Dead* (Gaumont, 1911). 14 minutes.
Notes: A girl impersonates a dead countess who was her twin sister.

342 *The Love of a Siren* (Cines, 1911). Italy. 10 minutes.
Notes: A boy is lured to his death by a siren's spell.

343 *The Man-Monkey* (C&M, 1911). Great Britain. 7 minutes.
Notes: A man acts like an ape after eating "monkey nuts."

344 *A Modern Yarn* (Pathé, 1911). France. 6 minutes.
Notes: A man driving a fantastic car that travels on the ocean floor encounters strange sea monsters.

345 *A Monkey Bite* (Pathé, 1911). France. 7 minutes.
Notes: The victims of a monkey's bite act like monkeys.

346 *The Moonstone* (Urbanora, 1911). 22 minutes.
Notes: Based on the novel by Wilkie Collins. Anyone stealing the jewel of the Moon God is cursed.

347 *The Mummy* (Pathé, 1911). France. 9 minutes.

Notes: A professor's assistant, as part of a plan to marry the professor's daughter, impersonates a mummy.

348 The Mummy (Thanhouser, 1911). 17 minutes.
Notes: A girl is turned into a mummy by electricity.

349 The Mummy (Urban, 1911). 16 minutes.
Notes: A professor dreams that a mummy comes to life.

350 The Mysterious Stranger (Eclipse, 1911). France. 10 minutes.
Notes: A girl struck by lightning is revived.

351 The Mystery of Souls (Itala, 1911). Italy. 50 minutes.
Notes: A hypnotist forces a girl to assist him in a crime.

352 Notre Dame de Paris (Pathé, 1911). France. 45 minutes.
Director: Albert Capellani.
Cast: Henri Krauss (Quasimodo), Stacia Napierkowska (Esmeralda), Claude Garry, Rene Alexandre.
Notes: This film was the first feature-length production of *The Hunchback of Notre Dame.*

353 An Old-Time Nightmare (Powers, 1911).
Notes: A boy is menaced by giant birds.

354 The Pied Piper of Hamlin (Pathé, 1911). France. 15 minutes.

355 The Pied Piper of Hamlin (Thanhouser, 1911).

356 Rosalie and Spiritisme (Pathé-Lux, 1911). [*Rosalie Fait du Spiritisme*]. France.
Director: Romeo Bosetti.

Rosalie Fait du Spiritisme
see *Rosalie and Spiritualism*

357 Satan Defeated (Pathé, 1911). France. 12 minutes.
Notes: Satan's face changes into grotesque masks.

358 Satana (1911). Italy.
Director: Luigi Maggi.
Screenplay: Guido Volante.
Cast: Antonio Grisanti, Mario Bonnard.
Notes: The Devil claims a victim.

359 The Saving of Faust (Pathé, 1911). France. 8 minutes.
Notes: From purgatory, Faust is allowed to see modern Babylon.

360 She (Thanhouser, 1911). 30 minutes.
Cast: James Cruze, Marguerite Snow.
Notes: Based on the novel by H. Rider Haggard. The queen of a lost kingdom is immortalized by a mystical flame.

361 A Spiritualistic Séance (Pathé, 1911). France. 6 minutes.
Notes: A man who scoffs at the supernatural is tormented by demons.

Strega de Siviglia, La see *The Witch of Seville*

362 Willy the Ghost (Éclair, 1911). [*Willy Fantôme*]. France. 7 minutes.
Cast: Willy Saunders.
Notes: A ghost haunts a household.

Willy Fantôme *see* **Willie the Ghost**

363 The Witch of Abruzzi (Le Lion, 1911). 12 minutes.
Notes: A girl is cursed by a witch.

364 The Witch of Seville (Itala, 1911). [*La Stréga de Siviglia*]. Italy. 13 minutes.
Notes: Spirits haunt the wearer of a witch's enchanted cap.

1912

À la Conquête du Pôle *see* **The Conquest of the North Pole**

365 Andalusian Superstition (Pathé, 1912). France. 13 minutes.
Notes: In a cavern hideous living creatures are sealed in bottles.

366 Bebe and Spiritualism (1912). [*Bébé Fait du Spiritisme*]. France.
Director: Louis Feuillade.

Bébé Fait du Spiritisme *see* **Bebe and Spiritualism**

367 Bertie's Book of Magic (Hepworth, 1912). Great Britain. 6 minutes.
Notes: A woman is transformed into a black cat and is changed back when a butcher cuts the cat's throat.

368 Billy's Séance (Imp, 1912). 13 minutes.
Notes: An electric generator is used in a séance.

369 Bobby, "Some" Spiritualist (Gaumont, 1912). 9 minutes.
Notes: A boy frightens people attending a séance.

370 Bob's Nightmare (Mono Film, 1912). 9 minutes.
Notes: A mysterious couple in white are seen in a dream; a huge knife cuts a person's head off.

371 The Brute (Champion, 1912).
Notes: The Grim Reaper claims a drunkard's soul.

372 The Conquest of the North Pole (Star Film, 1912). [*À la Conquête du Pôle*]. France. 20 minutes.
Production: Georges Méliès.

Notes: This Georges Méliès production depicts a threatening arctic snow giant confronting the hapless members of a polar expedition. This film differed little in technique and style from Méliès' first efforts of 16 years before, and it was his last production. After years of undeserved obscurity, Méliès was "rediscovered" upon a major retrospective showing of his work in 1929. The pioneering filmmaker was honored by the French government and awarded a measure of financial security; he died in 1938.

373 ***Conscience*** (Vitagraph, 1912). 10 minutes.
Alternate title: The Chamber of Horrors.
Director: Maurice Costello.
Producer: Albert E. Smith.
Cast: Rose Tapely, Maurice Costello.
Notes: A young woman (Tapely) elopes with her lover (Costello) and travels to New York with him. Complications ensue when she is deserted by her irresponsible husband. Desperate to feed her newborn child, she steals a bottle of milk. Chased by a policeman, she hides in a nearby chamber of horrors; coincidentally, her estranged husband has decided to spend a night in the chamber of horrors in order to win a bet. The next morning he awakes and, unexpectedly seeing his wife, dies of fright, with the experience driving her completely insane.

374 ***Convicted by Hypnotism*** (Éclair, 1912). France. 30 minutes.
Alternate title: A Double Life.
Cast: Cecile Guyon, Charles Krauss.
Notes: A wife, hypnotized by her husband, accidentally kills her father.

375 ***The Curse of the Hindoo Pearl*** (Standard, 1912). 37 minutes.
Notes: A pearl brings death to its owners.

376 ***Curse of the Lake*** (Vitagraph, 1912). 16 minutes.

377 ***The Diabolical Box*** (Urbanora, 1912). 6 minutes.
Notes: An imp transforms itself into an animal and frightens people.

Drama au Château d'Acre, Un; ou, Les Morts Reviennent-Ils? see *A Drama of the Castle; or, Do the Dead Return?*

378 ***A Drama of the Castle; or, Do the Dead Return?*** (1912). [*Un Drama au Château d'Acre; ou, Les Morts Reviennent-Ils?*] France.
Director/Screenplay: Abel Gance.

379 ***The Fatal Pact*** (Pathé, 1912). 7 minutes.
Notes: A gambler promises a genie that he will never gamble again; he fails to keep the pact and vanishes.

380 ***Feathertop*** (Éclair/American Standard, 1912). France. 15 minutes.

Notes: Based on the story by Nathaniel Hawthorne. A witch brings a scarecrow to life.

381 *Gavroche and the Ghosts* (Éclair, 1912). [*Gavroche et les Esprits*]. France.
Director: Romeo Bosetti.

Gavroche et les Esprits *see* Gavroche and the Ghosts

382 *The Ghost of Sulphur Mountain* (American Wild West, 1912). 17 minutes.
Notes: A man's ghost haunts a mine.

383 *Ghosts* (Essanay, 1912).
Notes: A haunted house is shown.

384 *Ghosts* (Hepworth, 1912). Great Britain. 7 minutes.
Notes: Ghosts and spirits are depicted.

385 *The Haunted House* (Pathé, 1912). 8 minutes.
Notes: Peasants in a Spanish inn see a haunted house revolve; faces of cats appear at the windows and fire leaps from the chimney.

386 *The Herncrake Witch* (Heron, 1912). Great Britain.
Director/Screenplay: Mark Melford.
Cast: Jakidawdra, Mark Melford.

387 *The Hindoo's Charm* (Lubin, 1912). 18 minutes.

Notes: When a wife sticks a pin in a clay voodoo figure, her husband feels it.

388 *Hop o' My Thumb* (Gaumont, 1912). France. 30 minutes.
Notes: Based on the fairy tale by Perrault. A giant is depicted.

389 *In the Grip of the Vampire* (Gaumont, 1912).
Screenplay: Leonce Perret.
Notes: A "vampire" guardian of a girl drives her insane with a drug, but a scientist restores her mind with hypnosis.

390 *An Indian Legend* (Mutual, 1912).
Notes: A lake is haunted by the spirit of an Indian girl.

391 *Jack and the Beanstalk* (Edison, 1912).
Notes: From the fairy tale.

392 *The Knight of the Snows* (Pathé, 1912). 22 minutes.
Notes: A baron sells his soul to the Devil in order to prevent a wedding.

393 *The Lady of Shallot* (Hepworth, 1912). Great Britain.
Director: Elwin Neame.
Screenplay: Elwin Neame (based on the poem by Tennyson).
Cast: Ivy Close.
Notes: A lady looks in a cursed mirror, sees a knight and dies.

394 *The Legend of Cagliostro* (Gaumont, 1912). 32 minutes.

Notes: Marie Antoinette's death on the guillotine is predicted by Cagliostro.

395 ***The Legend of Sleepy Hollow*** (Éclair/American Standard, 1912). 12 minutes.
Alternate title: Sleepy Hollow.
Notes: Based on Washington Irving's story of a headless ghost.

396 ***The Lion Tonic*** (Cines, 1912). Italy. 6 minutes.
Notes: A chemist's drug causes his wife to grow and transforms a dog into a lion.

397 ***Live Man's Tomb*** (Itala, 1912). Italy. 35 minutes.
Notes: A woman, believing a man dead, throws his body into a dungeon; she later sees him alive and thinks he is a ghost.

398 ***Magical Matches*** (Urbanora, 1912). 5 minutes.
Notes: Matches take the form of a skeleton, which then removes its own head.

399 ***A Magnetic Influence*** (Urbanora, 1912). 8 minutes.
Notes: A girl is under the influence of a hypnotist.

400 ***Man's Genesis*** (Biograph, 1912). 15 minutes.
Director: D. W. Griffith.
Screenplay: D. W. Griffith, Frank Woods.
Photography: Billy Bitzer.
Cast: Robert Harron (Weakhands), Mae Marsh (Lily White), Wilfred Lucas (Brute Force), William Chrystie Miller (Old Man), Charles Mailes (Boy), W. C. Robinson (Girl).
Notes: The lives of prehistoric cave people and their conflicts are depicted; the main theme is the superiority of intelligence over ignorance as the first tools and weapons are discovered. The following year, this film was expanded with additional footage and retitled *The Primitive Man.*

401 ***The Mystery of the Glass Coffin*** (Éclair/Tyler, 1912). 50 minutes.
Notes: A count unearths the preserved body of an Indian princess in a coffin.

402 ***The Mystical Maid of Jamasha Pass*** (American, 1912). 16 minutes.
Alternate title: The Myth of Jamasha Pass.
Cast: J. Warren Kerrigan.
Notes: A ghostly woman disappears through rock and lures men to their doom.

403 ***Nan in Fairyland*** (C&M, 1912). Great Britain. 19 minutes.
Notes: A giant's children decide to eat a girl for dinner.

404 ***Nursie and Knight*** (Thanhouser, 1912). 17 minutes.
Notes: A boy slays a dragon in a dream sequence.

405 ***One Too Exciting Night*** (Hepworth, 1912). Great Britain. 15 minutes.
Notes: A man buys a haunted house.

406 *Parsifal* (Ambrosio, 1912). Italy.
Notes: From the opera by Wagner. Magicians try to kill knights; a magic looking glass and an angel are depicted.

Polidor al Club Della Morte *see* **Polidor at the Death Club**

407 *Polidor at the Death Club* (Pasquali, 1912). [*Polidor al Club della Morte*]. Italy. 11 minutes.
Alternate title: Polidor, a Member of the Death Club.

408 *Queen of Spades* (Eclipse, 1912). France. 15 minutes.
Notes: A reporter joins a suicide club and draws the wrong card.

409 *The Raven* (Éclair/American Standard, 1912). 30 minutes.
Cast: Guy Oliver.
Notes: Based on scenes from Edgar Allan Poe's stories "The Gold Bug," "The Black Cat," "Murders in the Rue Morgue," "The Pit and the Pendulum," "In the Shadow of the Sea," "A Descent Into the Maelstrom," "The Raven" and "Buried Alive, or The Premature Burial."

410 *The Reincarnation of Karma* (Vitagraph, 1912). 30 minutes.
Notes: A mystic spell causes death; a human transformation into a snake is seen.

411 *St. George and the Dragon* (Milano, 1912). Italy. 45 minutes.
Notes: The legend of St. George and the Dragon is visualized. This film was hand-colored.

412 *Satan* (Ambrosio, 1912). Italy. 40 minutes.
Alternate title: Satan; *or,* The Drama of Humanity.
Director: Luigi Maggi.
Screenplay: Guido Volante.
Cast: Rina Alby, Mary Cleo Tarlarina, Antonio Grisanti.
Notes: This film was based on the poems "Paradise Lost" by John Milton and "The Messiah" by Fredrich Klopstock. The screenplay anticipates the basic structure of D. W. Griffith's *Intolerance* (1916) in its examination of Satan's influence on humanity through the ages.

Schatten des Meeres, Der *see* **The Sea's Shadow**

413 *The Sea's Shadow* (Messters, 1912). [*Der Schatten des Meeres*]. Germany. 40 minutes.
Director: Curt A. Stark.
Producer: Oscar Messter.
Photography: Carl Froehlich.
Cast: Henny Porten, Curt A. Stark, Fran Retzlag, Lizzy Krueger.
Notes: Death rises from the ocean and persuades a despondent young woman (Porten) to forsake life and commit suicide by following him back into the sea. Porten was one of the first German movie stars; the daughter of film director and opera singer Franz Porten, she was married to Curt A. Stark, who directed this film and also acted in

it. The producer, Oscar Messter, was a German film pioneer who directed his own pictures until UFA took control of his firm in 1917.

414 *The Secrets of House No. 5* (Pathé, 1912). Russia.
Notes: Mysticism and ghosts predominate.

415 *The Serpents* (Vitagraph, 1912). 17 minutes.
Cast: Ralph Ince, Edith Storey, Helen Gardner.
Notes: Prehistoric cave men are depicted.

416 *The Silent Castle* (Gaumont, 1912). France. 17 minutes.
Notes: Based on *Sleeping Beauty*. A sorcerer renders the inhabitants of a castle motionless.

417 *Simple Simon and the Devil* (1912). France. 8 minutes.
Director: Jean Durand.
Notes: A man's soul is claimed by the Devil in a dream sequence.

418 *The Skivvy's Ghost* (Lux, 1912).
Notes: A couple owns a house haunted by ghosts.

419 *Sleeping Beauty* (Hepworth, 1912). Great Britain. 17 minutes.
Director/Photography: Elwin Neame.
Cast: Ivy Close.
Notes: Based on the fairy tale by Charles Perrault.

420 *The Speckled Band* (SFFCE, 1912). Great Britain. 1700 feet.
Director: Georges Treville.
Cast: Georges Treville (Sherlock Holmes), Mr. Moyse (Dr. Watson).
Notes: Based on Conan Doyle's characters; murder in a country house.

421 *The Spectre of Jago* (Aquila, 1912). [*Lo Spettro di Jago*]. Italy.
Director: Alberto Carlo Lolli.

422 *Spell of the Hypnotist* (Helios, 1912).
Notes: A hypnotist causes a murder.

Spettro di Jago, Lo *see The Spectre of Jago*

423 *A Spider in the Brain* (Itala, 1912). Italy. 8 minutes.
Notes: A large spider that has burrowed into a person's head is located with an X-ray machine.

424 *Spiffkins Eats Frogs* (Lux, 1912). France. 8 minutes.
Notes: Title character eats frogs and changes into one.

425 *A Spiritualistic Convert* (Pathé, 1912). France. 7 minutes.
Notes: A maid studying mysticism gains occult powers.

426 *Spooks* (Pathé, 1912). 15 minutes.

Notes: A man sees his dead brother's ghost.

427 *The Stronger Mind* (Selig Polyscope Co., 1912). 17 minutes.
Notes: A hypnotic detective is featured.

428 *Supernatural Power* (Pathé, 1912). France. 7 minutes.
Notes: A séance is interrupted by spirits.

429 *The System of Dr. Tarr and Professor Fether* (Éclair, 1912). [*Le Système du Docteur Goudron et du Professeur Plume*]. France. 15 minutes.
Alternate titles: Le Docteur Goudron et le Professeur Plume, Dr. Goudron's System, The Lunatics.
Director: Maurice Tourneur.
Screenplay: Andre de Lord.
Cast: Henri Gouget, Henri Roussell, Renee Sylvaire.
Notes: Derived from Andre de Lord's play *Le Système du Docteur Goudron et du Professeur Plume,* which he had based on Edgar Allan Poe's story "The System of Dr. Tarr and Professor Fether." The story had been filmed before, in a diluted comedy version, by Edison in 1909 under the title *Lunatics in Power* (*q.v.*). This Éclair production was directed by Maurice Tourneur, one of the silent screen's great pictorialists. The story of rebelling inmates taking control of an insane asylum featured an unforgettable image of blood oozing suggestively from under a closed door, a vision of subdued, primal terror that was later used to equally impressive effect in producer Val Lewton's 1943 horror classic *The Leopard Man,* directed by Maurice Tourneur's son Jacques Tourneur.

Système du Docteur Goudron et du Professeur Plume, Le see *The System of Dr. Tarr and Professor Fether*

430 *The Thief and the Porter's Head* (Milano, 1912). Italy. 7 minutes.
Notes: Using electricity, a doctor restores a man's decapitated head.

431 *Trilby* (1912). Austria/Hungary. 50 minutes.
Directors: Luise and Anton Kolm, Jakob Fleck and Claudius Veltee.
Cast: Frau Galafres Hubermann, Paul Askonas.
Notes: Based on the book by Du Maurier.

432 *Trilby* (Standard, 1912). Great Britain.
Notes: Based on the book by Du Maurier.

Vengeance d'Edgar Poe, Une see *The Vengeance of Edgar Poe*

433 *The Vengeance of Edgar Poe* (Lux, 1912). [*Une Vengeance d'Edgar Poe*]. France. 30 minutes.
Director: Gerard Bourgeois.

Screenplay: Gerard Bourgeois, Abel Gance.
Notes: A drug drives Edgar Allan Poe insane.

434 *The Vengeance of Egypt* (Gaumont, 1912). Great Britain. 45 minutes.
Notes: Napoleon Bonaparte disinters an Egyptian mummy wearing a ring with a curse on it. The ring is stolen, and each subsequent owner of the ring dies. When an Egyptologist finally returns the ring to the mummy, the mummy's eyes glow in triumph.

435 *When Soul Meets Soul* (Essanay, 1912). 15 minutes.
Notes: The mummy of an Egyptian princess is acquired by her modern reincarnated lover.

436 *The Woman in White* (Universal, 1912). 35 minutes.
Cast: Janet Salzburg.
Notes: A woman's impersonator dies and is buried in her place.

1913

437 *The Adventures of Three Nights* (Eiko, 1913). 48 minutes.
Notes: A ghostly countess haunts an old castle.

438 *After Death* (Kleine/Cines, 1913). [*Dopo la Morte*]. Italy. 36 minutes.
Notes: Death is simulated with a drug.

439 *After the Welsh Rarebit* (Edison, 1913). 1 reel.
Alternate title: After the Welsh Rabbit.
Cast: William Wadsworth.
Notes: A man dreams that he is tortured in hell.

440 *The Airman's Enemy* (Film de Paris, 1913). France. 48 minutes.

Notes: Hypnotism is used in this story.

441 *The Alchemist* (Kinematograph, 1913). 30 minutes.
Notes: Astrology forecasts a girl's peril. This film was in color.

Andere, Der *see* **The Other**

442 *Atlantis* (Nordisk, 1913). Denmark/Germany.
Director: Ole Olsen.
Screenplay: Gerhardt Hauptmann (based on his novel).
Cast: Olaf Fons.

443 *Babes in the Woods* (Pathé Frères, 1913). France. 15 minutes.
Notes: Based on the fairy tale.

444 *Balaoo* (Éclair, 1913). [*Balaoo;*

ou, *Des Pas au Plafond*]. France. 45 minutes.
Alternate title: Balaoo, the Demon Baboon.
Director: Victorin Jasset.
Cast: M. Bataille (Balaoo), H. Gouget.
Notes: An ape-man is ordered to commit murder. Based on the newspaper serial by Gaston Leroux. Later remade in 1927 as *The Wizard* (*q.v.*).

Balaoo; *ou,* Des Pas au Plafond *see* **Balaoo**

445 Beauty and the Beast (Universal, 1913). 40 minutes.
Producer/Director: H. C. Mathews.
Cast: Elsie Albert.
Notes: Based on the fairy tales by Gabrielle Suzanne and the Brothers Grimm.

446 The Bells (Reliance, 1913). 30 minutes.
Director: Oscar C. Apfel.
Notes: A murderer is haunted by visions of his victim.

447 The Bewitched Matches (Éclair, 1913). France. 8 minutes.
Notes: A man is turned into a skeleton by a witch's curse.

448 The Black Opal (Ramo, 1913). 18 minutes.
Notes: An opal ring bears a curse.

449 Bloomer as a Ghost (Cines, 1913). Italy. 8 minutes.
Notes: Spiritualists are depicted.

450 Brand of Evil (Essanay, 1913). 30 minutes.
Director: H. Webster.
Screenplay: Edward T. Lowe.
Cast: Thomas Commerford.
Notes: When the eye of an idol is stolen, the thief's hand withers.

451 The Cave Dwellers' Romance (Bison, 1913). 33 minutes.
Notes: A man is mystically changed into a horse.

452 The Clown Hero (Imp, 1913). 13 minutes.
Notes: A boy is frightened by nightmares of strange animals.

Dama di Picche, La *see* **Queen of Spades**

453 Dante's Purgatorio (Cinema Productions, 1913).
Notes: A seven-headed beast is depicted.

454 The Dead Man Who Killed (Apex, 1913). France. 65 minutes.
Notes: A criminal's gloves are made of human skin.

455 The Dead Secret (Monopol, 1913). 50 minutes.
Notes: A girl is under a hypnotist's influence. Based on a story by Wilkie Collins.

456 The Death Stone of India (Bison, 1913). 45 minutes.

Notes: A band of coolies all die when they steal the cursed eye of a mysterious idol.

457 The Devil and Tom Walker (Selig, 1913). 15 minutes.
Director: Hardee Kirkland.
Screenplay: Edward McWade (based on the story by Washington Irving).
Cast: Harry Lonsdale, William Stowell (Satan).
Notes: A man sells his soul to the Devil for gold.

458 Dr. Jekyll and Mr. Hyde (Imp, 1913). 33 minutes.
Producer: Carl Laemmle.
Director/Screenplay: Herbert Brenon.
Cast: King Baggot (Dr. Jekyll/Mr. Hyde), Jane Gail (Alice), Matt Snyder (Alice's Father), Howard Crampton (Dr. Lanyon), William Sorelle (Lawyer Utterson).
Notes: This new screen version of the Stevenson novel was tepid and unremarkable. The producing company, Imp, later became Universal Pictures.

459 Dr. Jekyll and Mr. Hyde (Kineto-Kinemacolor, 1913). Great Britain. 30 minutes.
Notes: This rival production of *Dr. Jekyll and Mr. Hyde* was the first color horror film tinted by means other than frame-by-frame hand coloring. This production used a primitive color system involving two interlocked double-speed projectors fitted with revolving red/green filters. Because of the system's obviously cumbersome nature, this version of *Dr. Jekyll and Mr. Hyde* received only sparse distribution.

460 Dr. Trimball's Verdict (Hepworth, 1913). Great Britain. 18 minutes.
Notes: A skeleton takes the form of a doctor's murdered friend, scaring the doctor to death.

461 Don Juan's Compact (Milano, 1913). 35 minutes.
Notes: Don Juan sells his soul to the Devil in exchange for wealth and pleasure.

Dopo la Morte *see After Death*

462 The Egyptian Mummy (Kalem, 1913). 8 minutes.
Notes: A man impersonates a mummy.

d'Épouvante, Le *see Island of Terror*

463 The Evil Power (Rex, 1913). 30 minutes.
Notes: A doctor hypnotizes young women.

464 Eyes of Satan (Solax, 1913).
Notes: A skeleton is brought to life by a conjurer.

465 Faust and the Lily (Biograph, 1913). 8 minutes.
Notes: This film was a burlesque of Goethe's *Faust*.

466 Feathertop (Kinemacolor, 1913).

Notes: A scarecrow is brought to life. Based on the story by Nathaniel Hawthorne.

467 ***The Foreman's Treachery*** (Edison, 1913). 2 reels.
Director: Charles Brabin.
Cast: Miriam Nesbitt, Marc MacDermott, Charles Vernon.
Notes: A man pretends to be a ghost in order to protect his money.

468 ***From the Beyond*** (Éclair/American Standard, 1913). 35 minutes.
Notes: A ghost returns to haunt an ex-rival.

469 ***Funnicus and the Ghost*** (Éclair, 1913). 12 minutes.
Notes: Homeowners are terrified by a man disguised as a ghost.

470 ***The Ghost of Seaview Manor*** (1913). 17 minutes.
Notes: A fake ghost is depicted.

471 ***The Ghost of Self*** (Essanay, 1913).
Notes: A ghost tries to reform a corrupt man through spiritual manifestations.

472 ***Ghost of the Hacienda*** (1913).
Notes: Bandits are frightened by a girl disguised as a ghost.

473 ***The Ghost of the White Lady*** (Great Northern/Nordisk, 1913). 45 minutes.
Alternate title: The White Ghost.

Cast: Rita Sacchetto.
Notes: A woman frightens a man by disguising herself as a legendary ghost.

474 ***Grave Digger's Ambitions*** (1913).
Notes: A deal with the Devil is depicted.

475 ***The Great Ganton Mystery*** (Rex, 1913). 32 minutes.
Notes: Murder and hypnotism are brought into play.

476 ***The Great Physician*** (Edison, 1913). 1 reel.
Director: Richard Ridgely.
Screenplay: B. Merwin.
Cast: Charles Ogle (Death).

477 ***The Green Eye of the Yellow God*** (Edison, 1913). 1 reel.
Director: Richard Ridgely.
Cast: Charles Ogle.
Notes: A man dies after stealing the jeweled eye of a Hindu idol. Based on the poem by J. Milton Hayes.

478 ***The Haunted Bedroom*** (Edison, 1913). 1 reel.
Cast: Jack Strong, Mabel Trunelle, Harry Linson.
Notes: A ghost guards money in a haunted room.

479 ***The Haunted Chamber*** (Anderson, 1913). 45 minutes.

480 ***The Haunted Hotel*** (Pathé, 1913). 20 minutes.

481 The Haunted House (Kalem, 1913). 15 minutes.
Cast: Edgar Davenport, Olive Temple.
Notes: A burglar steals jewels from a haunted house guarded by a ghost.

482 The Haunted House (Mutual, 1913).
Notes: A beautiful girl announces that she will marry the first man who spends the night in a haunted house.

483 The Haunted House (Pathéplay, 1913). 17 minutes.
Notes: A little girl is afraid to walk past a haunted house.

Homme aux Figures de Cire, L' *see* **The Man of the Wax Figures**

484 In the Grip of a Charlatan (Kalem, 1913). 17 minutes.
Notes: A man with hypnotic powers holds a girl prisoner.

485 In the Long Ago (Selig Polyscope Co., 1913).
Director: Colin Campbell.
Screenplay: Lanter Bartlett.
Cast: Wheeler Oakman, Tom Santschi.
Notes: A spell of sleep is used.

486 In the Power of the Hypnotist (Warner's, 1913). 45 minutes.
Director: Sidney Olcott.
Cast: Sidney Olcott, Gene Gauntier.

487 In the Toils of the Devil (Milano, 1913). Italy. 40 minutes.
Notes: A deal with the Devil is depicted.

Insul der Seligen, Die *see* **The Islands of Bliss**

488 The Island of Bliss (Brandon, 1913). [*Die Insul der Seligen*]. Germany. 50 minutes.
Director: Arthur Kahane.
Cast: W. Diegelmann, W. Prager.
Notes: On an island of Roman gods, Circe turns two adventurers into pigs. Adapted from a play by Max Reinhardt.

489 Island of Terror (Kliene/Urbanora, 1913). [*Le d'Épouvante*]. France.
Notes: An insane physician conducts gruesome experiments. Based on the H. G. Wells novel *The Island of Dr. Moreau*.

490 The Isle of the Dead (1913). Denmark.
Director: Wilhelm Gluckstadt.
Notes: A ghost is shown.

491 Love from Out of the Grave (Film d'Art, 1913). 25 minutes.
Notes: An artist is haunted by the ghost of his wife's lover.

492 The Magic Skin (Victor, 1913). 35 minutes.
Cast: J. Warren Kerrigan.
Notes: Adapted from Balzac's *The Wild Ass's Skin*. A magical

skin shrinks as its owner's soul diminishes.

493 The Man in the White Cloak (Great Northern, 1913). Denmark. 45 minutes.
Notes: A spectre is depicted.

494 The Man of the Wax Figures (1913). [*L'Homme aux Figures de Cire*]. France. *Director:* Maurice Tourneur.

495 The Medium's Nemesis (Mutual, 1913). 17 minutes.
Notes: At a séance, a man who believes himself to be a murderer faces the spirit of his supposed victim.

496 The Mysterious Stranger (Essanay, 1913). 17 minutes.
Notes: A man is haunted by hypnotic visions.

497 The Mystery of the Haunted Hotel (Thanhouser, 1913). 17 minutes.
Notes: The title establishment is haunted by a ghost.

498 The Newsboy's Christmas Dream (C&M, 1913). Great Britain. 30 minutes.
Notes: In a dream, a flame-breathing, prehistoric monster is shown.

499 Notre Dame (Pathéplay, 1913). 45 minutes.
Notes: Based on Victor Hugo's novel *Notre Dame de Paris*.

500 The Occult (American/Flying A, 1913).
Notes: Hypnotism is depicted.

Onesime et la Maison Hantée *see Simple Simon and the Haunted House*

501 The Other (Vitascope, 1913). [*Der Andere*]. Germany. *Director:* Max Mack.
Cast: Albert Basserman, Emmerich Hanus, Reilly Ridon, Otto Collot.
Notes: A doctor suffers from a split personality. Based on a play by Paul Lindau.

502 Owana, the Devil Woman (Nestor, 1913). 17 minutes.
Notes: An Indian bridegroom is transformed into a horse.

503 'The Phantom Signal (Edison, 1913). 2 reels.
Director: George Lessey.
Screenplay: H. J. Collins.
Cast: Charles Ogle.
Notes: A skeleton's appearances predict railroad disasters.

504 The Picture of Dorian Gray (1913).
Director: Phillips Smalley.
Cast: Wallace Reid, Lois Weber.
Notes: Based on the novel by Oscar Wilde. A man remains eternally young while his sins are reflected in a hideous portrait of him.

505 The Pied Piper of Hamelin (Edison, 1913). 1 reel.

Director: George Lessey.
Cast: Herbert Prior, Robert Brower.

506 *The Pit and the Pendulum* (Solax, 1913). 50 minutes.
Director: Alice Guy Blanche.
Cast: Darwin Karr, Blanche Cornwall, Fraunie Fraunholz.
Notes: Based on the story by Edgar Allan Poe.

507 *Poisoned Waters* (Universal, 1913).
Notes: A witch curses a fountain so that whoever bathes in the water becomes beautiful and whoever drinks the water dies.

508 *Queen of Spades* (Celio/Kleine/Societa-Italiana, 1913). [*La Dama di Picche*]. Italy.
Cast: Leda Gys, Hesperia.
Notes: Based on the story by Pushkin.

509 *Queen of Spades* (Fidelity, 1913).
Notes: Based on Pushkin's story.

510 *Randin and Co.* (Ambrosio, 1913). Italy. 36 minutes.
Notes: A drug gives the appearance of death.

511 *The Reincarnation of a Soul* (Universal, 1913).
Cast: Edwin August.
Notes: A thief is reincarnated after being struck by lightning.

512 *The Roadside Inn* (Star Film, 1913). France. 4 minutes.
Notes: A man is frightened by fake ghosts.

513 *Satan's Castle* (Ambrosio, 1913).
Notes: Satan arrives to claim the soul of a man who has made a pact with him.

514 *Scrooge* (Big Features, 1913). Great Britain. 50 minutes.
Director: Leedham Bantock.
Screenplay: Sir Seymour Hicks.
Cast: Sir Seymour Hicks.
Notes: Based on Dickens' *A Christmas Carol.*

515 *Simple Simon and the Haunted House* (Gaumont, 1913). [*Onesime et la Maison Hantée*]. France.
Director: Jean Durand.

516 *Simple Simon and the Suicide Club* (Gaumont, 1913). France. 7 minutes.

517 *Sleeping Beauty* (Venus/Warner's, 1913). 45 minutes.
Notes: Based on the fairy tale by Perrault.

518 *Snow White* (Powers, 1913). 50 minutes.
Notes: Based on the Brothers Grimm fairy tale.

519 *The Spell* (Powers, 1913). 35 minutes.
Notes: A hypnotist imposes his will on a young girl.

520 *The Spell* (Vitagraph, 1913). 27 minutes.

Cast: Mary Chapelson.
Notes: A girl is under a hypnotist's spell.

521 *Star of India* (Blanche, 1913). 60 minutes.
Notes: The various owners of a stolen jewel die horribly.

522 *The Student of Prague; or, A Bargain with Satan* (Apex/Bioscop, 1913). [*Der Student von Prague*]. Germany.
Alternate title: From Life to Death; *or,* Flight to the Sun.
Director: Stellan Rye.
Screenplay: Hanns Heinz Ewers (based on the story *William Wilson* by Edgar Allan Poe).
Photography: Guido Seeber.
Art Direction: Robert A. Dietrich, K. Richter.
Cast: Paul Wegener (Baldwin), John Gottowt, Greta Berger, Lyda Salmonova, Lother Korner.
Notes: The story tells of Baldwin, a poor student who sells his soul to the Devil and is thus robbed of his own mirror reflection. Filmed on location in Prague, this movie was a global success and established a wider international market for German motion pictures.

Student von Prague, Der *see* The Student of Prague; or, A Bargain with Satan

523 *The Tenderfoot's Ghost* (Frontier, 1913). 17 minutes.
Notes: A robber is defeated by a ghost.

524 *Trilby* (Vitascope, 1913).
Notes: Based on the Du Maurier novel.

525 *Undine* (Thanhouser, 1913). 35 minutes.
Notes: A sea nymph's death is avenged by her own kind.

526 *The Vampire* (Kalem, 1913).
Cast: Alice Eis (the Vampire), Bert French.

527 *The Vampire* (Searchlight, 1913). Great Britain.
Notes: A girl transforms herself into a snake.

528 *The Vampire of the Desert* (1913). 26 minutes.
Notes: A woman casts a hypnotic spell.

529 *The Werewolf* (Bison/Universal, 1913).
Producer: Henry MacRae.
Notes: Watuma, an American Indian, transforms himself into a wolf, the scene using a simple dissolve to achieve this effect. To date, *The Werewolf* is the only werewolf film to examine the legend's American Indian variation.

530 *What the Gods Decree* (Éclair, 1913). France. 75 minutes.
Cast: Charles Krauss, Josette Andriot.
Notes: A statue of the goddess Kali comes to life.

1914

531 ***The Adventures of Pimple-Trilby*** (Folly, 1914). Great Britain. 21 minutes. *Director/Screenplay:* Fred Evans, Joe Evans. *Cast:* F. Evans (Trilby), J. Evans (Svengali). *Notes:* This film was a burlesque of the Du Maurier novel.

532 ***Alone with the Devil*** (Nordisk, 1914). 53 minutes. *Notes:* Hypnotism is depicted.

533 ***An Ancestor's Legacy*** (Ambrosio, 1914). 18 minutes. *Notes:* Visitors at an old castle are afflicted with horrific nightmares.

534 ***The Avenging Conscience*** (Mutual, 1914). 6 reels. *Alternate title:* Thou Shalt Not Kill. *Director/Screenplay:* D. W. Griffith (based on Edgar Allan Poe's "The Black Cat," "The Conquering Worm," "The Tell-Tale Heart," "The Pit and the Pendulum" and "Annabel Lee"). *Photography:* Billy Bitzer, Karl Brown. *Film Editors:* James Smith, Rose Richtell. *Cast:* Henry B. Walthall (the Nephew), Blanche Sweet (His Sweetheart), Spottiswoode Aitken (the Uncle), Josephine Crowell (Her Mother), George Siegmann (the Italian), Ralph Lewis (the Detective), Mae Marsh (Maid at the Garden Party), Robert Harron (the Grocery Boy), George A. Berranger. *Notes:* This was Griffith's last film before his milestone epic *The Birth of a Nation* in 1915. In this loose take-off from Poe's writings, Griffith veteran Henry B. Walthall plays a man whose love for his sweetheart (Blanche Sweet) is opposed by his overbearing uncle (Spottiswoode Aitken); it's only a matter of time before Walthall has murdered Aitken and hidden the corpse behind a wall. Haunted by this foul deed, Walthall is assailed by a crescendo of images—double-exposures and flash cuts—as his conscience overwhelms him. Although *The Avenging Conscience* still holds viewer interest today, its lame conclusion (a safe, happy "dream" ending) is as disappointing now as it was then. *Review:* "Artistically, Mr. Griffith has put on a beautiful picture in *Conscience*. It lives up to his reputation, from scenes and situations to photography."—*Variety*, August 7, 1914.

535 ***The Avenging Specter*** (Roma, 1914). [*Spèttro Vendicatóre*]. Italy.

536 ***The Basilisk*** (Hepworth,

The Avenging Conscience (1914).

(1914). Great Britain. 28 minutes.
Director/Producer/Screenplay/Photography: Cecil M. Hepworth.
Cast: William Felton, Alma Taylor, Tom Powers, Chrissie White, Cyril Morton.
Notes: A mesmerist pursues a beautiful woman and orders her to stab her fiancé, but the villain is killed by a poisonous snake.

537 *The Bells* (Gaumont, 1914). Great Britian.
Cast: H. B. Irving (Mathias), Frank Keenan, Joseph Dowling, Ed Coxen, Ida Lewis.
Notes: A murderer is driven insane by visions of his victim.

538 *The Bells* (Sawyer's Features, 1914). 40 minutes.
Notes: A murderer is haunted by visions of his victim. Based on the play by Leopold Lewis, derived from the novel by Erckmann-Chatrian.

539 *The Bride of Mystery* (Gold Seal, 1914). 40 minutes.
Notes: A doctor restores a seemingly dead girl to life.

Chien des Baskerville, Le *see* *The Hound of the Baskervilles* (French version)

540 *The Chimes* (Hepworth, 1914). Great Britain. 2500 feet.
Director/Screenplay: Thomas Bentley.

Notes: A spirit guides a man on a horrifying journey into the future.

541 ***A Christmas Carol*** (London, 1914). Great Britain. 22 minutes.
Director/Screenplay: Harold Shaw.
Cast: Charles Rock, George Bellamy, Edna Flugrath, Mary Brough.
Notes: Adapted from the novel by Charles Dickens.

542 ***The Crimson Moth*** (Biograph, 1914). 2 reels.
Cast: Jack Drumier, Louise Vale.
Notes: A curse decrees that when the "Crimson Moth" appears, one of a family's members must die.

543 ***The Curse of the Crimson Idol*** (Phoebus, 1914). 37 minutes.
Notes: A disappearing Hindu attempts to reclaim a Hindu idol.

544 ***The Curse of the Scarabee Ruby*** (Gaumont/Urban-Eclipse, 1914). 42 minutes.
Notes: An evil spirit turns into a girl.

545 ***A Deal in Real Estate*** (1914). 17 minutes.
Notes: A mansion is reputed to be haunted in order to reduce the sale price.

546 ***A Deal with the Devil*** (Nordisk, 1914). 37 minutes.
Notes: A man trades the devil ten years of his life in exchange for fame.

547 ***Diamond of Disaster*** (Thanhouser, 1914). 30 minutes.
Director: Carroll Fleming.
Screenplay: Phil Lonergan.
Cast: J. S. Murray, Ernest Warde, Morgan Jones.
Notes: A diamond causes death and destruction.

548 ***Dr. Jekyll and Mr. Hyde Done to a Frazzle*** (Warner's, 1914). 15 minutes.
Notes: A spoof of the Robert Louis Stevenson novel.

549 ***Doctor Polly*** (Vitagraph, 1914). 30 minutes.
Notes: A mansion is haunted by a ghost.

550 ***The Egyptian Mummy*** (Vitagraph, 1914). 1 reel.
Director: Lee Beggs.
Screenplay: A. A. Methley.
Cast: Billy Quirk, Constance Talmadge, Joel Day.
Notes: A living mummy acts as a matchmaker.

551 ***Ein Seltsamer Fall*** (Vitascope, 1914). Germany. 50 minutes.
Director: Max Mack.
Screenplay: Richard Oswald.
Cast: Alwin Neuss, Hanni Weisse, Lotte Neumann.
Notes: This German production was an unofficial adaptation of Stevenson's novel *The Strange Case of Dr. Jekyll and Mr. Hyde.*

552 The Exploits of Elaine

(Pathé, 1914).
Producers: Theodore W. Wharton, Leopold V. Wharton.
Directors: Louis Gasnier, George B. Seitz.
Screenplay: Arthur B. Reeve, Charles L. Goddard.
Cast: Pearl White (Elaine Dodge), Creighton Hale (Jameson), Arnold Daly (Craig Kennedy), Sheldon Lewis (the Clutching Hand), Floyd Buckley (Michael), William Riley Hatch (President Taylor Dodge), Raymond Owens (Perry Bennett), Robin Towney (Limpy Red), Edwin Arden (Wu Fang), M. W. Rale (Wong Long Sin).
Chapter Titles: (1) The Clutching Hand; (2) The Twilight Sleep; (3) The Vanishing Jewels; (4) The Frozen Safe; (5) The Poisoned Room; (6) The Vampire; (7) The Double Trap; (8) The Hidden Voice; (9) The Death Ray; (10) The Life Current; (11) The Hour of Three; (12) The Blood Crystals; (13) The Devil Worshippers; (14) The Reckoning.
Notes: Sheldon Lewis costarred in this serial as the monstrous "Clutching Hand," a villainous characterization he would repeat (at least in terms of mannerisms) when he appeared as Dr. Jekyll and Mr. Hyde in 1920 (*q.v.*). Lewis revived the character for a low-budget 1936 serial called *The Clutching Hand,* an independent production released by Stage and Screen.

553 The Fakir's Spell

(Dreadnought, 1914).
Director: Frank Newman.
Cast: I. Newman.
Notes: A murderous ape is depicted.

554 The Forbidden Room

(Universal, 1914). 45 minutes.
Notes: A hypnotized girl is ordered to kill.

555 The Forces of Evil; or, The Dominant Will

(Leading Players, 1914). 45 minutes.
Notes: A woman falls under the spell of a hypnotist.

556 The Ghost Breaker

(Paramount, 1914). 5 reels.
Producer: Jesse L. Lasky.
Directors: Cecil B. DeMille, Oscar C. Apfel.
Cast: H. B. Warner (Warren Jarvis), Rita Stanwood (Princess Maria Theresa), Theodore Roberts (Prince of Aragon), Betty Johnson (Carmen), Jode Mullally (Don Luis), Horace B. Carpenter (Carlos, Duke d'Alva), Jeanie MacPherson (Juanita, Carmen's Rival), Mabel Van Buren (Delores), Billy Elmer (Robledo), Dick La Strange (Maximo, the Ghost), Fred Montague (Gaspart, the Ghost), Lucien Littlefield (Judge Jarvis), J. W. Burton (Rusty), J. W. Johnson (Markham).
Notes: This tame comedic horror film involves ghosts haunting a Spanish castle, and, of course, the spirits on hand turn out to have been contrived in an underhanded scheme to steal hidden treasure. This story was filmed to better effect in 1922 (*q.v.*), improved even more as a slick Bob Hope vehicle in 1940, and

The Ghost Breaker (1914).

the same material saw service *again* as a 1952 Dean Martin-Jerry Lewis retread under the title *Scared Stiff*.

557 *The Ghost Club* (American, 1914).

558 *Ghost of the Mine* (Éclair, 1914). 15 minutes.
Notes: A girl's spirit solves her own murder.

559 *A Ghostly Affair* (Hepworth, 1914). Great Britain.
Notes: When a burglar robs a haunted castle, paintings come to life.

560 *Ghosts* (Ivy Close, 1914). Great Britain. 19 minutes.
Producer/Director: E. Neame.
Notes: A haunted house is featured.

561 *The Ghosts* (1914). [*Spiritisten*]. Denmark.
Director: Holger Madsen.
Notes: Ghosts and spiritualism are depicted.

562 *The Ghosts* (Vitagraph, 1914). 1 reel.
Alternate title: Ghosts; or, Who's Afraid?
Director: W. J. Bauman.
Notes: A mansion is supposedly haunted by the ghost of an old soldier.

563 *The God of Vengeance* (Chariot, 1914). 60 minutes.

564 *The Golem* (Deutsche-Bioscop, 1914). [*Der Golem und Wie auf de Welt Kam*]. Germany. 6 reels. *Alternate title:* The Monster of Fate (U.S.).
Directors: Paul Wegener, Henryk Galeen.
Photography: Guido Seeber.
Art Direction: R. A. Dietrich, R. Gliese.
Cast: Paul Wegener, Carl Ebert, Lyda Salmonova.
Notes: While on location filming *The Student of Prague* (1913) in that city, Paul Wegener had learned about the legend of the Golem, a massive clay statue magically brought to life by Rabbi Lowe in the late 16th century to save the city's Jews from persecution by Rudolph II of Hapsburg. In what was undoubtedly an economy move, Wegener set his film adaptation in contemporary times, casting himself as the Golem. The Golem is created as an avenging servant, but then rebels against his creator when he falls hopelessly in love with a beautiful girl, played by Lyda Salmanova (Wegener's wife). The similarities to later Frankenstein movies are obvious, and Wegener was so taken with the role that he played the hulking stone monster in two more features, made in 1917 and 1920. Only this last film, also entitled *The Golem,* survives today.

Golem und Wie auf de Welt Kam, Der *see* **The Golem**

565 *Guarding Britain's Secrets* (Walturdaw, 1914). Great Britain. 3300 feet. *U.S. Title:* The Fiends of Hell.
Director: Charles Calvert.
Screenplay: Dr. Nikola Hamilton.
Cast: Douglas Payne, Dr. Nikola Hamilton, Norman Howard.
Notes: A detective with occult powers battles a hypnotic medium.

566 *Hands Invisible* (Powers, 1914). 15 minutes.
Notes: A man's hands try to strangle his wife.

567 *The Haunted Attic* (Lubin, 1914). 1 reel.
Notes: An attic is haunted by a barber.

Haus Ohne Turen und Fenster, Das *see* **The House Without Doors or Windows**

568 *Henpeck's Nightmare* (Cosmograph, 1914). 8 minutes.
Notes: Strange apparitions are depicted.

569 *Hidden Death* (Gaumont, 1914). 35 minutes.
Notes: An all-powerful murderess dominates a castle in the Middle Ages.

570 *The Hound of the Baskervilles* (Pathé, 1914). [*Le Chien des Baskerville*]. France. 45 minutes.

571 *The Hound of the Baskervilles* (Vitascope, 1914). [*Der*

Hund von Baskerville]. Germany. In 2 parts: Part 1—65 minutes; Part 2—55 minutes.
Director: Rudolph Meinert.
Producer: Josef Greenbaum.
Screenplay: Richard Oswald.
Photography: Karl Freund, Werner Brandes.
Cast: Alwin Neuss, Friedrich Kuehne, Erwin Fichtner, Hanni Weisse, Andreas Von Horn.
Notes: This film adaptation of Sir Arthur Conan Doyle's novel was released in two parts. Oddly, the character of Dr. Watson did not appear in this film. The titular hound was described in reviews as "a monstrous Great Dane with flaming eyes and fire emerging from its mouth." This film was abridged and reissued in 1921.

572 The House of Fear (Lubin, 1914). 35 minutes.
Notes: Ghosts are shown.

573 The House Without Doors or Windows (1914). [*Das Haus Ohne Turen und Fenster*]. Germany.
Director: Stellan Rye.

574 The Hunchback of Cedar Lodge (Balboa, 1914). 45 minutes.
Notes: A ghost haunts a library.

Hund von Baskerville, Der *see* **The Hound of the Baskervilles** (German version)

575 The Hypnotic Violinist (Warner's, 1914). 45 minutes.
Notes: A doctor's wife is controlled by psychic power.

576 The Imp Abroad (Victor, 1914). 15 minutes.
Notes: An imp, eloping with an heiress, reverts to his true Satanic form.

577 The Invisible Power (Kalem, 1914).
Notes: A girl falls under a man's hypnotic influence.

578 A Lady of Spirits (Edison, 1914).
Cast: Harry Gripp (the Ghost), William Wadsworth.

579 Legend of the Phantom Tribe (Bison, 1914). 30 minutes.
Notes: A tribe of savages is reincarnated by witchcraft.

580 The Marriage of Psyche and Cupid (1914). 30 minutes.
Notes: Proserpine, the Queen of the Underworld, is visited by Psyche.

581 A Midnight Scare (Crystal, 1914). 8 minutes.
Notes: Ghost stories inspire a practical joke.

582 The Miser's Conversion (Thanhouser, 1914).
Cast: Sidney Bracy.
Notes: The story of a 75-year-old man obsessed with Darwinism, who regains his youth after drinking a special formula, and, when he

greedily drinks more of the concoction, devolves into an ape!

583 *Murders in the Rue Morgue* (Rosenberg, 1914).
Notes: Based on the story by Edgar Allan Poe; a gorilla kills for its master.

584 *The Mystery of Grayson Hall* (Éclair, 1914). 30 minutes.
Notes: A detective, impersonating a murdered man, "haunts" the man's killer.

585 *Mystery of the Death Head* (Monarch, 1914). 3 reels.

586 *The Mystery of the Fatal Pearl* (American Kineto, 1914). 5 reels.
Notes: The owners of a cursed pearl die.

587 *The Mystery of the Hidden House* (Vitagraph, 1914). 2 reels.
Notes: A girl with a dual personality is possessed by two souls.

588 *The Mystery of the Sleeping Death* (Kalem, 1914). 30 minutes.
Cast: Tom Moore.
Notes: Reincarnation and a curse of living death are featured.

589 *Naidra, the Dream Worker* (Edison, 1914). 3 reels.
Notes: A thief steals a mummy's cursed necklace only to find that he is unable to get rid of it.

590 *A Night in the Chamber of Horrors* (Éclair, 1914). 15 minutes.
Notes: Grand Guignol horror as another figure is added to the collection in a chamber of horrors.

591 *A Night of Thrills* (Universal/Rex, 1914). 25 minutes.
Director: Joseph De Grasse.
Cast: Lon Chaney.
Notes: This film was a haunted house comedy and one of the earliest screen appearances of Lon Chaney.

592 *Peter's Evil Spirit* (Urban-Eclipse, 1914). France. 8 minutes.
Notes: A man is tortured by a satanic tramp.

593 *The Phantom Light* (Bison, 1914). 30 minutes.
Notes: An American Indian is persecuted by the spirit of the brother he murdered.

594 *The Phantom Violin* (Universal, 1914).
Director: Francis Ford.
Notes: A maniac hides in a crypt.

595 *The Plot* (Vitagraph, 1914). 2 reels.
Directors: Robert Gaillord, Maurice Costello.
Cast: Estelle Mardo, Robert Gaillord.
Notes: A reporter is hypnotized and instructed to assassinate the Russian ambassador to the United States.

596 *The Princess of Darkness* (Aquila, 1914).

597 *Ruslan i Ljudmila* (1914). Russia. 82 minutes.
Director/Photography/Art Direction: Ladislas Starevich.
Cast: Ivan Mosjoukine (Devil), S. Vassilieva.
Notes: Based on Pushkin's narrative poem and filmed with stop-motion animation. Demons and the Devil are featured.

598 *Sinews of the Dead* (Gaston Méliès, 1914).
Notes: A man is driven insane by a graft from a dead strangler.

Spèttro Vendicatóre *see The Avenging Spectre*

Spiritisten *see The Ghosts*

599 *The Suicide Club* (Apex/British & Colonial, 1914). Great Britain.
Producer: Maurice Elvey.
Cast: Elizabeth Risdon.

600 *Svengali* (Wiener Kuntsfilm, 1914). Austria. 58 minutes.
Directors: Luise Kolm, Jakob Fleck.
Cast: Frl. Nording, Ferdinand Bonn.
Notes: Based on the novel *Trilby* by George Du Maurier.

601 *The Temptations of Joseph* (Kineto, 1914). 22 minutes.
Notes: A lustful mummy awakens in an antique shop.

602 *The Temptations of Satan* (Warner's, 1914). 75 minutes.
Director: Herbert Blache.
Cast: Binnie Burns, Joseph Lovering, James O'Neill (Satan).
Notes: A woman is tempted by Satan's helpers.

603 *The Terrible Two in Luck* (Phoenix, 1914). Great Britain. 13 minutes.
Director/Screenplay: James Read.
Cast: Joe Evans, James Read.
Notes: Ghosts are depicted in a search for treasure.

604 *Through the Centuries* (Selig Polyscope Co., 1914). 18 minutes.
Notes: Two scientists discover an ancient princess asleep in a catacomb.

605 *Trilby* (London, 1914). Great Britain.
Producer: Harold Shaw.
Cast: Sir Herbert Tree, Viva Birkett, Philip Merivale.
Notes: Based on the Du Maurier novel.

606 *The Unknown Country* (Lubin, 1914). 1 reel.
Notes: Spirits leave their bodies to gain control of other bodies.

607 *The Vampire* (Éclair, 1914). 32 minutes.
Notes: A psychologist is ordered by a mysterious sect to murder his wife using narcotics and a huge vampire bat.

608 ***Vendetta*** (Eclipse, 1914). France. 80 minutes.
Director: Louis Mereanton.
Cast: Regina Badet.
Notes: A supposedly dead man regains consciousness while he is buried. Based on the book by Marie Corelli.

609 ***The VIJ*** (Khanzhonkov, 1914). Russia. 82 minutes.
Director/Screenplay/Photography: Ladislas Starevitch.
Cast: Ivan Mosjoukine (Witch), Olga Obolenskaya, V. Turzhansky.
Notes: From Gogol's story about witches and Satan. Filmed using stop-motion animation, this was later made as a sound film, *Black Sunday,* in 1960.

610 ***When Spirits Walk*** (Frontier, 1914). 17 minutes.
Notes: A haunted house and a somnambulist cook are shown.

611 ***Whiffle's Nightmare*** (CGPC/Pathé, 1914). France. 8 minutes.
Notes: A haunted house is depicted.

612 ***While John Bolt Slept*** (Edison, 1914). 1 reel.
Notes: A spirit wanders through evil regions.

613 ***The White Spectre*** (General, 1914). 40 minutes.
Notes: A spectre is part of the scheme to foil blackmailers.

614 ***The White Wolf*** (Nestor/Universal, 1914).
Notes: A wolf in a trap is transformed into an Indian medicine man.

615 ***Woman of Mystery*** (Blanche, 1914). 65 minutes.
Director/Screenplay: Alice Guy Blanche.
Cast: Vinnie Burns, Fraunie Fraunholz.
Notes: A dual personality and spirit control are shown.

1915

616 ***The Agony of Fear*** (Selig Polyscope Co., 1915). 3 reels.
Director: Giles R. Warren.
Screenplay: William E. Wing.
Notes: A man dies of fright.

617 ***At the Signal of the Three Socks*** (1915).
Notes: This was episode #5 of *The Mysterious Lady Baffles and Detective Duck* series. A maid frightens a couple by dressing as a ghost.

618 ***The Black Box*** (Universal, 1915). 15 chapter serial.
Director: Otis Turner.
Cast: Herbert Rawlinson, Anna Little, Frank Lloyd, William Worthington.
Notes: A prehistoric ape-man, hypnotism and a cloak of invisibility are featured in this cliffhanger.

619 ***The Black Crook*** (Kalem, 1915). 60 minutes.
Screenplay: Phil Lang (based on the play by Charles M. Barras.
Cast: E. P. Sullivan.
Notes: A man promises Satan that he will deliver one soul a year to him.

620 ***The Blood Seedling*** (Selig, 1915). 3 reels.
Cast: Thomas Santschi, Leo Pierson, Thomas Bates.
Notes: A murderer is exposed at a séance.

621 ***The Bribe*** (Victor/Universal, 1915).
Cast: Charles Ogle, Mary Fuller.
Notes: A girl steals under the influence of hypnotism.

622 ***The Bridge of Time*** (Selig Polyscope Co., 1915). 3 reels. 35 minutes.
Director: Frank Beal.
Notes: A villainous ancestor's soul returns to his body.

623 ***Call from the Dead*** (Thanhouser, 1915). 15 minutes.
Notes: A murder is avenged by a corpse.

624 ***The Case of Becky*** (1915).
Director: Frank Reicher.
Cast: Blanche Sweet, Carlyle Blackwell, James Neill.
Notes: A split personality is imposed on a girl through hypnotism.

625 ***The Cheval Mystery*** (Victor, 1915). 35 minutes.
Cast: Harry Myers, Rosemary Theby.
Notes: A normal girl is transformed into a maniac by hypnotism.

626 ***Chronicles of Bloom Center*** (Selig Polyscope Co., 1915). 25 minutes.
Cast: Sidney Smith, William Hutchinson.
Notes: Spiritualists are frightened by a man dressed as a ghost, then real spirits appear.

627 ***The Circular Staircase*** (Selig Polyscope Co., 1915). 5 reels.
Director: Edward J. La Saint.
Cast: Eugenie Besserer, Stella Razeto, Guy Oliver, Edith Johnson.
Notes: Based on the novel by Mary Roberts Rinehart. A man is frightened to death by a ghost.

628 ***The Club Pest*** (Biograph, 1915). 8 minutes.
Notes: A man stays overnight in a haunted house on a bet.

629 ***Col. Heeza Liar, Ghost Breaker*** (Bray, 1915). 1 reel.
Notes: A haunted house is depicted in this animated cartoon.

630 Col. Heeza Liar in the Haunted House (Bray, 1915). 1 reel.
Notes: Ghosts and haunted houses are shown in this animated cartoon.

631 *A Cry in the Night* (New Agency, 1915). Great Britain. 20 minutes.
Director: Ernest G. Batley.
Cast: James Russell (the Thing).
Notes: A girl's father is killed by a winged gorilla under the control of a mad scientist.

632 *Destiny's Skein* (Lubin, 1915). 3 reels.
Director/Screenplay: George Terwilliger.
Cast: Tom Green, Ormi Hawley.
Notes: A man with a split personality commits crimes during periods of mental aberration.

633 *The Devil* (New York Motion Picture, 1915). 55 minutes.
Screenplay: Thomas H. Ince (based on the novel by Charles Swickard and the play by Franz Molnar).
Cast: Bessie Barriscale, Arthur Maude.
Notes: Several people are tempted by Satan.

634 *The Devil's Profession* (Arrow, 1915). Great Britain. 55 minutes.
Director/Screenplay: F. C. S. Tudor.
Cast: Alesia Leon.
Notes: Based on G. S. W. James' novel. A doctor injects wealthy people with a drug that causes insanity.

635 *Distilled Spirits* (MinA, 1915). 12 minutes.
Notes: A drunkard experiences visions of strange monsters.

636 *The Dream Dance* (Lubin, 1915). 30 minutes.
Notes: A man suffering from nightmares dies in his sleep.

637 *The Duel in the Dark* (Thanhouser, 1915).
Cast: Morris Foster, Flo LaBadie.
Notes: Long-distance hypnotism is depicted.

638 *The Dust of Egypt* (Vitagraph, 1915). 6 reels.
Director: George D. Baker.
Screenplay: Alan Campbell (based on his play *The Dust of Egypt*).
Photography: Joe Shelderfer.
Costumes: Jane Lewis.
Cast: Antonio Moreno (Geoffrey Lascelles), Edith Storey (Amenset), Hughie Mack (Billings), Charles Brown (Simpson), Jay Dwiggins (Mr. Manning), William Shea (Whiggins), Edward Elkas (Ani), J. Herbert Frank (Pinetum), Nicholas Dunaew (Slave), George Stevens (Dr. Jenkins), Jack Brawn (Benson), Mr. Sneeze, Mr. Pluto (Nubians), Cissy Fitzgerald (Mrs. Manning), Naomi Childers (Violet Manning), Ethel Corcoran (Maid).
Notes: The mummy of an Egyptian princess returns to life.

639 *The Eleventh Dimension* (Imp, 1915). 2 reels.
Screenplay: Raymond L. Shrock.
Notes: Attempts to restore the dead to life are depicted.

640 *Esther Redeemed* (Renaissance, 1915). Great Britain. 35 minutes.
Director/Screenplay: Sidney Morgan.
Cast: Julian Royce, William Brandon, Mona K. Harrison, Cecil Fletcher.
Notes: Based on the play *The Wolf Wife* by Arthur Bertram. A girl's immoral nature is altered by a surgical operation.

641 *The Experiment* (Edison, 1915). 1 reel.
Cast: Robert Brower, Bessie Learn.
Notes: A man nearly dies during an experiment in hypnosis.

642 *Foiled* (Kalem, 1915).
Cast: Ethel Teare.
Notes: A genie turns a man into a skeleton.

Folie du Docteur Tube, La *see* The Madness of Dr. Tube

643 *The Fox Woman* (Mutual, 1915). 45 minutes.
Cast: Elmer Clifton, Teddy Sampson.
Notes: Based on the novel by John Luther Long. When a vampirish "fox woman" dies, a man's soul is restored to him.

644 *Freaks* (Joker, 1915).
Director: Allen Curtis.
Screenplay: Clarence Badger.
Cast: Max Asher, William Franey, Gale Henry, Lilian Peacock.
Notes: Actors are made up as various freaks, including a human skeleton. No relation to the later Tod Browning film *Freaks* (1932).

645 *The Ghost Fakirs* (Starlight, 1915).
Notes: Two men stay overnight in a haunted house.

646 *Ghost of the Twisted Oaks* (Lubin, 1915). 35 minutes.
Director: Sidney Olcott.
Screenplay: Pearl Gaddis.
Cast: Valentine Grant, Florence Wolcott, James Vincent.
Notes: Voodooism and a ghost are depicted.

647 *Ghosts and Flypaper* (Vitagraph, 1915). 1 reel.
Producer: Ulysses Davis.
Screenplay: Louis B. Rose.
Cast: Anne Schaefer, Marguerite Reid, Otto Lederer.
Notes: A reportedly haunted house and fake ghosts are depicted.

648 *The Goddess* (Vitagraph, 1915). 15 chapter serial.
Director: Ralph Ince.
Cast: Anita Stewart, Earle Williams, Paul Scardon.
Notes: A girl is under the spell of a hypnotist in this cliffhanger.

649 *Graft* (Universal, 1915). 20 chapter serial.
Director: Richard Stanton.
Cast: Robert Henley, Harry D. Carey, Nanine Wright.
Notes: An apparently dead man returns to life in this cliffhanger.

650 *The Grasping Hand* (1915). [*La Main Qui Étreint*]. France. 35 minutes.
Alternate title: Max and the Clutching Hand (Max et la Main Qui Étreint).
Director: Louis Gasnier.
Cast: Max Linder.
Notes: A ghost is depicted in this comedy-horror outing.

651 *The Gray Horror* (Lubin, 1915). 3 reels.
Notes: A lawyer and his ward are frightened by ghosts in an old mansion.

652 *The Greater Will* (Pathé, 1915). 55 minutes.
Cast: Cyril Maude, Louis Meredith.
Notes: A hypnotic vision compels a man to commit suicide.

653 *The Hand of the Skeleton* (1915). [*La Main du Squelette*]. France.
Director: George Schneevoight.
Notes: A ghost is depicted.

654 *Haunted* (Superba, 1915). 7 minutes.
Notes: A man is tortured by visions of a dead man.

655 *The Haunting of Silas P. Gould* (Hepworth, 1915). Great Britain. 16 minutes.
Director: Elwin Neame.
Cast: Ivy Close.
Notes: Having sold her home to an American millionaire, an heiress then masquerades as a ghost in order to frighten him away.

656 *Haunting Winds* (Universal, 1915). 15 minutes.
Director: Carl M. Le Viness.
Screenplay: Earl R. Hewitt (story by G. E. Jenks).
Cast: Sydney Ayres, Doris Pawn.
Notes: A man who has murdered by accident is haunted by moaning winds, swaying tree limbs and banging doors.

657 *Heba the Snake Woman* (Excelsior, 1915).

658 *His Egyptian Affinity* (Nestor, 1915). 1 reel.
Screenplay/Producer: A. E. Christie.
Cast: Victoria Ford, Eddie Lyons.
Notes: A revived 3,000-year-old princess meets her reincarnated lover. They are both then pursued by thé reincarnated son of a shiek.

659 *Horrible Hyde* (Lubin, 1915).
Director: Jerold Hevener.
Screenplay: E. Sargent.
Notes: Based on the Robert Louis Stevenson novel *The Strange Case of Dr. Jekyll and Mr. Hyde*. An actor poses as the Mr. Hyde character.

660 *The Hound of the Baskervilles* (Greenbaum Film, 1915). [*Der Hund von Baskerville*]. Germany. Consisting of two parts. Part 1 – 50 minutes. Part 2 – 50 minutes.
Producer: Josef Greenbaum.
Director/Screenplay: Richard Oswald.

Cast: Alwin Neuss, Friedrich Kuehne, Erwin Fichtner, Andreas Van Horn, Tatjana Irrah, Hilde Borke.
Notes: German producer Josef Greenbaum left Vitascope to establish his own production company in 1915, and made a two-part rival version of *The Hound of the Baskervilles* to compete with the two-parter released the previous year by Vitascope (*q.v.*), using most of the same cast and crew from the Vitascope films. In retaliation, Vitascope, now renamed Pagu, released their *own* episode three, entitled *Der Hund von Baskerville: Das Dunkle Schloss.*

661 *The House of a Thousand Candles* (Selig Polyscope Co., 1915). 5 reels.
Director: T. N. Heffron.
Screenplay: Gilson Willets (based on the novel by Meredith Nicholson).
Cast: Harry Mestayer, Grace Darmond, George Backus.
Notes: A haunted house with secret panels is featured.

662 *The House of the Lost Court* (Edison, 1915). 5 reels.
Director: Charles R. Brabin.
Cast: Gertrude McCoy, Viola Dane, Duncan McRae.
Notes: Based on the novel by Mrs. C. M. Williamson. An oriental poison gives the appearance of death.

663 *The House with Nobody in It* (Rialto/Gaumont, 1915).
Director: Richard Garrick.
Screenplay: Dr. Clarence J. Harris.
Cast: Ivy Troutman, Bradley Barker, Frank Whitson.
Notes: Mysterious flashes of light emanating from an old house spur rumors that it is haunted.

Hund von Baskerville, Der *see* **The Hound of the Baskervilles**

664 *The Hypnotic Monkey* (Kalem, 1915). 15 minutes.
Director: Alfred Santell.
Cast: Lloyd Hamilton, Bud Duncan.
Notes: In a dream sequence, a man is transformed into a monkey and then back into a man.

665 *In Zululand* (1915).
Cast: Mattie Edwards, John Edwards.
Notes: A mother's daughters masquerade as ghosts in order to frighten away the man who intends to marry her.

666 *The Inner Brute* (Essanay, 1915). 2 reels.
Notes: A man whose mother was frightened by a tiger inherits beastial instincts.

667 *An Innocent Sinner* (Kalem, 1915). 40 minutes.
Cast: Katherine La Salle, Guy Coombs.
Notes: A villainous doctor exercises hypnotic powers.

668 *Inventing Trouble* (Cricks, 1915). Great Britain. 10 minutes.
Director: W. P. Kellino.
Screenplay: Reuben Gillmer.
Notes: An inventor who demonstrates labor-saving devices is eaten by a prehistoric monster.

669 *The Japanese Mask* (Pathé-Aetna, 1915). 40 minutes.
Notes: The Fates decree that anyone looking at the title mask will die an unnatural death.

670 *The Kidnapped Stockbroker* (Vitagraph, 1915). 2 reels.
Director: William Humphrey.
Notes: A haunted house is featured.

671 *The Legend of the Lone Tree* (Vitagraph, 1915). 1 reel.
Director: Ulysses Davis.
Cast: Myrtle Gonzalez, Alfred D. Vosburgh.
Notes: A murderer cursed by a tribal medicine man is transformed into a tree.

672 *Life Without Soul* (Ocean Distributing Co., 1915). 5 reels.
Director: John W. Smiley.
Screenplay: Jesse J. Goldberg (based on the novel *Frankenstein* by Mary W. Shelley).
Cast: William A. Cohill (Victor Frawley, a medical student), Percy Darrell Standing (his creation), George De Carlton (William Frawley, his father), Jack Hopkins (Richard Clerval, his friend), Lucy Cotton (Elizabeth Lavenza, ward of William Frawley), Pauline Curley (Claudia Frawley, his sister), David McCauley (Victor Frawley, as a child), Violet De Biccari (Elizabeth Lavenza, as a child).
Notes: Life Without Soul was the first feature-length adaptation of Mary W. Shelley's novel *Frankenstein*. The picture failed commercially, and Raver Film Corp. then acquired *Life Without Soul* and attempted to salvage the movie by re-cutting it with instructional "scientific" tedium (microscopic views of blood cells, etc.), only to repeat Ocean Distributing's box-office disaster, and *Life Without Soul* passed into a celluloid oblivion that was probably well-deserved.
Review: "...adapted from Mary Shelley's novel *Frankenstein* ... it is the familiar story of a physician who discovers a life-giving fluid and creates a superman of enormous physique but without conscience.... [H]ere is a subject worth the effort of a Griffith. The Ocean folks have done well with it, despite numerous inconsistencies.... [T]heir scenario is at times rather vague, but the novelty of the idea for filming will be sure to create a healthy demand for the picture...."—*Variety,* November 26, 1915.

673 *The Live Mummy* (Pathé, 1915). Great Britain. 15 minutes.
Notes: A man poses as an Egyptian mummy in order to fool a scientist.

674 *Lotta Coin's Ghost* (Ham Comedies, 1915). 12 minutes.
Cast: Maria Sais, Lloyd Hamilton, Bud Duncan.
Notes: Burglars are frightened by a woman dressed as a ghost.

675 *The Madness of Dr. Tube* (Les Films d'Art/Louis Nalpas, 1915). [*La Folie du Docteur Tube*]. France.
Alternate Titles: Le Docteur Tube; Story of a Madman.
Director/Screenplay: Abel Gance.
Photography: Wentzel.
Cast: Albert Dieudonne.
Notes: A scientist's attempts to break up light waves go awry. To represent the scientist's insanity, a few scenes in *The Madness of Dr. Tube* were photographed through a distorting lens, producing stylized visuals that almost predicted the expressionism of *The Cabinet of Dr. Caligari* (1919). Both Gance and Dieudonne would go on to direct and star, respectively, in Gance's sprawling 1927 historical epic *Napolean*.

676 *The Magic Skin* (Kleine/Edison, 1915). 5 reels.
Director/Screenplay: Richard Ridgely.
Notes: Based on Balzac's *The Wild Ass's Skin*.

Main du Squelette, La *see* **The Hand of the Skeleton**

Main Qui Étreint, La *see* **The Grasping Hand**

677 *The Midnight Specter* (Talia, 1915). [*Lo Spèttro di Mezzanòtte*]. Italy.

678 *Miss Jekyll and Madame Hyde* (Vitagraph, 1915). 3 reels.
Director: Charles L. Gaskill.
Cast: Helen Gardner, Paul Scardon (Satan).
Notes: A villain's soul is chained by Satan.

679 *Miss Trillie's Big Feet* (Novelty, 1915).
Cast: Edith Thornton, Joe Burke.
Notes: A spoof of George Du Maurier's novel *Trilby*.

680 *The Missing Mummy* (Kalem, 1915).
Cast: Bud Duncan, Charles Inslee, Ethel Teare.
Notes: A man disguises himself as a mummy.

681 *The Monkey's Paw* (Magnet, 1915). Great Britain. 45 minutes.
Cast: Jack Lawson.
Notes: Based on the story by W. W. Jacobs. A monkey's paw possesses supernatural powers.

682 *Mortmain* (Vitagraph, 1915). 1 reel.
Cast: Robert Edeson, Donald Hall.
Notes: In a dream sequence, a man loses his hand, and another is grafted in its place.

683 *Neal of the Navy* (Pathé, 1915). 14 chapter serial.

Director: W. M. Harvey.
Cast: Lillian Lorraine, William Conklin, William Courtleigh, Jr., Ed Brady.
Notes: A beastial apeman character is featured in this cliffhanger.

684 One Million Dollars (Rolfe-Metro, 1915). 5 reels.
Director: John W. Noble.
Cast: William Faversham, Henry Bergman, Charles Graham.
Notes: A detective with supernatural powers projects his astral spirit into the presence of suspects.

685 The Other Self (Lubin, 1915). 30 minutes.
Director: Leon D. Kent.
Screenplay: J. L. Lamothe.
Notes: A girl acquires a split personality through hypnosis.

686 The Phantom Witness (Thanhouser, 1915). 45 minutes.
Screenplay: Philip Lonergan.
Cast: Kathryn Adams.
Notes: A ward's ghost incriminates a murderer guardian.

687 The Picture of Dorian Gray (1915). [*Portrét Doriana Greja*]. Russia.
Director: Vsevolod Meyerhold.
Notes: Based on Oscar Wilde's novel.

688 The Picture of Dorian Gray (Thanhouser, 1915). 30 minutes.
Cast: Harris Gordon, A. Howard, Helen Fulton.
Notes: Based on Wilde's novel.

Portrét Doriana Greja *see* **The Picture of Dorian Gray**

689 The Raven (Essanay, 1915). 6 reels.
Cast: Henry B. Walthall, Wanda Howard.
Notes: Based on a play by George C. Hazelton and the writings of Edgar Allan Poe. In a vision, Poe kills his spirit double and sees the spirit of Lenore.

690 The Return of Richard Neal (Essanay, 1915). 3 reels.
Cast: Francis X. Bushman, Bryant Washburn, Neil Craig, Ernest Maupin.
Notes: A girl is influenced by hypnotism.

Rhapsodia Satanica *see* **Satanic Rhapsody**

691 *Satanic Rhapsody* (1915). [*Rhapsodia Satanica*]. Italy.
Cast: Lyda Borelli.
Notes: In order to regain her youth, a woman sells her soul to the Devil. This film was originally color-tinted.

692 The Secret Room (Kalem, 1915). 2 reels.
Director: Tom Moore.
Cast: Tom Moore, Marguerite Courtot, Robert Ellis.
Notes: A mad doctor attempts to transfer a man's soul to his retarded son's body.

693 The Silent Command (Universal, 1915). 4 reels.

Director/Screenplay: Robert Leonard.
Cast: Ella Hall, Harry Carter, Alan Forrest.
Notes: A doctor tries to hypnotize a girl into killing her own father.

694 The Soul of Phyra (Domino, 1915). 30 minutes.
Notes: After a maiden is mystically summoned to India in order to be sacrificed, her husband hears her soul calling to him and then dies himself.

695 The Specter of the Vault (Riviera, 1915). [*Lo Spettro del Sotterraneo*]. Italy.
Director: Ubaldo Maria Del Colle.

Spettro del Sotterraneo, Lo *see* **The Spectre of the Vault**

Spettro di Mezzanotte, Lo *see* **The Midnight Spectre**

696 A Spirited Elopment (Edison, 1915).
Cast: William Wadsworth, Viola Dane.
Notes: Ghosts are depicted.

697 Spirits Free of Duty (Horseshoe, 1915). Great Britain. 14 minutes.
Notes: A man scares a farmer by posing as a ghost.

698 The Spook Raisers (Kalem, 1915).
Cast: Ethel Teare.
Notes: Two con-men stage fake séances.

699 The Strange Unknown (Lubin, 1915). 3 reels.
Screenplay: William H. Ratterman.
Cast: L. C. Shumway, George Routh, Helen Eddy, Dorothy Barrett, Melvin Mayo.
Notes: A haunted house and a woman's ghost are featured.

700 The Three Wishes (Gaumont, 1915). 8 minutes.
Notes: A goblin grants three wishes to an elderly couple.

701 The Tragedies of the Crystal Globe (Edison, 1915). 3 reels.
Director: Richard Ridgely.
Cast: Robert Conness, Mabel Trunelle, Bigelow Cooper.
Notes: Hypnotically influenced by an Oriental mystic, a girl sees herself die three times in previous incarnations.

702 Trilby (Equitable-World, 1915). 5 reels.
Director: Maurice Tourneur.
Screenplay: I. M. Ingleton (based on the novel by George Du Maurier).
Art Director: Ben Carrer.
Assistant Director: Clarence L. Brown.
Cast: Clara Kimball Young (Trilby), Wilton Lackaye (Svengali), Chester Barnett (Little Billy), Paul McAllister (Gecko), James Young, Phyllis Neilsson Terry.

Review: "There are a number of faults to be found with *Trilby*. One expected much more of William Lackaye, who gave a most intelligent and not exaggerated conception of Svengali, but this was a distinct disappointment. He might have disregarded a modicum of consistency and contributed a bit of sensationalism. Clara Kimball Young as Tilby gave a most convincing characterization. — *Variety*, September 10, 1915.

703 The Unfaithful Wife
(Fox, 1915). 6 reels.
Director: J. Gordon Edwards.
Screenplay: Mary Murillo.
Cast: Robert B. Mantell, Genevieve Hamper, Stuart Holmes, Warner Oland.
Notes: A nobleman escapes after having been entombed alive.

704 The Warning
(Triumph/Equitable, 1915). 60 minutes.
Director: Edmund Lawrence.
Cast: Henry Kolker, Lily Leslie, Christine Mayo.
Notes: The suffering of the damned in hell is depicted in allegorical scenes.

705 Weird Nemesis
(Victor, 1915). 2 reels.
Director/Screenplay: Jacques Jaccard.
Cast: Alan Forrest.
Notes: Hypnotism is featured.

706 When the Mummy Cried for Help
(Nestor/Universal, 1915).
Cast: Lee Moran, Eddie Lyons.
Notes: A man disguises himself as a mummy.

707 When the Spirits Moved
(Universal, 1915). 1 reel.
Director/Screenplay: Al Christie.
Cast: Lee Moran, Eddie Lyons, Victoria Forde.
Notes: A man is cursed by spirits.

708 Which Is Witch?
(Martin, 1915). Great Britain. 533 feet.
Director: Edwin J. Collins.
Notes: A landowner is cursed by a witch.

709 The White Pearl
(Paramount, 1915).
Cast: Marie Doro.
Notes: A pearl stolen from an idol is cursed.

710 The Wraith of Haddon Towers
(Clipper, 1915). 45 minutes.
Cast: Constance Crawley, Arthur Maude, Beatrice Van.
Notes: A locked room is haunted by a ghost.

711 The Wraith of the Tomb
(Cricks, 1915). Great Britain. 3000 feet.
Alternate title: The Avenging Hand.
Director: Charles Calvert.
Screenplay: William J. Elliot.
Cast: Dorothy Bellew, Sydney Vautier, Douglas Payne.
Notes: The stolen hand of a mummified Egyptian princess commits murder.

1916

712 The Arrow Maiden (Mutual, 1916). 15 minutes.
Notes: An American Indian is revived from a spell by a medicine woman, and frightens another brave who thought he was dead.

713 Beauty and the Beast (International Film Service, 1916).
Director/Screenplay: H. E. Hancock.
Cast: Mineta Timayo.

714 Black Magic (Kalem, 1916). 25 minutes.
Director: James W. Horne.
Screenplay: George B. Howard.
Cast: Maria Sais, Ollie Kirkby.
Notes: This was an episode in the series *The Social Pirates*. A wealthy woman is under the power of a Hindu fakir.

715 Black Orchids (Bluebird, 1916). 5 reels.
Director/Screenplay: Rex Ingram.
Photography: Duke Hayward.
Cast: Cleo Madison (Marie De Severac/Zoraida), Richard La Reno (Emile De Severac), Francis McDonald (George Renoir/Ivan De Maupin), Wedgewood Nowell (Marquis De Chantal), Howard Crampton (Sebastian De Maupin), William J. Dyer (Proprietor of L'Hibour Blanc), John George (Ali Bara), Joe Martin (Hatim-Tai).
Notes: A flirtatious young woman is frightened into following a more virtuous path after her father relates a story in which a similar girl is entombed alive.

716 The Bogus Ghost (Kalem, 1916).
Notes: A woman believed drowned masquerades as a spirit for a mystic.

717 Chamber of Horrors (1916). 1 reel.
Notes: An animated cartoon in the *Mutt & Jeff* series.

718 Crime and Penalty (Martin, 1916). Great Britain. 57 minutes.
Director: R. H. West.
Cast: Alesia Leon, Jack Lovatt, Louis Nanten.
Notes: A woman is kidnapped with the aid of a chimpanzee that strangles when hypnotized.

719 The Crimson Stain Mystery (Consolidated Film Corp., 1916). 16 chapter serial.
Director: T. Hayes Hunter.
Screenplay: Albert Payson Terhune.
Photography: Ludwig G. B. Erb.
Cast: Maurice Costello (Harold Stanley), Ethel Grandin (Florence Montrose), Thomas J. McGrane

The Crimson Stain Mystery **(1916).**

(Dr. Burton Montrose), Olga Olonova (Vanya Tosca), Eugene Strong (Robert Clayton), William H. Cavanaugh (Doctor's Assistant), John Milton (Layton Parrish), N. J. Thompson (Jim Tanner).

Chapter Titles: (1) The Brand of Satan; (2) The Demon's Spell; (3) The Broken Spell; (4) The Mysterious Disappearance; (5) The Figure in Black; (6) The Phantom Image; (7) The Devil's Symphony; (8) In the Shadow of Death; (9) The Haunting Specter; (10) The Infernal Fiend; (11) The Tortured Soul; (12) The Restless Spirit; (13) Despoiling Brutes; (14) The Bloodhound; (15) The Human Tiger; (16) The Unmasking.

Notes: Mad scientist Dr. Burton Montrose's efforts to develop superior intelligence go predictably awry, resulting instead in the creation of horrible, mutated freaks. Banding together into a criminal organization, they initiate a reign of terror against society, opposed by a young detective, who eventually unmasks their leader – the mysterious "Crimson Stain" – as none other than Dr. Burton Montrose.

720 *The Dawn of Freedom*
(Vitagraph, 1916). 5 reels.
Director: Paul Scardon.
Screenplay: William J. Hurlbut.

Cast: Charles Richman, Arline Pretty, Joseph Kilgour, James Morrison.
Notes: Under the influence of hypnotism, a man goes into suspended animation.

721 *The Dead Alive* (Gaumont, 1916). 55 minutes.
Notes: The twin sister of a dead girl is forced by a crook to pose as her sister's ghost.

722 *A Deal with the Devil* (Hepworth, 1916). Great Britain. 17 minutes.
Director: Frank Wilson.
Notes: An elderly chemist sells his soul for youth.

723 *The Death Kiss* (Great Northern, 1916). Sweden.
Director: Victor Seastrom.

724 *The Devil's Toy* (Premo-Equitable, 1916). 55 minutes.
Screenplay: Edward Madden, Maurice Marks (based on the poem *The Mills of the Gods* by Edward Madden).
Cast: Adele Blood, Montagu Love, Edwin Stevens (Satan), Jack Halliday, Madge Evans.
Notes: A man influenced by visions of Satan commits murder.

725 *Double Dubs* (Pathé, 1916).
Notes: Two men masquerade as ghosts and frighten rivals who stole their girlfriends.

726 *Elixir of Life* (Joker, 1916). 11 minutes.
Director: Allen Curtis.
Screenplay: Harry Wulze.
Cast: William Franey, Gale Henry, Lilian Peacock.
Notes: A mummy is restored to life.

727 *Frilby Frilled* (Lubin, 1916). 1 reel.
Director/Screenplay: Edwin McKim.
Cast: David Don (Svengarlic), Patsy De Forest, George Egan.
Notes: This film was a spoof of George Du Maurier's novel *Trilby*.

728 *The Golem* (1916). Denmark.
Director: Urban Gad.

729 *The Green-Eyed Monster* (Fox, 1916). 5 reels.
Director: J. Gordon Edwards.
Screenplay: J. Gordon Edwards, Marie Murillo.
Cast: Robert B. Mantell, Stuart Holmes, Genevieve Hamper.
Notes: A woman dies of shock after seeing her murdered husband's corpse; a murderer later uncovers the decomposed skeleton and collapses from fright.

730 *Haunted* (E&R Jungle Film Co., 1916).
Cast: Lillian Leighton, Ralph McComas.
Notes: Newlyweds staying in a bungalow are frightened by the ghostly tricks of a mischievous chimpanzee.

731 *The Haunted Bell* (Universal, 1916). 2 reels.
Director: Henry Otto.

Screenplay: J. Grubb Alexander (based on a story by Jacques Futrelle).
Cast: King Baggot, Edna Hunter, Joseph Smiley.
Notes: A woman believes that a sacred bell is haunted.

732 Haunts for Rent (Paramount, 1916).
Alternate Title: Haunts for Hire.
Screenplay: C. Allan Gilbert.
Animation: L. M. Glackens.
Notes: A girl insists that she will marry the suitor who can spend the night in a haunted house. This film combined live-action and animation.

733 Her Father's Gold (Thanhouser, 1916). 55 minutes.
Cast: Barbara Gilroy, Harris Gordon, William Burt, Louise Bates.
Notes: A reporter encounters a sea monster in Florida.

734 Her Invisible Husband (Universal, 1916). 1 reel.
Producer: Matt Moore.
Notes: In a dream, a sorceress gives a man a magic ring, which renders him invisible without his knowledge.

735 Homunculus (Deutsch-Bioscop, 1916). [*Die Rache des Homunculus*]. Germany. 6 chapter serial.
Director: Otto Rippert.
Screenplay: Otto Rippert, Robert Neuss.
Photography: C. Hoffmann.
Art Direction: R. Dietrich.
Cast: Olaf Fons (Homunculus), Aud E. Nissen, Theodor Loos, Lupu Pick.
Notes: A doctor creates an artificial being. Loosely based on Mary W. Shelley's novel *Frankenstein,* each chapter of this German serial was feature-length.

736 The Jewel of Death (1916). 22 minutes.
Director: M. J. Fahrney.
Screenplay: James Dayton.
Cast: William Clifford, Bud Osborne.
Notes: The magical eye of an idol causes death.

737 Lola (World, 1916).
Alternate Title: Without a Soul.
Cast: Clara Kimball Young, James Young, Alec Francis.
Notes: Based on the play by Owen Davis. The daughter of a doctor who has invented a life-restoring machine dies and is brought back to life by the device.

738 Luke's Double (Pathé, 1916).
Notes: A man reading Robert Louis Stevenson's novel *The Strange Case of Dr. Jekyll and Mr. Hyde* falls asleep, dreaming that he is tormented by an evil twin.

739 The Man Without a Soul (London, 1916). Great Britain.
Director: George Loane Tucker.
Cast: Barbara Everest, Milton Rosmer, Edward O'Neill, Kitty Cavendish, Hubert Willis, Charles Rock.
Notes: A man revived from the dead lacks any trace of morality.

740 *Midnight* (Universal/Imp, 1916). 1 reel.
Screenplay: E. J. Clawson.
Notes: A priest is led to a dying man by a girl who is really a ghost.

741 *Mingling Spirits* (Nestor, 1916). 1 reel.
Producer: Al Christie.
Screenplay: Al Christie, Robert McGowan.
Cast: Lee Moran, Eddie Lyons, Betty Compson.
Notes: A spiritualist is frightened by a man disguised as the Devil.

742 *Mr. Tvardovski* (1916). [*Pan Tvardovski*]. Russia.
Director/Photography: Ladislas Starevitch.
Cast: N. Saltikoff, S. Tchapelski.
Notes: Based on the story by I. J. Kraszevski. A deal with the Devil is depicted.

743 *The Modern Sphinx* (American, 1916). 33 minutes.
Director: Charles Bennett.
Cast: Winifred Greenwood, Edward Coxen, Robert Klein, George Field, Nan Christy, Charles Newton.
Notes: An Egyptian girl is placed in suspended animation for 3,000 years by her astrologer father. She awakens in the present to have a tragic love affair, commits suicide, and reawakens unharmed in the past.

744 *The Mysteries of Myra* (Pathé, 1916). 15 chapter serial.
Directors: Theodore Wharton, Leo Wharton.
Cast: Jean Sothern (Myra), Howard Estabrook, Allen Murname, M. W. Rale, Bessie Wharton.
Chapter titles: (1) Unknown Title; (2) Unknown Title; (3) The Mystic Mirrors; (4) Unknown Title; (5) Unknown Title; (6) Unknown Title; (7) Unknown Title; (8) Unknown Title; (9) The Invisible Destroyer; (10) Levitation; (11) The Fire-Elemental; (12) The Elixir of Youth; (13) Witchcraft; (14) Suspended Animation; (15) The Thought Monster.
Notes: A character named "The Thought Monster," created by "The Grand Master of the Black Order," was described in publicity for *The Mysteries of Myra* as "a sort of psychic Frankenstein. This monster is a huge and powerful creation. But his disposition is sort of like a child, in that he is easily distracted from his purpose. He starts to smash things up in the laboratory and to kill Myra. He sees his reflection in the mirror and forgets what he is after."

745 *The Mysterious Mrs. M* (Bluebird, 1916). 55 minutes.
Cast: Harrison Ford, Mary McLaren, Willie Marks.
Notes: A fortune-teller predicts that both she and a customer will soon die. The customer believes in the prophecy when he learns that the fortune-teller has died.

Nachte des Grauens *see Night of Terror*

746 *Night of Terror* (1916). [*Nachte des Grauens*]. Germany.

Alternate titles: A Night of Horror; A Night of Horror in the Menagerie.
Director: Arthur Robison.
Cast: Werner Krauss, Emil Jannings, Lupu Pick.
Notes: Vampire-like people are depicted.

747 *The Ocean Waif* (International/Golden Eagle, 1916). 5 reels.
Screenplay: Frederick Chapin.
Cast: Doris Kenyon, Carlisle Blackwell, Fraunie Fraunholz.
Notes: A girl pretends to be a ghost in a haunted house.

748 *Only a Room-er* (Cricks, 1916). Great Britain. 10 minutes.
Director: Toby Cooper.
Screenplay: E. Dangerfield.
Cast: Jack Jarman.
Notes: Men play tricks on a friend sleeping in a haunted room.

Pan Tvardovski *see* **Mr. Tvardovski**

749 *The Picture of Dorian Gray* (Barker-Neptune-Browne, 1916). Great Britain. 6 reels.
Director: Fred W. Durant.
Screenplay: Rowland Talbot (based on the novel by Oscar Wilde).
Cast: Henry Victor (Dorian Gray), Pat O'Malley (Sybil Vane), Jack Jordon (Lord Henry Wooton), Sydney Bland (Basil Hallward), A. B. Imeson (Satan), Douglas Cox (James Vane), Dorothy Fane (Lady Marchmont), Miriam Ferris.

750 *The Queen of Spades* (PFA, 1916). 53 minutes.
Screenplay: F. Otsep.
Photography: Y. Slavkinsky.
Art Direction: V. Ballieuzek.
Notes: The ghost of a Countess frightened to death by a man tells him the secret of winning at cards.

Rache des Homunculus, Die *see* **Homunculus**

751 *Rah, Rah, Rah* (Vitagraph, 1916). 1 reel.
Director: Larry Semon.
Screenplay: Larry Semon, Graham Baker.
Cast: Hughie Mack, James Aubrey, Patsy de Forrest.
Notes: In this comedy, robbers and actors confront each other in a haunted house.

752 *The Real Thing at Last* (British Actors, 1916). Great Britain. 33 minutes.
Directors; James M. Barrie, L. C. MacBean.
Screenplay: James M. Barrie.
Cast: Ernest Thesiger (Witch), Gladys Cooper (American Witch), Edmund Gwenn. Godfrey Tearle, Owen Nares, A. E. Matthews.
Notes: This film was a contemporized adaptation of Shakespeare's *Macbeth,* emphasizing the witches and supernatural aspects.

753 *The Right to Be Happy* (Bluebird, 1916). 5 reels.
Director: Rupert Julian.
Screenplay: E. J. Clawson (based on Charles Dickens' *A Christmas Carol*).

Cast: Rupert Julian (Scrooge), John Cook, Claire McDowell.

Rubezahl's Hochzeit *see Rubezahl's Marriage*

754 *Rubezahl's Marriage* (Wegener, 1916). [*Rubezahl's Hochzeit*]. Germany.
Director/Screenplay: Paul Wegener.
Art Direction: Rochus Gliese.
Cast: Paul Wegener, Lyda Salmonova, Marianne Niemeyer.
Notes: A phantom giant terrorizes a family on a mountain outing by creating a monstrous storm.

755 *The Ruling Passion* (Fox, 1916). 5 reels.
Director: Joseph MacKay.
Producer/Screenplay: Herbert Brenon.
Cast: Claire Whitney, Stephen Grattan, Edward Boring.
Notes: The wife of an English officer is hypnotized by an Indian prince.

756 *The Scorpion's Sting* (Victor, 1916). Great Britain. 3 reels.
Cast: George Bellamy, Fay Temple.
Notes: An ex-convict sells his soul to Satan.

757 *Secret of the King* (Nordisk, 1916). Denmark. 35 minutes.
Notes: A cursed ring brings death to its owner.

758 *A Shadowed Shadow* (Joker, 1916).
Screenplay: Jack Byrne.
Notes: Fake ghosts are featured.

759 *She* (Barker, 1916). Great Britain.
Director: Lisle Lucoque.
Screenplay: Nellie Lucoque (based on H. Rider Haggard's novel *She*).
Cast: Alice Delysia, Henry Victor, Jack Denton, Sidney Bland, Blanche Forsythe.

760 *The Shielding Shadow* (Pathé, 1916). 15 chapter serial.
Directors: Louis Gasnier, Donald MacKenzie.
Screenplay: George B. Seitz.
Cast: Grace Darmond, Ralph Kellard, Leon Barry.
Notes: A girl is protected by a shadowy figure with burning eyes. Hypnotism and a cloak of invisibility are also featured.

761 *The Silent Stranger* (Universal, 1916).
Screenplay: Frank Smith.
Cast: King Baggot, Irene Hunt.
Notes: Satan restores a dead girl to a man with the condition that he must not smile or laugh. The girl dies when the man fails to keep his unholy bargain.

762 *Skelley's Skeleton* (American, 1916). 11 minutes.
Notes: A haunted house, a magician, a skeleton and a torch-lit visit to a forest are featured.

763 *Snow White* (Educational, 1916). 45 minutes.

764 *Snow White* (Paramount, 1916). 70 minutes.
Director: J. Searle Dawley.
Photography: H. L. Broening.
Cast: Creighton Hale, Marguerite Clark.
Notes: Based on the Brothers Grimm fairy tale.

765 *Sold to Satan* (Lubin, 1916). 3 reels.
Screenplay: R. P. Rifenborich, Jr.
Cast: Edward Sloman (Satan), L. C. Shumway.
Notes: A man sells his soul to Satan in exchange for youth and wealth.

766 *The Soul's Cycle* (Centaur, 1916). 55 minutes.
Director: Ulysses Davis.
Cast: Margaret Gibson, Roy Watson (Satan).
Notes: A man reincarnated as a lion and a bargain with Satan are depicted.

767 *Thinnen Stout* (Mutual, 1916).
Cast: Orral Humphrey, Lucille Ward, John Gough.
Notes: A diet specialist reduces a patient to skeleton form.

768 *The Treasure of Cibola* (Kalem, 1916).
Notes: This film was episode #6 in *The Girl from 'Frisco* series. A girl masquerades as a ghost in order to frighten people.

769 *20,000 Leagues Under the Sea* (Universal, 1916). 8 reels.
Director: Stuart Paton.
Assistant Director: Martin Murphy.
Screenplay: Stuart Paton (based on the novel by Jules Verne).
Photography: Eugene Gaudio.
Assistant Photographers: Friend Baker, Milton Loryea.
Art Direction: Frank D. Ormston.
Technical Directors: H. H. Barter, James Milburn.
Cast: Allan Holubar (Captain Nemo/Prince Daaker), Jane Gail (a Child of Nature/Princess Daaker), Dan Hanlon (Professor Aronnax), Edna Pendleton (Aronnax's daughter), Curtis Benton (Ned Land), Matt Moore (Lieutenant Bond), Howard Crampton (Cyrus Harding), Wallace Clark (Pencroft), Martin Murphy (Herbert Brown), Leviticus Jones (Neb), William Welch (Charles Denver), Lois Alexander (Prince Daaker's daughter, as a child), Joseph W. Girard (Major Cameron), Ole Jansen.
Notes: Sea monsters were seen in this adaptation of Jules Verne's 1870 novel, filmed over two years at a cost of $500,000. The underwater scenes were photographed by the Williamson Submarine Film Corp. in the Bahamas.

Vampires, Les *see The Vampires, the Arch Criminals of Paris*

770 *The Vampires, the Arch Criminals of Paris* (Gaumont, 1916). [*Les Vampires*]. France. 9 chapter serial; 3 reels each.
Director/Screenplay: Louis Feuillade.

Photography: Manichoux.
Cast: Musidora (Irma Vep), Marcel Levesque, Louis Leubas (Satanas), Jean Ayme (Le Grand Vampire).
Chapter titles: (1) The Detective's Head; (2) The Red Notebook; (3) The Ghost; (4) The Dead Man's Escape; (5) The Eyes That Hold; (6) Satanas; (7) The Master of Thunder; (8) The Poison Man; (9) The Terrible Wedding.
Notes: Hypnosis and various super-scientific gadgets are utilized by a cadre of super-criminals in this French cliffhanger.

771 *Witch of the Dark House* (Kalem, 1916).
Notes: This film was episode #14 of *The Girl from 'Frisco* series. A haunted house and a witch are featured.

772 *The Witch of the Mountains* (Knickerbocker, 1916). 35 minutes.
Cast: Marguerite Nichols, Gordon Sackville, Richard Johnson.
Notes: A ghostly witch guards a mountainside cave.

773 *The Witching House* (Frohman, 1916).
Cast: C. Aubrey Smith, Marie Shotwell.
Notes: Based on the book *Caleb Powers*. A man is compelled to murder the owner of a cat's eye pin. Psychic power and telepathy are featured.

Yoghi, Der *see The Yogi*

774 *The Yogi* (1916). [*Der Yoghi*]. Germany.
Cast: Paul Wegener.
Notes: This film starred Wegener in the dual roles of a youthful inventor and a yogi who becomes invisible.

1917

775 *Aladdin and the Wonderful Lamp* (Fox, 1917). 8 reels.
Directors: C. M. Franklin, S. A. Franklin.
Screenplay: Bernard McConville.
Cast: Violet Radcliffe, Virginia Corbin, Buddy Messinger, Elmo Lincoln.
Notes: An evil magician and an evil spirit are featured.

776 *Avarice* (Imp/Universal, 1917).
Director/Screenplay: E. Magnus Ingleton.
Cast: Claire McDowell, T. D. Crittenden (Death), Leo Pearson, Betty Schade.
Notes: Death reviews the life of a miserly woman.

777 *Babes in the Woods* (Fox, 1917). 6 reels.
Directors: C. M. Franklin, S. A. Franklin.
Screenplay: Bernard McConville (based on the fairy tale *Hansel and Gretel*).

Bildnis des Dorian Gray, Das see *The Picture of Dorian Gray*

778 *Brand of Satan* (Peerless-World, 1917). 55 minutes.
Director: George Archianbaud.
Screenplay: J. F. Looney.
Cast: Montagu Love.
Notes: A strangler is afflicted with a split personality.

779 *Conscience* (Fox, 1917). 6 reels.
Director: Bertram Bracken.
Screenplay: Adrian Johnson (based on a story by J. Searle Dawley and E. Lloyd Sheldon).
Cast: Gladys Brockwell (Serama/Ruth Somers/Conscience/Lust/Avarice/Hate/Revenge/Vanity), Marjorie Daw (Madge), Eugenie Forde (her mother), Eve Southern (Alice Marsh), Genevieve Blinn (Mrs. Marsh), Douglas Gerrard (Cecil Brooke), Edward Cecil (Alan Mackay), Harry G. Lonsdale (Rupert Cowdray), Colin Chase (Ned Langley), Bertram Grassby (Dr. Norton/the Devil).
Notes: Serama, Lucifer's consort, is barred from Paradise by the Archangel Michael, who commands Conscience to enter human souls so that mankind may be judged and punished. Elements of John Milton's *Paradise Lost* were also woven into this allegorical melodrama.

780 *The Darling of Paris* (Fox, 1917). 5 reels.
Director: J. Gordon Edwards.
Screenplay: Adrian Jackson (based on the novel *Notre Dame de Paris* by Victor Hugo).
Photography: Phil Rosen.
Cast: Theda Bara (Esmeralda), Glen White (Quasimodo), Walter Law (Claude Frallo), Herbert Hayes (Capt. Phoebus), Miss Carey Lee (Pacquette), Alice Gale (Gypsy Queen), John Webb Dillon (Clopin), Louis Dean (Gringouier).
Review: "...Its main weakness is the casting of Theda Bara in the role of an innocent gypsy girl, with no opportunity to wear modern alluring costumes or give her any opportunity to 'vamp.' The first portion of the photoplay is merely a series of 'high spots' from the famous novel, but culminates in the trial of Esmeralda for murder, her being tortured until she confesses to a crime she didn't commit, her rescue by the gypsies, etc."— *Variety,* January 26, 1917.

781 *The Devil-Stone* (Artcraft Pictures Corp., 1917). 5 reels.
Producer: Jesse L. Lasky.
Director: Cecil B. DeMille.
Assistant Director: Cullen Tate.
Screenplay: Jeanie MacPherson (story by Beatrice C. DeMille and Leighton Osmun).
Photography: Alvin Wyckoff.
Art Direction: Wilfred Buckland.
Cast: Geraldine Farrar (Marcia Manot), Wallace Reid (Guy Sterling), Hobart Bosworth (Robert

The Darling of Paris (1917): Theda Bara as Esmeralda.

Judson), Tully Marshall (Silas Martin), James Neill (Simpson), Gustav von Seyffertitz (Stephen Densmore), Ernest Joy, Mabel Van Buren, Lillian Leighton, Burwell Hamrick, Horace B. Carpenter, Theodore Roberts, Raymond Hatton.

Notes: A girl finds a priceless emerald cursed by the Devil.

782 *The Devil's Assistant*
(Pollard Picture Plays/Mutual, 1917). 5 reels.

Producer/Director: Harry Pollard.

Screenplay: J. Edward Hungerford.

Cast: Margarita Fisher (Marta), Monroe Salisbury (Dr. Lorenz), Kathleen Kirkham (Marion Dane), Jack Mower (John Lane), Joseph Harris (Butler).

Notes: In this surprisingly raw melodrama, an evil doctor addicts a woman to drugs and attempts to rape her in a mountain cabin during a thunderstorm, when the cabin is struck by lightning and both are buried in the crumbling ruins.

783 *The Dinosaur and the Missing Link* (Edison, 1917).
5 minutes.

Producer/Director: Willis H. O'Brien.

Notes: Under the production banner of Conquest Pictures, the Edison Studios produced a series of comedy shorts with prehistoric themes featuring animated models of dinosaurs and cavemen, brought to life through stop-motion animation, with the figures photographed one frame at a time. Model animation for these shorts was provided by Willis H. O'Brien, a former sculptor with the 1915 San Francisco World's Fair who, after holding various odd jobs, had drifted into the film industry. O'Brien's tenure with Edison was brief-faced with rising competition from the newly established major studios, the company abandoned film production in 1918. In *The Dinosaur and the Missing Link,* the titular missing link bears more than a passing resemblance to a much later and considerably more impressive ape-like O'Brien creation — *King Kong.*

Elet Kiralya, Dorian Gray, Az see *The Picture of Dorian Gray* [802]

784 *The Enchanted Kiss* (General, 1917). 20 minutes.
Cast: Chet Ryan, Frances Parks.
Notes: In a dream sequence, a man finds the secret of eternal youth by devouring the flesh of a maiden once a year.

785 *Eyes in the Dark* (Imp/Universal, 1917). 22 minutes.
Director: Frank H. Crane.
Screenplay: Stuart Paton.
Notes: A mysterious ruby has occult powers.

786 *The Fighting Gringo* (Universal, 1917). 5 reels.
Director: Fred Kelsey.
Screenplay: Maud Grange (story by H. W. Philips).
Cast: Harry Carey, Claire Du Bray, George Webb, T. D. Crittendon, Rex de Rosselli.
Notes: A man with political ambitions holds a girl under his hypnotic influence.

787 *Gertie on Tour* (1917). 2 minutes.
Director: Winsor McKay.
Notes: Gertie the dinosaur rides on a streetcar in this animated cartoon, a sequel to *Gertie the Dinosaur* (1909).

788 *Ghost Hounds* (Kalem, 1917).
Notes: Thieves are sentenced to spend the night in a haunted house.

789 *The Ghost House* (Paramount, 1917).
Director: William C. deMille.
Screenplay: Beulah Dix.
Photography: Paul Perry.
Notes: Bank robbers hide out in a haunted house.

790 *Ghost of Old Morro* (Edison, 1917). 55 minutes.
Director: Richard Ridgely.
Screenplay: James Oppenheim.
Cast: Mabel Trunnelle, Robert Conness, Helen Strickland.
Notes: An old castle, a witch and murders are depicted.

791 *The Ghost of Rosie Taylor* (American, 1917). 52 minutes.

Director: Edward Sloman.
Screenplay: Elizabeth Mahoney.
Cast: Marion Lee, Helen Howard, Mary Miles Minter, Kate Price.
Notes: A house is rumored to be haunted.

792 The Golem and the Dancer (Bioscop, 1917). [*Der Golem und der Tänzerin*]. Germany.
Director: Paul Wegener.
Cast: Paul Wegener (the Golem).
Notes: In this off-beat sequel, Wegener plays himself, as he attends a screening of his previous success *The Golem,* and is then inspired to make himself up as his monstrous film character in order to frighten a beautiful dancer and seduce her. *The Golem and the Dancer* bears the distinction of being the first horror movie sequel.

Golem und der Tänzerin, Der *see* **The Golem and the Dancer**

793 The Haunted House (Triangle, 1917).

794 The Heir of the Ages (Paramount, 1917). 5 reels.
Cast: House Peters, Eugene Pallette, Adele Farrington.
Notes: A caveman is reincarnated.

795 Her Temptation (Fox, 1917). 5 reels.
Director: Richard Stanton.
Screenplay: Norris Shannon.
Cast: Gladys Brockwell, Bertram Grassby, Ralph Lewis, James Cruze, Beatrice Burnham.
Notes: A girl is hypnotized into believing herself a murderess.

796 Hilde Warren and Death (May Films, 1917). [*Hilde Warren und der Tod*]. Germany. 80 minutes.
Producer/Director: Joe May.
Screenplay: Fritz Lang.
Photography: Kurt Courant.
Cast: Mia May (Hilde Warren), Hans Mierendorff, Bruno Kastner, Ernst Matray, Fritz Lang (Death), Georg John.
Notes: Hilde Warren, an actress, murders her newborn child when she realizes that the father is a condemned murderer. She is then haunted by spectral visions of Death (played by Fritz Lang), and finally offers herself willingly to him while awaiting her own end in a prison cell.

Hilde Warren und der Tod *see* **Hilde Warren and Death**

797 I Believe (Cosmotofilm, 1917). 75 minutes.
Producer/Screenplay: George Loane Tucker.
Cast: Milton Rosmer.
Notes: A man revived from the dead has no soul.

798 Jack and the Beanstalk (Fox, 1917). 10 reels.
Directors/Screenplay: C. M. Franklin, S. A. Franklin.
Cast: Francis Carpenter, Virginia Lee.

799 *Little Red Riding Hood* (Edison, 1917). 8 minutes.

800 *The Man of Mystery* (Vitagraph, 1917). 5 reels.
Director: Frederick A. Thompson.
Cast: E. H. Sothern, Charlotte Ives, Vilda Varesi.
Notes: An aging, deformed man trapped in the intense heat and sulfur fumes caused by an eruption of Mt. Vesuvius finds his youth restored and his deformities cured.

801 *The Mystic Hour* (Art Drama/Apollo, 1917). 55 minutes.
Director: Richard Ridgely.
Cast: Charles Hutchinson, Alma Hanlon, John Sainpolis.
Notes: A man obsessed with the desire to kill another man dreams that he murders him and awakens to find that the man is actually dead.

802 *The Picture of Dorian Gray* (1917). [*Az Elet Kiralya, Dorian Gray*]. Hungary.
Director: Alfred Deesy.
Notes: Bela Lugosi's presence in the cast is rumored, but unconfirmed.

803 *The Picture of Dorian Gray* (Richard Oswald Film, 1917). [*Das Bildnis des Dorian Gray*]. Germany. 80 minutes.
Producer/Director/Screenplay: Richard Oswald.
Photography: Max Fassbender.
Cast: Bernd Aldor, Lupu Pick, Ernst Pittaschau, Andreas Van Horn, Lea Lara, Ernst Ludwig.
Notes: Based on Oscar Wilde's novel.

804 *The Pied Piper of Hamelin* (1917). [*Der Rattenfänger von Hamelin*]. Germany.
Director: Paul Wegener.
Screenplay: Henryk Galeen.
Art Direction: Rochus Gliese.
Cast: Paul Wegener, Lyda Salmonova, Wilhelm Diegelmann, Jakob Tiedtke.

805 *Prehistoric Poultry* (Edison, 1917).
Notes: An animated model short by Willis O'Brien.

806 *The Primrose Ring* (Lasky, 1917). 5 reels.
Director: Robert Leonard.
Screenplay: Marion Fairfax, C. Carr (based on a book by Ruth Sawyer).
Cast: Mae Murray, Tom Moore.
Notes: In a children's hospital, a nurse relates the story of a giant ogre to the young patients.

Rattenfänger von Hamelin, Der *see The Pied Piper of Hamelin*

807 *The Reward of the Faithless* (Bluebird, 1917). 5 reels.
Producer: Rex Ingram.
Screenplay: Rex Ingram (from a story by E. Magnus Ingleton).
Cast: Betty Schade, Wedgewood Nowell, Claire Du Bray, Nicholas Dunaew.
Notes: An entranced princess is buried alive, but escapes and re-

turns to "haunt" her would-be murderer.

808 *The Scarlet Crystal* (Red Feather, 1917). 5 reels.
Screenplay: J. Grubb Alexander.
Cast: Betty Schade, Herbert Rawlinson.
Notes: Scenes of horror are depicted in a magic crystal.

809 *The Seven Swans* (Paramount, 1917). 5 reels.
Director: J. Searle Dawley.
Cast: Maguerite Clark, Richard Barthelmess, William Danforth.
Notes: Seven swans are cursed by an evil witch.

810 *She* (Fox, 1917). 5 reels.
Director: Kenean Buel.
Screenplay: Mary Murillo (based on H. Rider Haggard's novel).
Photography: Frank G. Kugler.
Cast: Valeska Suratt (Ayesha, also known as "She"), Ben L. Taggart (Leo), Miriam Fouche (Ustane), Wigney Percyval (Billali), Tom Burrough (Holly), Martin Reagan (Job).
Notes: The 3,000-year-old queen of a lost kingdom maintains her youth by immersion in a mysterical flame.

811 *Snow White* (Rex, 1917). 35 minutes.

812 *The Sorrows of Satan* (Samuelson, 1917). Great Britain.
Producer/Director: Alexander Butler.
Cast: Owen Nares, Gladys Cooper, Lionel D'Aragon, Cecil Humphreys.
Notes: Based on the novel by Marie Corelli. Satan appears in mortal guise to lure his victims. A prologue and epilogue are set in hell.

813 *Spooks and Spasms* (Vitagraph, 1917). 1 reel.
Director/Screenplay: Larry Semon.

814 *Unconquered* (Paramount, 1917). 5 reels.
Cast: Mabel Van Buren, Fannie Ward, Hobart Bosworth, Tully Marshall, Jane Wolfe.
Notes: A voodoo-crazed savage pursues human sacrifices.

815 *The Voice on the Wire* (Universal, 1917). 15 chapter serial.
Director: Stuart Paton.
Cast: Ben Wilson, Neva Gerber, Francis McDonald, Joseph W. Girard.
Notes: This cliffhanger was based on a novel by Eustace Hale Ball. Mummification, limb transplants and a disembodied hand are the horrific gimmicks exploited.

1918

816 *Alraune* (Neutral Film, 1918). Germany. 88 minutes.
Director/Photography: Eugen Illes.
Cast: Hilde Wolter (Alraune), Gustav Adolf Semler, Friedrich Kuehne, Max Auzinger, Ernst Rennspies.
Notes: In this adaptation of Hanns Heinz Ewers' 1913 novel of the same title, a beautiful but deadly female monster is created when a prostitute is artificially inseminated with the sperm of a hanged murderer. Using her sexual wiles, the soulless Alraune lures men to their doom.

817 *Alraune* (Phoenix, 1918). Austria-Hungary. 80 minutes.
Directors: Mihaly Kertesz (Michael Curtiz), Fritz Odon.
Screenplay: Richard Falk (based on the novel by Hanns Heinz Ewers).
Cast: Guyla Gal (Alraune), Rozsi Szollosi, Jeno Torzs, Margit Lux, Kalman Kormendy, Geza Erdelyi, Andor Kardos, Violette Szlatenyl, Karoly Arnyai, Boske Malatinszky.
Notes: In this competing version of *Alraune,* a mad scientist creates a Frankenstein-like creature by forcing a prostitute to copulate with a mandrake root. The alluring creation, Alraune, captivates her male admirers and then destroys them. Co-director Mihaly Kertesz later changed his name to Michael Curtiz, and became a top-flight director at Warner Bros. in the 30s and 40s, helming classics like *Angels with Dirty Faces* and *Casablanca.* Earlier in his Warner Bros. career, Curtiz directed the horror films *Doctor X* (1932), *Mystery of the Wax Museum* (1933), and *The Walking Dead* (1936).

Ander Ich, Das *see* **The Other Self**

Augen der Mumie Ma, Die *see* **The Eyes of the Mummy**

818 *The Bells* (Pathé, 1918). 5 reels.
Director: Ernest C. Warde.
Screenplay: Gilson Willets, Jack Cunningham (based on the play by Emile Erckmann and Alexander Chatrian, adapted by Leopold Lewis).
Cast: Frank Keenan (Mathias), Lois Wilson (Annette), Edward Coxen (Christian), Carl Stockdale (Gari), Albert Cody (Nickel), Joseph J. Dowling (Lisparre), Ida Lewis (Catherine), Bert Law (Koveski).
Notes: A murderer is haunted by visions of his victim.

819 *The Eyes of the Mummy*

(Union, 1918). [*Die Augen der Mumie Ma*]. Germany. 55 minutes.
Alternate title: Die Mumia Ma.
Director: Ernst Lubitsch.
Screenplay: Hans Kraly, Emil Rameau.
Photography: Alfred Hansen.
Set Designer: Kurt Richter.
Cast: Emil Jannings (Ma, the Mummy), Pola Negri, Harry Liedtke, Max Lawrence.
Notes: Ma the mummy is resurrected from the slumber of eons to seek vengeance on the defilers of his tomb. Both Jannings and Negri enjoyed brief Hollywood careers. A more successful Hollywood immigrant was director Ernst Lubitsch, famed for his sophisticated comedies.

820 *Flames* (Butchers, 1918). Great Britain. 65 minutes.
Director: Maurice Elvey.
Screenplay: Eliot Stannard (based on the novel by Robert Hichens).
Cast: Owen Nares, Margaret Bannerman, Edward O'Neill, Clifford Cobb.
Notes: A good and an evil man exchange souls.

821 *Ghost of the Rancho* (Pathé, 1918). 6 reels.
Director: William Worthington.
Screenplay: Jack Cunningham (story by Arthur Gooden).
Cast: Bryant Washburn, Rhea Mitchell.
Notes: A ghostly posse is depicted.

822 *The Haunted Hotel* (Kinekature, 1918). Great Britain. 11 minutes.
Producer: Fred Rains.
Cast: Will Asher, Marion Peake, Lupino Lane.

823 *The Haunted House* (Frazee, 1918). 22 minutes.
Producer/Screenplay: Edwin A. Frazee.
Notes: Mystical illusions and magic are featured.

824 *The House of Hate* (Pathé, 1918). 20 chapter serial.
Producer: Louis J. Gasnier.
Director: George B. Seitz.
Screenplay: Bertram Millhauser.
Cast: Pearl White (Pearl Waldon), Antonio Moreno (Harvey Gresham), Paul Clerget (the Hooded Terror), J. H. Gilmour (Winthrop Waldon), John Webb Dillion (Haynes Waldon), Peggy Shanor (Zelda Waldon).
Chapter titles: (1) The Hooded Terror; (2) The Tiger's Eye; (3) A Woman's Perfidy; (4) The Man from Java; (5) Spies Within; (6) A Living Target; (7) Germ Menace; (8) The Untold Secret; (9) Poisoned Darts; (10) Double-Crossed; (11) Haunts of Evil; (12) Flashes in the Dark; (13) Enemy Aliens; (14) Underworld Allies; (15) The False Signal; (16) The Vial of Death; (17) The Death Switch; (18) At the Pistol's Point; (19) The Hooded Terror Unmasked; (20) Following Old Glory.
Notes: A masked fiend known only as "The Hooded Terror" attempts to kill with germ warfare in this Pearl White cliffhanger.

825 *House of Silence* (Paramount, 1918).

Director: Donald Crisp.
Screenplay: Margaret Turnbull.
Cast: Wallace Reid, Anna Little, Winter Hall, Ernest Joy.
Notes: A haunted house is featured.

826 *I Accuse* (1918). [*J'Accuse*]. France.
Director/Screenplay: Abel Gance.
Notes: Dead men rise from the graveyards of World War I to march on the world. Later remade by Gance as a talkie.

J'Accuse *see I Accuse*

827 *The Other Self* (Sascha-Film, 1918). [*Das Ander Ich*]. Austria. 66 minutes.
Director: Fritz Freisler.
Screenplay: Ladislaus Tuszinsky.
Cast: Raoul Asian, Fritz Kortner, Magda Sonja.
Notes: A professor has a split personality.

828 *Queen of the Sea* (Fox, 1918). 5 reels.
Cast: Annette Kellerman, Hugh Thompson.
Notes: Mermaids and demons are depicted.

829 *The Silent Mystery* (Silent Mystery Corp./Burston, 1918). 15 chapter serial.
Director: Francis Ford.
Cast: Francis Ford, Rosemary Theby, Mae Gaston, Elsie Van Neame.
Notes: A jewel stolen from an Egyptian mummy is cursed.

1919

830 *The Beetle* (Barker, 1919). Great Britain.
Director: Alexander Butler.
Cast: L. Douglas, Maudie Dunham.
Note: The soul of an Egyptian princess, reincarnated in a beetle, seeks revenge.

831 *The Cabinet of Dr. Caligari* (Decla-Bioscop, 1919). [*Das Kabinett des Dr. Caligari*]. Germany. 5 reels.
Producer: Erich Pommer.
Director: Robert Wiene.
Screenplay: Carl Mayer, Hans Janowitz, (and, uncredited) Fritz Lang.
Photography: Willy Hameister.
Art Direction: Hermann Warm, Walter Reimann, Walter Rohrig.
Costumes: Walter Reimann.
Cast: Werner Krauss (Dr. Cali-

The Cabinet of Dr. Caligari (1919): **Lil Dagover and Werner Krauss.**

gari), Conrad Veidt (Cesare, the Somnambulist), Friedrich Feher (Francis), Lil Dagover (Jane), Hans Heinz von Twardowski (Alan), Rudolph Lettinger (Dr. Olsen), Rudolph Klein-Rogge (a criminal).

Notes: While appearing on a television talk show in his later years, Orson Welles was asked how it felt to have made, in *Citizen Kane,* "the greatest movie ever made." With a touch of perhaps false modesty, Welles replied that it was "a little like being in the 'Top 10' in the music business — it just lasts a little longer, that's all. When I was a young man everyone thought the greatest movie ever made was a pictured called *The Cabinet of Dr. Caligari,* but now it's not talked about much."

Perhaps, but *The Cabinet of Dr. Caligari* was, almost from the day it was released in 1919, one of the towering landmarks of motion picture history, and it remains so today. Directed by Robert Wiene (1881-1938), this internationally acclaimed German film is known not for its stars or plot, but for its style. German expressionism in film was an artistic movement advancing the theory that every component of a movie — the photography, scenery, lighting, costuming and acting — should be intentionally stylized and even wildly exaggerated in order to achieve a unified emotional impact.

Although the faltering post-

The Cabinet of Dr. Caligari (1919): **Werner Krauss, Conrad Veidt and Lil Dagover.**

World War I German economy undoubtedly had a partial influence on the widespread adoption of this technique — the flat, painted backdrops and crazily stylized scenery of *Caligari* were, after all, very economical, no matter how creatively designed — it is a valid artistic theory, and this film provides a textbook example of the style.

After the opening credits for *The Cabinet of Dr. Caligari,* we are shown a cryptic but intriguing title card informing us that the story we are about to see is: "A modern representation of an 11th century myth in which a mountebank monk bears a strange and mysterious influence over a somnambulist."

The opening scene then focuses on two well-dressed men, one young and the other elderly, seated on a bench in what appears to be a garden. The older man turns to his companion and ominously intones: "Spirits surround us on every side — they have driven me from hearth and home, from wife and child."

A young woman clad in a shapeless white gown then wanders trance-like past the two men. The young man remarks: "My betrothed ... what she and I have experienced is yet more remarkable than the story you have told me. I will tell you...."

The wandering girl is then shown again in a strangely evocative soft-focus shot as she staggers off-screen. The young man continues: "In Holstenwall, where I was born...."

The Cabinet of Dr. Caligari (1919): Werner Krauss in a typical set.

So begins *The Cabinet of Dr. Caligari*. For such an influential film, *Caligari*'s plot is amazingly simple. Dr. Caligari (Werner Krauss), a fairground mesmerist, exhibits a sleepwalker, Cesare (Conrad Veidt), who makes predictions for the audience; after the show, Caligari regularly sends Cesare forth to do his sinister bidding — including murder. Woven into this premise is a romantic triangle subplot involving a girl, Jane Olsen (Lil Dagover), and her two young suitors, Francis (Friedrich Feher) and Alan (Hans Heinz von Twardowski). Framing the central plot is the previously described introduction and a matching epilogue revealing that the entire story has been a delusion imagined by Francis, and that the garden seen in the prologue is really the grounds of an insane asylum. Most of the cast is then glimpsed wandering the grounds, with Caligari presiding as the administrator.

Most feature-length movies of this period were based on either novels or stage plays, but *The Cabinet of Dr. Caligari* was a true screen original, written by Carl Mayer and Hans Janowitz. A contribution to the script was made by Fritz Lang, who imposed—over the objections of Mayer and Janowitz—the insane asylum framing device, which was really unnecessary, since the distorted, almost cartoonish sets designed by Hermann Warm and Walter Reimann provided more than enough indication of madness.

These sets are cunningly designed; though highly stylized and flat, they somehow manage to present a convincing environment, perhaps because the entire film is shot in this manner on a soundstage, with no "reality" intruding to disrupt the atmosphere. Light, shadow and other details are starkly painted on the scenery flats, even the *actors* seem painted, with Caligari sporting dark brush strokes in his hair and wearing lined Mickey Mouse-style gloves.

The acting, when viewed today, ranges from silent movie outrageousness to almost internalized low-key realism, with Krauss, Dagover and Veidt coming off best. Conrad Veidt (1893-1943), perhaps best known today for his supporting role as Major Strasser in *Casablanca* (1942), was a front-rank talent deserving a thorough biographical reappraisal. Veidt was a talented, expressive, physically imposing performer capable of some wonderful things; witness his performance as Jaffar, the evil magician in Alexander Korda's Technicolor fantasy *The Thief of Bagdad* (1940). Like Boris Karloff, Veidt could improve a film, even a mediocre one, simply by appearing in it.

Before 1914, Veidt studied and performed with the Max Reinhardt company, serving in the German army during World War I. As a result of illness, the military reassigned him to duty in Berlin in 1916; his film debut was in *The Spy* (*Der Spion*) in 1917. His role as Cesare in *The Cabinet of Dr. Caligari* two years later focused international attention on him, and in 1920 he formed his own production company, starring in and sometimes directing his own films. Veidt became a British citizen in 1939; he worked in both England and America, fleeing Germany after the Nazis harassed him because his wife was Jewish.

Veidt manages some genuinely creepy moments as Cesare in *Caligari,* staggering across the painted, stylized landscapes, his mascara-highlighted eyes bulging with menace. Veidt's finest moment, though, occurs via a well-placed title card when the character of Alan (Hans Heinz von Twardowski) requests a prediction during Cesare's exhibition at the fair. "How long will I live?" Alan timorously inquires. Cesare leans forward ominously, and in a superb moment of black humor intones: "The time is short—you die at dawn!" after which he validates the prophecy by murdering Alan the next morning! Cesare's general appearance, black clothing and stiff, hesitant gait influenced Boris Karloff's monster in *Frankenstein* (1931). Director James Whale and his crew were very much under the spell of Caligari's visual design as well, although the expressionism in *Frankenstein* is far gentler, and the

The Cabinet of Dr. Caligari (1919): Conrad Veidt and Lil Dagover in an exaggerated set.

sets — though still exaggerated — far more realistic.

On its first release, *The Cabinet of Dr. Caligari* was an instant world-wide sensation. The film was exhibited in Paris non-stop for seven years, and as late as 1958 it was chosen by a panel of 117 film historians from 26 countries at the Brussels World's Fair as one of the 12 most important films of all time.

Because his other work is uneven, exhibiting little or no outstanding talent, and because he never again directed a film to equal *The Cabinet of Dr. Caligari,* some have tended to belittle Robert Wiene's contributions to this milestone film. But while the input of *Caligari*'s art directors, performers and scenarists was of major importance, Wiene's tightly controlled handling of these elements is obvious and undeniable. Although Wiene, who made his directorial debut in 1912 with *Die Waffen der Jugend,* helmed many crass and trivial films before and after *Caligari,* his careful supervision of *The Hands of Orlac* (*q.v.*) in 1924 verifies his talent.

The influence of *The Cabinet of Dr. Caligari* has been widespread, and was especially obvious in the 30s and 40s, when the film was closely studied and copied. Besides the aforementioned *Frankenstein,* later films that were most obviously indebted to *Caligari* included the excellent Universal horror movies *Murders in the Rue Morgue* (1932) and *Son of Frankenstein* (1939), not to overlook Welles' *Citizen Kane* (1941), which used exaggerated set design both to impart atmosphere and provide visual commentary on the baroque, ostentatious life-style of its ruthless newspaper-baron antagonist.

A 1962 "remake" of *The Cabinet of Dr. Caligari,* scripted by Robert Bloch (*Psycho*), was a remake in name only and had little to do with the original, though Bloch did make a commendable effort to duplicate the silent film's emphasis on the unreality of madness by placing the action in an asylum.

Reviews: "It is not only a step in a new direction — it is a misconception to call it a step in advance — but also in the way of direction and acting. It is so completely and skillfully organized and handled as to compel attention and study. ... Of first importance is the direction and cutting. This has resulted in a series of actions so perfectly dovetailed as to carry the story through to its conclusion ... at a perfect tempo. ... The director's name is Robert Wiene. Among the few preeminent in the world today he may justly be included because of what he has done with this story. ... Nowhere is there a shot of nature itself. Everything is designed and painted and there is everywhere a sense of the widening and narrowing of the attention. ... The best performance unquestionably is that given by Werner Krauss as Dr. Caligari...." — *Variety,* April 8, 1921.

"[E]verything has an air of exaggeration which makes the characters seem unreal as human beings, but extraordinarily real as embodying qualities of goodness and evil, peace and terror." — *The New York Times,* March 20, 1921.

"The picture is significant ... not because it is expressionistic in any special sense, but because it is expressionistic in the general sense that all of its elements, its settings, its plot, its people, are expressive, eloquent, and, for the most part, harmoniously so." — *The New York Times,* April 4, 1921.

832 Dance of Death (Helios Film, 1919). [*Tötentanz*]. Germany. 84 minutes.
Producer: Erwin Rosner.
Director: Otto Rippert.
Screenplay: Fritz Lang.
Photography: Willy Hameister.
Cast: Sascha Gura, Werner Krauss, Joseph Roemer, Richard Kirsch.
Notes: In this German *Svengali*-like horror fantasy, Sascha Gura was cast as a beautiful dancer, her will dominated and controlled by a tyrannical, crippled mastermind, played by Werner Krauss. The Krauss character uses Gura's beauty to ensnare his victims, who are lured to destruction by her wiles.

833 The Devil's Locksmith (Regent-Film, 1919). [*Der Teufelsschlosser*]. Austria.

Director: Franz Ferdinand.
Cast: Franz Ferdinand, Herr Ruibar, Eugen Jensen (Satan), Armin Seydelmann.
Notes: A group of locksmiths make a deal with the Devil.

834 ***Do the Dead Talk?*** (1919).
Notes: Spirits are depicted.

835 ***The Ghost of Slumber Mountain*** (World Film Corp., 1919). 12 minutes.
Producer: Herbert M. Dawley.
Director/Special effects: Willis H. O'Brien.
Cast: Herbert M. Dawley (Uncle Jack).
Notes: The story of *The Ghost of Slumber Mountain* is told in flashback as Uncle Jack, a writer, spins a yarn for his two young nephews, recalling an encounter with dinosaurs still living in a hidden valley, including a brontosaurus, a triceratops, and a tyrannosaurus ("His fevered breath was in my face! I could almost feel his fangs tearing my flesh!!"). Rumors persist that Willis O'Brien played the character of an old hermit, but existing prints of *The Ghost of Slumber Mountain* are of such poor quality that verification of this is impossible.
  The construction of O'Brien's dinosaur models (the technical supervisor was Dr. Barnum Brown) marked a great improvement over the crude shorts he had made for Edison before, looking forward to his infinitely more sophisticated work on *The Lost World* in 1925.
Reviews: "*The Ghost of Slumber Mountain* is a one-reel dream play with its leading actors the named and nameless creatures of forest and stream of the ages of the earth when the old ball was in the first processes of its cooling stage and life in the spawn was beginning to come out of the mist. The idea is a big one, capable of infinite extension, and, even as achieved in the initial attempt, embodied in the present sketch, of strange and shuddering interest.... [T]hese dinosaurs that suggest impossible lengths and heights, as well as the horned animal hobgobblins of the period ... walk, twist, gaze and eat, as we might imagine they must have in the long, long ago." – *Variety,* April 18, 1919.
  "*The Ghost of Slumber Mountain,* presented by Herbert M. Dawley ... shows animals, said to be prehistoric, in remarkably lifelike activity." – *The New York Times,* November 18, 1918.

836 ***The Haunted Bedroom*** (Paramount, 1919). 6 reels.
Producer: Thomas H. Ince.
Director: Fred Niblo.
Screenplay: C. Gardner Sullivan.
Cast: Lloyd Hughes, Enid Bennett, Dorcas Mathews, Otto Hoffman, Jack Nelson.
Notes: Ghostly figures plague a haunted room.

Kabinett des Dr. Caligari, Das *see* ***The Cabinet of Dr. Caligari***

Kökarlen *see* ***The Phantom Chariot***

837 Lilith and Ly (Fiat Films, 1919). Austria.
Director: Erick Kober.
Screenplay: Fritz Lang.
Photography: Willy Hameister.
Cast: Elga Beck, Hans Marschall, Ernst Escherich, Franz Kammauf.

Notes: The nominal hero of *Lilith and Ly,* Frank Landow, discovers how to create life through the mystical powers of a strange ruby, and falls in love with a statue—Lilith—when the sculpture is endowed with life under the gem's influence. Lilith's doppelganger then appears as a vampirish image on a futuristic television screen. She steadily grows more powerful and nearly drains the life from Landow and his lover Ly, before Landow disposes of the magic ruby, destroying Lilith.

838 Madness (Veidt Film, 1919). [*Wahnsinn*]. Germany. 70 minutes.
Producer/Director: Conrad Veidt.
Screenplay: Margarete Lindau-Schulz, Hermann Fellner.
Photography: Carl Hoffman.
Cast: Conrad Veidt, Reinhold Schuenzel, Gussy Hole, Grit Hegesa.

Notes: Veidt plays a banker who deteriorates mentally when a sinister gypsy predicts that he will be given a trunk, the possession of which will bring either happiness or death. Veidt is then locked inside the trunk and suffocates. Based on a novella by Kurt Muenzer.

839 The Master Mystery (Octagon, 1919). 15 chapter serial.
Producer: Benjamin A. Rolfe.
Director: Burton King.
Assistant Director: William Haddock.
Screenplay: Arthur B. Reeve, Charles A. Logue.
Cast: Harry Houdini (Quentin Lock), Marguerite Marsh (Eva Brent), William Pike (Peter Brent), Ruth Stonehouse (Deluxe Dora), Charles Graham (Madagascar Strangler), Floyd Buckley ("Q," the Automoton), Jack Burns (Chemist), Edna Britton (Maid).

Chapter titles: The first 14 episodes of this serial were registered for copyright *without* titles; chapter 15 was registered *with* the title *Unmasking of the Automoton.*

Notes: In this cliffhanger, famed real-life magician Harry Houdini tried his hand at acting as he battled "Q," the Automoton, a clunky, boiler-plated robot.

Pest in Florenz, Die *see* **The Plague in Florence**

840 The Phantom Chariot (Svensk Bio, 1919). [*Körkarlen*]. Sweden. 110 minutes.
Alternate titles: The Phantom Carriage; Thy Soul Shall Bear Witness; The Stroke of Midnight.
Director/Screenplay: Victor Seastrom.
Producer: Charles Magnusson.
Photography: Julius Jaenzon.
Cast: Victor Seastrom, Hilda Borgstrom, Astrid Holm, Tore Svennberg, Concordia Selander, Lisa Lundholm, Olaf Aas, Nils Arehn, Tor Weijden.

Notes: This film related the tale of an unrepentant drunkard, and was distinguished by its elegant imagery, particularly the concept of Death driving a ghostly carriage, roaming the countryside in search of victims. *The Phantom Chariot* was reissued in 1921 in a shorter version running 80 minutes. The film was remade as a talkie, by director Julien Duvivier in 1939, and by director Arne Mattson in 1958.

841 *Phantom Honeymoon* (Hallmark, 1919). 6 reels.
Director: J. Searle Dawley.
Notes: A professor who debunks superstition is startled by the appearance of three ghosts in a castle.

842 *The Plague in Florence* (Decla Film, 1919). [*Die Pest in Florenz*]. Germany. 96 minutes.
Producer: Erich Pommer.
Director: Otto Rippert.
Screenplay: Fritz Lang.
Photography: Willy Hameister, Emile Schunemann.
Cast: Otto Mannstedt, Anders Wikman, Theodor Becker, Marga Kierska, Julietta Brandt, Karl Bernhard, Franz Knaak, Erner Huebsch, Hans Walter.
Notes: This film was an unofficial adaptation of Edgar Allan Poe's *The Masque of the Red Death,* with the judgmental figure of Death here represented by a beautiful woman (Marga Kierska), who uses her wiles to degrade an entire city, transforming even the churches into sites of sexual debauchery.

843 *The Poison Pen* (World, 1919). 50 minutes.
Director: Edwin August.
Screenplay: J. C. Miller (story by Edwin August).
Cast: June Elvidge, Earle Metcalfe, Joseph Smiley, George Bunny.
Notes: A patient with a split personality is cured by hypnosis and strange rays.

844 *Satanas* (1919). Germany.
Director: F. W. Murnau.
Photography: Karl Freund.
Cast: Conrad Veidt (Satan).

845 *Scream in the Night* (Selznick, 1919). 6 reels.
Directors: Burton King, Leander De Cordova.
Screenplay: Charles A. Logue.
Photography: William Reinhart, A. A. Caldwell.
Cast: Ruth Budd, Ralph Kellard.
Notes: Darwa, a wild jungle girl, is created by a mad scientist intent on proving Darwin's theory of evolution.

846 *The Spiders* (Decla-Bioscop, 1919). [*Die Spinnen*]. Germany.
Director/Screenplay: Fritz Lang.
Photography: Emile Schunemann (Part One), Karl Freund (Part Two).
Set Designers: Otto Hunte, Carl Kirmse.
Cast: Lil Dagover, Carl de Vogt, Ressel Orla, Georg John, Paul Morgan, Bruno Lettinger.
Notes: Released in two feature-length installments; Part One: *The Golden Lake* (*Der Goldene See*); Part Two: *The Diamond Ship* (*Das Brillanten Schiff*). Director Fritz Lang generated some atmospheric horror effects in this tale of a society of super criminals.

Spinnen, Die *see* **The Spiders**

847 *Tales of the Uncanny*
(Richard Oswald Film, 1919). [*Unheimliche Geschichten*]. Germany. 112 minutes.
Alternate titles: Tales of Horror; Five Sinister Stories.
Producer/Director: Richard Oswald.
Screenplay: Richard Oswald, Robert Liebmann.
Photography: Carl Hoffman.
Cast: Conrad Veidt, Anita Berber, Reinhold Schuenzel, Georg John, Hugo Doeblin, Paul Morgan.
Notes: This film is available on video under still another alternate title, *Weird Tales*. Stories by Edgar Allan Poe and Robert Louis Stevenson were adapted for this five-part horror omnibus.

Teufelsschlosser, Der *see* **The Devil's Locksmith**

848 *The Thirteenth Chair*
(Pathé, 1919).
Director/Screenplay: Leonce Perret.
Cast: Yvonne Delva, Creighton Hale, Marie Shotwell, Christine Mayo, Suzanne Colbert, George Deneubourg, Marc MacDermott, Walter Law.
Notes: Adapted from the stage play by Bayard Veiller. A man sitting in the thirteenth chair at a séance is murdered. Later remade as a talkie by director Tod Browning, with Bela Lugosi in a leading role.

849 *To Let* (Harma, 1919). Great Britain. 22 minutes.
Director: James Reardon.
Screenplay: Reuben Gillmer.
Notes: A retired conjurer attempts to frighten a couple into leaving his house.

Tötentanz *see* **Dance of Death**

850 *Trail of the Octopus* (Hallmark, 1919). 15 chapter serial.
Director: Duke Worne.
Screenplay: J. Grubb Alexander.
Cast: Ben Wilson, Neva Gerber, William Dyer, Howard Crampton.
Notes: An ape-man character is featured in this cliffhanger.

851 *The Trembling Hour* (Universal, 1919). 6 reels.
Director: George Siegmann.
Cast: Kenneth Harlan, Helen Eddy.
Notes: A man suffers from memory losses and murderous impulses. When he is suspected of killing someone, he compels the victim's twin brother to masquerade as the victim's ghost in order to force a confession from the true murderer.

Unheimliche Geschichten *see* **Tales of the Uncanny**

Wahnsinn *see* **Madness**

1920

852 *Algol* (Deutsche Licht., 1920). Germany.
Director: Hans Werckmeister.
Screenplay: Hans Brenert.
Photography: H. Kricheldorff, Axel Graatkjar.
Art Direction: Walter Reimann.
Cast: Emil Jannings, John Gottowt, Kathe Haack, Hanna Ralph.
Notes: An evil being travels to Earth from the star Algol, giving a human an omnipotent machine that will allow him to conquer the world.

853 *Along the Moonbeam Trail* (1920).
Producer: Herbert M. Dawley.
Notes: This film contained dinosaur footage, animated by Willis O'Brien, lifted from the 1919 film *The Ghost of Slumber Mountain* (*q.v.*).

854 *Anita* (Wiener Kunstfilm, 1920). Austria.
Alternate title: Trance.
Directors: Luise Kolm, Jakob Fleck.
Screenplay: Fritz Lohner-Beda.
Cast: Lola Urban-Kneidinger, Wilhelm Klitsch, Julius Strobl, Nora Herbert.
Notes: An existence under the influence of hypnosis is depicted.

855 *The Barton Mystery* (Stoll, 1920). Great Britain. 72 minutes.
Director: Harry Roberts.
Screenplay: R. Byron-Webber.
Photography: E. Harvey Harrison.
Cast: Lyn Harding, Edward O'Neal, Arthur Pusey, Little Enid Bell.
Notes: A murder is solved by a psychic.

856 *Black Shadows* (Fox, 1920). 5 reels.
Director: Howard M. Mitchell.
Screenplay: J. Anthony Roach.
Cast: Estella Evans, Peggy Hyland, Albert Roscoe.
Notes: A victim of hypnosis is compelled to steal.

Bucklige und die Tänzerin, Der *see* **The Hunchback and the Dancer**

857 *Cagliostro* (Micco-Film, 1920). [*Der Graf von Cagliostro*].
Director: Reinhold Schuenzel.
Screenplay: Reinhold Schuenzel, Robert Liebmann.
Photography: Karl Hoffman.
Art Direction: O. F. Werndorff.
Cast: Conrad Veidt, Reinhold Schuenzel, Anita Berber, Carl Gotz.
Notes: The infamous mesmerist is depicted. The nationality of this film is uncertain; it is either Austrian or German in origin.

858 *The Dark Mirror* (Paramount/Artcraft, 1920). 5 reels.
Director: Charles Giblyn.
Cast: Dorothy Dalton, Pedro de Cordoba, Huntley Gordon.
Notes: When he sees a girl who he believes is a ghost, a gangster drowns himself.

859 *Desire* (B&C, 1920). Great Britain. 54 minutes.
Alternate title: The Magic Skin.
Director/Screenplay: George Edwardes Hall.
Cast: Dennis Neilson-Terry, Yvonne Arnaud.
Notes: Derived from Balzac's *The Wild Ass's Skin.* An ass's hide grants a man's wishes at the expense of his soul.

860 *Dr. Jekyll and Mr. Hyde* (Arrow, 1920).
Cast: Hank Mann.
Notes: A short comedy version of the Stevenson novel.

861 *Dr. Jekyll and Mr. Hyde* (Paramount/Artcraft, 1920). 7 reels.
Director: John S. Robertson.
Screenplay: Clara S. Beranger (based on the novel *The Strange Case of Dr. Jekyll and Mr. Hyde* by Robert Louis Stevenson).
Photography: Roy Overbaugh.
Cast: John Barrymore (Dr. Jekyll/Mr. Hyde), Martha Mansfield (Milicent Carew), Brandon Hurst (Sir George Carew), Charles Lane (Dr. Richard Lanyon), J. Malcolm Dunn (John Utterson), Cecil Clovelly (Edward Endfield), Nita Naldi (Gina), George Stevens (Poole), Louis Wolheim (Music Hall Proprietor).
Notes: Paramount's 1920 production of *Dr. Jekyll and Mr. Hyde,* starring John Barrymore in the dual title role, was hardly the first adaptation of Robert Louis Stevenson's novel (see other entries for previous versions), but it was the first *major* adaptation of Stevenson's tale, and the definitive silent film interpretation of this classic story. Not that the Barrymore film remains entirely faithful to the original novel. The picture seems to draw equal inspiration from both Stevenson's book and Oscar Wilde's novel *The Picture of Dorian Gray,* this latter story having obviously inspired the intriguing character of Sir George Carew (Brandon Hurst), whose goading criticism of Dr. Jekyll's virtuous morals prompts Jekyll into first attempting his experimental separation of man's good and evil natures, resulting in the emergence of his own monstrous alter ego, Edward Hyde.

Paramount's *Dr. Jekyll and Mr. Hyde* begins: "In each of us, two natures are at war—the good and the evil. All our lives the fight goes on between them, and one of them must conquer. But in our own hands lies the power to choose—what we most want to be, we *are.*"

This is star John Barrymore's film all the way, and his theatrically overt but powerful dramatics are undeniably impressive as he creates two distinctly separate and morally opposed personalities; the ascetic, compassionate, almost saintly Dr. Jekyll, and the foul, corrupt Hyde, scuttling crablike through the London fog, leaving a trail of debauchery

Dr. Jekyll and Mr. Hyde (1920): John Barrymore.

and violence in his wake. While he was filming *Dr. Jekyll and Mr. Hyde* at Paramount's New York studios, Barrymore was also starring in *Richard III* on Broadway; the added strain of performing nightly in this difficult Shakespearean role while filming *Dr. Jekyll and Mr. Hyde* (a demanding enough role in its own right) each day proved too much, and Barrymore suffered a nervous breakdown as a result. This physically strenuous and emotionally draining

Dr. Jekyll and Mr. Hyde **(1920): Martha Mansfield and John Barrymore.**

role is one of Barrymore's finest silent movie performances; filmed when the actor was 38 years old, *Dr. Jekyll and Mr. Hyde* offers Barrymore at the height of his powers, and hints at how impressive his Richard III must have been.

Although the 1932 Fredric March sound remake is undoubtedly the best *over-all* film adaptation of Stevenson's book, March gets some tough competition from Barrymore in this earlier version. Barrymore's Hyde is less "made-up" than March's, less ape-like, more grotesquely "human" in appearance and, arguably, more horrifying because of this.

Martha Mansfield is pretty and capable, but rather bland (perhaps intentionally so) as "good girl" heroine Millicent Carew, Jekyll's fiancée. Her reaction when she finally confronts Hyde is surprisingly off-beat and very well-acted; instead of the expected shrieking histrionics, she simply turns away from the monster in underplayed disgust. Nita Naldi, in the role of Gina, an exotic Italian music hall dancer, is amazingly provocative and sensual; whenever she is on-screen her startling, contemporary sex appeal makes the film seem almost modern. Naldi should have taken some dancing lessons, though—her amatuerish gyrations in a couple of scenes detract from ther believability of her character—or perhaps *enhance* it, depending on how the viewer interprets her stated "profession."

It was this 1920 production of the story that established the device of representing Jekyll and Hyde's moral division by introducing "good girl" (Mansfield) "bad girl" (Naldi) characters into the narrative (this was not in Stevenson's book) and the subsequent sound film versions, instead of returning to the original novel, simply remade the Barrymore film. Over the years, a degree of inexplicable confusion seems to have arisen over the names of the female characters in Barrymore's version. In contemporary reviews, "Gina" was referred to as "Therese," while decades later, a half-hour narrated abridgment for the TV series *Silents Please* (also marketed under the series title *The History of the Motion Picture*) renamed both girls "Carla" (Naldi) and "Barbara" (Mansfield).

If the physical assets of *Dr. Jekyll and Mr. Hyde* were not outstandingly lavish (a few of the sets, most noticeably Jekyll's laboratory, are serviceable but look a little on the economical side), the production values for the most part were solid enough, with a convincingly foggy evocation of London's 19th-century streets and byways. James S. Robertson's direction, although naturalistic and straightforward for the most part, occasionally reaches stylistic heights as in the fantasy sequence where a weakened, bedridden Jekyll, fighting his approaching transformation into Hyde, is tormented by the vision of a symbolic giant spider with Hyde's face (played, through an adept in-camera double-exposure, by Barrymore himself, wearing a spider costume), the surreal, malignant apparition illuminated by an other-worldly tracking spotlight as it approaches the reclining Jekyll.

The version of Barrymore's *Dr. Jekyll and Mr. Hyde* available on Kino International Video is recommended to the reader, as it is the most complete available (containing a few minutes of scenes missing from other public domain versions), is presented at the correct projection speed, and is enhanced with a good music score and appropriate color tints.

Reviews: "A fine, dignified production.... The story is ridiculous, judged by modern standards, but that doesn't alter its value as a medium for Mr. Barrymore. He is certainly a picturesque actor and the opportunity for contrast between the philanthropic and high-minded physician and the fiendish 'Mr. Hyde' is one of those roles a star revels in." – *Variety,* April 2, 1920.

"...[T]he excellence of the photoplay, everything that distinguishes it as ... something special and extraordinary, is centered in Mr. Barrymore's flawless performance. It is what Mr. Barrymore himself does that makes the dual character of Jekyll and Hyde tremendous. His performance is one of pure motion picture pantomime on as high a level as has ever been attained by anyone ... he creates such a genuinely beautiful Jekyll and compellingly hideous Hyde, and emphasizes the contrast between the two with such a sure eye for essentials, that one must believe in both while he sees them and afterwards admire a work of art. The production, aside from his performance, is uninspired." – *The New York Times,* March 29, 1920.

862 *Dr. Jekyll and Mr. Hyde*
(Pioneer, 1920). 5 reels.
Producer: Louis B. Mayer.
Director/Screenplay: Charles J. Hayden.
Cast: Sheldon Lewis (Dr. Jekyll/Mr. Hyde), Alexander Shannon (Dr. Lanyon), Dora Mills Adams (Mrs. Lanyon), Gladys Field (Bernice Lanyon), Harold Forshay (Edward Utterson), Leslie Austin (Danvers Carewe).
Notes: A rival *Dr. Jekyll and Mr. Hyde* was also released at the same time as Barrymore's version. This 5 reel picture starred Sheldon Lewis in a poor updating of the story, filmed in economical contemporary settings and ending with Jekyll waking from a nightmare – just as Hyde is about to be executed in an electric chair – only to find that the preceding events had been a dream! This film was so awful that director-scenarist Charles J. Hayden declined on-screen credit; more readily admitting his participation was Louis B. Mayer, the cynical producer of this quickie knock-off, who was then on the verge of founding his M-G-M studio empire. It is interesting to compare Gladys Field's (playing Jekyll's fiancée, "Bernice") reaction when she sees Hyde to Martha Mansfield's acting in the Barrymore version's similar scene. Whereas Mansfield was subdued in her expressed terror, Field bulges her eyes and gesticulates in the sort of over-the-top emoting that most people today mistakenly consider the norm in silent movie acting. Star Sheldon Lewis had played Hyde-like "monster" roles in silent serials like Pearl White's *The Exploits of Elaine* (1914). His performance here is stiff, unimaginative and more than a little desperate, with the Hyde "make-up" consisting of little more than dishevelled hair and a set of false teeth.

863 *The Dream Cheater* (Hodkinson, 1920).
Director: Ernest C. Warde.
Cast: J. Warren Kerrigan.

Notes: Based on Balzac's *The Wild Ass's Skin.*

864 Genuine (Decla-Bioscop, 1920). Germany.
Director: Robert Wiene.
Screenplay: Carl Mayer.
Photography: Willy Hameister.
Set Designer: Cesar Klein.
Cast: Fern Andra, Harald Paulsen, Ernst Gronau, John Gottowt, Hans Heinz von Twardowski.
Notes: An Oriental Princess is enslaved by a wealthy old man, who imprisons her in a glass case. From this cell, she controls others telepathically, and mentally orders her captor's nephew to murder his uncle. Robert Wiene's follow-up to *The Cabinet of Dr. Caligari (q.v.), Genuine* was unsuccessful, both artistically and financially.

865 Go and Get It (Neilan, 1920). 7 reels.
Directors: Marshall Neilan, Henry Symonds.
Screenplay: Marion Fairfax.
Cast: Pat O'Malley, Wesley Barry, Noah Beery, Bull Montana (gorilla).
Notes: A dead convict's brain is transplanted into the body of a gorilla. Bull Montana's simian make-up in *Go and Get It* was very similar to his ape-man disguise in *The Lost World* (1925). *Go and Get It* scenarist Marion Fairfax also scripted *The Lost World* and, recalling Montana's performance in *Go and Get It,* recommended him for the ape-man role.

Golem: Wie Er in de Welt Kam, Der *see* **The Golem**

866 The Golem (UFA, 1920). [*Der Golem: Wie Er in de Welt Kam*]. Germany. 6 reels.
Directors: Paul Wegener, Carl Boese.
Screenplay: Paul Wegener, Henryk Galeen (based on a story by Gustav Meyrink).
Photography: Karl Freund.
Set Designer: Hans Poelzig.
Costumes: Rochus Gliese.
Cast: Paul Wegener (the Golem), Albert Steinbruck (Rabbi Lowe), Ernst Deutsch, Lyda Salmonova, Hans Sturm, Greta Schroeder, Lothar Meuthel, Otto Gebuhr, Max Kronert, Dore Paetzold.
Notes: In the opening scenes of *The Golem,* Rabbi Lowe stands in blackness, surrounded by a mystic circle of flame, and calls forth the powers of darkness. Suddenly the bulbous, disembodied head of the demon Astaroth floats in the void before him, and speaks the magic words that will bring a clay statue to life. The Golem hesitantly draws his first breath, and walks forth. This 1920 film was star, co-director and co-writer Paul Wegener's third foray into the ancient European legend, and the only film of the trilogy that survives today.

For this version, subtitled *Wie Er in de Welt Kam (How He Came into the World),* Wegener and co-scenarist Henryk Galeen wisely returned the story to its period source instead of attempting to contemporize it as they had done before. As the Golem, Wegener cuts a powerful figure, literally appearing as solid as a rock, and his performance is marred only by some excessive facial grimacing in the close-ups.

The Golem (1920): Paul Wegener (center).

It is established when the Golem is created by Rabbi Lowe (Albert Steinbruck) that his life-force is contained in a mystic Star of David amulet the creature wears about his neck. In a scene that must have inspired the similar passage in James Whale's *Frankenstein,* the Golem meets a little girl who befriends him, offers him an apple, and then innocently removes the amulet, draining his life away.

The special photographic effects for *The Golem,* such as the floating vision of the demon Astaroth, were devised by Wegener's co-director Carl Boese and filmed through in-camera double-exposures. The chief cinematographer was Karl Freund (1890-1969), later a top Hollywood cameraman who also directed the Boris Karloff classic *The Mummy* (1932). The cluttered, detailed and highly evocative sets for this film were by Hans Poelzig, and the period costumes were designed by Rochus Gliese.

The character of the Golem has seen three subsequent film incarnations; a 1936 French version directed by Julian Duvivier, a 1951 Czechoslovakian version entitled *The Emperor and the Golem,* directed by Mac Fric, and a negligible 1966 film entitled *It,* starring Roddy McDowell and Jill Haworth.

Reviews: "The production is an impressively dignified one and the scenes of medieval times are well-visualized, with some magnificent mob scenes. The cast has been carefully selected with a view to the depiction of ancient types and are all excellent screen players."—*Variety,* June 24, 1921.

"The black magic of the Middle Ages, sorcery, astrology and all of the superstitious realities of people so legendary in appearance and manners that the unnatural seems natural among them have been brought to the screen ... in *The Golem,* the latest motion picture to come from the explorative innovators of Germany. The photoplay gives the impression of some fabulous old tale of strange people in a strange world, fascinating, exciting to the imagination, and yet so unfamiliar in all of its aspects that it always seems remote, elusive even, when one would like to get closer to its meaning. Paul Wegener, who directed ... has shown his greatest artistry ... in maintaining the consistency of his production ... one cannot lose interest in a work so strangely engrossing and with such power as *The Golem* has in many of its scenes. This power is derived mainly from a combination of exceptional acting and the most expressive settings yet seen in this country."—*The New York Times,* June 20, 1921.

Graf von Cagliostro, Der *see* *Cagliostro*

867 *The Great London Mystery* (T&P, 1920). Great Britain. 12 chapter serial.
Director: Charles Raymond.
Screenplay: Charles Raymond, Hope Loring.
Cast: David Devant (the Master Magician), Lady Doris Stapleton, Lester Gard (the Man Monkey), Lola de Liane (Froggie the Vampire).
Notes: Spiritualism, snake-worshippers and the living dead are a few of the plot elements featured in this British cliffhanger.

868 *Happy Hooligan in Dr. Jekyll and Mr. Zip* (IFS, 1920). 6 minutes.

The Golem (1920): Paul Wegener (right).

Director: Bill Nolan.
Notes: This animated cartoon spoofed the Robert Louis Stevenson novel.

869 Haunted Spooks (Pathé, 1920). 20 minutes.
Director: Alf Goulding.
Titles: H. M. Walker.
Cast: Harold Lloyd, Mildred Davis.
Notes: This Harold Lloyd comedy takes place in a haunted house.

870 The Hawk's Trail (Burston, 1920). 15 chapter serial.
Director: W. S. Van Dyke.
Cast: King Baggot, Rhea Mitchell, Grace Darmond.
Notes: A criminal has hypnotic powers.

871 The Head of Janus (Decla-Bioscop, 1920). [*Der Januskopf*]. Germany. 107 minutes.
Alternate titles: Janus-Faced; Love's Mockery.
Director: F. W. Murnau.
Screenplay: Hans Janowitz.
Photography: Carl Hoffman, Karl Freund.
Cast: Conrad Veidt (Dr. Warren/Mr. O'Connor), Margarete Schlegel, Willy Kayser-Heyl, Margarete Kupfer, Gustav Botz, Bela Lugosi, Jaro Fuerth, Manus Stifter, Marga Reuter, Lansa Rudolph, Danny Gurtler.
Notes: This film was an unofficial adaptation of Robert Louis Stevenson's novel *The Strange Case of Dr. Jekyll and Mr. Hyde,* renaming the main characters Dr. Warren and

Mr. O'Connor. In the supporting cast was future Dracula Bela Lugosi, playing a butler. He was still several years away from his immigration to America.

872 His Brother's Keeper
(Pioneer, 1920). 6 reels.
Director: Wilfred North.
Screenplay: N. Brewster Morse.
Cast: Gladden James, Anne Drew.
Notes: Mind control is used to commit murder.

Homme Qui Vendit Son Âme au Diable, L' *see* **The Man Who Sold His Soul to the Devil**

873 The Hound of the Baskervilles (Greenbaum Film, 1920). [*Der Hund von Baskerville*]. Germany. Part 1—73 minutes; Part 2—84 minutes.
Producer: Julius Greenbaum.
Director: Willy Zehn.
Screenplay: Robert Liebmann.
Cast: Willy Kayser-Titz (Sherlock Holmes), Lu Juergens, Erwin Fichtner, Ludwig Rex.
Notes: This film continued the German Sherlock Holmes series begun at Vitascope in 1914.

874 House of the Tolling Bell
(Pathé, 1920).
Producer/Director: J. Stuart Blackton.
Screenplay: Edith S. Tupper.
Cast: Bruce Gordon, May McAvoy, William Jenkins.
Notes: Ghosts and spirits are featured.

875 The House of Whispers
(Brunton-Hodkinson, 1920).
Director: Ernest C. Warde.
Screenplay: Jack Cunningham.
Photography: Arthur L. Todd.
Cast: J. Warren Kerrigan, Joseph J. Dowling, Fritzi Brunette, Fred C. Jones.
Notes: The tenants of an apartment house are frightened by disembodied whispers.

876 The Hunchback and the Dancer (Helios, 1920). [*Der Bucklige und die Tänzerin*]. Germany.
Director: F. W. Murnau.
Screenplay: Carl Mayer.
Set Designer: Robert Neppach.
Cast: Sascha Gura.

Hund von Baskerville, Der *see* **The Hound of the Baskervilles**

Januskopf, Der *see* **The Head of Janus**

877 Jorinde and Joringel
(1920). Germany.
Notes: A witch is featured in this animated cartoon.

878 Love Without Question
(Jans-Rolfe, 1920). 7 reels.
Producer/Director: B. A. Rolfe.
Screenplay: Violet Clark (based on the novel *The Abandoned Room* by C. Wadsworth Camp).
Cast: Olive Tell, James W. Morrison, Mario Marjaroni, Ivo Dawson, Charles MacKay, George S. Stevens.
Notes: A man is killed in a haunted room.

879 *The Man Who Sold His Soul to the Devil* (1920). [*L'Homme Qui Vendit Son Âme au Diable*]. France.
Director: Pierre Caron.
Photography: Andre A. Dantan.

880 *The Master Mind* (1920). 6 reels.
Director: Kenneth Webb.
Cast: Lionel Barrymore, Gypsy O'Brien, Ralph Kellard, Bradley Barker.
Notes: A man seeking revenge forces secrets from his enemies through telepathy.

881 *The Monster of Frankenstein* (Albertini Film, 1920). [*Il Mostro di Frankenstein*]. Italy.
Alternate title: Frankenstein's Monster.
Producer: Luciano Albertini.
Director: Eugenio Testa.
Screenplay: Giovanni Drivetti.
Cast: Luciano Albertini (the Baron), Umberto Guarracino (the Creature).
Notes: An adaptation of Mary W. Shelley's novel.

Mostro di Frankenstein, Il *see* **The Monster of Frankenstein**

882 *The Mystery Mind* (Pioneer, 1920). 15 chapter serial.
Directors: William Davis, Fred Sittenham.
Cast: J. Robert Pauline, Peggy Shanor, Paul Panzer, Ed Rogers.
Notes: An ape-man, hypnotism and the occult are depicted in this cliffhanger.

883 *Nachtgestalten* (Richard Oswald Film, 1920). Germany. 106 minutes.
Alternate title: Eleagable Kuperus.
Producer/Director: Richard Oswald.
Screenplay: Richard Oswald (based on the story *Eleagable Kuperus* by Karl Hans Strobl).
Photography: Carl Hoffmann.
Cast: Paul Wegener, Conrad Veidt, Erna Morena, Anita Berber, Reinhold Schuenzel, Erik Charell, Theodor Loos.
Notes: Karl Hans Strobl, whose original story provided the basis for this film, was Austria's leading author of horror stories in the Poe tradition. Little is known about the plot of this film, but actor Erik Charell appeared in the role of a gorilla, indicative of the picture's horrific content.

884 *One Hour Before Dawn* (Pathé, 1920).
Director: Henry King.
Cast: H. B. Warner.
Notes: Based on the novel *Behind Red Curtains* by Mansfield Scott. Under the influence of a hypnotist, a man commits murder an hour before dawn.

885 *The Penalty* (Goldwyn, 1920). 6 reels.
Director: Wallace Worsley.
Screenplay: Charles Kenyon, Philip Lonegran (based on the story by Governeur Morris).
Photography: Don Short.
Cast: Lon Chaney (Blizzard), Claire Adams (Barbara), Kenneth Harlan (Wilmot), Charles Clary (Doctor), Ethel Grey Terry (Rose),

Lon Chaney.

The Penalty (1920): Original poster.

Edouard Trebaal (Bubbie), Milton Ross (Lichtenstein), James Mason (Pete), Doris Pawn (Barbary Nell), Lee Phelps (Cop), Wilson Hummel, Montgomery Carlyle, Madelaine Travers.

Notes: *The Penalty* is not really overtly "horrific" in story or content, but this Lon Chaney vehicle, directed by Wallace Worsley (who would later direct Chaney in *The Hunchback of Notre Dame*), is a crime melodrama with a decidedly morbid slant. Chaney stars as Blizzard, an underworld mastermind whose legs have been amputated at the knees; vengefully declaring war on society, his influence grows until he dominates San Francisco's criminal element. The picture's ending is weak; Chaney eventually reforms after an operation conveniently relieves a blood clot on his brain. What makes this otherwise pedestrian film remarkable is its leading man.

Chaney (1883-1930), born to deaf mute parents and coming to movies from a vaudeville-theatre background, had a unique perspective on society's outcasts, the deformed and the crippled. This rare insight imbued his pantomimic skills and his expertise in creating startling, and at times horrific make-up were invaluable qualities that would make him a top screen star.

Chaney had made an impression in 1919 playing a contorted, fake cripple in *The Miracle Man,* and his future collaboration with director Tod Browning (1882-1962), beginning with *Outside the Law* in 1921, would result in a string of pictures remarkable for their sustained macabre atmosphere. Unfortunately, Chaney's celluloid legacy survives only in shreds and tatters now — only his most famous pictures exist in high quality prints, with many of his films either completely lost or available only in abridged or incomplete form.

Reviews: "It is needless to say that the picture is Chaney more than anyone else...." — *Variety,* November 19, 1920.

"*The Penalty,* an altogether incredible melodrama that, by its excesses, mocks even the friendliest spectator's love of life ... is from a story by Gouverneur Morris, which, if it is anything like its motion picture version, must have taxed the author's rampant imagination ... it will undoubtedly win the active interest, and even the regard, of many — because of Lon Chaney in the principle role, and the direction of Wallace Worsley. When they saw *The Miracle Man* some were struck at first by Chaney's ability to make himself seem a hopeless cripple, but before the picture was finished they forgot his stunt as such and their interest was all in the person he seemed to be. Likewise, when Chaney appears in *The Penalty* with both of his legs apparently sawed off above the knees, some will exclaim, 'How in the world can he do that?' but after they have followed his acting awhile, and felt the force of his presence on the screen, they will take it as just a part of his role that his legs are missing." — *The New York Times,* November 15, 1920.

886 The Perils of Paul (Keefe-Arrow, 1920). 22 minutes.
Screenplay: William Keefe.
Notes: Ouija boards and the spirit world are depicted.

887 The Phantom Foe (Pathé, 1920). 15 chapter serial.
Director: Bertram Millhauser.
Cast: Juanita Hansen, William N. Bailey, Warner Oland, Harry Semmels.
Notes: Hypnotism and the occult are featured in this cliffhanger.

888 Phantom Melody (Universal, 1920). 5 reels.
Director: Douglas Gerrard.
Cast: Monroe Salisbury.
Notes: After he is struck by lightning, a count regains consciousness in his tomb.

889 Spiritism (1920). [*Spiritismo*]. Italy.
Cast: Francesca Bertina.

Spiritismo *see* Spiritism

890 The Star Rover (Metro, 1920). 70 minutes.
Director: Edward Sloman.
Screenplay: A. S. LeVino (based on the novel by Jack London).
Photography: Jackson Rose.
Art Direction: Edward Shulter.
Cast: Courtenay Foote, Thelma Percy, Jack Carlysle.

Notes: An accused murderer, interrogated by the police, lives through his previous incarnations.

891 Sumurun (Union/UFA, 1920). [*One Arabian Night*]. Germany. 60 minutes.
Director: Ernst Lubitsch.
Screenplay: Hans Kraly (based on the pantomime *Sumurun* by F. Freska and V. Hollander).
Photography: Theodor Sparkuhl.
Art Direction: Kurt Richter, Erno Metzner.
Music: Victor Hollander.
Costumes: Ali Hubert.
Cast: Ernst Lubitsch (Yeggar, the Hunchback), Paul Wegener, Pola Negri, Jenny Hasselquist, Harry Liedtke, Jakob Tiedtke, Aud Egede Nissen.
Notes: Future Hollywood comedy director Ernst Lubitsch starred as a hunchback in this film. The 1920 film *The Hunchback and the Dancer* (*q.v.*), directed by F. W. Murnau, was similar to *Sumurun*.

892 Torgus, the Coffin Maker (Union/UFA, 1920). Germany.
Director: Hans Kobe.
Screenplay: Carl Mayer.
Photography: Karl Freund.
Art Direction: Robert Neppach.
Cast: Eugen Klopfer, Maria Leiko.
Notes: A coffin containing a body is sent to an old woman.

1921

Blade am Satan's Bog *see* **Leaves from Satan's Book**

893 The Conquering Power (Metro, 1921). 7 reels.
Producer/Director: Rex Ingram.
Screenplay: June Mathis (based on Honoré de Balzac's *Eugenie Grandet*).
Photography: John F. Seitz.
Technical Directors: Ralph Barton, Amos Meyers.
Cast: Alice Terry (Eugenie Grandet), Rudolph Valentino (Charles Grandet), Eric Mayne (Victor Grandet), Ralph Lewis (Pere Grandet), Edna Demaurey (his wife), Edward Connelly (Notary Cruchot), George Atkinson (his son), Willard Lee Hall (the Abbe), Mark Fenton (Monsieur des Grassins), Bridgetta Clark (his wife), Ward Wing (Adolph), Mary Hearn (Nanon), Eugene Pouyet (Cormoiller), Andree Tourneur (Annette).
Notes: A miser driven mad by the death of his wife suffers a horrifying demise himself when he is killed by a trunkful of his own gold.
Review: "For an American production, the atmospheric detail has been admirably worked out. The

acting is brilliant ... the photography ... is wonderfully effective...." — *Variety,* July 8, 1921.

Crime de Lord Arthur Savile, Le see **Lord Arthur Savile's Crime**

894 Death (1921). [*Gevatter Tod*]. Austria.
Director: Heinz Hanus.
Screenplay: Hans Berger, L. Gunther (based on *Der Pate des Todes* by Baumbach).
Photography: Hans Androschin, Eduard Hosch.
Art Direction: Hans Berger.
Cast: Armin Seydelmann, Artur Ranzenhofer (Death), Erika Wagner, Fritz Strabny, Louise Nerz.
Notes: The personification of Death is depicted.

895 The Devil (Pathé, 1921). 70 minutes.
Director: James Young.
Screenplay: Edmund Goulding (based on Ferenc Molnar's *Az Ordog*).
Photography: Harry Fischbeck.
Art Direction: Charles O. Seesel.
Cast: George Arliss, Sylvia Breamer, Lucy Cotton, Mrs. Arliss, Edmund Lowe.
Notes: Satan is repelled by a crucifix.

896 Dr. Hallin (Lampel-Film, 1921). Austria.
Direction: Alfred Lampel.
Screenplay: Alfred Lampel, J. C. Hoger.
Cast: Franz Herterich, Traute Carlsen, Karl Schopfer, Paul Kronegg.
Notes: Brain transplants are depicted.

897 The Dollar-a-Year Man (Paramount, 1921). 5 reels.
Director: James Cruze.
Screenplay: Walter Woods.
Photography: Karl Brown.
Cast: Roscoe "Fatty" Arbuckle, Lila Lee, Winifred Greenwood, Edward Sutherland, J. M. Dumont.
Notes: A haunted house provides the setting for this comedy.

898 Faust (1921).
Director: Frederick A. Todd.

Gevatter Tod see **Death**

899 The Ghost in the Garret (Paramount, 1921). 5 reels.
Director: F. Richard Jones.
Screenplay: Wells Hastings, Fred Chaston.
Cast: Dorothy Gish, William Parke, Jr., Tom Blake, Porter Strong, Mrs. David Landau, Downing Clarke.
Notes: A gang of thieves uses a haunted house as a hideout.

900 The Golem's Last Adventure (Sascha Film, 1921). [*Der Golem's Letzte Abenteuer*]. Austria.
Alternate title: Der Dorfgolem.
Director: Julius Szomogyl.

Golem's Letzte Abenteuer, Der see **The Golem's Last Adventure**

Grinsende Gesicht, Das see *The Man Who Laughs*

901 *The Haunted Castle*
(Decla-Bioscop, 1921). [*Schloss Vogelod*]. Germany.
Director: F. W. Murnau.
Photography: Fritz Arno Wagner.
Screenplay: Carl Meyer, Berthold Viertel (based on the novel by Rudolf Stratz).
Cast: Paul Hartmann, Olga Tschechowa, Arnold Korff, Paul Bildt.

902 *The Haunted House*
(Metro, 1921). 22 minutes.
Director/Screenplay: Buster Keaton, Eddie Kline.
Cast: Buster Keaton.
Notes: Counterfeiters masquerade as ghosts in a haunted house in this comedy.

903 *The Hole in the Wall*
(Metro, 1921). 6 reels.
Producer/Director: Maxwell Karger.
Screenplay: June Mathis (based on a play by Fred Jackson).
Photography: Allan Stegler.
Art Direction: Joseph Calder.
Cast: Alice Lake, Alan Forrest, Frank Brownlee, Claire DeBrey.
Notes: A medium, Madame Mysteria, dies in a train wreck.

904 *The Hound of the Baskervilles* (Stoll, 1921). Great Britain. 64 minutes.
Director: Maurice Elvey.
Screenplay: William J. Elliott (based on the novel by Sir Arthur Conan Doyle).
Photography: G. Burger.
Art Direction: Walter W. Murton.
Cast: Ellie Norwood, Hubert Willis, Allen Jeayes, Lewis Gilbert, Betty Campbell, Mme. D'Esterre.

905 *The House Without Doors or Windows* (1921). Germany.
Director: Friedrich Feher.
Notes: This film's art direction was influenced by *The Cabinet of Dr. Caligari* (*q.v.*).

906 *The Indian Tomb* (May Film, 1921). [*Das Indische Grabmal*]. Germany.
Alternate title: The Hindu Tombstone.
Director: Joe May.
Screenplay: Thea von Harbou, Fritz Lang.
Cast: Conrad Veidt, Lya de Putti, Mia May, Olaf Fons, Bernhard Goetzke.
Notes: A prince plans a Poe-like fate for his wife by entombing her alive.

Indische Grabmal, Das see *The Indian Tomb*

907 *Leaves from Satan's Book*
(Nordisk, 1921). [*Blade am Satan's Bog*]. Denmark.
Director: Carl Theodor Dryer.
Screenplay: Edgar Hoyer (based on the novel by Marie Corelli).
Photography: George Schneevoight.
Art Direction: Carl Theodor Dryer, Axel Bruun, Jens G. Lind.

Cast: Helge Nissen, Halvard Hoff (Jesus Christ), Jacob Texiere, Erling Hansson, Ebon Strandin, Tenna Kraft, Clara Pontoppidan, Karina Bell, Elith Pio.
Notes: Satan is followed through four separate stories, each laid in a different historical era, as he claims the soul of a victim in each time period—only to fail when he encounters Jesus Christ in one segment.

908 *Little Red Riding Hood* (Blanton, 1921). 11 minutes.

909 *Lord Arthur Savile's Crime* (1921). [*Le Crime de Lord Arthur Savile*]. France.
Director: Renee Hervil.
Notes: A palm reader predicts that a man will commit murder.

910 *The Lost Shadow* (UFA/Film Union, 1921). [*Der Verlorene Schatten*]. Germany. 64 minutes.
Director: Rochus Gliese.
Screenplay: Paul Wegener.
Photography: Karl Freund.
Art Direction: Kurt Richter.
Cast: Paul Wegener, Hannes Sturm, Lyda Salmonova.
Notes: A musician sells his soul to Satan in exchange for a magic violin.

911 *The Man from Beyond* (1921). 7 reels.
Director: Burton King.
Screenplay: Harry Houdini, Coolidge Streeter.
Photography: Frank Zucker, I. B. Ruby, Harry Fischbeck, A. G. Penrod, L. Dunmyre, L. D. Littlefield.
Cast: Harry Houdini, Nita Naldi, Arthur Maude, Luis Alberni.
Notes: A man is frozen alive in suspended animation for 100 years.

912 *The Man Who Laughs* (Olympic Film, 1921). [*Das Grinsende Gesicht*]. Austria. 90 minutes.
Director: Julius Herzka.
Screenplay: Louis Nerz (based on the novel by Victor Hugo).
Photography: Eduard Hosch.
Art Direction: Ladislaus Tuszinsky.
Cast: Franz Hobling, Nora Gregor, Lucienne Delacroix, Anna Kallina, Eugen Jensen, A. Seydelmann, Fritz Strabny.
Notes: A man's face is frozen in a hideous grin after he is mutilated by bandits. Remade in 1928 (*q.v.*).

913 *A Message from Mars* (Metro, 1921). 6 reels.
Producer: Maxwell Karger.
Screenplay: Arthur Zellner, Arthur Maude (based on the play by Richard Gathoney).
Photography: Arthur Martinelli.
Cast: Bert Lytell, Raye Dean, Leonard Mudie, Frank Currier, Maude Milton, Gordon Ash.
Notes: A spectral messenger from Mars wanders through the streets of earth, pointing out the needs of the poor.

914 *A Midnight Bell* (First National, 1921). 6 reels.
Director: Albert Ray.
Cast: Charles Ray, Donald MacDonald.

Notes: A man spends the night in a haunted church on a dare.

Müde Tod, Der *see* **The Weary Death**

915 *The Other Person* (Granger-Binger, 1921). Great Britain. 66 minutes.
Director: B. E. Doxat-Pratt.
Screenplay: B. James (based on the novel by Fergus Humes).
Cast: Zoe Palmer, A. Migliar, Arthur Pusey, Ivo Dawson, N. Hayden.
Notes: At a séance, it is proven that a spiritualist was compelled to murder his father by a ghost.

916 *The Pet* (1921). 7 minutes.
Alternate title: The Monster Dog.
Director: Winsor McKay.
Notes: In this animated cartoon, a pet dog grows to immense size, eventually destroying a city.

917 *The Price of Silence* (Sunrise, 1921). 65 minutes.
Director: F. L. Granville.
Photography: Leland Lancaster.
Cast: Peggy Hyland, Campbell Gullan, Tom Chatterton, Dorothy Grodon.
Notes: A murder scene is etched on a window pane by ghostly lightning.

918 *Queen of Spades* (1921). Hungary.
Director: Paul Fejos.
Notes: Based on the story by Pushkin.

919 *The Resident Patient* (Stoll, 1921). Great Britain. 22 minutes.
Director: Maurice Elvey.
Cast: Eille Norwood, Hubert Willis, Mme. D'Esterre, C. Pitt Chatham.
Notes: An entry in the British *Adventures of Sherlock Holmes* series. Based on the story by Sir Arthur Conan Doyle.
A man lives in fear until he is found hanged.

Schlöss Vogelod *see* **The Haunted Castle**

920 *A Spectre Haunts Europe* (1921). Russia.
Director: Vladmir R. Gardin.
Notes: This film was based on Edgar Allan Poe's *The Masque of the Red Death*.

Velorene Schatten, Der *see* **The Lost Shadow**

921 *The Weary Death* (Decla-Bioscop, 1921). [*Der Müde Tod*]. Germany. 11 reels.
Alternate titles: Destiny; Beyond the Wall; The Light Within; The Three Lights; Between Worlds.
Producer: Erich Pommer.
Director: Fritz Lang.
Screenplay: Thea von Harbou, Fritz Lang.
Photography: Fritz Arno Wagner, Erich Nitzschmann, Herman Salfrank.
Set Designers: Hermann Warm, Robert Herlth, Walter Rohrig.
Cast: Bernhard Goetzke, Lil Dagover, Walter Janssen, Rudolph

Klein-Rogge, George John, Edward von Winterstein, Max Adalbert, Wilhelm Diegelmann, Karl Platen, Hans Sternberg.
Notes: Death (Bernhard Goetzke) relates a trilogy of nightmarish tales to a young newlywed (Lil Dagover), eventually driving her to suicide.

922 *The Witching Hour* (Paramount, 1921). 7 reels.
Director: William Desmond Taylor.
Screenplay: Julia Ivers (based on the play by Augustus Thomas).
Photography: James Van Trees.
Cast: Elliott Dexter, Winter Hall, Edward Sutherland, Mary Alden, Ruth Renick, Robert Cain.
Notes: Hypnosis and telepathy are depicted.

923 *The Yellow Face* (Stoll, 1921). Great Britain. 20 minutes.
Screenplay: William J. Elliott.
Cast: Eille Norwood, Hubert Willis, Clifford Heatherley.
Notes: An entry in the British *Adventures of Sherlock Holmes* series. Based on the story by Sir Arthur Conan Doyle. Holmes is mystified by a strange creature with a yellow face inhabiting a cottage.

1922

924 *At the Sign of the Jack o' Lantern* (Hodkinson/ Renco, 1922). 5 reels.
Director: Lloyd Ingraham.
Screenplay: Lloyd Ingraham, David Kirkland.
Cast: Betty Ross Clark, Earl Schenk, Wade Boteler, Victor Poten, Mrs. Raymond Hatton, Monte Collins.
Notes: Ghostly events occur in a country home.

925 *A Blind Bargain* (Goldwyn, 1922). 5 reels.
Director: Wallace Worsley.
Screenplay: J. G. Hawks (based on *The Octave of Claudius* by Barry Pain).
Photography: Norbert Brodin.
Cast: Lon Chaney (Dr. Arthur Lamb/the Ape Man), Jacqueline Logan (Angela Marshall), Raymond McKee (Robert Sandrell), Virginia True Boardman (Mrs. Sandell), Fontaine La Rue (Mrs. Lamb), Aggie Herring (Bessie), Virginia Madison (Angela's Mother).
Notes: A Blind Bargain, based on the 1897 story *The Octave of Claudius* by Barry Pain, contained plot elements that would later be exploited to fuller advantage in Paramount's *Island of Lost Souls* (1932). Chaney's simian monster disguise, although a relatively light make-up, was impressive and extremely well-designed. A charity

ball scene was filmed in two-strip Technicolor.

Reviews: "Another addition to the 'horror' situation so prevalent in fiction, theatre and on the screen for the past year. The script is shy of originality in plot and in telling, seemingly having borrowed numerous instances from at least one novel, as well as a stage production which has only been out of New York about three weeks.... [B]eyond the work of the star himself there is nothing to raise this film above the average feature. Chaney, doubling as the doctor and the hunchback, gives a creditable performance.... Always at his best in a grotesque make-up, Chaney predominates in the character of the man-ape, using the ungainly lope of the supposed animal as a means of locomotion throughout the interpretation of the character...." — *Variety,* December 8, 1922.

"Lon Chaney, having demonstrated ... his ability to impersonate a variety of characters, has been made one of the favorite trick actors of the screen and is seldom allowed to appear as a plausible human being.... [I]n *A Blind Bargain* ... he is further exhibited at his stunts...." — *The New York Times,* December 4, 1922.

926 *Danse Macabre* (Mac-Gowan, 1922). 11 minutes.

Cast: Adolph Bolm, Olin Howland.

Notes: Based on the composition by Saint-Saens. The spectre of Death is depicted.

927 *Doctor Mabuse* (Ullstein-UCO Films/UFA, 1922). Germany. 110 minutes for each installment.

Director: Fritz Lang.

Screenplay: Fritz Lang, Thea von Harbou (based on the novel by Norbert Jacques).

Photography: Carl Hoffmann.

Set Designers: Otto Hunte, Stahl-Urach.

Cast: Rudolph Klein-Rogge, Alfred Abel, Aud Egede Nissen, Gertrud Welcker, Bernhard Goetzke, Paul Richter, Forster Larinaga, Hans Adalbert von Schlettow, Georg John, Karl Huszar, Greta Berger, Julius Falkenstein, Lydia Potechina, Anita Berber, Adele Sandrock, Max Adalbert, Paul Biensfeldt, Hans J. Junkermann, Auguste Prasch-Grevenberg, Karl Platen.

Notes: Dr. Mabuse (Rudolph Klein-Rogge) is a sophisticated, gadget-laden master-criminal with far-reaching influence not unlike the James Bond supervillains of a later film era. His only worthy opponent is District Attorney Wenk (Bernhard Goetzke), who is not above stooping to Mabuse's debased level in order to combat his machiavellian schemes, which are international in scope. Director Lang managed some nice, moody atmosphere, with horrific overtones, in this slowly paced but fascinating picture that had two feature-length parts: Part One entitled *The Great Gambler* (*Der Spieler*) and Part Two entitled *Inferno* (*Menschen der Zeit*).

Review: "The direction of Fritz Lang has moments — at last through the consciousness of the picture world is beginning to filter the idea that what you see is worth at least

A Blind Bargain (1922): Lon Chaney as the ape-man.

twenty times what you read. For instance, the handling of a scene in which Mabuse tries to hypnotize Wenk and force him to play a card, the rest of the characters dim out, leaving only the face of Mabuse visible, and this becomes larger and larger, until it covers the whole screen. This is tremendously effective film technique." — *Variety,* June 3, 1922.

928 *Don Juan and Faust* (1922). France.
Director: Marcel L'Herbier.
Cast: Philippe Heriat.

929 *Esmeralda* (Master, 1922). Great Britain. 1100 feet.
Alternate title: The Hunchback of Notre Dame.
Director: Edwin J. Collins.
Screenplay: Frank Miller (based on the novel *Notre Dame de Paris* by Victor Hugo).
Cast: Sybil Thorndike (Esmeralda), Booth Conway (Quasimodo), Arthur Kingsley (Phoebus), Annesley Hely (Priest).
Notes: This film was an entry in the *Tense Moments from Master Plays* series.

930 *Faust* (Master, 1922). Great Britain. 14 minutes.
Director: Challis Sanderson.
Screenplay: Frank Miller (based on Gounod's opera).
Cast: Dick Webb, Sylvia Caine, Lawford Davidson (Mephistopheles).

931 *The Ghost Breaker* (Paramount/Famous Players–Lasky, 1922). 6 reels.
Producer: Jesse L. Lasky.
Director: Alfred Green.
Screenplay: Jack Cunningham, Walter de Leon.
Photography: William Marshall.
Cast: Wallace Reid (Warren Jarvis), Lila Lee (Maria Theresa), Walter Hiers (Rusty Snow), Arthur Edmund Carewe (Duke D'Alva), J. Farrell McDonald (Sam Marcum), Snitz Edwards (Maurice).
Notes: Based on the 1909 Paul Dickey and Charles W. Goddard horror-comedy play filmed previously in 1914 (*q.v.*); even at a scant 57 minutes, this version, loosely directed by Alfred Green, seemed too long.
Reviews: "... [F]airly well-done, with considerable comedy element that prevents the picture from falling into the classification of ordinary. The sets are elaborate and the photography good, but it looks as though Reid had made up his mind that he was going to do as little work in this picture as possible, and possibly conspired with the script writer and director to help him out." — *Variety,* September 15, 1922.
"... [T]he Dickey-Goddard play offered almost boundless opportunities for fun and thrills on the screen, and they have been taken advantage of only half-way and half-heartedly. The main fault seems to be in the direction. Alfred Green has not enlivened the film. ... Instead, he has made many meaningless scenes that let the spectator's imagination go to sleep, while he is flatly informed in words just what they are all about. When the picture finally does get to the

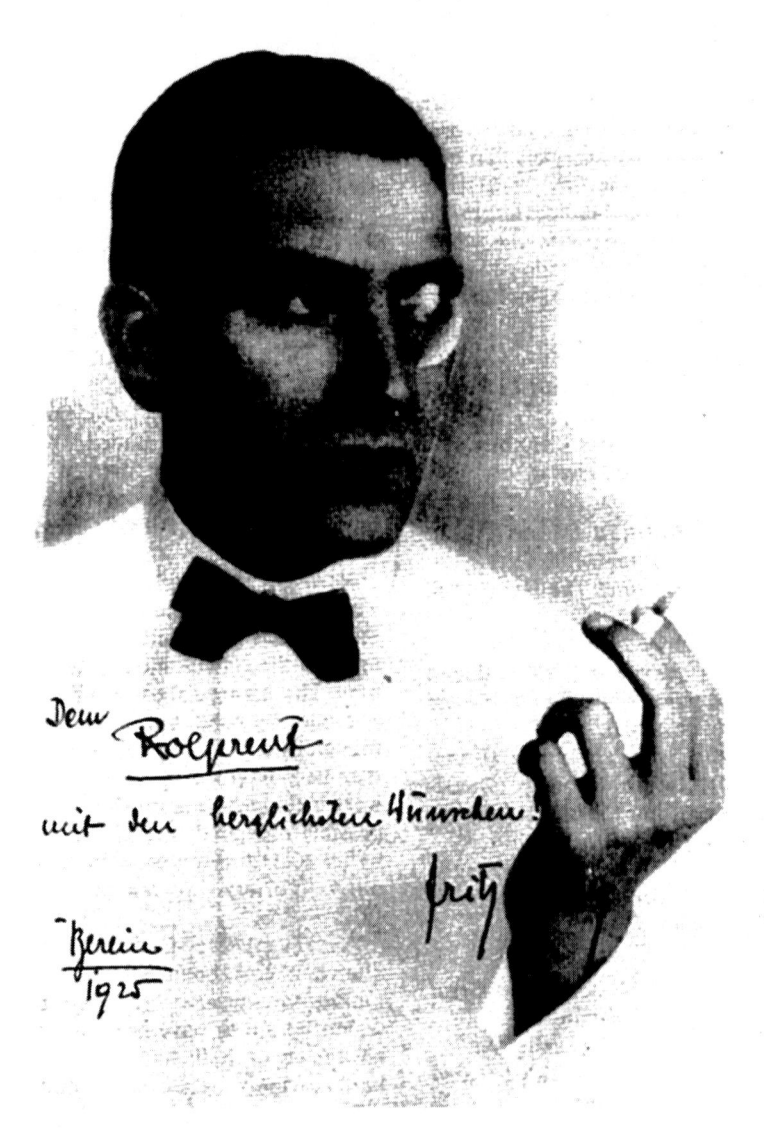

Fritz Lang: A 1920s portrait of the director.

business of the ghosts and the treasure it picks up a little, and although it never has the pictorial vitality one is always expecting of it, it takes on a certain intensity of life that makes it fairly interesting and amusing." – *The New York Times,* September 11, 1922.

The Ghost Breaker (1922): Original poster.

932 ***The Haunted Castle*** (Educational, 1922). 11 minutes.

933 ***The Haunted House*** (Fox, 1922). 22 minutes.
Director: Erle C. Kenton.

Häxan *see* **Witchcraft Through the Ages**

934 ***The Headless Horseman*** (Hodkinson, 1922).
Director: Edward Venturini.
Cast: Will Rogers.
Notes: Based on *The Legend of Sleepy Hollow* by Washington Irving.

935 ***Little Red Riding Hood*** (Hepworth, 1922). Great Britain.
Notes: This adaptation of the fairy tale was an animated cartoon.

936 ***Little Red Riding Hood*** (Selznick, 1922).

Macht der Finsternis, Die *see* **The Power of Darkness**

937 ***Money to Burn*** (Fox, 1922). 5 reels.
Director: Rowland V. Lee.
Screenplay: Jack Strumwasser.
Photography: David Abel.
Cast: William Russell, Sylvia Breamer, Hallam Cooley, Harvey Clark.
Notes: A man buys a supposedly haunted country estate.

938 *My Friend the Devil* (Fox, 1922). 100 minutes.
Director: Harry Millarde.
Screenplay: Paul H. Sloane (based on the novel *Dr. Rameau* by Georges Ohnet).
Photography: Joseph Ruttenberg.
Cast: Charles Richman, Ben Grauer, Alice May, Robert Frazer, William Tooker.
Notes: A boy prays to God for the death of his step-father, but lightning strikes his mother instead.

939 *Nosferatu* (Prana, 1922). [*Nosferatu eine Symphonie des Grauens*]. Germany. 8 reels.
Director: F. W. Murnau.
Screenplay: Henryk Galeen.
Titles: Ben de Casseres.
Photography: Fritz Arno Wagner.
Set Designer: Albin Grau.
Cast: Max Schreck (Graf Orlok), Alexander Granach (Knock, a real estate agent), Gustav von Wangenheim (Jonathan Hutter), Greta Schroeder (Ellen Hutter), G. H. Schnell (Harding, shipowner), Ruth Landshoff (Anne), John Gottowt (Prof. Buluer), Gustav Botz (Prof. Sievers), Max Nemetz (Captain of the *Demeter*), Wolfgang Heinz, Albert Venohr (Seamen), Guido Herzfeld (Innkeeper), Hardy von Francois (Doctor).
Notes: Directed by F. (Friedrich) W. Murnau (1899-1931) – real name F. W. Plumpe – *Nosferatu,* subitlted *Eine Symphonie des Grauens* (*A Symphony of Horror*) is the first screen version of Bram Stoker's novel *Dracula.* The first and only production of Germany's Prana Film Company, a financially troubled organization that folded soon after completion of this film, *Nosferatu* was unofficially adapted from Stoker's novel, with the names of the characters changed in an effort to disguise the source. "Count Dracula" became "Graf Orlok," "Jonathan Harker" became "Jonathan Hutter," and so on. It's unfortunate that a filmmaker of Murnau's talent had to resort to this subterfuge in order to acquire material, but he was shooting on a limited budget, and had successfully pulled off the same routine two years earlier when he filmed *Der Januskopf* (*q.v.*), an unofficial adaptation of *Dr. Jekyll and Mr. Hyde.*

In the case of *Nosferatu,* though, the ruse failed, and on the film's release Bram Stoker's widow sued, seeking the destruction of all prints. Fortunately, for the sake of posterity as well as anyone who just enjoys a well-made film, she did not achieve her goal, and *Nosferatu* survives today as one of the great silent classics.

Looking at *Nosferatu* now, and comparing it to American films of the same period, it is surprising how much *older* Murnau's film looks, and its lack of studio gloss and polish is entirely to its advantage, since the story is set in 1843. Another surprise in comparing *Nosferatu* to *German* films of its period is Murnau's unconventional use of real scenery in lieu of the exaggerated studio sets prevalent at the time. This was, after all, only three years after *The Cabinet of Dr. Caligari.* But although *Nosferatu* was economically filmed on

Nosferatu (1922): Max Schreck.

actual locations, those locations were carefully chosen and expertly photographed to the fullest possible advantage. Murnau's shrewd use of existing landscapes and structures in establishing mood and building atmosphere is impressive; his affinity for natural scenery and meticulous, painterly compositions reveal a visual sophistication equal to D. W. Griffith's. Murnau's sensitivity and talent, so abundantly evident in this and his other surviving films, particularly *Faust* (*q.v.*) and the docudrama *Tabu* (1931), make it all the more tragic that so few of his pictures exist today.

After completing his education at the universities of Berlin and Heidelberg where he studied art history and literature, Murnau attended the Max Reinhardt theatre school, later joining the company. In 1914 he was drafted into the military and was soon promoted to lieutenant and transferred to the Air Force. In 1917 he was imprisoned in Switzerland after crashing in a fog; through the German embassy he was able to direct stage productions, and was introduced to movies when he began compiling and editing propaganda film material. Murnau made his official directorial bow with *The Boy in Blue* (1919); one of his productions was *The Haunted Castle* (*Schlöss Vogelod*), a 1921 release, which, from published descriptions of its grimmer passages, would seem to foreshadow *Nosferatu*. In 1926, after directing *Faust* in Germany, Murnau was invited to Hollywood by William Fox; after directing the lyrical *Sunrise* (1927) and *Tabu* (1931), he was killed in a car accident on March 11, 1931.

If there is any fault at all to be found in *Nosferatu*, it is in the script's somewhat lop-sided construction. After much expository (though atmospheric) footage with the real estate agent Hutter journeying to Transylvania, falling prey to the vampire, and escaping from the castle after Orlok has apparently left him for dead and travelled to Wisborg in search of fresh prey—including Hutter's wife—the film doesn't really begin to move forward in a narrative sense until it is nearly two-thirds over. Orlok does not even threaten Ellen Hutter until the last scene, in which, martyr-like, she willingly allows him to feed on her blood until the sun rises and Orlok dissolves in the first shafts of light entering the room.

This seems like nit-picking, though, when discussing a film that is so rich visually; otherwise, there are only minor lapses of directorial judgement, such as the scene in which Hutter, delirious from the vampire's attack, watches from a castle window as Orlok loads a wagon with coffins in the courtyard below in preparation for his journey to Wisborg. The scene is shot downward from Hutter's point of view, but in speeded-up fast motion, with Orlok madly scurrying back and forth, stacking the coffins at a frenetic pace. The technique is intended to suggest the supernatural, but the effect is unintentionally comical instead, and must have seemed so even in 1922.

As Orlok, Max Schreck is a genuinely frightening character; his bald-headed, pointy-eared make-up,

Nosferatu (1922): Max Schreck (right) emerges from his coffin.

with obscene, rat-like fangs protruding from the mouth and grasping, clawed hands adding up to one of the foulest, most repulsive creatures in the annals of screen horror. Schreck is seemingly centuries old; surprisingly, he was only 43 when he appeared in this film. Orlok's very appearance suggests pestilence and death. Fittingly enough, he is trailed by an accompanying horde of rats wherever he goes. Gustav von Wangenheim as Hutter and Greta Schroeder as Ellen are adequate in their roles, while Max Schreck gets some tough competition from Alexander Granach as Knock, Hutter's employer and Orlok's mad servant, a character patterned after the maniac Renfield in the novel. Granach is flamboyant and wildly over the top with his drooling, cackling performance, but, after all, he *is* supposed to be mad.

Comparisons between *Nosferatu* and the much more famous Bela Lugosi *Dracula* of 1931 are inevitable but pointless. Even though *Dracula* did rely on *Nosferatu* for the structuring of its opening two reels, while the rest of the film was based on a 1927 Broadway play adaptation (which also starred Lugosi), the two films approach the same material from opposing conceptual directions. Schreck's Orlok truly is one of the "children of the night," to quote Lugosi, and could never, under any circumstances, be mistaken for a human being, while Lugosi's Dracula is capable of being accepted in high society and even welcomed into his victims' homes, blending perfectly in his formal evening attire.

In a dramatic sense, the Lugosi concept is superior, imparting greater flexibility to the vampire's interactions with his potential victims and adversaries. While *Dracula* is undeniably a flawed movie in terms of dramatic pacing, its opening passages still thrill, and it remains a great classic; instead of choosing one over the other, both *Dracula* and *Nosferatu* should be accepted together, as equally interesting variants of the same theme.

Without Murnau's knowledge (he had since gone to Hollywood), *Nosferatu* was extensively reedited and reissued, with a soundtrack, under the title *The Twelfth Hour* in 1929.

Nosferatu was remade in 1979 under the title *Nosferatu, the Vampyre* by German director Werner Herzog, whose serious if artistically pretentious approach was welcome after a decade of vampire spoofs and comedies, but star Klaus Kinski's physique was ill-suited for the vampire make-up, based on Schreck's original. Lovely actress Isabele Adjani's beauty was put to good use as Kinski's victim, but despite Herzog's good intentions, his film was miscalculated and failed to equal Murnau's classic, even with the addition of color and sound.

The video release of *Nosferatu* available on Kino International Video is highly recommended to the reader, since this version is accurately reconstructed, with restored, translated titles and appropriate color tinting; it is also accompanied by an excellent music score.

Reviews: "Skillfully mounted and directed, this symbolical legendary cinema story of reanimated ghosts in a period set about a century or so ago when vampirism was pretty well entrenched in the world's beliefs, is a depressive piece of art.... [T]he picture is a shivery melodrama spilling ghostlike impossibilities from beginning to end. Murnau proved his directorial artistry in *Sunrise* for Fox about three years ago, but in this picture he's a master artisan demonstrating not only a knowledge of the subtler side of directing but in photography. One shot of the sun cracking at dawn is an eye filler. Max Schreck as the vampire is an able pantomimist and works clocklike, his make-up suggesting everything that's goose-pimply." — *Variety*, December 25, 1929.

"This would-be spine-chiller neglects little in its desire to make somebody or other look around for werewolves, ghosts or vampires. The chief figure in this orgy of gooseflesh ... is a vampire, according to this story. Prior to disturbing a peaceful village, he contents himself by sleeping in a coffin. ... Max Schreck's movements are too deliberate to be lifelike." — *The New York Times*, June 4, 1929.

Nosferatu eine Symphonie de Grauens *see* **Nosferatu**

940 **One Exciting Night** (United Artists, 1922). 11 reels.
Director: D. W. Griffith.
Screenplay: Irene Sinclair (pseudonym for D. W. Griffith).

One Exciting Night (1922).

Photography: Hendrick Sartov, Irving B. Ruby.
Set Designer: Charles M. Kirk.
Special Effects: Edward Scholl.
Cast: Carol Dempster (Agnes Harrington), Henry Hull (John Fairfax), Porter Strong (Romeo Washington), Morgan Wallace (J. Wilson Rockmaine), C. H. Crocker-King (the neighbor), Margaret Dale (Mrs. Harrington), Frank Sheridan (the detective),

Frank Wunerlee (Samuel Jones), Grace Griswold (Auntie Fairfax), Irma Harrison (the maid), Herbert Sutch (Clary Johnson), Percy Carr (the butler), Charles E. Mack (a guest).

Notes: For *One Exiciting Night,* cinematic pioneer D. W. Griffith, faltering commercially and desperate for a popular hit, unofficially "borrowed" the general plot of the successful Broadway play *The Bat* and cobbled up this haunted house imitation.

Reviews: "It is a melodramatic hodge-podge of every mystery thriller from serial, dime novel . . . etc., right up to the modern *The Bat* and *The Cat and the Canary.* Although Griffith may take violent exception to the statement, it looks as if he wanted to make a little money for himself this time. . . . Hidden safes, sliding panels, masked figures, revolving bookcases, guns, knives, hidden hands groping out of doorways, all . . . are present."—*Variety,* October 13, 1922.

"The film is somewhat too long; it hasn't the photographic finish in all of its scenes one has come to expect from a Griffith production . . . but . . . despite everything, *One Exciting Night* is a hilarious thriller."—*The New York Times,* October 24, 1922.

941 ***One Glorious Night*** (Paramount, 1922). 56 minutes.

Alternate title: Souls Before Birth.

Director: James Cruze.

Screenplay: A. B. Baringer, Walter Woods.

Photography: Karl Brown.

Cast: Lila Lee, Will Rogers, Alan Hale, John Fox.

Notes: When a professor obsessed with spiritualism ejects his spirit from his body, a new spirit enters his empty form, and his own spirit wanders aimlessly, searching for its owner.

942 ***The Power of Darkness*** (Neumann, 1922). [*Die Macht der Finsternis*]. Germany. 72 minutes.

Director: Robert Wiene.

Notes: Adapted from a play by Leo Tolstoy. A man has strange powers over women.

943 ***Sherlock Holmes*** (Goldwyn, 1922). 9 reels.

Director: Albert Parker.

Screenplay: Marion Fairfax (based on the play by William Gillette and the character created by Sir Arthur Conan Doyle).

Cast: John Barrymore (Sherlock Holmes), Roland Young, Carol Dempster, Hedda Hopper, Gustav von Seyffertitz (Prof. Moriarty), William H. Powell, Reginald Denny, David Torrence, Lumsden Hare, Louis Wolheim.

Notes: Director Albert Parker injected a horrific atmosphere into this film's conclusion, with plenty of exaggerated shadows, secret panels and low-key lighting.

944 ***Singed Wings*** (Paramount, 1922). 8 reels.

Director: Penrhyn Stanlaws.

Screenplay: Ewart Adamson, Edfrid A. Bingham (based on a novel by Katharine Burt).

Cast: Bebe Daniels, Conrad

Nagel, Adolphe Menjou, Ernest Torrence.
Notes: A witch on a broomstick is depicted.

945 *The Spirit of '23* (C.B.C., 1922). 25 minutes.
Notes: A skeleton is featured.

946 *Spooks* (Mermaid, 1922).
Directors: Jack White, Robert Kerr.
Cast: Lige Conley.
Notes: A person spends a night in a wax museum in order to win a prize.

947 *Trifling Women* (Metro, 1922). 9 reels.
Direction/Screenplay: Rex Ingram.
Photography: John F. Seitz.
Art Direction: Leo E. Kuter.
Production Manager: Starret Ford.
Cast: Barbara La Marr (Jacqueline de Severac/Zareda), Ramon Novarro (Henri/Ivan de Maupin), Pomeroy Cannon (Leon de Severac), Edward Connelly (Baron Francois de Maupin), Lewis Stone (the Marquis Ferroni), Hughie Mack (Pere Alphonse Bidondeau), Gene Pouyet (Colonel Roybet), John George (Achmet), Jess Weldon (Caesar), B. Hyman (Hassan), Joe Martin (Hatim-Tai, a chimpanzee).
Notes: A remake of the same director's 1916 film *Black Orchids* (*q.v.*). A promiscuous young woman (Barbara La Marr) is frightened into adopting a more conservative life when her father tells her a horrifying story in which a similar character (also played by La Marr) suffers a gruesome death in payment for her sins.
Review: "The greatest difficulty this picture must overcome is the title, *Trifling Women,* as the title is too big and encompasses too much for this film to stand up under it. . . . [T]here is nothing striking in the film's acting." — *Variety,* October 6, 1922.

948 *Trilby* (Master, 1922). Great Britain. 1300 feet.
Cast: Phyllis Nelson-Terry (Trilby), Charles Garry (Svengali).
Notes: This short subject was an entry in the *Tense Moments with Great Authors* series. Based on the novel *Trilby* by George Du Maurier.

949 *Vendetta* (Cosmopolitan/ Famous Players, 1922).
Director: Alan Crossland.
Screenplay: Frances Marion (based on the novel by Marie Corelli).
Cast: Lionel Barrymore, Alma Rubens.
Notes: A man returns from the dead.

950 *Whispering Shadows* (Peacock-States' Rights/Peerless, 1922). 72 minutes.
Director: E. Chautard.
Screenplay: Walter Hackett.
Photography: Jacques Bizeul.
Titles: William B. Loeb, Harry Chandlee.
Cast: Lucy Cotton, Charles A. Stevenson, Robert Barrat, Mrs. Celestine Saunders (the medium), Philip Merivale.
Notes: At a séance, a girl is warned

Witchcraft Through the Ages (1922): An explicit black mass.

by an unseen presence that her sweetheart is in danger.

951 *Witchcraft Through the Ages* (Svensk Filmindustri, 1922). [*Häxan*]. Sweden. 10 reels.
Producer: Ernest Mattison.
Director/Screenplay: Benjamin Christensen.
Photography: Joan Ankerstjerne.
Cast: Maren Pederson, Oscar Stribolt, Clara Pontoppidan, Benjamin Christensen, Tora Teje, Elith Pio, Karen Winther, Emmy Schoenfeld, Johs Andersen, Poul Reumert, Astrid Holm, Alice O'Fredericks.
Notes: In this film, director Benjamin Christensen's intent was to expose the hypocrisy of organized religion through a historical examination of witchcraft and the church's reaction to it through the years. In this goal Christensen was only partially successful; his structural approach, which anticipated the "docudrama" style of more recent years, is turgid and boring. The film is nearly saved by its startling visuals; a few scenes are unforgettable pictorially, such as a black mass with a skeletonized horse capering through the proceedings and the Devil (played by the director!) suddenly appearing in a church. The picture's frequent use of nudity, while justified and relatively tasteful, is surprising considering its vintage, and certainly did not help its distribution in

The Young Diana (1922): Marion Davies.

the United States at the time. Although a fascinating oddity, *Witchcraft Through the Ages* is ultimately defeated by its flawed construction. The film was not improved when it was reissued in 1966, pruned from 94 to 76 minutes, with narration by author William Burroughs (*Naked Lunch*) and an irritating free-form jazz score added.

Reviews: "Swedish and Danish pictures easily hold the palm for morbid realism, and in many cases for brilliant acting and production. *Witchcraft Through the Ages,* made by Benjamin Christensen, leaves all the others beaten. It is in reality a pictorial history of black magic; of witches, of the inquisition, and the thousand and one inhumanities of the superstition-ridden Middle Ages. Many of its scenes are unadulterated horror." — *Variety,* September 6, 1923.

"This film of the supernatural delves into the mechanics of sorcery, revealing the devious machinations of the Devil from a steam model of Hell to an orgy of Satan's disciples. Benjamin Christensen, author and director of the film, depicts various types of witches, their work and their subsequent trial and burning at the stake. The picture is, for the most part, fantastically conceived and directed, holding the onlooker in a sort of medieval spell." — *The New York Times,* May 28, 1929.

952 *The Young Diana* (Paramount, 1922). 7 reels.
Directors: Albert Capellani, Robert G. Vignola.
Screenplay: Luther Reed (based on the novel *The Young Diana: An Experiment of the Future, a Romance* by Marie Corelli).
Photography: Harold Wenstrom.
Set Designer: Joseph Urban.
Cast: Marion Davies (Diana May), Maclyn Arbuckle (James P. May), Forrest Stanley (Commander Cleeve), Gypsy O'Brien (Lady Anne), Pedro De Cordoba (Dr. Dimitrius).
Notes: Rejuvenation was the theme of this Marion Davies vehicle. Diana May, an embittered spinster, is restored to youth with an elixer administered by Dr. Dimitrius.
Review: "Miss Davies ... plays with poise, surety and splendid artistry. ... With its superb photography, sumptuous settings and regal costuming *The Young Diana* shines...." — *Variety,* September 1, 1922.

1923

953 *Aaron's Rod* (Stoll, 1923). Great Britain. 20 minutes.
Director: A. E. Colby.
Cast: Harry Agar Lyons, Fred Paul.
Notes: This short subject was an entry in *The Mystery of Dr. Fu-Manchu* series, based on the oriental villain created by Sax Rohmer. Each installment in the series was directed by A. E. Colby and starred Harry Agar Lyons and Fred Paul.

954 *Au Secours!* (Abel Gance, 1923). France. 18 minutes.
Alternate title: Help!

Producer/Director: Abel Gance.
Screenplay: Abel Gance, Max Linder.
Photography: Georges Specht.
Cast: Max Linder, Gina Palerme, Jean Toulot.
Notes: A Grand Guignol spoof starring French comic Linder.

955 *The Bishop of the Ozarks* (FBO/Cosmopolitan, 1923). 6 reels.
Director: Finis Fox.
Screenplay: Finis Fox (story by Milford W. Howard).
Photography: Sol Polito.
Cast: Milford W. Howard, Derelys Perdue, Cecil Holland, Fred Kelsey, William Kenton.
Notes: A doctor controls a girl telepathically. A séance is also featured in this occult melodrama.

956 *Black Oxen* (First National, 1923). 8 reels.
Director: Frank Lloyd.
Photography: Norbert Brodin.
Cast: Corinne Griffith, Conway Tearle, Alan Hale, Clara Bow, Kate Lester.
Notes: Based on the novel by Gertrude Atherton. A 58-year-old woman is rejuvenated by a doctor's radiation treatments. Included in the cast was scandalous actress Clara Bow—known as the "It" girl—then on her way up in Hollywood.

957 *The Call of Siva* (Stoll, 1923). Great Britain. 20 minutes.
Notes: An entry in *The Mystery of Dr. Fu-Manchu* series.

958 *The Cardboard Box* (Stoll, 1923). Great Britain. 30 minutes.
Art Director: Walter W. Murton.
Cast: Eille Norwood, Hubert Willis, Tom Beaumont.
Notes: When a woman receives a package containing a pair of human ears, Sherlock Holmes investigates. Based on Sir Arthur Conan Doyle's character.

959 *The Chronicle of the Gray House* (Union-UFA, 1923). [*Chronik von Grieschuus*]. Germany.
Director: Arthur von Gerlach.
Screenplay: Thea von Harbou (based on a story by Theodor Storm).
Photography: Karl Drews, Fritz Arno Wagner, Erich Nitzchmann.
Set Designers: Hans Poelzig, Robert Herlth, Walter Rohrig.
Cast: Paul Hartmann, Lil Dagover, Gertrud Arnold, Rudolph Forster, Gertrud Welcker, Arthur Kraussneck.
Notes: Two brothers of noble heritage are rivals for the same woman in a trifling romantic plot completely overshadowed by horrific, atmospheric sets depicting a brooding castle and its surrounding moors.

Chronik von Grieshuus *see* ***The Chronicle of the Gray House***

960 *The Clue of the Pigtail* (Stoll, 1923). Great Britain. 22 minutes.

Notes: An entry in *The Mystery of Dr. Fu-Manchu* series.

961 Col. Heeza Liar and the Ghost (Bray, 1923).
Notes: An animated cartoon.

962 The Cry of the Night Hawk (Stoll, 1923). Great Britain. 20 minutes.
Director: A. E. Colby.
Screenplay: A. E. Colby, Frank Wilson (based on the character created by Sax Rohmer).
Photography: D. P. Cooper.
Cast: Harry Agar Lyons, Joan Clarkson, Fred Paul, Humbertson Wright.
Notes: An entry in *The Mystery of Dr. Fu-Manchu* series.

963 Drums of Jeopardy (Truart/Hoffman, 1923). 7 reels.
Director: Edward Dillon.
Screenplay: Arthur Hoerl (based on a story by Harold McGrath).
Cast: Elaine Hammerstein, Jack Mulhall, Wallace Beery, David Torrence.
Notes: Emeralds have a strange and mysterious influence over their owner. Remade as a talkie in 1931.

964 Faust (Butcher, 1923). Great Britain. 22 minutes.
Director: Bertram Phillips.
Screenplay: Frank Miller.
Cast: Queenie Thomas, Frank Stanmore.

965 The Fiery Hand (Stoll, 1923). Great Britain. 25 minutes.
Director: A. E. Colby.
Screenplay: A. E. Colby, Frank Wilson (based on the character created by Sax Rohmer).
Photography: D. P. Cooper, Phil Ross.
Art Direction: Walter W. Murton.
Cast: Harry Agar Lyons, Joan Clarkson.
Notes: A haunted house was featured in this entry in *The Mystery of Dr. Fu-Manchu* series.

966 The Flying Dutchman (FBO, 1923). 6 reels.
Director: Lloyd B. Carleton (based on the opera *Der Fliegende Hollander* by Richard Wagner).
Photography: Andra Barlatier.
Cast: Lawson Butt, Lola Luxford, Edward Coxen.
Notes: A phantom ship and a ghost are featured.

967 The Fungi Cellars (Stoll, 1923). Great Britain. 20 minutes.
Director: A. E. Colby.
Screenplay: A. E. Colby, Frank Wilson (based on the character created by Sax Rohmer).
Photography: D. P. Cooper.
Cast: Harry Agar Lyons, Joan Clarkson, Humbertson Wright.
Notes: An entry in *The Mystery of Dr. Fu-Manchu* series. Fu-Manchu grows a fungus that emits poisonous fumes.

968 The Ghost of Tolston's Manor (Micheaux, 1923). Japan.
Director: Keisuke Kinoshita.
Cast: Ken Uehara, Kinuyo Tanaka.

The Hunchback of Notre Dame (1923): Lon Chaney.

969 Hansel and Gretel (Universal, 1923). 22 minutes.

970 The Hunchback of Notre Dame (Universal, 1923). 12 reels.
Producer: Carl Laemmle; Irving Thalberg.
Director: Wallace Worsley.
Screenplay: Edward T. Lowe, Jr., Perley Poore Sheehan (based on the novel *Notre Dame de Paris* by Victor Hugo).
Photography: Robert Newhard, Tony Kornman.
Assistant Directors: Jack Sullivan, William Wyler.
Cast: Lon Chaney (Quasimodo), Ernest Torrence (Clopin), Patsy Ruth Miller (Esmeralda), Norman Kerry (Phoebus), Kate Lester (Mme. De Gondelaurier), Brandon Hurst (Jehan), Raymond Hatton (Grin-

The Hunchback of Notre Dame (1923): Patsy Ruth Miller, Lon Chaney.

goire), Tully Marshall (Louix XI), Nigel De Brulier (Dom Claude), Harry Van Meter (Mons Neufchatel), Gladys Brockwell (Godule), Eulalie Jensen (Marie), Winifred Bryson (Fleur de Lys), Nick De Ruiz (Mons, le Torteru), Edwin Wallock (King's Chamberlain), W. Ray Meyers (Chamolou's Assistant), William Parke, Sr. (Josephus), John Cossar (Judge of Court), Roy Laidlaw (Charmolie), George MacQuame, Jay Hunt, Harry De Vere, Pearl Tupper, Eva Lewis, Jane Sherman, Helen Bruneau, Gladys Johnston, Cesare Gravina.

Notes: This film, along with *The Phantom of the Opera* (1925), is one of Lon Chaney's best-known pictures, and was also one of the most lavish movies produced by

Universal in the 1920s, taking three months to film in an era when many pictures were shot in less than a week. The scenarists of this production made a number of changes in adapting Victor Hugo's original novel, *Notre Dame de Paris*. In Hugo's book, Quasimodo, the hideously deformed bell-ringer of Notre Dame cathedral, was a relatively minor character, and the general thrust of the work was a scathing critique of organized religion's hypocrisies and injustices, with the ostensibly pious but secretly perverse cleric Jehan lusting after the beautiful gypsy girl Esmeralda. No Hollywood studio in the 1920s was about to risk producing a film even faintly critical of religion, even in a historical context, so the fascinating character of Quasimodo was brought forward and thrown into bolder relief as a starring role for Chaney, and Hugo's general theme was downplayed somewhat, although—and this must be noted to Universal's credit—the author's central intent remains in the background and the film, in spite of these changes, holds basically true to the tone and spirit of its source.

The Hunchback of Notre Dame was produced by the legendary Irving Thalberg before he left Universal for M-G-M. No expense was spared in terms of massive set construction, costume design and historical detail. This is a far more coherent picture than Chaney's later *The Phantom of the Opera*. Where that movie failed in the script department, *The Hunchback of Notre Dame* succeeds. It is well-constructed dramatically throughout, and meticulously calculated to emphasize its star.

Admirably faithful to the novel's description, Quasimodo is Chaney's heaviest and most intricately detailed make-up creation; he is virtually unrecognizable beneath pounds of clay and rubber. Still—and this is a tribute to Chaney's infinite skills, both as performer and make-up artist—the effect is never stiff or mask-like, and Chaney's emotional sincerity never fails to come through the grotesque disguise.

Mention should also be made of the very capable supporting cast, particularly Brandon Hurst as Jehan and Ernest Torrance as Clopin, the self-styled King of Thieves. Patsy Ruth Miller is excellent as Esmeralda, the gypsy dancing girl who captures Quasimodo's heart, offering just the right combination of innocence and sex appeal. This is one Hollywood star vehicle where the supporting actors rival the leading man in effectiveness.

Critics have tended to minimize director Wallace Worsley's contributions to the film, and while it is true that Worsley often deferred to Chaney during production, Worsley's expert handling of the massive crowd scenes (assisted by a young William Wyler, who would later direct the 1959 version of *Ben-Hur*) and his attention to historical detail cannot be faulted. It was Worsley who insisted that the period clothing worn by the actors had to look like *clothing,* not *costumes,* and the film's remarkable verisimilitude in this area is one of its greatest achievements.

The Hunchback of Notre Dame,

The Hunchback of Notre Dame (1923): Lon Chaney and Brandon Hurst.

originally shown in a long 12 reel (over two hours) roadshow version, was shortened for general release, and had been cut still further by the time it was reissued in 1930; it is this shortened version, running about 100 minutes, that survives today. The tinted and scored version of the film available on Kino International Video is recommended to the reader.

RKO produced a solid, well-done remake of *The Hunchback of Notre Dame* in 1939, with Charles Laughton as Quasimodo and Maureen O'Hara as Esmeralda. Although filmed on a large budget, the picture did not equal Chaney's silent original, in spite of Charles Laughton's superlative performance and grotesque make-up.

A 1957 version with Anthony Quinn and Gina Lollobrigida, filmed in wide-screen and color, lacked conviction and detail, while an even weaker 1982 made-for-tv production starring Anthony Hopkins and Leslie Anne-Down was totally unconvincing and instantly forgettable.

The Hunchback of Notre Dame (1923): Patsy Ruth Miller, Lon Chaney and (in the background) Brandon Hurst.

Reviews: "*The Hunchback of Notre Dame* is a two-hour nightmare. It's murderous, hideous and repulsive. No children can stand its morbid scenes, and there are likely but few parents seeing it first who will permit their young to see it afterward. Mr. Chaney's performance as a performer entitles him to starring honors—it makes him forever more on the screen, but his make-up as the Hunchback is propaganda for the wets. His misshapened figure from the hump on his back to the deadeyed eye on his face cannot stand off his acting nor his acrobatics, nor his general work of excellence throughout this film. *The Hunchback of Notre Dame* is misery all of the time, nothing but misery, tiresome, loathsome misery that doesn't make you feel any the better for it."—*Variety*, September 6, 1923.

"Lon Chaney portrays Quasimodo, the ape-like bell-ringer of the famed cathedral, as a fearsome, frightful, crooked creature. . . . Chaney throws his whole soul into making Quasimodo as repugnant as anything human could very well be. . . . He is remarkably agile and impressive. . . . There are a number of changes, obviously necessary, which have been made in this adaptation. The story is subservient to the atmosphere and the acting. . . . However, the film holds interest because of the excellent acting and sets, and the splendid atmosphere throughout the drama."—*The New York Times*, September 3, 1923.

The Hunchback of Notre Dame (1923).

Inhumaine, L' *see* **The Living Dead Man**

971 *Itching Palms* (FBO/R-C Pictures, 1923). 6 reels.
Director: James W. Horne.
Art Direction: W. L. Heywood.
Film Editor: J. Wilkinson.
Cast: Tom Gallery, Virginia Fox, Tom Wilson, Victor Poten.
Notes: Based on the play *When Jerry Comes Home* by R. Briant. A haunted house is featured.

972 *The Last Moment* (J. Parker Read/Goldwyn, 1923). 6 reels.
Producer/Director: J. Parker Read, Jr.
Screenplay: J. Clarkson Miller (story by Jack Boyle).
Photography: J. O. Taylor.
Cast: Henry Hull (Hercules Napolean Cameron), Doris Kenyon (Alice Winthrop), Louis Wolheim ("The Finn"), Louis Calhern (Harry Gaines), William Nally ("Big Mike"), Mickey Bennett (Danny), Harry Allen (Pat Rooney), Donald Hall (Mr. Winthrop), Danny Hayes (Bartender), Jerry Peterson ("The Thing"), Robert Hazelton (the butler).
Notes: A meek bookworm is shanghaied with his girlfriend by a sadistic ship's captain who keeps an ape-like monster known as "The Thing" caged aboard his vessel.

973 *Legally Dead* (Universal, 1923). 6 reels.
Director: William Parke.
Screenplay: Harvey Gates (story by Charles Furtham).

The Last Moment (1923): Henry Hull, Doris Kenyon.

Photography: Richard Fryer.
Cast: Milton Sills, Claire Adams, Margaret Campbell, Joseph Girard, Robert Homans, Edwin Sturgis, Brandon Hurst.
Notes: An executed man is revived from the dead by a drug injected into his heart.

974 *The Little Red Schoolhouse* (Arrow, 1923). 6 reels.
Director: John G. Adolfi.
Screenplay: J. S. Hamilton (based on the play by Hal Reid).
Photography: George F. Webber.
Notes: A murderer is revealed when his face is etched on a window pane by a bolt of lightning.

975 *The Living Dead Man* (1923). [*L'Inhumaine*]. France.
Director: Marcel L'Herbier.

Art. Direction: Fernand Legar, R. Mallet-Stevens, Alberto Cavalcanti.
Cast: Eve Francis, Jacques Catelain, Georgette Leblanc.
Notes: A strange laboratory experiment saves the life of a singer who has been poisoned.

976 *The Lost Soul; or, The Dangers of Hypnosis* (Astra Film, 1923). [*Das Verlorene Ich; or, Gefahren der Hypnose*]. Austria.
Director: Hugo Werner-Kahle.
Screenplay: L. Thomas, J. Malina.
Photography: R. Mayer, H. Pebal.
Cast: Hugo Werner-Kahle, Paul Kronegg, Anne Marie Steinsleck.

Loup-Garou, Le *see The Werewolf*

Puritan Passions (1923): An original theater lobby card.

977 The Miracle (Stoll, 1923). Great Britain. 21 minutes.
Director: A. E. Colby.
Screenplay: A. E. Colby, Frank Wilson (based on the character created by Sax Rohmer).
Photography: D. P. Cooper.
Cast: Harry Agar Lyons, Joan Clarkson, Stacey Gaunt Wilson, Humbertson Wright, Fred Paul.
Notes: An entry in *The Mystery of Dr. Fu-Manchu* series.

978 The Monkey's Paw (Selznick, 1923). Great Britain. 55 minutes.
Director: Manning Haynes.
Screenplay: Lydia Hayward (based on the story by W. W. Jacobs).
Notes: A monkey's paw is cursed.

979 One Spooky Night (Pathé/Sennett, 1923).
Notes: A comedy short set in a haunted house.

980 Puritan Passions (Film Guild/Hodkinson Corp., 1923). 7 reels.
Director: Frank Tuttle.
Screenplay: James Ashmore Creelman, Frank Tuttle (based on the novel *The Scarecrow; or The Glass of Truth, a Tragedy of the Ludicrous* by Percy Mackaye).
Photography: Fred Waller, Jr.
Cast: Glen Hunter (Lord Ravensbane/the scarecrow), Mary Astor (Rachel), Osgood Perkins (Dr. Nicholas), Maude Hill (Goody Rickby), Frank Tweed (Gillead Wingate), Dwight Wiman (Bugby), Thomas Chalmers (the minister).

Notes: A young Puritan woman makes a deal with the Devil in order to gain revenge on a man who fathered her illegitimate child and then abandoned her; Satan then brings a scarecrow to life in an effort to frame the man and his ward for witchcraft.

981 *The Queen of Hearts* (Stoll, 1923). Great Britain. 22 minutes.
Director: A. E. Colby.
Screenplay: A. E. Colby, Frank Wilson (based on the character created by Sax Rohmer).
Photography: D. P. Cooper.
Cast: Harry Agar Lyons, Fred Paul, Humbertson Wright, Joan Clarkson.
Notes: An entry in *The Mystery of Dr. Fu-Manchu* series. Fu-Manchu undergoes a strange operation.

982 *The Sacred Order* (Stoll, 1923). Great Britain. 20 minutes.
Director: A. E. Colby.
Screenplay: A. E. Colby, Frank Wilson (based on the character created by Sax Rohmer).
Photography: D. P. Cooper.
Cast: Harry Agar Lyons, Fred Paul, Humbertson Wright, Joan Clarkson.
Notes: An entry in *The Mystery of Dr. Fu-Manchu* series.

983 *The Scented Envelopes* (Stoll, 1923). Great Britain. 30 minutes.
Notes: An entry in *The Mystery of Dr. Fu-Manchu* series.

Schatten *see* **Warning Shadows**

984 *The Shrine of Seven Lamps* (Stoll, 1923). Great Britain. 20 minutes.
Director: A. E. Colby.
Screenplay: A. E. Colby, Frank Wilson (based on the character created by Sax Rohmer).
Photography: D. P. Cooper.
Cast: Harry Agar Lyons, Fred Paul, Humbertson Wright, Joan Clarkson.
Notes: An entry in *The Mystery of Dr. Fu-Manchu* series.

985 *The Silver Buddha* (Stoll, 1923). Great Britain. 20 minutes.
Director: A. E. Colby.
Screenplay: A. E. Colby, Frank Wilson (based on the character created by Sax Rohmer).
Photography: D. P. Cooper.
Cast: Harry Agar Lyons, Fred Paul, Humbertson Wright, Joan Clarkson.
Notes: An entry in *The Mystery of Dr. Fu-Manchu* series.

986 *Slave of Desire* (Goldwyn, 1923). 7 reels.
Director: George Baker.
Cast: Bessie Love, Carmel Meyers, George Walsh.
Notes: Based on *The Wild Ass's Skin* by Balzac. An ass's hide grants wishes at the expense of the owner's soul.

987 *A Spooky Romance* (Century, 1923). 2 reels.
Director/Screenplay: Al Herman.
Notes: A horror-comedy short.

The Unknown Purple (1923).

Steinerne Reiter, Der *see* **The Stone Rider**

988 *The Stone Rider* (Decla-Bioscop, 1923). [*Der Steinerne Reiter*]. Germany.
Director: Fritz Wendhausen.
Screenplay: Thea von Harbou.
Photography: Karl Hoffman.
Set Designer: Heinrich Heuser.
Cast: Rudolf Klein-Rogge, Lucie Mannheim, Georg John, Fritz Kampers, Gustav von Wangenheim, Paul Biensfeldt, Otto Framer.
Notes: A man pays for his sins when he and his wife are turned to stone.

989 *Trilby* (First National, 1923). 8 reels.
Producer: Richard Walton Tully.
Director: James Young.
Screenplay: Richard Walton Tully (based on the novel by George Du Maurier).
Photography: George Benoit.
Cast: Andree Lafayette (Trilby), Arthur Edmund Carewe (Svengali), Creighton Hale (Little Billy), Philo McCullough (Taffy), Wilfred Lucas (the laird), Francis McDonald (Geko), Maurice Cannon (Zouzou), Gordon Mullen (Durien), Martha Franklin (Madame Vinard), Gilbert Clayton (Reverend Bagot), Edward Kimball (Impressario), Max Constant (Dodor), Gertrude Olmstead (Miss Bagot), Evelyn Sherman (Mrs. Bagot), Rose Dione (Laundress), Robert De Vilbiss (Jeannot).
Notes: Arthur Edmund Carewe, cast as Svengali in this version of *Trilby*, would later contribute

memorable support in horror films like *The Phantom of the Opera* (1925), *Doctor X* (1932) and *Mystery of the Wax Museum* (1933).

Review: "Richard Walton Tully has filmed an especially satisfying version of *Trilby,* notable in respect to the playing of two roles — Mlle. Lafayette and the Svengali of Arthur Edmund Carewe. Andree Lafayette is an ideal Trilby in face and figure." — *Variety,* July 26, 1923.

990 *Tut-Tut and His Terrible Tomb* (Butcher, 1923). Great Britain. 25 minutes.
Director: Bertram Phillips.
Screenplay: Frank Miller.
Cast: Queenie Thomas, Frank Stanmore.
Notes: Revived mummies stalk through this comedy short.

991 *The Unknown Purple* (Truart Film Corp., 1923). 7 reels.
Director: Roland West.
Screenplay: Roland West, Paul Schofield (based on the play *The Unknown Purple* by Roland West).
Titles: Alfred A. Cohn.
Photography: Oliver T. Marsh.
Set Designers: Horace Jackson.
Film Editor: Alfred A. Cohn.
Cast: Henry B. Walthall (Peter Marchmont/Victor Cromport), Alice Lake (Jewel Marchmont), Stuart Holmes (James Dawson), Helen Ferguson (Ruth Marsh), Frankie Lee (Bobbie), Ethel Grey Terry (Mrs. Freddie Goodlittle), James Morrison (Leslie Bradbury), Johnny Arthur (Freddie Goodlittle), Richard Wayne (George Allison), Brinsley Shaw (Hawkins), Mike Donlin (Burton).
Notes: An eerie purple light renders its inventor invisible, enabling him to seek revenge on his unfaithful wife.

992 *The Untameable* (Universal, 1923). 5 reels.
Director: Herbert Blache.
Continuity: Hugh Hoffman (based on *The White Cat* by Gelette Burgess).
Photography: H. Oswald, Ben Kline.
Cast: Gladys Walton, Malcolm McGregor, John Sainpolis, Etta Lee.
Notes: A woman acquires a split personality from a hypnotist.

Verlorene Ich, Das; *or,* Gefahren der Hypnose *see* **The Lost Soul;** or, **The Dangers of Hypnosis**

993 *Warning Shadows* (Pan Film, 1923). [*Schatten*]. Germany. 10 reels.
Alternate title: Die Nacht Der Erkenntnis.
Director: Arthur Robison.
Screenplay: Rudolf Schneider, Arthur Robison.
Photography: Fritz Arno Wagner.
Cast: Fritz Kortner, Ruth Weyher, Gustav von Wangenheim, Alexander Granach, Fritz Rasp, Ferdinand von Alten, Karl Platen, Lilli Herder, Eugen Rex, Max Guelstoff.

While Paris Sleeps (1923): Original poster.

Notes: Warning Shadows, dealing with an unfaithful wife, her husband and her lover—all three placed under a trance by a magician as a form of therapy—depends entirely on shadowy cinematography and distorted visuals to achieve its horrific effects, as the main characters experience their secret fears and desires while under hypnosis. Although surviving prints of *Warning Shadows* contain traditional dialogue intertitles, the film was entirely visual in its original European version, and was shown without title cards.

Review: "Whether or not *Warning Shadows* arouses intense admiration or intense dislike, there is no half-way attitude; no one will deny that it is unlike any other film ever shown. ... Throughout, the perfection of detail shows the hand of a master. The photography, too, is excellent."—*Variety,* December 3, 1924.

994 *The Werewolf* (1923). [*Le Loup-Garou*]. France.
Cast: Jean Marau, Madeleine Guitty.
Notes: A cursed murderer becomes a werewolf.

995 *While Paris Sleeps* (Hodkinson, 1923). 6 reels.
Director: Maurice Tourneur.
Photography: Rene Guissart.
Cast: Lon Chaney (Henri Santodos), Mildred Manning (Bebe Larvache), Jack Gilbert (Dennis O'Keefe), Hardee Kirkland (his father), Jack McDonald (Father

Marionette), J. Farrell McDonald (Georges Morier).

Notes: Chaney plays an insane sculptor intent on adding his model's fiancé (John Gilbert) to the collection of figures in his wax museum. This film predates the similar 1924 German movie *Waxworks* (*q.v.*), and the later sound film *Mystery of the Wax Museum* (1933) in its central theme. *While Paris Sleeps* had originally been produced by Paramount in 1920 under the somewhat misleading title *The Glory of Love,* but the studio, wary of the film's unconventional, horrific subject matter, had refused to release it.

Review: "This feature looks as though it ... had been lying around for some little time, finally patched up and released to salvage whatever could be got from it. ... The story is weird ... Lon Chaney plays the heavy and from the role it is quite evident it must have been shot long before the day he started starring." — *Variety,* January 19, 1923.

1 9 2 4

996 *Aelita* (Mezhrabpom, 1924). Russia. 77 minutes.

Alternate title: Revolt of the Robots.

Director: Jacob Protazanov.

Screenplay: Fyodor Otzep, Alexei Falko (based on the novel by Alexei Tolstoy).

Photography: Yuri Zhelyabuzhky, E. Schonemann.

Set Designers: Victor Simov, Isaac Rabinovitch, Alexandra Exeter, Sergei Kozlovsky.

Cast: Igor Illinsky, Yulia Solntseva, Nikolai Tseretelly, Nikolai Batalov, Konstantin Eggert, V. Orlova, Valentina Kuinzhi.

Notes: A civilization of robots is discovered on Mars. This film's art direction was influenced by *The Cabinet of Dr. Caligari* (1919).

997 *Alice's Spooky Adventure* (Disney, 1924).

Notes: Alice visits Spooksville in this cartoon, which combines live action and animation.

998 *Behind the Curtain* (Universal, 1924). 5 reels.

Director: Chester M. Franklin.

Screenplay: Emil Forest, Harvey Gates (story by William J. Flynn).

Photography: Jackson Rose.

Cast: Lucille Rickson, Johnny Harron, George Cooper, Winifred Bryson, Charles Clary.

Notes: A phony spiritualist is guilty of murder.

999 *Bonzolino* (Ward, 1924). Great Britain.

Dante's Inferno (1924).

Notes: In this animated cartoon, the character Bonzo appears as famous actor "Bon" Chaney.

1000 The Cafe l'Egypte (Stoll, 1924). Great Britain. 28 minutes.
Notes: This film was an entry in *The Further Mysteries of Dr. Fu-Manchu* series.

1001 The Coughing Horror (Stoll, 1924). Great Britain. 23 minutes.
Director: Fred Paul.
Screenplay: Fred Paul (based on the character created by Sax Rohmer).
Photography: Frank Canham.
Art Direction: Walter W. Murton.
Cast: Harry Agar Lyons, Fred Paul, Humbertson Wright.
Notes: An entry in *The Further Mysteries of Dr. Fu-Manchu* series.

1002 Cragmire Tower (Stoll, 1924). Great Britain. 21 minutes.
Director: Fred Paul.
Screenplay: Fred Paul (based on the character created by Sax Rohmer).
Photography: Frank Canham.
Art Direction: Walter W. Murton.
Cast: Harry Agar Lyons, Fred Paul, Humbertson Wright.
Notes: An entry in *The Further Mysteries of Dr. Fu-Manchu* series.

1003 Dante's Inferno (Fox, 1924). 6 reels.
Director: Henry Otto.
Screenplay: Edmund Goulding (based on a story by Cyrus Wood and the composition by Dante).

Dante's Inferno (1924).

Photography: Joseph August.
Cast: Lawson Butt (Dante), Howard Gaye (Virgil), Ralph Lewis (Mortimer Judd), Pauline Starke (Marjorie Vernon), Josef Swickard (Eugene Craig), Gloria Grey (Mildred Craig), William Scott (Ernest Judd), Robert Klein (a friend), Winifred Landis (Mrs. Judd), Lorimer Johnston (the doctor), Lon Poff (secretary), Bud Jamison (the butler).
Notes: Ruthless industrialist Mortimer Judd literally goes to hell before repenting his misdeeds after reading Dante's *Inferno*. What makes the otherwise preachy film interesting is its highly erotic depiction of purgatory, with hundreds of nude sinners writhing in the smoldering pits. Actually, these unclothed hordes wore body stockings that only implied nudity — except for actress Pauline Starke, who was perfectly willing to cavort on the set *without* wearing a body stocking — or much of anything else!
Review: "The tour of Satan's dominions ... is alarmingly well-pictured. There are glistening coal-black rocks and furnaces sending their red glow on the squirming sinners, many of whom appear to be clad in little more than shadows." — *The New York Times,* September 30, 1924.

1004 *Fools in the Dark* (FBO, 1924). 7 reels.
Director: Alfred Santell.
Screenplay: John Grey, Bertram Millhauser (from the story *Peaceful Percy* by Bertram Millhauser).
Photography: Leon Eycke, Blake Wagner.

Cast: Tom Wilson, Matt Moore, Patsy Ruth Miller, Charles Belcher, Bertram Grassby.
Notes: A skeleton chases a man through a haunted house.

1005 The Golden Pomegranates (Stoll, 1924). Great Britain. 37 minutes.
Director: Fred Paul.
Screenplay: Fred Paul (based on the character created by Sax Rohmer).
Photography: Frank Canham.
Art Direction: Walter W. Murton.
Cast: Harry Agar Lyons, Fred Paul, Humbertson Wright.

1006 Greywater Park (Stoll, 1924). Great Britain. 30 minutes.
Notes: An entry in The Further Mysteries of Dr. Fu-Manchu series.

1007 The Hands of Orlac (Pan Film, 1924). [Orlac's Hände]. Germany. 8 reels.
Director: Robert Wiene.
Screenplay: Louis Nerz.
Photography: Hans Androschin, Gunther Krampf.
Cast: Conrad Veidt, Fritz Kortner, Carmen Cartellieri, Alexandra Sorina, Fritz Stassny, Paul Askonas.
Notes: Robert Wiene, who directed The Cabinet of Dr. Caligari (q.v.) was also responsible for The Hands of Orlac (Orlac's Hände). This was the story of a successful concert pianist, Orlac (Conrad Veidt), whose hands are mutilated in a train accident and then replaced with the hands of a murderer in a transplant operation. Orlac becomes convinced that the murderer's hands have a sinister life of their own, but the entire affair is eventually revealed to have been a plot hatched by a greedy hospital aide in order to drive Orlac mad and steal his money.

Scripted by Louis Nerz and photographed by Hans Androschin and Gunther Krampf, The Hands of Orlac is not in the same league as The Cabinet of Dr. Caligari, but director Wiene handles the material expertly, and this is a very well-done horrific mystery, with an excellent performance by Veidt, whose tight, gaunt features are put to good use as he wavers on the edge of sanity, growing increasingly more unstable as the story progresses.

As good as The Hands of Orlac is, though, the definitive version of this story is director Karl Freund's 1935 remake for M-G-M, Mad Love, starring Peter Lorre in the Conrad Veidt role. There the story was altered somewhat, with the spotlight on Lorre as a demented surgeon who attempts to drive Orlac (Colin Clive) mad after the operation because he is obsessed with Orlac's beautiful wife (Frances Drake). Although Veidt's performance in The Hands of Orlac is impressive, Lorre's character in Mad Love incorporates a perverse sexual angle that improves the story and heightens its believability.

Long thought to be unavailable, The Hands of Orlac is available on video, although in crude, public-domain form.

Reviews: "Were it not for Veidt's masterly characterization, The

Hands of Orlac would be an absurd fantasy in the old-time mystery-thriller class. The salvaging of a train wreck by torchlight is one of the production's most vivid sequences." — *Variety,* June 27, 1928.

"Although it is raw, hardly the sort of thing some people want to look at . . . *The Hands of Orlac* . . . is not without merit. It has a grim theme, a story reminiscent of Balzac, and as one may never know how a man would act in the same circumstances in which Paul Orlac is placed, it is hardly fair to say that Conrad Veidt goes a bit far in his efforts to strike terror into the hearts of his spectators. Nevertheless, one can assert with safety that Mr. Veidt and the others would have added to the realism of their grand guignol tale if they had been a wee bit more restrained. Most of the plot is worked out adroitly...." — *The New York Times,* June 5, 1928.

1008 Hansel and Gretel (1924). Austria. 80 minutes.

1009 The Haunted Hills (Educational, 1924). 11 minutes.
Cast: Jim Bemis.
Notes: A villain is driven to his own death by mysterious events.

1010 Hot Water (Pathé, 1924). 5 reels.
Directors: Sam Taylor, Fred Newmeyer.
Screenplay: Sam Taylor, John Grey, Tommy Gray, Tim Whelan.
Photography: Walter Lundin.
Cast: Harold Lloyd, Jobyna Ralston, Charles Stevenson, Josephine Crowell.
Notes: A spoof of D. W. Griffith's *One Exciting Night* (1922).

1011 Interplanetary Revolution (SFT, 1924). [*Mezhplanetnaya Revolutsiya*]. Russia. 6 minutes.
Art Direction: E. Komissarenko.
Notes: In this bizarre, propagandistic animated comedy, capitalist and national socialist "ghouls" drink a woman's blood through straws.

Lebende Buddahs *see* **Living Buddahs**

1012 Living Buddhas (1924). [*Lebende Buddhas*]. Germany.
Director: Paul Wegener.
Screenplay: Paul Wegener, Hans Sturm.

Mezhplanetnaya Revolutsiya *see* **Interplanetary Revolution**

1013 On Time (Truart, 1924). 6 reels.
Director: Henry Lehrman.
Screenplay: Garret Fort (from a story by Al Cohn).
Titles: Ralph Spence.
Photography: William Marshall.
Film Editor: Ralph Spence.
Cast: Richard Talmadge (Harry Willis), Billie Dove (Helen Hendon), Stuart Holmes (Richard Drake), George Siegmann (Wang Wu), Tom Wilson (Casanova Clay), Charles Clary (Horace Hendon), Douglas Gerard (Mr. Black), Fred Kirby (Dr. Spinks), Frankie Mann (Mrs. Spinks).
Notes: In this tongue-in-cheek

Siegfried (1924): Siegfried (Paul Richter) gains immortality by bathing in the blood of a dragon he has slain.

melodrama, a young man, after promising his fiancée that he will make a fortune in six months, is embroiled in a series of misadventures — including a crazed doctor's attempt to perform a brain transplant on him, using a gorilla as the donor.

Orlac's Hände *see The Hands of Orlac*

1014 *The Shadow of the East*
(Fox, 1924). 6 reels.
Director: George Archainbaud.
Cast: Frank Mayo, Norman Kerry, Evelyn Brent, Joseph Swickard.
Notes: A man is haunted by the ghost of an Indian girl.

1015 *Siegfried* (UFA, 1924).
Germany. In two feature-length installments: *Siegfried* (Siegfried's Tod), 11 reels; *Kriemhild's Revenge* (Kriemhild's Rache), 12 reels.
Producer: Erich Pommer.
Director: Fritz Lang.
Screenplay: Thea von Harbou (based on Nordic legend).
Photography: Carl Hoffmann, Gunther Rittau.
Art Direction: Otto Hunte, Eric Kettlehut, Karl Volbrecht.
Costumes: Paul Gerd Gudenan, Anne Willkom.
Make-up: Otto Genath.
Animation: Walther Ruttman.

Cast: Paul Richter (Siegfried), Margaret Schon (Kriemhild), Theodor Loos (King Gunther), Hanna Ralph (Brunhild), Georg John (Mime, the Smith/Alberich), Gertrud Arnold (Queen Ute), Hans Carl Muller (Gerenot), Erwin Biswanger (Giselher), Bernhard Goetzke (Volker von Alzey), Hans Adalbert von Schlettow (Hagen Tronje), Hardy von Francois (Dankwart), Hubert Heinrich (Werbel), Frieda Richard (Lecturer), Georg Jurowski (Priest), Iris Roberts (Page), Rudolph Rittner (Markgraf Rudiger von Bechlam), Fritz Alberti (Dietrich von Bern), Georg August Koch (Hildebrand), Rudolph Klein-Rogge (King Etzel), Greta Berger (a hun, Rose Lichtenstein).

Notes: Drawn from German legend by scenarists Fritz Lang and his wife Thea von Harbou, *Siegfried* is deeply rooted in epic fantasy, with titanic heroes and monolithic sets, but, as always with Lang, there are recurring moments of horror as the Aryan warrior-hero Siegfried battles a giant dragon (an impressive full-scale articulated prop) and encounters a race of malignant trolls.

Review: "It's an artistic but not a commercial film. Paul Richter plays the title role and does a magnificent job of it at most times, although there are moments when the portrayal grows too effeminate. ... The rave about these German pictures is that the directors are artists to their fingertips. ... But after looking at *Siegfried* the only conclusion is that their artistry consists in playing the film story before settings of a very stagey nature and in playing the various scenes in a slow and stodgy pace, not only tiresome to an American audience, but ruinous to the picture." — *Variety,* December 23, 1925.

1016 *A Son of Satan* (Micheaux, 1924). 65 minutes.
Cast: Andrew Bishop, Ida Anderson.
Notes: A haunted house is featured.

1017 *The Story of Hansel and Gretel* (1924). Germany. 23 minutes.
Notes: From the Brothers Grimm fairy tale.

1018 *That's the Spirit* (Universal, 1924). 11 minutes.
Cast: Bert Roach.
Notes: In this comedy short, rotund comic Roach is beset by spooks, spirits, skeletons, and a flying chicken with a human skull.

1019 *The Thief of Bagdad* (United Artists, 1924). 12 reels.
Director: Raoul Walsh.
Screenplay: Lotta Woods, Elton Thomas (pseudonym for Douglas Fairbanks).
Photography: Arthur Edeson, P. H. Witman, Kenneth MacLean.
Art Direction: William Cameron Menzies, Irvin J. Martin.
Film Editor: William Nolan.
Costumes: Mitchell Leisen.
Cast: Douglas Fairbanks (the thief of Bagdad), Snitz Edwards (his evil associate), Charles Belcher (the Holy Man), Julanne Johnston (the princess), Anna May Wong

(the Mongol slave), Winter-Blossom (the slave of the lute), Etta Lee (the slave of the sand board), Brandon Hurst (the caliph), Tote Du Crow (the soothsayer), Sojin (the Mongol prince), K. Nambu (his counselor), Sadakichi Hartmann (his court magician), Nobel Johnson (the Indian prince), Mathilde Comont (the Persian prince), Charles Stevens (his awaker), Sam Baker (the sworder), Jess Weldon, Scotty Mattraw, Charles Sylvester.

Notes: Although primarily a fantasy-adventure, Douglas Fairbanks' magnificently designed *The Thief of Bagdad* contains many horror elements as well, including Fairbanks' encounter with a huge fire-breathing dragon.

1020 *Those Who Dare* (Creative, 1924). 70 minutes.
Director: John B. O'Brien.
Screenplay: Frank Beresford (story by I. W. Irving).
Cast: John Bowers, Marguerite De La Motte, Joseph Dowling, Claire McDowell, Spottiswoode Aitken, Sheldon Lewis.
Notes: Aboard a ship, the leader of the mutinous crew practices voodoo.

1021 *Unseen Hands* (Associated Exhibitors, 1924). 6 reels.
Director: Jacques Jaccard.
Producer/Screenplay: Walker Coleman Graves, Jr.
Cast: Wallace Beery (Jean Scholast), Joseph J. Dowling (Georges Le Quintrec), Fontaine La Rue (Madame Le Quintrec), Jack Rollins (Armand Le Quintrec), Cleo Madison (Matoaka), Jim Corey (Wapita), Jamie Gray (Nola).
Notes: A scheming adventurer dies of heart failure when he is confronted by the ghost of a man he murdered.

1022 *Vanity's Price* (FBO, 1924). 6 reels.
Director: Roy William Neill.
Screenplay: Paul Bern.
Photography: Hal Mohr.
Assistant Director: Joseph von Sternberg.
Cast: Anna Q. Nilsson (Vanna Du Maurier), Stuart Holmes (Henri De Greve), Wyndham Standing (Richard Dowling), Arthur Rankin (Teddy, Vanna's son), Lucille Rickson (Sylvia, Teddy's fiancée), Robert Bolder (Bill Connors, theatrical manager) Cissy Fitzgerald (Mrs. Connors), Dot Farley (Katherine, Vanna's maid), Charles Newton (butler).
Notes: An aging actress is rejuvenated by a doctor's experiments.

Wachsfigurenkabinett *see Waxworks*

1023 *Waxworks* (Neptune, 1924). [*Wachsfigurenkabinett*]. Germany. 7 reels.
Alternate title: Three Wax Men (U.S.).
Director: Paul Leni.
Screenplay: Henryk Galeen.
Photography: Helmar Lerski.
Set Designers: Paul Leni, Ernst Stern.
Cast: Emil Jannings (Haroun-al-Raschid), Conrad Veidt (Ivan the

Terrible), Werner Krauss (Jack the Ripper), Wilhelm (later William) Dieterle, Olga von Belajeff, John Gottowt, Georg John.

Notes: The German film *Waxworks* (Wachsfigurenkabinett) was directed by Paul Leni (1885-1929) three years before he immigrated to Hollywood. Every horror movie variation on the wax museum theme, from *Mystery of the Wax Museum* (1933) on down, can be traced back to this film, with its novel central premise — an unemployed writer (Wilhelm — later Hollywood director William — Dieterle) is hired by the proprietor of a wax museum to concoct promotional yarns about three of the figures in his exhibit. As the writer formulates each tale, the story appears on-screen with Dieterle and the proprietor's daughter as characters in it. Emil Jannings appears as Sultan Haroun-al-Raschid in the opening segment, Conrad Veidt as Ivan the Terrible in the second tale, and Werner Krauss as Jack the Ripper in the third story.

Any sustained atmosphere is impossible due to the film's episodic nature, but Leni does manage some effective touches; of the three starring actors Conrad Veidt comes off best as Ivan the Terrible, who enjoys forcing his poisoned victims to watch the sand drain from an hourglass, pin-pointing the exact moment of their death.

Leni also had a hand in the set design for *Waxworks* (the film was retitled *Three Wax Men* in America), but the sets, constructed along the same expressionistic lines as those for *The Cabinet of Dr. Caligari,* lack the strange functional conviction of the scenery in Wiene's film, looking simply flat and cartoonish instead.

As interesting as it is, *Waxworks* falls short of director Michael Curtiz's 1933 Warner Bros. film *Mystery of the Wax Museum* as a leading example of the wax museum horror movie premise. The Curtiz picture, about an insane sculptor (Lionel Atwill) who encases dead bodies in wax, had a queasy sexual edge not present in Leni's film, and benefited from stylized two-strip Technicolor photography (it was later remade as the 3-D color Vincent Price thriller *House of Wax* in 1953).

Nevertheless, *Mystery of the Wax Museum* owes a real debt to Leni's *Waxworks,* and it is unfortunate that the prints of *Waxworks* available on video from public-domain distributors are of poor quality, with Werner Krauss' Jack the Ripper segment edited and missing footage.

Reviews: "Three stories in one are hitched together. ... Ivan the Terrible is largely a costume affair with a gripping scene of the Czar torturing victims in Kremlin. ... Much triple exposure work which made German photography the Hollywood rage for a time. All sets are freakish."—*Variety,* February 6, 1929.

"This fantastic film consisted of three weird tales, the last of which was by all means the most interesting. In it Emil Jannings gives a startlingly fine performance as a grotesque Caliph who is wont to leave a waxwork figure of himself in his bed while he goes forth under

Waxworks (1924): Conrad Veidt (left) as Ivan the Terrible.

cover of darkness seeking romance and adventure. ... Conrad Veidt renders an excellent portrayal in the role of Ivan the Terrible, and Werner Krauss is quite impressive as Jack the Ripper."—*The New York Times,* March 19, 1926.

1024 *What an Eye* (Universal, 1924). 22 minutes.
Director/Screenplay: Edward L. Luddy.
Cast: Buddy Messinger.
Notes: A neighborhood is haunted by a creature with a huge eye; a haunted house is also featured.

1925

1025 *Babes in the Woods* (FBO, 1925). 20 minutes.
Notes: An animated cartoon version of *Hansel and Gretel.*

1026 *Dr. Jekyll and Mr. Hyde* (Standard, 1925).
Notes: A *comedy* version of the Robert Louis Stevenson novel.

Possibly the same film as entry #1027.

1027 Dr. Pyckle and Mr. Pryde (Standard, 1925). 20 minutes.
Producer: Joe Rock.
Cast: Stan Laurel.
Notes: Comedian Stan Laurel — in his pre-Oliver Hardy days — stars in this spoof of *Dr. Jekyll and Mr. Hyde,* cavorting on the sets from Lon Chaney's *The Hunchback of Notre Dame.*

1028 Evolution (Red Seal, 1925). 45 minutes.
Notes: Clips from the 1919 film *The Ghost of Slumber Mountain* (*q.v.*), depicting a fight between two dinosaurs, were incorporated into this film.

Fantôme du Moulin Rouge, Le *see* **The Phantom of the Moulin Rouge**

1029 The Green Archer (Pathé, 1925). 10 chapter serial.
Director: Spencer Gordon Bennet.
Cast: Ailene Ray, Walter Miller, Frank Lackteen, Burr McIntosh.
Notes: Based on the novel by Edgar Wallace. A mysterious masked man in green archer's garb signifies death. Plenty of shadowy atmosphere and "haunted house" trappings; later remade as a Columbia serial in 1940.

1030 The Haunted Honeymoon (Roach, 1925). 22 minutes.
Alternate title: Billy Gets Married.

Director: Fred Guiol.
Cast: Glenn Tryon, Blanche Mehaffy, James Finlayson, George Rowe.
Notes: Honeymooners find themselves in a haunted house.

1031 The Haunted House (1925).
Notes: An animated cartoon produced by Paul Terry.

1032 The Imaginary Voyage (de Mare, 1925). [*Le Voyage Imaginaire*]. France. 62 minutes.
Director/Screenplay: Rene Clair.
Photography: Jimmy Berliet, A. Morin.
Set Designer: Robert Gys.
Cast: Jean Borlin, Dolly Davis, Albert Prejean, Maurice Schutz.
Notes: Bluebeard, clutching hands, an evil fairy and a mutant "alligafrog" are featured.

1033 Just Spooks (Bray, 1925).
Notes: An animated cartoon short.

1034 Koko Sees Spooks (Paramount/Fleischer, 1925). 6 minutes.
Notes: This animated cartoon was an entry in the *Out of the Inkwell* series.

1035 Little Red Riding Hood (Century, 1925). 22 minutes.
Cast: Baby Peggy.
Notes: Based on the fairy tale.

1036 The Lost World (First National, 1925). 10 reels with existing prints in 5 reels.

The Lost World (1925): A dinosaur battle.

Director: Harry O. Hoyt.
Production Supervisor: Earl Hudson.
Screenplay: Marion Fairfax (based on the novel by Sir Arthur Conan Doyle).
Photography: Arthur Edeson.
Film Editor: George McGuire.
Set Designer: Milton Menasco.
Special Effects: Willis H. O'Brien.
Assistant Director: William Dowling.
Cast: Bessie Love (Paula White), Lloyd Hughes (Edward J. Malone), Lewis Stone (Sir John Roxton), Wallace Beery (Prof. Challenger), Arthur Hoyt (Prof. Summerlee), Margaret McWade (Mrs. Challenger), Finch Smiles (Austin, Challenger's butler), Jules Cowles (Zambo, Roxton's servant), Bull Montana (Ape Man), George Bunny (Colin McArdle), Charles Wellesley (Maj. Hibbard), Alma Bennett (Gladys Hungerford), Virginia Browne Faire (Marquette, the half-caste girl), Nelson MacDowell (attorney).

Notes: Although not a horror film, First National's *The Lost World* certainly had its share of horrific moments. The adventure-fantasy, based on Sir Arthur Conan Doyle's 1912 novel about living dinosaurs found on an isolated South American plateau, featured an impressive array of stop-motion animated monsters brought to life by special effects technician Willis O'Brien. The explicit violence of the dinosaur battles, with a surfeit of torn flesh and blood, not to mention Bull Montana as a hairy, snarling ape-man, was topped by the climactic near-destruction of London by a marauding brontosaurus! Although O'Brien's stop-frame effects are obvious today, the film retains its charm and a large degree of its original excitement.

The high-quality tinted and scored version of *The Lost World* available on Lumivision laser-disc is recommended to the reader; this version has been telecast on the American Movie Classics (AMC) cable network and is also available from Milestone Video.

Reviews: "Without doubt an unusual and interesting picture. A picture that will get a load of money at the box office, create a tremendous amount of discussion and achieve as much word of mouth advertising as anything ever had in motion picture history. This fantastical tale was made possible for the screen through the perfection of mechanical reproduction of the animals done in miniature and so superimposed on the actual scenes that were photographed that they appeared to be there full size." — *Variety*, February 11, 1925.

"Through wonderful photographic skill and infinite patience in the camera work ... *The Lost World* makes a memorable motion picture. . . . This photoplay ... is a unique production which will create a lot of talk, as some of the scenes are as awesome as anything that has ever been shown...." — *The New York Times*, February 9, 1925.

1037 *Maciste in Hell* (Excelsior/Olympia, 1925). Italy.
Director: Guido Brignone.
Special effects: Segundo de Chomon.
Cast: Bartolomeo Pagano.
Notes: The Italian "muscleman" adventure films that proliferated in the 1960s (*Hercules*, etc.) had their origins in that country's silent film era. This particular silent epic, loosely adapted from Dante's *Inferno*, had particularly horrific overtones; Satan is depicted as a huge demon frozen in a lake of ice, with Brutus, Cassius and Judas in his three mouths. *Maciste in Hell* was released in the United States in 1931.

1038 *The Monster* (Metro-Goldwyn, 1925). 7 reels.
Director: Roland West.
Screenplay: Willard Mack, Albert Kenyon (based on the play by Crane Wilbur).
Titles: C. Gardner Sullivan.
Photography: Hal Mohr.
Film Editor: A. Carle Palm.
Cast: Lon Chaney (Dr. Ziska), Gertrude Olmstead (Betty Watson), Hallam Cooley (Watson's head clerk), Johnny Arthur (the under clerk), Charles A. Sellon (the constable), Walter James (Caliban), Knute Erickson (Daffy Dan), George Austin (Rigo), Edward

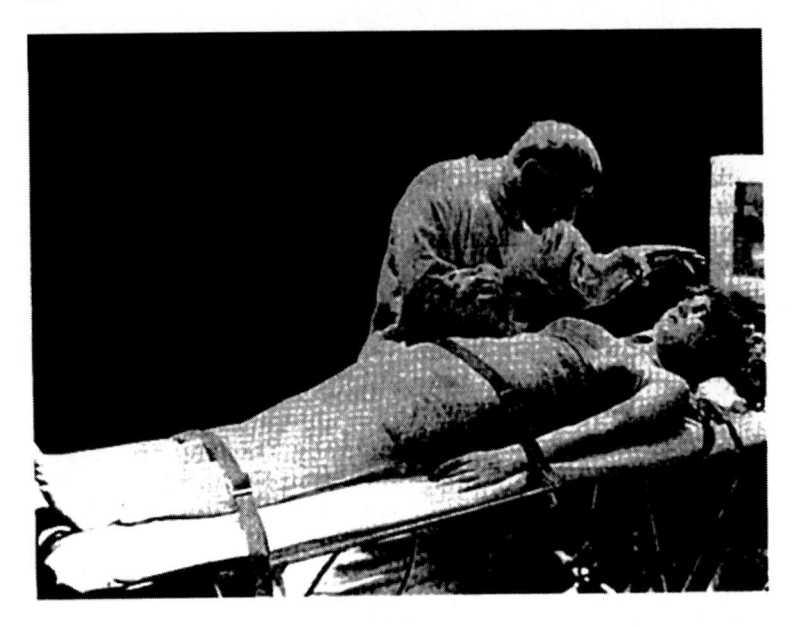

The Monster (1925): Lon Chaney menaces a victim.

McWade (Luke Watson), Ethel Wales (Mrs. Watson).

Notes: An unexpectedly spoofy horror comedy, *The Monster* starred Lon Chaney as the insane Dr. Ziska, who lures unsuspecting motorists to his isolated sanitarium and uses them as lab subjects in his crazed experiments — until he is defeated by an amateur detective, played by Johnny Arthur. Directed by the interesting but erratic Roland West (*The Bat*), *The Monster* was based on a Broadway play by Crane Wilbur, an old hand at this type of subject, who was still at work on similar projects as late as the 1950s (*House of Wax*).

Reviews: "Lon Chaney does not make the crazed surgeon as terrifying ... as he might have, and in that the film lets down to a certain extent. The picture ends rather abruptly with a fade-out of the hero and the girl in a motor car. ... A slower tempo in the playing of the scenes in the sanitarium would have added much to the suspense qualities of the picture. ... One thing that Roland West must be given credit for was the selection of a cast to enact the characters of the piece." — *Variety,* February 18, 1925.

"The starch seems to have been taken out of ... *The Monster* by the inclusion of too much light comedy. The result is that, although this film possesses a degree of queer entertainment, it is neither fish, fowl, nor good red herring. ... Mr. Chaney does not have very much to do, but his various appearances are effective. There is a good deal about this picture that reminds one of *One Exciting Night,* but one feels rather disappointed with the timidity with which the drama has been approached and the constant injection of slapstick comedy." — *The New York Times,* February 16, 1925.

1039 The Mystic (M-G-M, 1925). 7 reels.
Director: Tod Browning.
Screenplay: Waldemar Young.
Photography: Ira Morgan.
Art Direction: Cedric Gibbons, H. Libbert.
Film Editor: Frank Sullivan.
Cast: Aileen Pringle, Conway Tearle, Mitchell Lewis, Robert Ober, David Torrence DeWitt Jennings.
Notes: A fraudulent clairvoyant is frightened by a ghost.

1040 One Way Street (First National, 1925). 6 reels.
Producer: Earl Hudson.
Director: John F. Dillon.
Screenplay: Arthur Statter, Mary Scully (adaptation by Earl Hudson).
Photography: Arthur Edeson.
Cast: Dorothy Cumming, Ben Lyon, Anna Q. Nilsson, Marjorie Daw, Lumsden Hare.
Notes: An aging woman's youth is restored when she is treated with monkey glands.

1041 The Phantom of the Moulin Rouge (Fernand, 1925). [*Le Fantôme du Moulin Rouge*]. France. 80 minutes.
Director/Screenplay: Rene Clair.
Photography: Jimmy Berliet, Louis Chair.
Art Direction: Robert Gys.
Assistant Director: G. Lacombe.
Cast: George Vaultier, Jose Davert, Albert Prejean, Sandra Milowanoff, M. S. Schutz, Paul Oliver.
Notes: A psychologist wills a man's spirit to leave his body.

1042 The Phantom of the Opera (Universal, 1925). 10 reels.
Producer: Carl Laemmle.
Director: Rupert Julian.
Screenplay: Raymond Schrock, Elliott J. Clawson (based on the novel by Gaston Leroux).
Titles: Tom Reed.
Photography: Virgil Miller, Milton Bridenbecker, Charles J. Van Enger.
Art Direction: Charles D. Hall.
Film Editor: Maurice Pivar.
Additional Direction: Edward Sedgwick.
Cast: Lon Chaney (Erik, the Phantom), Mary Philbin (Christine Daae), Norman Kerry (Raoul de Chagny), Snitz Edwards (Florine Papillon), Gibson Gowland (Simon), John Sainpolis (Philippe de Chagny), Virginia Pearson (Carlotta), Arthur Edmund Carewe (Ledoux, the Persian), Edith Yorke (Mama Valerius), Anton Vaverka (prompter), Bernard Siegel (Joseph Buguet), Olive Ann Alcorn (La Sorelli), Cesare Gravina (manager), George B. Williams (M. Ricard), Bruce Covington (M. Moncharmin), Edward Cecil (Faust), John Miljan (Valentin), Alexander Bevani (Mephistopheles), Grace Marvin (Martha), Ward Crane (Count Ruboff),

The Phantom of the Opera (1925): **Lon Chaney and Mary Philbin.**

Chester Conklin (orderly), William Tryoler (director of Opera Orchestra), Carla Laemmle (Prima Ballerina).

Notes: Gaston Leroux wrote *The Phantom of the Opera* in 1911, and it is surprising that the story was not filmed for the first time until 1925, when Universal Pictures adapted it as a vehicle for Lon Chaney.

Nearly all great horror movies are also great romances, and Leroux's tale of a deformed, masked composer, haunting the labyrinthine Paris Opera like a ghost, redeemed only by his love for a pretty young singer, has both qualities — horror and romance — in abundance. Erik, the Phantom (Chaney), may exhibit occasional homicidal tendencies, but like most of the screen's great "monsters," he is also in love, and this is his saving grace.

In adapting the novel, Universal was somewhat clumsy; the first half of the movie is uneventful, and there are too many extraneous characters throughout. Character background is also neglected; the audience should at least be filled in on Erik's origins, exactly who he is and how he came to be, but in one scene, after it is established that Erik's activities are being investigated by the police, we are shown a close-up of a file card, with one paragraph informing us that

Erik (no surname) is criminally insane, a prison escapee and a "master of black art" — whatever *that* means.

The physical attributes of the movie cannot be faulted; the sets are big and impressive, the art direction imaginative and the costumes expensive and detailed. But, as noted, the film is sloppily constructed, and not at all as good an adaptation as Chaney's *The Hunchback of Notre Dame*. At times the picture has a frantic, slap-dash editing style, almost like a serial, and this haphazard cutting may be due to difficulties that arose during production. According to *Phantom* cinematographer Charles Van Enger's statements in a published interview, Chaney and director Rupert Julian were in constant disagreement, and the animosity between them on the set was almost palpable. Eventually Chaney, a top star with real clout, wound up directing some of the picture himself. He may well have been justified in doing so, since Julian, though a competent enough director, simply wasn't the outstanding craftsman that flamboyant material like this demands. In fact, Julian almost completely botches one of the film's most famous scenes in which Erik ruthlessly saws through the chain suspending a massive chandelier over the opera auditorium, sending it crashing into the audience below. Julian filmed this potentially exciting thrill-piece in a bland and unimaginative manner, but the same scene was filmed much better in the 1943 remake.

It is unclear exactly who shaped the picture's most famous scene in which the Phantom, in his underground lair, is unmasked by the young opera singer Christine (Mary Philbin) after he has abducted her. This mid-point showstopper is cunningly devised, both photographically and editorially, with the camera positioned so that both Christine and the Phantom are facing forward when the unmasking occurs, allowing the *audience* to see the Phantom's monstrous, cadaverous visage first, and *then* Christine's shocked reaction when he turns around to confront her.

The scene packs a jolt even today, after the rest of the film has lost much of its power to frighten, and the effect on audiences in 1925 must have been overwhelming. Chaney's make-up is fascinating, although a much lighter application than his make-up for Quasimodo, really little more than an extension of his own features. Much has been written about the complexity of Chaney's various make-ups, and while some of this commentary is true, a good deal of it is also publicity hyperbole, endlessly repeated.

Chaney's genius lay not in piling layer after layer of make-up on his face, but in the *artfulness* of his designs — he used only the materials needed, when and where they were needed, in order to achieve the desired characterization. It has been claimed that for his *Phantom* role, Chaney used chemicals to dilate his eyes and give them a crazed, bulging look, but a close study of the publicity photos reveals that, for the most part, he simply painted half-moon white crescents on his

The Phantom of the Opera (1925): Lon Chaney and Mary Philbin.

face below the eyes, making them appear larger on-screen. More complicated methods *were* used for tight close-ups, but Chaney achieved most of his effects through the simple but cunning use of facial distortion, greasepaint, wigs and false teeth. Chaney's enormous talent is readily apparent when comparisons are made between *his* film make-ups and the unsuccessful *reproductions* of them in the 1957 biographical drama *Man of a Thousand Faces,* starring James Cagney as Chaney. In this film, a soapy but generally accurate and more or less sincere tribute to Chaney from Universal Pictures (the studio that intentionally destroyed all of his movies when they junked their silent film inventory in the 1940s), the various make-ups all look stiff, mask-like (because they *are* masks) and not at all convincing.

Aside from Chaney, the casting for *The Phantom of the Opera* leaves a lot to be desired. Mary Philbin is pretty as Christine, but not as good an actress as Patsy Ruth Miller in *The Hunchback of Notre Dame*. Although adequate, she falls short occasionally, coming across as too emotional in some scenes, and not emotional enough in others. Norman Kerry, Philbin's leading man, was a good enough actor, but looks shockingly middle-aged to be playing the hero romantically involved with Philbin, who was only 23.

The Phantom of the Opera has had a checkered distribution history; the version most commonly in circulation today is *not* the one seen by the public in 1925. The original 1925 release version *does* exist, but only in prints of very poor quality. By 1930, Universal had prepared *two* new reedited versions of the film, one recut from the original release version, the other with newly shot dialogue scenes, for which Mary Philbin and Norman Kerry were recalled, five years after the fact (since Chaney was under contract to M-G-M by this time, the Phantom spoke—but not with Chaney's voice). The part-talkie version does not survive, but the reedited silent version does. Although the recutting plays havoc with the film's original continuity, changing the order of shots and even altering the identity of at least one character (the opera prima donna Carlotta becomes her own *mother* in this version), the existing prints are derived from 35mm materials and are of excellent quality. The release of this version on Kino International Video, with a vibrant organ score by Gaylord Carter, is recommended to the reader.

In the 1970s, a two-strip Technicolor print of the masked ball sequence (in which Chaney appears in masquerade, garbed in crimson as Poe's Red Death) resurfaced and has been restored to most prints (including Kino International's). Although it is of excellent quality and fascinating to see, this color scene really does a disservice to the film, since originally the *entire* movie was full of tints and tones, and not in basic black-and-white.

Despite its structural flaws, Chaney's *The Phantom of the Opera* remains the best screen adaptation of the novel, and there have been plenty of others. In 1943, Claude Rains appeared in a big-budget full-color sound remake for Universal, starring Susannah Foster and directed by Arthur Lubin. Because of the large budget and glossy treatment, the horror elements were intentionally deemphasized in favor of music and romance between Foster and her leading man Nelson Eddy; when Rains' make-up *was* finally revealed, it proved to be tame, sketchy, and not at all frightening.

A new version, starring Herbert Lom and Heather Sears, was produced by England's Hammer Films in 1962, but the movie, although returning to the horrific intent of the original, was cheap and ineffective,

The Phantom of the Opera (1925): Lon Chaney.

with Lom's make-up no better than Rains' had been.

A low-budget made-for-television version, starring Maxmilian Schell and Jane Seymour, appeared in 1983. Schell's make-up consisted of a stiff, lifeless rubber mask, and director Robert Markowitz seemed incapable of generating any melodramatic atmosphere or of disguising Seymour's lack of singing talent.

Due to the success of composer Andrew Lloyd Webber's musical stage production of *The Phantom of the Opera* in the late 1980s, a new theatrical version, directed by Dwight H. Little and starring Robert Englund, was released in 1989, but the film was tasteless and gory, failing at the box office.

A 200 minute made-for-television version also inspired by the popularity of the stage musical was broadcast in 1990, starring Charles Dance, Teri Polo and Burt Lancaster—who was cast for name value as the Phantom's father! Director Tony Richardson, clearly aware that he could add little to this well-worn material, and that nothing conceived for the inevitable unmasking scene could possibly startle an audience overly familiar with the story, opted for a unique solution—the Phantom is never unmasked at all!

But the most unconventional version of *The Phantom of the Opera* was director Brian DePalma's 1974 spoof *The Phantom of the Paradise,* starring Paul Williams, in which the oft-filmed story was reworked with a rock music theme.

Reviews: "Universal has turned out another horror . . . Lon Chaney is again the 'goat' in the matter, no matter if it is another tribute to his character acting. His make-up as the hunchback . . . was morbid enough, but this is infinitely worse, as in this instance his body is normal with a horrible face solely relied upon for the effect. Universal is evidently out to establish itself as the champ ghost story-telling firm among film producers. There can be no question of its supremacy after seeing this one . . . the kick of the picture is in the unmasking of the Phantom by the girl. Between Chaney's horrible facial make-up and the expression thereon it's a wallop that can't miss its objective. Julian has done well enough with his directing . . . views of the auditorium of the opera house, entrance and foyer have been done in natural colors. Also included in this is a masque ball."—*Variety,* September 16, 1925.

". . . [A]n ultra-fantastic melodrama, an ambitious production in which there is much to marvel at in the scenic effects. The most dramatic touch is where Christine in the cellar abode is listening to the masked Phantom . . . then . . . steals up behind him, as he is apparently entranced with his own playing, and, after hesitating, suddenly snatches the mask from the Phantom's face and at once faints at the horrible ugliness of the man. In the theatre last night a woman behind us stifled a scream when this happened. . . ."— *The New York Times,* September 7, 1925.

1043 *The Power God* (Davis, 1925). 15 chapter serial.
Director: Ben Wilson.
Screenplay: Rex Taylor, Harry Haven.
Cast: Ben Wilson, Neva Gerber, Mary Brooklyn.
Notes: This cliffhanger offered occasional horrific touches, including a huge jungle idol and revived corpses.

1044 *Spook Ranch* (Universal, 1925). 6 reels.

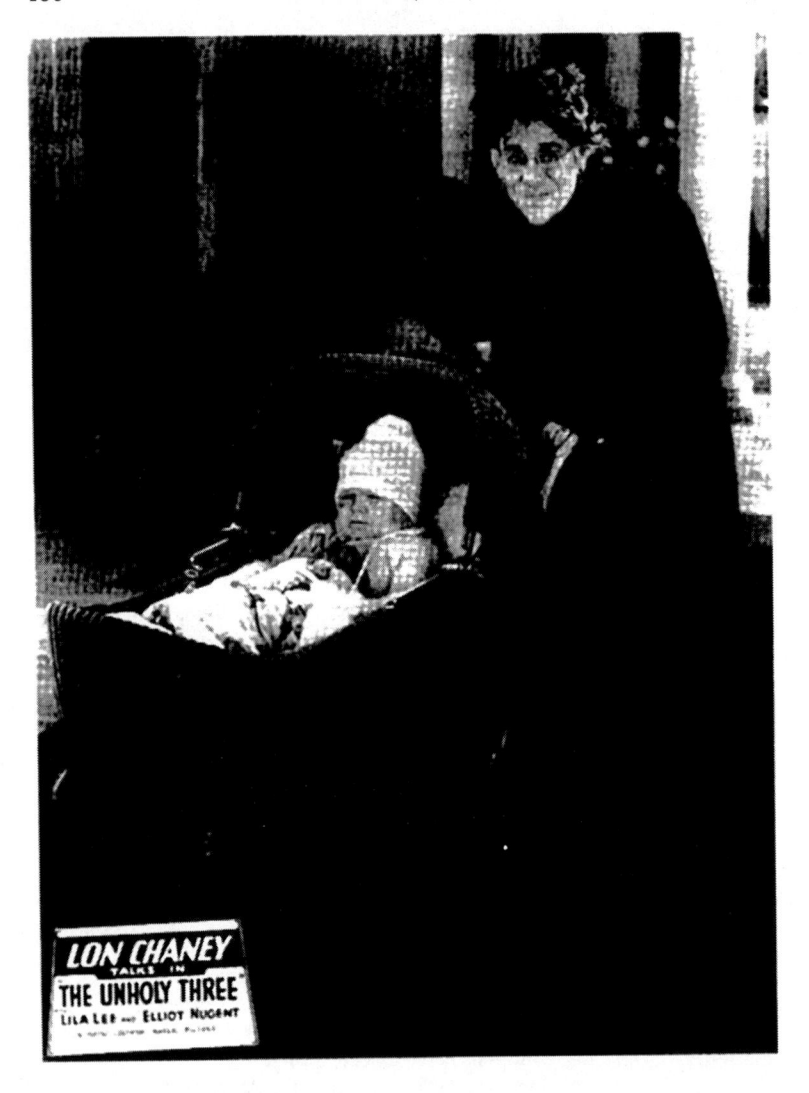

The Unholy Three (a photo from the sound remake of 1930): Harry Earles, Lon Chaney.

Director: Edward Laemmle.
Screenplay: Raymond L. Schrock, Edward Sedgwick.
Photography: Harry Neumann.

Cast: Hoot Gibson, Tote Du-Crow, Ed Cowles, Helen Ferguson, Robert McKim, Frank Rice.
Notes: A western with horror

overtones. Bandits kidnap a girl and her father, holding them hostage at a haunted mine.

1045 *The Unholy Three* (M-G-M, 1925). 7 reels.
Producer: Louis B. Mayer.
Director: Tod Browning.
Screenplay: Waldemar Young (based on the novel *The Unholy Three* by Clarence Aaron Robbins).
Photography: David Kesson.
Set Design: Cedric Gibbons, Joseph Wright.
Film Editor: Daniel J. Gray.

Cast: Lon Chaney (Echo), Mae Busch (Rosie O'Grady), Matt Moore (Hector McDonald), Victor McLaglen (Hercules), Harry Earles (Tweedledee), Harry Betz (Regan), Edward Connelly (judge), William Humphreys (attorney), A. E. Warren (prosecuting attorney), John Merkyl (jeweler), Charles Wellesley (John Arlington).

Notes: Lon Chaney was Echo, a circus ventriloquist, in *The Unholy Three,* one of director Tod Browning's best silents. The plot deals with three circus performers, Echo, Hercules (Victor McLaglen), a strongman, and Tweedledee (Harry Earles), a midget, who combine their unique talents to commit burglaries. Browning later remade this film with Chaney as a talkie in 1930, and this remake was Chaney's only sound film. Like many of Browning's pictures, *The Unholy Three* was not overtly horrific, but this crime melodrama was embued with a sinister atmosphere and colored by the usual Browning morbidity.

Review: "Here is about the best bet from a box-office standpoint that has come along in a while.... It is a wow of a story. ... It has everything—hoke, romance, crook stuff, murder, suspense, trick stuff and, above all is as cleverly titled as has been any production in many moons. ... Lon Chaney stands out like a million dollars. He's done that before, but always with a more or less grotesque make-up. No make-up this time. He isn't all hunched up, he isn't legless, he isn't this, that or the other thing in deformities. He's just Lon Chaney, and he's great."—*Variety,* August 5, 1925.

Voyage Imaginaire, Le *see* ***The Imaginary Voyage***

1046 *Wolf Blood* (Ryan Brothers/Lee-Bradford Corp., 1925). 6 reels.
Directors: George Chesebro, George Mitchell.
Screenplay: C. A. Hill.
Cast: Marguerite Clayton (Edith Ford), George Chesebro (Dick Bannister), Ray Hanford (Dr. Eugene Horton), Roy Watson (Jules Deveroux), Milburn Morante (Jacques Lebeq), Frank Clark (Pop Hadley).
Notes: A man who receives the blood of a wolf in an emergency transfusion fears that he is becoming a half-human beast-man. An interesting and early variation on the werewolf theme.

1926

1047 *Bachelor Brides* (PDC, 1926). 6 reels.
Producer: Cecil B. DeMille.
Director: William K. Howard.
Screenplay: Garrett Fort, C. Gardner Sullivan (based on a play by C. H. Malcolm).
Photography: Lucien Andriot.
Art Direction: Max Parker.
Assistant Director: Henry Hathaway.
Cast: Rod LaRoque, Eulalie Jensen, Sally Rand, Elinor Fair, George Nichols, Lucien Littlefield, Eddie Gribbon.
Notes: A mysterious castle with secret passages is featured.

1048 *The Bat* (United Artists, 1926). 9 reels.
Producer/Director/Screenplay: Roland West (based on the play by Mary Roberts Rinehart).
Titles: George Marion, Jr.
Photography: Arthur Edeson.
Art Direction: William Cameron Menzies, Ned Mann.
Cast: Jack Pickford (Brooks Bailey), Jewel Carmen (Miss Dale Ogden), Louise Fazenda (Lizzie Allen, the maid), Andre de Beranger (Gideon Bell), Charles Herzinger (Courtleigh Fleming), Emily Fitzroy (Mrs. Cornelia Van Gorder), Arthur Houseman (Richard Fleming), Robert McKim (Dr. Wells), Kamiyama, Sojin (Billy, the Japanese Butler), Tulio Carminati (Moletti), Eddie Gribbon (Detective Anderson), Lee Shumway (the unknown).
Notes: A haunted house mystery adapted from the stage hit by Mary Roberts Rinehart, *The Bat*, was the first of three films based on that play. The aforementioned mystery centers on a homicidal criminal mastermind known only as "The Bat," and it is up to the audience to decide which of the several likely characters is really the murderous villain after they are all conveniently gathered in a spooky old mansion. All the expected and all-too-familiar characters are here; the rich old dowager (Emily Fitzroy), the perky, cute heroine (Jewel Carmen), the earnest young hero (Jack Pickford), the frightened servant (Louise Fazenda), and the usual half-dozen or so suspects. This plot is so old that it must have seemed tiresome even in 1926; as a matter of fact, it is so old that it was being *spoofed* only a year later in *The Cat and the Canary* (*q.v.*).

The Bat seems very tame now, and the film has been remade and imitated so often that it would hardly be worth viewing if not for the stunning art direction by William Cameron Menzies. The sets and miniatures (by Ned Mann) are meticulously designed, photographed by Arthur Edeson with a bold, graphically clean look that almost compensates for this otherwise tedious film's many shortcomings. Those shortcomings, by the way, include a clichéd, exasperating "comedy" performance by Louise Fazenda as a constantly terrified maid allocated far too much screen time.

The title character's hideous bat disguise is so overdone, consisting of an out-sized full-head bat mask complete with huge erect ears and snarling, toothy face, that it is unintentionally funny instead of horrifying.

It is said that cartoonist Bob Kane, the creator of Batman, was partially inspired by this film in devising his own similar, but heroic, character. This would seem to be the case, not only because of the villainous Bat's disguise and athletic prowess, but particularly because of one scene in which the Bat frightens his victims by projecting a spotlight containing a bat silhouette into the room, anticipating Batman's bat-signal.

Director Roland West was a noteworthy but inconsistent talent; he lavishly remade this film as a talkie, *The Bat Whispers,* in 1930 before his career sputtered into oblivion and he attained a degree of scandalous attention with his involvement in the 1935 death of his wife, actress Thelma Todd, which was officially ruled a "suicide."

The Bat was, incredibly, remade a *second* time, under the original title, as a 1959 vehicle for Vincent Price. The already thin material hadn't improved after gathering dust for an additional 30 years, and the film was so cheaply made that not even Price, assisted by Agnes Moorehead in a supporting role, could help; in a hapless attempt to add some contemporary life to an old chestnut, the producers even added an incongruous jazz score under the opening credits!

Reviews: "This picture ran 91 minutes—a long time for anybody's film, but it was interesting every minute of the way. Its maker, Roland West, has made several other mystery films before *The Bat,* and the story is that he paid heavy money for the film rights to this long-run legit show ... an excellent picture, *The Bat,* and one which looks to have been made on an economical scale, aside from the heavy money for rights. But what the film costs is West's business alone and the exhibitor buying it can depend on real value."—*Variety,* March 17, 1926.

"Doubtless the film conception of *The Bat* will prove both entertaining and exciting despite the mechanical twists employed. ... Nobody is permitted to forget The Bat in this subject. If this thief does not appear in his ungainly make-up, then a moth on the headlight of an automobile is magnified into a bat against the ceiling. ... People in the theatre yesterday were distinctly affected by the spine-chilling episodes, and they were relieved by the comedy interludes."—*The New York Times,* March 15, 1926.

1049 The Bells (Chadwick, 1926). 7 reels.
Producer: I. E. Chadwick.
Director: James Young.
Screenplay: James Young (based on a play by Erckmann-Chatrian).
Photography: William O'Connell.

The Bat (1926): Jack Pickford and Jewel Carmen.

Cast: Lionel Barrymore (Mathias), Edward Phillips (Christian), Lola Todd (Annette), Gustav von Seyffertitz (Frantz), Boris Karloff (Mesmerist), Fred Warren (Kowelski), Otto Lederer, Lorimer Johnston.

Notes: Another remake of the tale about a murderer haunted by his misdeeds. Remarkable only for the presence of Boris Karloff, cast as a fairground mesmerist similar in appearance to Werner Krauss in *The Cabinet of Dr. Caligari*.

1050 *Faust* (UFA, 1926). 8 reels.
Director: F. W. Murnau.
Screenplay: Hans Kyser (based on German folklore and the writings of Christopher Marlowe and Johann Wolfgang von Goethe).
Photography: Carl Hoffman.
Art Direction: Robert Herlth, Walter Rohrig.
Cast: Emil Jannings (Mephistopheles), Gosta Ekman (Faust), Camilla Horn (Margueritte), Yvette Gilbert (Martha), Wilhelm Dieterle (Valentine), Frieda Richard (Margueritte's Mother), Eric Barclay (the Duke), Hanna Ralph (the Duchess).

Notes: This impressive film was F. W. Murnau's last directorial effort in Germany before his immigration to America, and a fitting climax to his European career. *Faust* is a superlative film, brimming with chaotic, apocalyptic imagery, beautifully photographed and precisely edited for maximum effect. Narratively, the film is a straightforward retelling of the "Faust" legend. Mephistopheles

The Bells **(1926): Boris Karloff in a Caligariesque make-up.**

(Emil Jannings) challenges a heavenly emissary to a wager: that the earth and all humanity will fall under his dominion if he succeeds in corrupting the soul of Faust. Mephistopheles then descends earthward and, spreading his immense black cloak over an unsuspecting town, infects the populace with a deadly plague. The saintly Faust (Gosta Ekman), an elderly man who has spent his entire life among books, attempts to save the townspeople, but cannot find a cure for the disease.

Emil Jannings.

Finally, in desperation, Faust renounces God and calls forth Mephistopheles, who appears before him in the guise of a corrupt old man, and offers to banish the plague in exchange for a bargain with Faust. Faust is granted eternal youth and the love of a beautiful girl, Margueritte (Camilla Horn) in exchange for his soul. Through Mephistoph-

Faust (1926): Gosta Ekman, Emil Jannings.

eles' efforts, Margueritte is eventually accused of murdering both a former lover and her own child, and she is condemned to be burned at the stake. Mephistopheles' corruption of Faust is nearly complete when Faust renounces his youth — and his pact with the Devil — reverts to his true elderly form, and earns redemption through the sacrifice of his own life in an attempt to save Margueritte.

Refusing to admit defeat, Mephistopheles storms the gates of Heaven, demanding mankind as his prize, only to be halted by an angel, who tells Mephistopheles that he has been beaten by "The word reverberating jubilantly all over the universe — The word appeasing every pain and every grief — The word expiating all human guilt — The eternal word...." A stark title card then drifts into focus, containing only the word "Love," and Mephistopheles is hurled toward the inferno below in defeat.

Although *Nosferatu* gets most of the attention whenever Murnau's work is discussed, *Faust* is every bit as good, and is even more ambitious in its photography and editing. The individual shots are impeccably framed and lighted, the cutting, and the rapid editing of certain scenes in particular, is surprisingly modern. The visuals, especially in the first half hour or so, are lush and intense; the heavenly prologue, as Mephistopheles confronts the angel, the enormous Devil enfolding the sleeping town in his black, wing-like cloak, and the symbolic "Four Horsemen of the Apocalypse" view of death and disease infecting the world ("The gates of darkness are open and the shades of the nations chase over the earth...") are stunning pictorial highlights.

Photographically and editorially, *Faust* seems to have inspired a more recent filmmaker, Francis Ford Coppola, whose *Bram Stoker's Dracula* (1992) shows evidence of having been influenced in these respects by Murnau's film, even more so than by any previous vampire movie, including Murnau's *Nosferatu*.

Although *Faust is* available for viewing in bootleg video form, there is no high-quality official tape or disc version on the market, which is unfortunate, because this is one of the greatest silent films ever made, and it certainly deserves a wider audience.

Reviews: "*Faust* is not a performer's picture. With or without Emil Jannings it would be pictorially as good. Murnau, directing, and Hoffman, at the camera, have made the cast secondary. It's really a cameraman's picture. How much trick photography and how many fantastic sets go to make up this release is guess work. Murnau has taken the story of Heaven and Hell at cross purposes over the soul of Faust and symbolized it with a production that must have cost all kinds of money. It's a corking picture that holds tension from start to finish. One of the best that Germany has sent over and worth an hour and a quarter of anybody's time." — *Variety,* December 8, 1926.

"If any picture is calculated to lift the abused screen out of a rut, it is this radiant jewel, for not in a single instance has anyone connected with this picture bowed to the usual commercial conventionalities. While gazing upon this delicate and easy-flowing masterpiece, one is impelled to wonder what Mr. Murnau's next film will be like. No writer need be ashamed of saying that there are countless scenes in this production that virtually defy description. ... There are fanciful flights through the skies and a sight of Satan's awe-inspiring wings closing over a town, darkening the skies." — *The New York Times,* December 7, 1926.

1051 ***The Haunted House***
(Davis Dist., 1926). 5 reels.
Director: Paul Hurst.
Screenplay: Frank Howard Clark.
Photography: Frank Cotner.
Cast: Ken Maynard (Terry Baldwin), Alma Rayford (Judith Kellard), Harry Moody (Alex Forester), Al Hallett (executor), Fred Burns (Charlie Titus), Bob Williamson (Ralph Kellard), Tarzan (horse).
Notes: In this western melodrama a ranch is supposedly haunted.

1052 ***The Hound of the Baskervilles*** (Suedfilm/Erda Film, 1926). [*Der Hund von Baskerville*]. Germany. 115 minutes.
Director: Richard Oswald.

Screenplay: Georg C. Klaren, Herbert Juttke (based on the story by Sir Arthur Conan Doyle).
Photography: Frederik Fuglsang.
Cast: Carlyle Blackwell, George Seroff, Fritz Rasp, Alexander Murski, Livio Pavanelli, Betty Bird, Alma Taylor.
Notes: This film was the last silent Sherlock Holmes movie; it was not a commercial success.

Hund von Baskerville, Der *see* **The Hound of the Baskervilles**

1053 Jim Hood's Ghost (Universal, 1926). 22 minutes.
Director: John O'Brien.
Screenplay: William Lester.
Notes: In this western short, a twin pretends to be the ghost of his dead brother so that he can obtain a confession.

Kyoren no Onna Shisho *see* **Passion of a Woman Teacher**

1054 The Lodger (Gainsborough, 1926). 8 reels.
Producer: Michael Balcon.
Director: Alfred Hitchcock.
Screenplay: Alfred Hitchcock, Eliot Stannard (based on the novel by Mrs. Belloc Lowndes).
Titles: Ivor Montagu.
Photography: Baron (Giovanni) Ventigmilla.
Film Editor: Ivor Montagu.
Art Direction: C. Wilfred Arnold, Bertram Evans.
Set Designer: Ishlington.
Cast: Ivor Novello (the lodger/Jonathan Drew), June (Daisy Bunting), Marie Ault (Mrs. Bunting, Daisy's mother), Arthur Chesney (Mr. Bunting), Malcolm Keen (Joe Betts, policeman and Daisy's fiancé).
Notes: The Lodger tells of a roominghouse tenant (Ivor Novello) believed to be Jack the Ripper—until it is discovered he is innocent at the film's conclusion. This film was effectively directed by young Alfred Hitchcock, who made full use of exaggerated shadows and dramatic camera angles to heighten suspense. In one scene, Novello's landlady imagines him pacing back and forth in the room above her, and Hitchcock visualized this by shooting upward through a glass floor at the actor's pacing feet. Considered the first true Hitchcock film in the director's established style, reviewers of that time called *The Lodger* the best British film to date.

1055 The Magician (M-G-M, 1926). 7 reels.
Producer/Director/Screenplay: Rex Ingram (based on a play by Somerset Maugham).
Photography: John Seitz.
Set Designer: Henri Menessier.
Film Editor: Grant Whytock.
Production Manager: Harry Lachman.
Director's Assistant: Michael Powell.
Cast: Alice Terry (Margaret Dauncey), Paul Wegener (Dr. Oliver Haddo), Ivan Petrovich (Dr. Arthur Aurdon), Firmin Geier (Dr. Pohoet), Gladys Hamer (Susie Bond), Stowitz, Henry Wilson, Michael Powell.
Notes: A mad doctor (Paul Wegener) discovers the secret of creating

The Magician (1926): Paul Wegener attacks Ivan Petrovich.

life, only to find that a vital ingredient for the procedure is the blood of a maiden's heart. The maiden is blonde Alice Terry, and Wegener spends most of the film in pursuit of her (even taking her on an imagined tour of Hell at one point) before Terry is finally rescued and Wegener defeated by hero Ivan Petrovich.

Although the magician is not officially available on video, the film does exist and has been preserved by the Museum of Modern Art in New York. What makes the film additionally interesting today is that it appears to have inspired James Whale's *Frankenstein* to some extent. Whale must have seen the film; there are marked similarities to *Frankenstein,* not only in locale and character—Dr. Haddo resides in a tower laboratory and is assisted by a dwarf—but in the Ingram film's use of humor, used in a couple of instances to lighten the horror.

1056 *Metropolis* (UFA, 1926).
10 reels.
Director: Fritz Lang.
Screenplay: Fritz Lang, Thea von Harbou (based on her novel).
English titles: Channing Pollock.
Photography: Karl Freund, Gunther Rittau.
Art Direction: Otto Hunte, Erich Kettlehut.
Special Effects: Eugene Shuftan.
Costumes: Ann Wilkomm.
Cast: Alfred Abel (Joh Freder-

Metropolis (1926): Hot times for Brigitte Helm as the robot Maria is burned at the stake.

sen), Gustav Frolich (Freder), Rudolf Klein-Rogge (Rotwang), Brigitte Helm (Maria/robot), Fritz Rasp (Slim), Theodor Loos (Josaphat/Joseph), Erwin Biswanger (Georg, No. 11811), Heinrich George (Grot, the foreman), Olaf Storm (Jan), Hans Leo Reich (Marinus), Heinrich Gotho (Master of Ceremonies), Margarete Lanner (woman in car/woman in eternal garden), Max Dietze, Georg John, Walter Kuhle, Arthur Reinhard, Erwin Vater (workers), Greta Berger, Olly Boheim, Ellen Frey, Lisa Gray, Rose Lictenstein, Helene Weigel (female workers), Beatrice Garga, Anny Hintze, Helen von Munchofen, Hilde Woitscheff (women in eternal garden), Fritz Alberti (robot), 750 bit players, 30,000 (plus) extras.

Notes: Director Fritz Lang's futuristic epic *Metropolis* was grounded firmly in science fiction, but merits inclusion here for its incongruous horror elements. Although Thea von Harbou's screenplay is set in the future, and deals with a capital vs. labor dispute in which an omnipotent technocrat (Alfred Abel) seeks to control rebelling workers by creating an evil robotic twin of their evangelical leader (Brigitte Helm in both roles), Lang injects aspects of horror amidst the futuristic splendor; the crazed inventor of the robot (Rudolf Klein-Rogge) lives in a mystical, decaying old house located in the heart of the city, and when he abducts the girl Maria in order to duplicate her as a robot, she is pursued through the cobwebs of a musty, subterranean dungeon.

Review: "Nothing of the sort has ever been filmed before; its effect is positively overwhelming. From a photographic and directorial standpoint it is something entirely original. Brigitte Helm ... is a find." — *Variety,* February 23, 1927.

1057 *Mummy Love* (FBO, 1926). 22 minutes.
Director: Joe Rock.
Cast: Neely Edwards, Alice Ardell.
Notes: A comedic horror short about a party of explorers investigating a tomb.

1058 *Passion of a Woman Teacher* (Nikkatsu Shingekibu, 1926). [*Kyoren no Onna Shisho*]. Japan. 85 minutes.
Director: Kenji Mizoguchi.
Screenplay: Kawaguchi Matsutaro.
Photography: Tatsuyuki Yokota.
Cast: Yoneko Sakai, Eiji Nakano, Yoshiko Okada.
Notes: The ghost of a woman teacher gains vengeance on her faithless lover.

1059 *Pete's Haunted House* (Bray, 1926).
Notes: Ghosts and skeletons cavort in this animated cartoon.

1060 *The Prince of Tempters* (First National, 1926). 8 reels.
Director: Lothar Mendes.
Screenplay: Paul Bern (based on *The Ex-Duke* by E. Phillips Oppenheim).
Photography: Ernest Haller.
Cast: Lois Moran, Lya de Putti, Ben Lyon, Ian Keith (Satan), Mary Brian, J. Barney Sherry, Olive Tell, Sam Hardy.
Notes: Satan attempts to ruin a young man with the assistance of a promiscuous woman.

1061 *The Savage* (First National, 1926). 7 reels.
Director: Fred Newmeyer.
Screenplay: Jane Murfin, Charles E. Whittaker.
Cast: Ben Lyon, May McAvoy.
Notes: The Savage was a semi-spoof of *The Lost World,* produced by the same studio. A young journalist (Ben Lyon) accompanies a scientific expedition to the remote Mariposa islands, where he discovers a friendly dinosaur that follows him back to New York. The special effects for this film were not by Willis O'Brien, and are uncredited.

1062 *Scared Stiff* (Pathé/Roach, 1926). 25 minutes.

Director: James W. Horne.
Cast: Clyde Cook, Eileen Percy, Stuart Holmes.
Notes: A haunted house, a mad scientist and a gorilla are featured.

1063 *She* (Lee-Bradford/Samuelson, 1926). Great Britain. 64 minutes.
Director: Leander Cordova.
Screenplay: Walter Summers (based on the novel by H. Rider Haggard).
Photography: Sidney Blythe.
Art Direction: Heinrich Richter.
Cast: Betty Blythe, Carlyle Blackwell, Marjorie Statler.
Notes: The queen of a lost city in Africa gains immortality by immersion in a mystical column of fire. This is the most elaborate silent version of this story.

1064 *Shivering Spooks* (Pathé/Roach, 1926). 16 minutes.
Notes: An *Our Gang* comedy short set in a haunted house.

1065 *Sorrows of Satan* (Paramount, 1926). 12 reels.
Director: D. W. Griffith.
Screenplay: Forrest Halsey, John Russell, George Hull (based on the novel by Marie Corelli).
Titles: Julian Johnson.
Photography: Harry Fishbeck, Arthur De Titta.
Film Editor: Julian Johnson.
Art Direction: Charles Kirk.
Cast: Adolph Menjou (Prince Lucio de Rimanez), Ricardo Cortez (Geoffrey Tempest), Lya de Putti (Princess Olga), Carol Dempster (Mavis Claire), Ivan Lebedeff (Amiel), Marcia Harris (the landlady), Lawrence D'Orsay (Lord Elton), Nellie Savage (dancing girl), Dorothy Hughes (Mavis' Chum), Josephine Dunn, Dorothy Nourse, Jeanne Morgan, Raymond Griffith, Owen Nares.
Notes: When director Cecil B. DeMille stormed out of Paramount after a dispute, *Sorrows of Satan,* which had been prepared for him, was assigned to D. W. Griffith instead. Griffith's professional fortunes were in decline, and it is possible that hard-nosed studio executives believed the fading director would be easier to handle than DeMille, while the lingering prestige of his name would prove helpful in selling the picture. By 1926, Griffith was considered to be passé and out of touch with the public, and it had become fashionable for critics and even the industry press to deride his sensibilities and techniques. Although *some* of this criticism may have been justified in terms of Griffith's Victorian moral tone, over-all it was largely undeserved.

Griffith desperately wanted *Sorrows of Satan* to be a hit, working long hours to please the studio brass, only to have the film fail miserably at the box office on release. *Sorrows of Satan,* based on a popular novel by Marie Corelli, is the tale of two poverty-stricken, aspiring writers (Ricardo Cortez and Carol Dempster), very much in love. Cortez, frustrated by constant publisher rejections and nagging poverty, is offered a deal by Satan (Adolphe Menjou): reject Dempster's love and marry a beautiful princess (Lya de Putti) in order to gain instant wealth and success.

Sorrows of Satan (1926): Original ad.

This Cortez does, only to find that de Putti does not love him. Eventually, a repentant Cortez and Dempster are reunited, and Satan is defeated by the purity of their love.

This film's obscurity is unfortunate; its pictorial elegance belies contemporary rejection of Griffith's directorial style; particularly memorable is a scene with the satanic Menjou pursuing Cortez in the form of an immense, shadowy bat.

Reviews: "D. W. Griffith again symbolizes good and evil ... meanwhile out-DeMilling DeMille in sets and Bacchanalian revels, plus liberal suggestiveness. For all of that the picture is overshadowed in story and cast by its superb photography. Limited action comes very close to trying the patience more than once. ... Harry Fishbeck's work at the camera dominates the film." — *Variety,* October 20, 1926.

"A silk-hatted Satan glides across the screen in ... *The Sorrows of Satan.* In swinging from squalor to pomp, depicting wretchedness on one side and passionate orgies on the other, Mr. Griffith reveals himself a master, and in this present offering he ... excels anything he has done in recent years. It is a marvelously beautiful film, in which Mr. Griffith has obtained some gorgeous lighting effects. Adolphe Menjou is remarkably fine as the Prince who enjoys the ruin of his victims. He is distinctive,

Sparrows (1926): Gustav von Seyffertitz (left) threatens Mary Pickford and the children.

almost gentle in setting forth his temptations." – *The New York Times,* October 13, 1926.

1066 *Sparrows* (United Artists, 1926). 9 reels.
Director: William Beaudine.
Screenplay: C. Gardner Sullivan, Tom McNamara, Carl Harbaugh, Earle Browne (based on a story by Winifred Dunn).
Titles: George Marion, Jr.
Photography: Charles Rosher, Karl Struss, Hal Mohr.
Art Direction: Harry Oliver.
Cast: Mary Pickford (Moma Mollie), Gustav von Seyffertitz (Grimes), Roy Stewart (Richard Wayne), Mary Louise Miller (Doris Wayne), Charlotte Mineau (Mrs. Grimes), Spike O'Donnel (Ambrose Grimes), Lloyd Whitlock (Bailey), A. L. Schaeffer (his confederate), Mark Hamilton (hog buyer), Monty O'Grady (Splutters), Muriel McCormac, Billy "Red" Jones, Cammilla Johnson, Mary McLane, Billy Butts, Jack Lavine, Florence Rogan, Seesel Ann Johnson, Sylvia Bernard (the sparrows).

Notes: A lushly mounted Mary Pickford vehicle, *Sparrows* was about an assortment of mistreated orphans who escape from their monstrously cruel guardian (Gustav von Seyffertitz) by fleeing through an alligator-infested swamp. Although *Sparrows* can hardly be considered a "horror" film, it contains more horrific scenes than the average Tod Browning-Lon Chaney collaboration! Although its sharply defined contrasts between "good" (Pickford) and "evil" (von Seyffertitz) are simplistic and overdrawn at times, *Sparrows* is beautifully photographed by Charles Rosher and Karl Struss, with tight direction by William Beaudine, an underrated craftsman who has been unfairly maligned in recent years for his later work on negligible low-budget horror movies like *Billy the Kid vs. Dracula* and *Jesse James Meets Frankenstein's Daughter* (both 1965).

The commanding Gustav von Seyffertitz walks away with all acting honors as Grimes, the film's inhuman villain; far less effective is Mary Pickford as Mollie, the orphans' unofficial leader and surrogate mother (the children call her "Moma Mollie"). Although a star of the first magnitude and an influential behind-the-scenes production executive as well, Pickford's shrewdly calculated screen personna has not worn well over the years. It's a little bizarre to see a woman past 30 playing a teenager; nevertheless, Pickford's boundless energy and spirited personality — the qualities that made her popular with audiences of the day — are obvious and fully in evidence here.

Reviews: "The truth is the production is one of the few duds put out by Mary Pickford ... in *Sparrows* there isn't a ray of brightness. For once a Pollyanna is submerged, smothered and muffled in sinister gloom. The surroundings are those of a terrifying nightmare. ... The photography is done in dim half lights and the whole business drips desolation. Miss Pickford's special style of sentimental comedy can make no headway against the penetrating gloom of the subject and locale. ... Grimes, who looks like Dr. Jekyll in one of his worst moments, misuses his charges cruelly ... everything is overshadowed by the horror and wretchedness, which supplies the controlling element and makes all else incidental." — *Variety,* September 22, 1926.

"Miss Pickford's excellent portrayal of the little mother leaves only the desire for a more plausible story. Gustav von Seyffertitz, with a suspicion of Lon Chaney's penchant for deformity, is emphatically capable as Mr. Grimes." — *The New York Times,* September 20, 1926.

1067 The Student of Prague
(Sokal, 1926). Germany. 9 reels.

Alternate title: The Man Who Cheated Life (U.S.).

Director/Screenplay: Henryk Galeen (based on a novel by Hanns Heinz Ewers, derived from the story *William Wilson* by Edgar Allan Poe).

Photography: Gunther Krampf, Erich Nitzschmann.

Set Designer: Hermann Warm.

Cast: Conrad Veidt (Baldwin), Werner Krauss (Mr. Scapinelli/Satan), Agnes Esterhazy, Elizza La Porte, Ferdinand von Alten, Erick Kober, Fritz Albert, Sylvia Torf, Max Maxmillian, Marian Alma.

Notes: The Student of Prague is the second film version of the Hanns Heinz Ewers novel about a student who sells his soul to Satan in exchange for riches, Conrad Veidt was cast as the student, Baldwin; the film was directed by

The Student of Prague (1926): Conrad Veidt.

Henryk Galeen, with cinematography by Gunther Krampf and Erich Nitzchmann.

Veidt is brilliantly subdued and understated as Baldwin, who finds that he has lost his mirror reflection after signing his pact with Satan (Werner Krauss), only to have that reflection enter the real world and haunt him as an evil twin "doppelganger." Veidt's division of these two physically identical characters is superb, and his enactment of the mirror reflection, as it lurches slowly and inexorably about the countryside on windswept roads in search of its "owner," is particularly adept. The trick mirror shots are all nicely done, too, with, for instance, Veidt appearing in a roomful of people while his reflection alone fails to register in the mirrors he passes.

This film has a degree of historical significance, coming as it does at the end of Germany's Gothic Romance period in film, and it uses both stylized expressionistic sets and natural locations.

A third version of the story, starring Anton Walbrook, was produced in 1936.

Reviews: "Gruesome thriller which might have emanated from the imagination of Poe. Not a bad story for the Caligari type of treatment. Werner Krauss was the best possible choice for the Devil, and Conrad Veidt might be supposed an adequate one for the student. But the director, Heinrich Galeen, hasn't been able to get much out of his actors and only the last half-reel chase of the student by his reflection is really thrilling." — *Variety,* November 4, 1926.

"It is a ... German production with a modicum of interest due to the plot of the story and, to a certain extent, to Conrad Veidt's careful and intelligent interpretation of the leading role." — *The New York Times,* February 11, 1929.

1068 ***Tin Hats*** (M-G-M, 1926). 80 minutes.
Director: Edward Sedgwick.
Screenplay: Edward Sedgwick, Albert Lewin (adaptation by Lew Lipton, Donald W. Lee).
Titles: Ralph Spence.
Art Direction: Cedric Gibbons, F. Hope.
Cast: Conrad Nagel, Claire Windsor, George Cooper, Bert Roach, Eileen Sedgwick.
Notes: A haunted castle and a ghost in armor are featured.

1069 ***Unknown Treasures*** (Sterling, 1926). 6 reels.
Director: Archie Mayo.
Screenplay: Charles A. Logue (based on the story *The House Behind the Hedge* by Mary Spain Vigus).
Photography: Harry Davis.
Cast: Gladys Hulette, Robert Agnew, John Miljan, Gustav von Seyffertitz, Jed Prouty.
Notes: Hidden treasure in an old house and a murderous ape inject horror into the plot of this melodrama.

1070 ***While London Sleeps*** (Warner Bros., 1926). 6 reels.
Director: Howard P. Bretherton.
Screenplay: Walter Morosco.
Photography: Frank Kesson, Fred West.
Assistant Director: William Cannon.
Cast: Rin-Tin-Tin (Rinty), Helene Costello (Dale Burke), Walter Merrill (Thomas Hallard), John Patrick (Foster), Otto Matieson (London Letter), George Kotsonaros (the monk), De Witt Jennings (Inspector Burke), Carl Stockdale (Stokes), Les Bates (Long Tom).
Notes: Canine idol Rin-Tin-Tin starred in *While London Sleeps,* a 6 reel Warner Bros. production in which the daughter (Helene Costello) of a Scotland Yard Inspector (De Witt Jennings) encounters a notorious master criminal (Otto Matieson) known as "London Letter," who harbors a monstrous apeman (George Kotsonaros), trained to do his bidding. Kotsonaros would play a similar monster character in the 1927 Fox production *The Wizard* (*q.v.*).
Review: "Technique pretty terrible. Long stretches of action that amount almost to close-ups of still life. ... Acting also terrible. ... The melodrama is laid on so thick it gets into unintended comedy." — *Variety,* December 22, 1926.

1071 ***Whispering Wires*** (Fox, 1926). 6 reels.
Director: Albert Ray.
Screenplay: L. G. Rigby.
Titles: William Conselman.
Photography: George Schneiderman.
Assistant Director: Horace Hough.
Cast: Anita Stewart (Doris Stockbridge), Edmund Burns (Barry McGill), Charles Clary (Montgomery Stockbridge), Otto Matieson (Bert Norton), Mack Swain (Cassidy), Arthur Houseman (McCarthy),

Charles Conklin (Jasper, the butler), Frank Campeau (Andrew Murphy), Scott Welsh (Triggy Drew), Mayme Kelso (Ann Cartwright), Charles Sellon (Tracy Bennett), Cecile Evans.

Notes: In this melodrama, a whispering voice on the telephone predicts murders.

1927

1072 *The Cat and the Canary*
(Universal, 1927). 8 reels.
Producer: Carl Laemmle.
Director: Paul Leni.
Screenplay: Robert F. Hill, Alfred A. Cohn (based on the play by John Willard).
Titles: Walter Anthony.
Photography: Gilbert Warrenton.
Set Designer: Charles D. Hall.
Cast: Laura LaPlante (Annabel West), Creighton Hale (Paul Jones), Forrest Stanley (Charles Wilder), Tully Marshall (Roger Crosby), Gertrude Astor (Cecily Young), Arthur Edmund Carewe (Harry Blythe), Flora Finch (Susan Silsby), Martha Mattox ("Mammy" Pleasant), Lucien Littlefield (Dr. Patterson), George Siegmann (Hendricks), Joe Murphy (milkman), Billy Engle (taxi driver).
Notes: Based on a successful mystery play by John Willard, Universal's *The Cat and the Canary* was director Paul Leni's first movie after arriving in America from Germany. The plot centers on the pretty young heiress to a fortune (Laura LaPlante) who will be denied her bequest only if her sanity is called into question; soon other characters are mysteriously disappearing and monstrous clutching hands are emerging from secret wall panels in a gloomy old mansion as one of the other legatees spares no effort in attempting to drive LaPlante mad.

This highly cinematic film is Leni's best, with Gilbert Warrenton's mobile camera gliding smoothly through the atmospheric sets, and Leni using bizarre angles and distorted shadows at every opportunity. The high vertical sets (a couple of which were later used briefly in *Frankenstein*) were designed by Charles D. Hall, who was to supervise the set construction on many of Universal's 1930s sound horror chillers.

The Cat and the Canary is successful not because of its story, which was old hat even then, but because of its bold visual style and the self-effacing nature of its presentation. Laced with just the right amount of humor, this picture, for better or worse, almost single-handedly established the haunted house horror-comedy subgenre, a category that would be

The Cat and the Canary (1927): Gertrude Astor and Laura LaPlante.

thoroughly mined by directors of considerably lesser stature than Paul Leni.

The Cat and the Canary would be remade *three* times; as a Universal talkie with Helen Twelvetrees under the title *The Cat Creeps*, as a Paramount vehicle for Bob Hope in 1939, and as a low-budget thriller with Carol Lynley in 1978.

Reviews: "What distinguishes Universal's film version of the ... play is Paul Leni's intelligent handling of a weird theme, introducing some of his novel settings and ideas with which he became identified. ... The story and the Leni direction could carry almost any cast. ... The film runs a bit overlong. ... Otherwise it's a more than average satisfying feature...."— *Variety,* September 14, 1927.

"...[T]he film transcription of John Willard's play, *The Cat and the Canary* ... has been turned into one of the finest examples of motion picture art. Mr. Leni has not lost a single chance in this new film to show what can be done with the camera. He creates excitement by pitching his camera high and low, or rolling it along. He makes you feel that you are one of the characters in the haunted house of the story. There are scenes in this piece of work that are amazing,

THE PLAY THAT STARTLED THE WORLD

becomes the greatest mystery special the screen has ever seen! A sensationally successful stage play surpassed in a screen masterpiece!

Spooks! Thrills! Shrieks! Laughs!

A Paul Leni Production

It's a Universal "Long Run" Special

With Universal's Challenge Cast: LAURA LA PLANTE, Creighton Hale, Forrest Stanley, Tully Marshall, Gertrude Astor, Flora Finch, Martha Mattox, Arthur Edmund Carew, etc. Based on John Willard's play

The Cat and the Canary (1927): Original ad.

especially those in which Mr. Leni photographs his characters through the backs of chairs and first gives one an impression that the books on a shelf are long, narrow, deep-sunken windows ... while the lines of the furniture bring to mind the interior of a cathedral. This is the first time that a mystery melodrama has been lifted into the realms of art, for this feature is something that those who rave about cinematics will find delightful and those who are only anxious for a movie probably will find almost bloodcurdling." — *The New York Times*, September 10, 1927.

1073 *The Chinese Parrot*
(Universal, 1927). 7 reels.
Producer: Carl Laemmle.
Director: Paul Leni.
Screenplay: J. Grubb Alexander (based on the novel by Earl Derr Biggers).
Titles: Walter Anthony.
Photography: Ben Kline.
Cast: Marian Nixon (Sally Phillimore), Florence Turner (Sally Phillimore, older), Hobart Bosworth (Philip Madden/Jerry Delaney), Edward Burns (Robert Eden), Albert Conti (Martin Thorne), K. Sojin (Charlie Chan), Fred Esmelton (Alexander Eden), Ed Kennedy (Maydorf), George Kuwa (Louie Wong), Slim Summerville, Dan Mason (prospectors), Anna May Wong (Nautch Dancer), Etta Lee (Gambling Den Habitue), Jack Trent (Jordan).
Notes: The Oriental sleuth Charlie Chan investigates stolen pearls and a kidnapping in this melodrama, which Paul Leni directed with unexpectedly heavy atmosphere, aided by the excellent cinematography of Ben Kline.

1074 *Faust* (1927). Great Britain. 20 minutes.
Director: H. B. Parkinson.
Cast: Herbert Langley, A. B. Imeson, Margot Lees.
Notes: Adapted from Gounod's opera, this short was an entry in the *Cameo Operas* series.

1075 *Felix Switches Witches*
(Educational, 1927). 10 minutes.
Notes: A witch and hobgoblins are featured in this cartoon.

1076 *The Gorilla* (First National, 1927). 8 reels.
Director: Alfred Santell.
Screenplay: Alfred A. Cohen, James T. O'Donahue, Henry McCarthy (based on the play by Ralph Spence).
Titles: Sidney Lazarus, Al Boasberg.
Photography: Arthur Edeson.
Production Manager: Edward Small.
Cast: Charlie Murray (Garrity), Fred Kelsey (Mulligan), Alice Day (Alice Townsend), Tully Marshall (William Townsend), Claude Gillingwater (Cyrus Townsend), Walter Pidgeon (Stevens), Gaston Glass (Marsden), Brooks Benedict (the reporter), Aggie Herring (the cook), Syd Crossley (the butler), John Gough (sailor).
Notes: The Gorilla was based on a hit Broadway play by Ralph Spence. Photographed by Arthur Edeson, the picture was little more than standard haunted house tedium about a series of murders supposedly committed by the marauding title simian. At this late date (and since the film does not exist anyway), it can do no any harm to reveal that the murderer was really future M-G-M romantic lead Walter Pidgeon, disguised as an ape. The cast included Charles

Murray and Alice Day; the film was remade as a talkie in 1930 (with Pidgeon returning), and again in 1939 as a comedy vehicle for the Ritz Brothers, co-starring Bela Lugosi in a wasted red-herring role.

Reviews: "*The Gorilla* is a box office tonic for more reasons than one. It is an entertaining picture, the title boasts a reputation gained from the stage play, and the story makes good exploitation material. Except in a few serious instances, the story is done in broad comedy. Technically the picture is distinctive in photography, being handled with an expert treatment of lighting values and perspective. Sets are highly atmospheric. Effective direction by Santell...." — *Variety,* November 23, 1927.

"Excitement and amusement are linked in the screen translation of *The Gorilla,* Ralph Spence's stage burlesque on the mystery play. In quite a number of spots, Alfred Santell's easy and imaginative touch is apparent, but here and there this film slumps into horseplay and silly stunts. *The Gorilla* is very much as if Mack Sennett in a restrained mood had turned to Edgar Allan Poe's *The Murders in the Rue Morgue* and decided to adapt it to the screen. . . . Mr. Santell . . . makes very good use of his settings in this production...." — *The New York Times,* November 21, 1927.

1077 *High Spirits* (Cameo-Educational, 1927). 11 minutes.
Notes: In this short subject, a fake medium holds séances.

1078 *London After Midnight* (M-G-M, 1927). 7 reels.
Producer/Director: Tod Browning.
Screenplay: Tod Browning, Waldemar Young (based on a story by Tod Browning).
Titles: Joe Farnham.
Photography: Merritt B. Gerstad.
Film Editor: Harry Reynolds.
Set Designers: Cedric Gibbons, Arnold Gillespie.
Costumes: Lucia Coulter.
Cast: Lon Chaney (Burke), Marceline Day (Lucille Balfour), Henry B. Walthall (Sir James Hamlin), Percy Williams (butler), Conrad Nagel (Arthur Hibbs), Polly Moran (Miss Smithson), Edna Tichenor (bat girl), Claude King (the stranger), Jules Cowles (Gallagher), Andy MacLennan (Scotland Yard Inspector).

Notes: London After Midnight starred Chaney as a Scotland Yard inspector who stages a bizarre plot in order to force a confession from a murderer by convincing the killer that his victim's death had actually been caused by a vampire! Chaney's saw-toothed make-up as the phony vampire remains impressive in surviving still photos, although the film itself (no longer in existence) was reportedly dull and slowly paced. Browning later had the script reworked a bit, and remade it as *Mark of the Vampire* in 1935, with Bela Lugosi as the pretend vampire.

Reviews: "Will add nothing to Chaney's prestige as a trouper, nor increase the star's box office value. With Chaney's name in lights, however, this picture, any picture with

Chaney, means a strong box-office draw. Young, Browning and Chaney have made a good combination in the past but the story on which this production is based is not of the quality that results in broken house records." — *Variety*, December 14, 1927.

"Tod Browning ... evidently does not believe in delaying a murder. It happens in the first scene. It is a somewhat incoherent narrative, which, however, gives Lon Chaney an opportunity to turn up in an uncanny disguise and also to manifest his powers as Scotland Yard's expert hypnotist. You are therefore treated to close-ups of Mr. Chaney's rolling orbs, which, fortunately, do not exert their influence on the audience. Mr. Chaney is sound and sure of his acting, but this detective character does not give him anything in the way of a big opportunity. His other role is shrewdly made-up and portrayed." — *The New York Times*, December 31, 1927.

1079 *The Missing Link* (Warner Bros., 1927). 7 reels.
Director: Charles F. Reisner.
Screenplay: Darryl F. Zanuck.
Photography: Devereaux Jennings, Fred West.
Assistant Director: Sandy Roth.
Cast: Syd Chaplin (Arthur Wells), Ruth Hiatt (Beatrice Braden), Tom McGuire (Colonel Braden), Crauford Kent (Lord Dryden), Nick Cogley (captain), Sam Baker ("The Missing Link"), Akka (chimp), Otto Fries, Kewpie Morgan.
Notes: Sam Baker appears as a bestial ape-man monster in this otherwise tame farce.

1080 *Mr. Wu* (M-G-M, 1927). 9 reels.
Director: William Nigh.
Screenplay: Lorna Moon (based on the 1914 play *Mr. Wu* by Maurice Vernon and Harold Owen).
Photography: John Arnold.
Cast: Lon Chaney (Mr. Wu), Renee Adoree, Louise Dresser, Holmes Herbert.
Notes: Chaney's portrayal of a sinister Oriental sparked this melodramatic tale of seduction, revenge and murder.

1081 *Mockery* (M-G-M, 1927). 7 reels.
Director/Screenplay: Benjamin Christensen.
Continuity: Bradley King.
Titles: Joe Farnham.
Photography: Merritt B. Gerstad.
Set Designers: Cedric Gibbons, Alexander Toluboff.
Film Editor: John W. English.
Wardrobe: Gilbert Clark.
Cast: Lon Chaney (Sergei), Ricardo Cortez (Dimitri), Barbara Bedford (Tatiana), Mack Swain (Mr. Gaidaroff), Emily Fitzroy (Mrs. Gaidaroff), Charles Puffy (Ivan), Kai Schmidt (butler).
Notes: Mockery, involving revolution and torture in Czarist Russia, was not horrific in nature, but Christensen's precise imagery was so atmospheric in effect that the title originally chosen by the studio — *Terror* — would probably have been more appropriate.

London After Midnight (1927): Lon Chaney.

1082 *The Monkey Talks* (Fox, 1927). 6 reels.
Producer: William Fox.
Director: Raoul Walsh.
Screenplay: L. G. Rigby (based on a play by Rene Frauchois).
Photography: L. William O'Connell.
Assistant Director: R. Lee Hough.
Cast: Olive Borden (Olivette), Jacques Lerner (Jocko Lerner/Fano), Don Alvarado (Sam Wick/Pierre), Malcolm Waite (Bergerin), Raymond Hitchcock (Lorenzo), Ted McNamara (Firmin), Jane

Mr. Wu (1927): **Lon Chaney.**

Winton (Maisie), August Tollaire (Mata).

Notes: Directed by Raoul Walsh, *The Monkey Talks* was the story of a midget, Jocko (Jacques Lerner) who masquerades as a talking monkey in a circus. Falling in love with a beautiful high-wire performer (Borden), Jocko eventually sacrifices himself to save her when she is threatened by a rampaging circus animal. The script by L. G. Rigby (based on a play by Rene Frauchois) was worthy of Browning

Mockery (1927): Lon Chaney.

and Chaney; the monkey-man make-up was by Jack P. Pierce, later noted for his remarkable work on horror films at Universal in the 30s and 40s.

Reviews: "It's a picture that is a decided novelty, has a wealth of suspense, a tremendous love interest, and sufficient comedy. ... Raoul Walsh has turned this out full of atmosphere and replete with suspense. Olive Borden, as the youthful wire-walker, is a joyous bit of beauty and the performance of Jacques Lerner is a marvel." — *Variety,* February 23, 1927.

"Raoul Walsh ... sometimes shows his fine hand in ... *The Monkey Talks.* The story, however, is hardly satisfying and the characters are not as clearly defined as they might be. Mr. Lerner bows his legs, lengthens his arms and stoops, thus making his impersonation as seen on the screen almost uncanny." — *The New York Times,* April 5, 1927.

1083 *Prelude* (Knight, 1927). Great Britain. 8 minutes.
Director: Castleton Knight.
Screenplay: Castleton Knight (based on the Edgar Allan Poe Story *The Premature Burial*).
Cast: Castleton Knight.
Notes: After listening to Rachmanioff's *Prelude,* a man dreams that he is buried alive.

1084 *Queen of Spades* (Phoebus-Film, 1927). Germany.
Notes: A ghostly woman helps a gambler win at cards.

1085 *Scared Silly* (Educational, 1927). 25 minutes.

Cast: Johnny Arthur.
Notes: A ghost assists a hindu with his séances.

1086 *The Show* (M-G-M, 1927). 7 reels.
Director: Tod Browning.
Screenplay: Waldemar Young (based on a story by Charles Tenny Jackson).
Titles: Joe Farnham.
Photography: John Arnold.
Set Designers: Cedric Gibbons, Richard Day.
Film Editor: Errol Taggart.
Wardrobe: Lucia Coulter.
Cast: John Gilbert (Cock Robin), Renee Adoree (Salome), Lionel Barrymore (the Greek), Edward Connelly (the soldier), Gertrude Short (Lena), Andy MacLennan (the ferret), Edna Tichenor.
Notes: The Show features a plot involving a romantic triangle between the three stars — John Gilbert, Renee Adoree and Lionel Barrymore — set against the backdrop of a carnival freak show. Directed by Browning and scripted by Waldemar Young, *The Show* is almost a blueprint for Browning's later M-G-M picture *Freaks* (1932). Gilbert is actually beheaded at one point — strong stuff for 1927 — although this on-screen decapitation takes place in a fantasy sequence.
Reviews: "Gilbert and Miss Adoree certainly play their roles right up to the hilt, and Barrymore as the heavy furnished a flock of menace where it was most needed. ... Tod Browning handled the direction very skillfully." — *Variety*, March 16, 1927.
"Once again the crafty and imaginative Tod Browning ... fails to stir his audiences. The shining lights of this production are Renee Adoree and Lionel Barrymore. ... Barrymore is splendid as the Greek." — *The New York Times*, March 14, 1927.

1087 *Spione* (Fritz Lang Film/ G.M.B.H.-UFA/M-G-M, 1927). Germany. 5 reels.
Alternate titles: The Spy; Spies (U.S. title).
Director: Fritz Lang.
Screenplay: Fritz Lang, Thea von Harbou.
Photography: Fritz Arno Wagner.
Art Direction: Otto Hunte, Karl Volbrecht.
Cast: Rudolf Klein-Rogge (Haghi), Gerda Maurus (Sonia), Willy Fritsch (the detective, Agent 326), Lupu Pick (Masimoto), Fritz Rasp (Ivan Stepanov), Lien Deyers (Kitty), Craighall Sherry (Burton Jason), Julius Falkenstein (hotel manager), Georg John (train conductor), Paul Rehkopf (Strotch), Paul Horbiger (Valet), Louis Ralph (Hans Morriera), Herman Valentin, Greta Berger, Hertha von Walther.
Notes: It is superspy Haghi vs. Agent 326 in this intense melodrama directed by Fritz Lang after he had finished *Metropolis*.

1088 *Spook Spoofing* (1927). 2 reels.
Notes: An *Our Gang* comedy short set in a graveyard.

1089 *Spooks* (Bray, 1927). 2 reels.

The Show (1927): Renee Adoree and John Gilbert.

Director: Robert B. Wilcox.
Notes: A haunted house comedy short.

1090 *Svengali* (Terra-Film, 1927). Germany.
Directors: Gennaro Righelli, H. Grund.
Screenplay: Max Glass (based on the novel *Trilby* by George Du Maurier).
Art Direction: Hans Jacoby.
Cast: Paul Wegener, Anita Dorris, Andre Mattoni, Alexander Granach.

1091 *The Thirteenth Hour* (M-G-M, 1927). 6 reels.
Director: Chester Franklin.
Screenplay: Douglas Furber, Chester Franklin.
Continuity: Edward T. Lowe, Jr.
Titles: Wellyn Totman.
Photography: Maximillian Fabian.
Set Designer: Eugene Hornbostel.
Film Editor: Dan Sharits.
Cast: Lionel Barrymore (Prof. Leroy), Jacqueline Gadsdon (Mary Lyle), Charles Delaney (Matt Gray), Fred Kelsey (Detective Shaw), Napolean (dog), Polly Moran (Polly).
Notes: A respected criminologist is actually a mass-murderer; he is finally tracked down by a detective and his dog.
Review: "Why don't the boys

The Unknown (1927): Joan Crawford, Lon Chaney.

give Pearl White a break and bring her back? She's gotten out of more traps, dungeons, cages and torture cells than Houdini. And she did it years ago; so these modern mysteries and dilemmas wouldn't faze her. They are not liable to faze anyone else, either, if this one is an example. ... Plain unadulterated melodrama ... Barrymore probably snickers to himself over these roles." — *Variety,* November 30, 1927.

1092 *The Unknown* (M-G-M, 1927). 6 reels.
Director: Tod Browning.
Screenplay: Tod Browning, Waldemar Young.
Titles: Joe Farnham.
Photography: Merritt Gerstad.
Art Direction: Cedric Gibbons, Richard Day.
Film Editors: Harry Reynolds, Errol Taggart.
Wardrobe: Lucia Coulter.
Cast: Lon Chaney (Alonzo), Norman Kerry (Malabar), Joan Crawford (Estrellita), Nick De Ruiz (Zanzi), John George (Cojo), Frank Lanning (Costra).
Notes: In *The Unknown,* a Lon Chaney vehicle directed by Tod Browning, Chaney stars as Alonzo the Armless Wonder, an escaped killer who, masquerading as an armless circus performer, hurls knives with his feet and lusts after fellow big-top artiste Joan Crawford. The leggy Crawford suffers

from a psychological fear of being fondled by men, and Chaney, believing that she is attracted to him because he cannot touch her, has his arms amputated *for real* — only to find that, meanwhile, Crawford has overcome her aversion and fallen for handsome Norman Kerry. In a bizarre conclusion to an already weird yarn, Chaney plots to murder Kerry by having him torn apart while he is chained between two horses during a circus act, only to die himself when he slips and is trampled beneath their hooves.

Reviews: "A good Chaney film that might have been great. Chaney and his characterizations invite stories that have power behind them. Everytime Browning thinks of Chaney he probably looks around for a typewriter and says 'let's get gruesome.' Chaney does various things with his feet during the picture, such as eating, smoking, etc. Some are obviously not Chaney's legs, and in one or two instances the large dimension of features before a close lens makes some of this work seem out of physical proportion. At that, the effect on the whole is good and well-done. Browning has chopped to the bone in the cutting room ... and that's smart, too, because it crams the picture with action and interest, something Chaney's preceding vehicles didn't always hold. Miss Crawford never looked better in her life...." — *Variety,* June 15, 1927.

"Although it has strength and undoubtedly sustains the interest, *The Unknown* ... is anything but a pleasant story. It is gruesome and at times shocking, and the principal character deteriorates from a more or less sympathetic individual to an arch-fiend." — *The New York Times,* June 13, 1927.

1093 *The Wizard* (Fox, 1927). 6 reels.
Director: Richard Rosson.
Screenplay: Harry O. Hoyt, Andrew Bennison (based on the story *Balaoo* by Gaston Leroux).
Titles: Malcolm Stuart Boylan.
Photography: Frank Good.
Assistant Director: Park Fame.
Cast: Edmund Lowe (Stanley Gordon), Leila Hyams (Anne Webster), Gustav von Seyffertitz (Dr. Paul Coriolos), E. H. Calvert (Edwin Palmer), Barry Norton (Reginald Van Lear), Oscar Smith (Sam), Perle Marshall (Detective Murphy), Norman Trevor (Judge Webster), George Kotsonaros (the ape), Maude Turner Gordon (Mrs. Van Lear).

Notes: The Wizard was a direct remake of the 1913 French film *Balaoo* (*q.v.*), and was itself remade as *Dr. Renault's Secret* (20th Century-Fox, 1942), featuring J. Carrol Naish as the ape-man.

Reviews: "More horror. Laid on thick. But the great American public brought it on themselves. They 'went' for the serials back in the early days of screendom, and it looks as if the cycle has come around again. The new dish is evidently gorillas sprinkled with apes. Shake well, add the mental power of a tabloid reader and be horrified. Silly and a waste of time...." — *Variety,* November 30, 1927.

"This new combination of laughter

and excitement ... is quite a good entertainment weakened by the levity forced upon it. This subject really has enough of a story to deserve more serious treatment. ... The scenes with a mad surgeon and a queer gorilla are quite cleverly pictured, especially when the spectator is taken through a room by means of the camera. Edmund Lowe as Stanley Gordon does quite well in some scenes ... Leila Hyams is graceful and attractive as the girl with whom Gordon is in love. Gustav von Seyffertitz, who impersonates the mad surgeon, does some capital acting." — *The New York Times,* November 22, 1927.

1928

1094 *Alraune* (AMA Film, 1928). Germany. 14 reels.
Alternate title: Unholy Love.
Producer: Helmut Schreiber.
Director: Henryk Galeen.
Screenplay: Henryk Galeen, Hanns Heinz Ewers (based on the novel by Hanns Heinz Ewers).
Photography: Franz Planer.
Set Designers: Walter Reimann, Max Hellbronner.
Cast: Brigitte Helm (Alraune), Paul Wegener, Ivan Petrovich, Mia Pankau, Georg John, Valeska Gert, Wolfgang Lilzer, Louis Ralph, Hans Trautner, John Loder, Heinrich Schroth, Alexander Sascha.
Notes: Alraune, released by AMA Film in Germany, was a new version of the Hanns Heinz Ewers tale about an evil, artificial woman created when a prostitute is impregnated with the semen of an executed killer. This time Brigitte Helm (Fritz Lang's erotic robot from *Metropolis*) played the title role, and was so impressive that she repeated the part for an inferior sound remake two years later. This first Helm version was directed and co-scripted by Henryk Galeen, with script contribution by Hanns Heinz Ewers. Paul Wegener costarred.
Reviews: "Titilation for the gooseflesh. All the horrors of *Metropolis* and quite a lot more ... Hanns Heinz Ewers, scenario writer, makes Edgar Allan Poe look like an amateur. A coldblooded doctor brings to life a child, the daughter of a hanged criminal and a prostitute, in a fashion which cannot be printed, even if screened. ... Heinrich Galeen squeezes all the horror juice out of it, and Brigitte Helm, the vamp, is at least 200 percent. When will some American director take a look at this extraordinarily fascinating girl? She has an individuality of her own." — *Variety,* May 2, 1928.

1095 *The Ape* (Collwyn Pictures, 1928). 5 reels.

Director: B. C. Rule.
Cast: Gladys Walton, Ruth Stonehouse, Basil Wilson, Bradley Barker.
Notes: There isn't must information available on *The Ape*. The story apparently involved a rampaging simian and was "claimed to be based on an actual police record."
Review: "Shot in the old Triangle Arts studio in Riverdale, *The Ape* is a little inferior in technique. . . . The story, a jumbled mess of cart before the horse detail, is brought to the screen with a schoolboy's appreciation for technicalities. Messed up with this is a cartload of the most explanatory titles. These take up half of the footage. All kinds of hands that are played upon by a baby spot and figures that shadow themselves on window sills attempt to provide the mystery. The action confines itself to four sets with a fleeting shot of the Hudson. . . . The thing is blah all the way." — *Variety,* May 2, 1928.

1096 *The Black Pearl* (Rayart, 1928). 6 reels.
Director: Scott Pembroke.
Screenplay/Titles: Arthur Hoerl.
Photography: Hap Depew.
Film Editor: J. S. Harrington.
Cast: Lila Lee (Eugenie Bromley), Ray Hallor (Robert Lathrop), Carlton Stockdale (Ethelbert/Bertram Chisolm), Howard Lorenz (Dr. Drake), Adele Watson (Sarah Runyan), Thomas Curran (Silas Lathrop), Sybil Grove (Miss Sheen), Lew Short (Eugene Bromley), George French (Stephen Runyan), Baldy Belmont (Wiggenbottom), Art Reynolds (Claude Lathrop).
Notes: A mysterious gem stolen from an Indian idol exerts a baleful influence on its owners, resulting in several deaths.

Büchse der Pandora, Die *see* ***Pandora's Box***

1097 *Cagliostro* (1928).
Cast: Renee Heribel, Rina De Liguoro.

Chute de la Maison Usher, La *see* ***The Fall of the House of Usher***

1098 *The Coffin Maker* (1928).
Producer/Screenplay: Robert Florey.
Notes: Death and the revived dead are the themes explored.

1099 *The Fall of the House of Usher* (Epstein, 1928). [*La Chute de la Maison Usher*]. France. 55 minutes.
Producer/Director/Screenplay: Jean Epstein (based on *The Fall of the House of Usher* and *The Oval Portrait* by Edgar Allan Poe).
Photography: Lucas Y. Herbert.
Set Design: Pierre Kefer.
Cast: Marguerite Abel Gance, Jean Debucourt, Charles Lamyn.
Notes: Poe has always been a difficult source for filmmakers, since his writings are largely introspective and rely on sustained mood rather than conventional narrative techniques, and the Epstein film, though largely shallow and unsuccessful, suggests that the

The Haunted House (1928).

short feature may be the ideal medium for adapting Poe. As a further example, the 1934 Universal film *The Black Cat,* directed by Edgar G. Ulmer and starring Boris Karloff and Bela Lugosi, sustains a Poe-like mood admirably for the duration of its brief 65 minutes — although, admittedly, the film is weak on character development and has almost nothing to do with Poe's original story.

1100 *The Fall of the House of Usher* (Webber, 1928). 20 minutes.
Screenplay: Melville Webber (based on the story by Edgar Allan Poe).
Photography: James Sibley Watson.
Cast: Melville Webber, Herbert Stem, Hildegarde Watson.

1101 *Goofy Ghosts* (Paramount/Christie, 1928). 2 reels.
Director: Harold Beaudine.
Screenplay: Sig Herzig.
Notes: Spirits cavort in this comedy short.

1102 *Habeas Corpus* (M-G-M/Roach, 1928). 20 minutes.
Director: Leo McCarey.
Cast: Stan Laurel, Oliver Hardy.
Notes: A mad scientist hires Laurel and Hardy to steal corpses from a graveyard in this comedy short.

1103 *The Haunted House* (First National, 1928). 7 reels.
Producer: Wid Gunning.
Director: Benjamin Christensen.
Screenplay: Richard Bee, Lajos Biro.
Titles: William Irish.

The Leopard Lady (1928): Jacqueline Logan, Alan Hale and ape.

Photography: Sol Polito.
Film Editor: Frank Ware.
Cast: Larry Kent (Billy), Thelma Todd (the nurse), Edmund Breese (James Herbert), Sidney Bracy (Tully), Barbara Bedford (Nancy), Flora Finch (Mrs. Rackham), Chester Conklin (Mr. Rackham), William V. Mong (the caretaker), Montagu Love (the mad doctor), Eve Southern (sleepwalking girl), Johnny Gough (Jack the chauffer).

Notes: The Haunted House— complete with a mad doctor, among other horrific characters— was directed by *Witchcraft Through the Ages'* Benjamin Christensen for First National. The screenplay by Richard Bee was adapted from a 1926 three-act stage play by Owen Davis.

1104 *The Leopard Lady*
(Pathé, 1928). 7 reels.
Producer: Bertram Millhauser.
Director: Rupert Julian.
Screenplay: Beulah Marie Dix (based on the play by Edward Childs Carpenter).
Photography: John Mescall.
Film Editor: Claude Berkeley.
Cast: Jacqueline Logan (Paula), Alan Hale (Caesar), Robert Armstrong (Chris), Hedwig Reicher (Fran Holweg), James Bradbury, Sr. (Herman Berlitz), Dick Alexander (Hektor, the lion tamer), William Burt (Presner), Sylvia Ashton (Mama Lolita), Kay Deslys, Willie May Carson (Austrian Maids).

Notes: The Leopard Lady, released by Pathé, starred Jacqueline

Conrad Veidt.

Logan as Paula, a leopard trainer who, working with the police, joins a circus in order to unmask a killer supposedly employed by the travelling show. Eventually, Paula discovers that the murders were the work of a gorilla, controlled by villainous animal trainer Alan Hale.

Directed by Rupert Julian and scripted by Beulah Marie Dix and scripted by Beulah Marie Dix from a play by Edward Childs Carpenter, the film seems oddly similar, in general plot, to the much later and similarly titled Val Lewton horror film *The Leopard Man* (1943).

Reviews: "Film features like this don't make it tough for the opposition. Here's a mystery thriller that's a perfect fit for the third-grade houses. ... Johnny Mescall ... has tricked up the photography to snare early attention, and Rupert Julian, directing, has undone that good work by stringing out, endlessly, a deal between the secret service head and Miss Logan, which takes place in the latter's dressing room. Very dramatic most all the way, Miss Logan, like the rest, is prone to overplay. A much hoked dramatic release that occasionally shows flashes of what it might have been." — *Variety,* February 29, 1928.

1105 *The Lost Whirl* (Bray, 1928). 15 minutes.
Director: Glen Lambert.
Screenplay: Glen Lambert, Frank Terry.
Model Animation: J. L. Roop.
Notes: This comedy short was a parody of *The Lost World* (1925), complete with an animated dinosaur.

1106 *The Man Who Laughs* (Universal, 1928). 10 reels.
Producer: Carl Laemmle.
Director: Paul Leni.
Production Supervisor: Paul Kohner.
Screenplay: J. Grubb Alexander and (uncredited) Charles E. Whittaker, Marion Ward, May McLean (based on the novel *L'Homme Qui Rit* by Victor Hugo).
Story Supervision: Dr. Bela Sekely.
Titles: Walter Anthony.
Photography: Gilbert Warrenton.
Film Editors: Maurice Pivar, Edward Cahn.
Art Direction: Charles D. Hall, Joseph Wright, Thomas F. O'Neill.
Costumes: David Cox, Vera West.
Song Lyrics: "When Love Comes Stealing," by Walter Hirsch, Lew Pollack, Erno Rapee.
Production Staff: John M. Voshell, Jay Merchant, Louis Friedlander.
Technical Research: R. H. Newlands.
Cast: Conrad Veidt (Gwynplaine), Mary Philbin (Dea), Olga Baclanova (Duchess Josiana), Josephine Crowell (Queen Anne), George Siegmann (Dr. Hardquanone), Brandon Hurst (Barkiphedro, the jester), Sam De Grasse (King James II), Stuart Holmes (Lord Dirry Noir), Cesare Gravina (Ursus), Nick De Ruiz (Wapentake), Edgar Norton (Lord High Chancellor), Torben Meyer (the spy), Julius Molnar, Jr. (Gwynplaine, as a child), Charles Puffy (Innkeeper), Frank Puglia, Jack Goodrich (clowns), Carmen Costello (Dea's mother), Zimbo (Homo, the wolf), Lon Poff.
Notes: Although not exactly a horror film, Universal's *The Man Who Laughs* certainly has enough visual scares to merit its inclusion here. With *The Hunchback of Notre*

The Man Who Laughs (1928): Conrad Veidt and Mary Philbin.

Dame, The Man Who Laughs (also based on a novel by Victor Hugo), is one of Universal's most expensive and prestigious films of the 1920s, produced on a grand scale that overshadows any of the studio's 1930s horror pictures.

Conrad Veidt is Gwynplaine, who as a child was tortured and mutilated by bandits so that his face is locked in a permanent, hideous grin; he is in love with Dea (Mary Philbin), a blind girl who can see only the beauty of his soul. Ultimately, Gwynplaine and Dea are separated when it is learned that he is of noble ancestry, but after various developments, including court intrigue and the attempted seduction of Gwynplaine by a lustful countess (Olga Baclanova), the unlikely lovers are reunited at the fade-out.

A sprawling historical melodrama with a wealth of convincing historical detail, *The Man Who Laughs* was beautifully photographed by Gilbert Warrenton, and it is director Paul Leni's glossiest, most polished film. One interesting aspect of Universal's movies during this period that is seldom discussed is their geographic conviction. It seems hard to believe that *The Man Who Laughs,* as well as *The Hunchback of Notre Dame* and such later classics as *Dracula* and *The Invisible Man* were all filmed on the same back lot, so convincing is their

The Man Who Laughs (1928): Conrad Vedit.

sense of time and place, and this close attention to detail is a real tribute to the photographers and set designers involved.

Although Conrad Veidt is excellent as Gwynplaine, his performance seems a little too remote and understated for material as rich as this, and it is possible that Lon Chaney could have brought more passion and energy to the role if he had been cast instead.

Cartoonist Bob Kane, the creator of Batman, has admitted that

Veidt's eternally grinning visage in *The Man Who Laughs* was a major influence in the creation of Batman's grotesque foe The Joker.
Reviews: "The toothy clown with his perpetual grin makes an interesting, if gruesome character. The grin makes it difficult for Conrad Vedit to do much acting. Glycerine tears do not quite succeed in conveying soul torture nor in creating romantic illusion. *The Man Who Laughs* will appeal to the Lon Chaney mob and to those who like quasi-morbid plot themes. To others it will seem fairly interesting, a trifle unpleasant, and intermittently tedious. ... Mary Philbin, incidentally, is zero in this picture. Any pretty girl would have done as well. ... Production, direction and photography are excellent. Indeed, the ... work of Paul Leni puts the picture over even where the script leaves loose ends...." — *Variety*, May 2, 1928.
"... [A] gruesome tale in which the horror is possibly moderated but none the less disturbing... Mr. Leni's handling of the subject is in many passages quite expert, for he revels in light and shadows, and takes advantage of the full details of a man, who, through mutilation ... goes through life with a hideous grin on his countenance. This part is portrayed with astounding cleverness by Conrad Veidt ... part of the time he covers his abnormal mouth, but on other occasions, through wearing huge false teeth, Mr. Veidt sends a chill down one's spine." — *The New York Times*, April 28, 1928.

1107 *The Mystic Mirror* (UFA, 1928). Germany.
Director/Photography: Carl Hoffman.
Cast: Fritz Rasp, Felicitas Malten, Rina de Kigoure.
Notes: When the moon rises, a magical mirror in an old castle predicts the future through visions.

1108 *Pandora's Box* (Nero/Moviegraphs, 1928). [*Die Büchse der Pandora*]. Germany. 9 reels.
Producer: George C. Horsetzky.
Director: G. W. Pabst.
Screenplay: Ladislaus Vajda (based on the plays *Erdgeist* and *Die Büchse der Pandora* by Frank Wedekind).
Titles: Joseph R. Fliesler.
Photographer: Gunther Krampf.
Film Editor: Joseph R. Fliesler.
Art Direction: Andrei Andreiev.
Costumes: Gottlieb Hesch.
Cast: Louise Brooks (Lulu), Fritz Kortner (Dr. Peter Schon), Franz Lederer (Alwa Schon, his son), Carl Gotz (Schigolch/Papa Brommer), Alice Roberts (Countess Anna Geschwitz), Daisy d'Ora (Marie de Zarniko), Kraft Rashig (Rodrigo Quast), Michael von Newlinsky (Marquis Cast-Piani), Siegfried Arno (the stage manager), Gustav Diessi (Jack the Ripper).
Notes: A promiscuous young woman, after ruining the lives of those around her, meets her end at the hands of Jack the Ripper. Remarkable for Pabst's incisive direction and Brooks' remarkable performance in the lead.

1109 *Phantom City* (First National, 1928). 6 reels.

Director: Albert Rogell.
Screenplay: Adele Buffington.
Photography: Harry J. Brown.
Cast: Ken Maynard, James Mason, Eugenia Gilbert, Jackie Coombs, Jack McDonald.
Notes: In this horrific western, a town is haunted by a black-robed phantom.

1110 *Sweeney Todd* (Ideal, 1928). Great Britain. 7 reels.
Director: Walter West.
Cast: Moore Marriott (Sweeney Todd), Zoe Palmer, Charles Ashton, Iris Darbyshire, Judd Green.
Notes: A homicidal barber bakes meat pies from the bodies of his victims. Incredibly, later a successful musical on stage!

1111 *The Tell-Tale Heart* (1928).
Director/Screenplay: Charles Klein (based on the story by Edgar Allan Poe).
Photography: Leon Shamroy.
Cast: Otto Matiesen, Darvas.
Notes: A guilt-ridden murderer is haunted by the imagined beating of his victim's heart.

1112 *The Terrible People* (Pathé, 1928). 10 chapter serial.
Director: Spencer Gordon Bennet.
Cast: Ailene Ray, Walter Miller, Wilfred North.
Notes: A ghost-like villain with monstrous clawed hands is featured.

1113 *Terror* (FBO, 1928). 55 minutes.
Director: Louis King.
Screenplay: Wyndham Gittens.
Continuity: F. H. Clark.
Titles: Helen Gregg.
Photography: Nicholas Musuraca.
Cast: Tom Tyler, Jane Reid, Al Ferguson, Frankie Darro.
Notes: Ghostly figures are seen around a deserted house in this horror-western.

1114 *The Thief in the Dark* (Fox, 1928). 6 reels.
Director: Albert Ray.
Screenplay: C. Graham Baker (story by Andrew Bennison, Albert Ray, Kenneth Hawks).
Titles: William Kernell.
Photography: Arthur Edeson.
Cast: George Meeker, Doris Hill, Gwen Lee, Marjorie Beebe.
Notes: A haunted house with sliding wall panels and secret passages and fake spiritualists are featured. Some scenes were tinted.

1115 *West of Zanzibar* (M-G-M, 1928). 7 reels.
Director: Tod Browning.
Screenplay: Elliott Clawson, Waldemar Young (based on a story by Chester De Vonde, Kilbourne Gordon).
Titles: Joe Farnham.
Photography: Percy Hilburn.
Film Editor: Harry Reynolds.
Set Designer: Cedric Gibbons.
Cast: Lon Chaney (Phroso/Flint), Lionel Barrymore (Crane), Warner Baxter (Doc), Mary Nolan (Maizie), Jane Daly (Anna), Roscoe Ward (Tiny), Kalia Pasha (Babe), Curtis Nero (Bumbo), Jacqueline Gadsdon (Anna).

West of Zanzibar (1928): **Lon Chaney plots revenge.**

Notes: The Lon Chaney vehicle *West of Zanzaibar,* directed by Tod Browning for M-G-M, featured Chaney as a vaudeville magician who, his fiancée stolen by Lionel Barrymore, is crippled when the two rivals clash in a fight. The story then picks up with Chaney relocated in a jungle outpost, operating as a trader and dominating the natives with his old magic tricks. Having lost the use of his legs, Chaney dreams of revenge on Barrymore, which he achieves by

West of Zanzibar (1928): Lon Chaney, with Warner Baxter (center).

luring Barrymore's daughter into his sphere of influence, then degrading her and turning her into a prostitute. Eventually, Chaney discovers that the girl is actually *his* daughter, and gives up his own life at the hands of rebelling natives so that she can escape with an associate of Chaney's, a reformed alcoholic doctor who loves her. Synchronized music and sound effects were added.

The Chaney-Browning films are almost always excessively morbid and depressing, but *West of Zanzibar* is at least buoyed periodically by its black (very black) humor, and Chaney is a joy to watch. His character is so malevolent and perverse, and his performance so emotionally intense, that he manages to almost completely overshadow a very capable supporting cast. Warner Baxter is very good as the washed-up doctor ruined by drink and (by implication) drug addiction, and Mary Nolan is outstanding as the degraded girl.

Nolan's sexual exploitation is also implied rather than openly stated, but the film gets away with a lot through implication, and this is probably one of the rawest dramas ever made in Hollywood before censorship was tightened in the mid-thirties.

West of Zanzibar was remade as a talkie, *Kongo*, with Walter Huston in the Chaney role in 1932.

Reviews: "*West of Zanzibar*

indicates an over-worked Chaney. The star is there, but the rush of getting his quota on the release schedule is taking its toll in the most important phase of production-preparation. . . . Jungle scenes with crocodiles oozing through slime and a score or so of vaselined black extras doing their dances and attending to their funeral pyres are what will get this by."—*Variety,* January 9, 1929.

"In a grim, ingenious, but somewhat artificial tale, with a background of an African swamp festooned with cannibals, Lon Chaney once again returns to the impersonation of a cripple. . . . It is a well-concocted narrative and Mr. Chaney gives one of his most able and effective portrayals as he drags himself through scene after scene without using his legs. Warner Baxter acts the role of a derelict doctor. . . . Mr. Baxter handles this part with considerable artistry. Miss Nolan is attractive and competent."—*The New York Times,* December 31, 1928.

1929

1116 ***Buster's Spooks*** (Universal, 1929). 2 reels.
Director: Sam Newfield.
Notes: An entry in the *Buster Brown* series, based on the comic strip character. A haunted house is featured.

1117 ***Cagliostro*** (1929). Germany.
Director: Richard Oswald.
Cast: Alfred Abel.

1118 ***The Faker*** (Columbia, 1929). 6 reels.
Director: Phil Rosen.
Screenplay: Howard J. Green.
Photography: Ted Tetzlaff.
Art Direction: Harrison Wiley.
Film Editor: William Hamilton.
Cast: Warner Oland, Jacqueline Logan, Charles Delaney, Fred Kelsey, Gaston Glass, Flora Finch, Charles Mailes.
Notes: Harry Cohn's newly established Columbia Pictures produced this melodrama about a fake spiritualist.

1119 ***The Fire Detective*** (Pathé, 1929). 10 chapter serial.
Directors: Spencer Gordon Bennet, Thomas L. Storey.
Cast: Gladys McConnell, Hugh Allan, Frank Lackteen.
Notes: Chapter 7 of this cliffhanger featured a beastial apeman.

Frau im Mond, Die *see* ***The Woman in the Moon***

1120 The House of Horror

(First National, 1929). 7 reels.
Producer: Richard A. Rowland.
Director: Benjamin Christensen.
Screenplay/Story: Richard Bee.
Dialogue: William Irish.
Titles: Tom Miranda.
Photography: Ernest Haller, Sol Polito.
Film Editor: Frank Ware.
Music Score: Louis Silvers.
Cast: Louise Fazenda (Louise), Chester Conklin (Chester), James Ford (Joe), Thelma Todd (Thelma), William V. Mong (Mystery Man), Emile Chautard (Old Miser), William Orlamond (Miller), Dale Fuller (Gladys), Tenen Holtz (Brown), Michael Visaroff (Chauffeur).

Notes: Although nominally a sound film, First National's *The House of Horror* only contained one dialogue sequence and was 99 percent silent. Directed by Benjamin Christensen and scripted by Richard Bee, the story recalled Christensen's *Seven Footprints to Satan* in that the horrific mystery involved (concerning a haunted mansion and a missing diamond) is weakened and almost casually dismissed at the picture's conclusion.

Review: "*The House of Horror* is one of the weakest and most boring afterbirths of pseudo-mystery-comedy ground out of Hollywood. ... If the thing ever had a script Christensen apparently never knew it, judging strictly from the finished product...."—*Variety,* June 19, 1929.

1121 The Last Performance

(Universal, 1929). 7 reels.
Producer: Carl Laemmle.
Director: Paul Fejos.
Production Supervisor: Carl Laemmle, Jr.
Screenplay: James Ashmore Creelman.
Titles: Walter Anthony, Tom Reed.
Photography: Hal Mohr.
Film Editors: Edward Cahn, Robert Carlisle, Robert Jaans.
Cast: Conrad Veidt (Erik, the Great), Mary Philbin (Julie), Leslie Fenton (Buffo), Fred MacKaye (Mark Royce), Gustav Partos (theatre manager), William H. Turner (booking agent), Anders Randoe (judge), Sam De Grasse (district attorney), George Irving (defense attorney).

Notes: In Universal's *The Last Performance,* Conrad Veidt starred as a master magician in love with a young woman (Mary Philbin) appearing in his show. Jealous because she loves another, younger member of the troupe (Fred MacKaye), Veidt plans to murder her lover, but only succeeds in killing his own assistant (Leslie Fenton) instead. The police arrest MacKaye for the crime, but he is exonerated when Veidt confesses, before committing suicide. *The Last Performance* was directed by Paul Fejos and was shot by Hal Mohr on some of the standing sets from *The Phantom of the Opera.* Those same *Phantom* sets were dusted off again for Universal's similarly titled *The Last Warning,* a talkie, directed by Paul Leni that same year just before his untimely death from blood poisoning. A spoof horror yarn in a theatrical setting, the film was hardly worthy of Leni's talents, although cameraman Hal Mohr of *The Last Performance* did manage to keep the proceedings visually interesting. Laura LaPlante, Montagu Love and Roy D'Arcy starred.

1122 Little Red Riding Hood (1929). [*Le Petit Chaperon Rouge*]. France.
Director/Screenplay: Alberto Cavalcanti.
Cast: Catherine Hessling, Jean Renoir.

Petit Chaperon Rouge, Le see **Little Red Riding Hood**

1123 Queen of the North Woods (Pathé, 1929). 10 chapter serial.
Directors: Spencer Gordon Bennet, Thomas L. Storey.
Cast: Ethlyne Clair, Walter Miller.
Notes: A beastial wolf-devil and a cult of devil worshippers are featured in this cliffhanger.

1124 Seven Footprints to Satan (First National, 1929). 6 reels.
Producer: Wid Gunning.
Director: Benjamin Christensen.
Screenplay: Richard Bee (based on a story by Abraham Merritt).
Titles: William Irish.
Photography: Sol Polito.
Film Editor: Frank Ware.
Cast: Thelma Todd (Eve), Creighton Hale (Jim), William V. Mong (the professor), Sheldon Lewis (the spider), Sojin (himself), Laska Winters (Satan's Mostress), Ivan Christy (Jim's valet), DeWitt Jennings (Uncle Joe), Nora Cecil (Old Witch), Kalla Pasha (Professor Von Viede), Harry Tenbrooke (Eve's chauffer), Cissy Fitzgerald (Old Lady), Alonzo (Angelo) Rositto (the dwarf), Thelma McNeill (tall girl).
Notes: Released by First National as a follow-up to *The Haunted House* (1928), *Seven Footprints to Satan,* also directed by Benjamin Christensen, offered the panoply of dazzling images one would expect from the man who had filmed *Witchcraft Through the Ages* (*q.v.*). The story follows heroic young Creighton Hale and his pretty girlfriend Thelma Todd as they search for a missing gem in a spook-infested castle; unfortunately, the plot crumbles with the usual denouement revealing the accumulated horrors (a gorilla, witches, assorted maniacs, etc.) to be fakes, staged as an elaborate joke on Hale, a resolution made all the more disappointing by the sophisticated visuals (photographed by Sol Polito) employed in their presentation. Abraham Merritt's original novel (which did *not* have the film's "cheater" ending) was adapted by scenarist Richard Bee (who had also scripted *The Haunted House*); Sheldon Lewis (doing his patented "Mr. Hyde" monster act) and William V. Mong costarred with Hale and Todd. The film had synchronized music and sound effects.
Review: "Another of those fright producers, wholly baffling from start to finish. Elucidation of mystery which encompasses the production reveals the salacious scenes a frame-up, which doubtless accounts for its not being censored.

Seven Footprints to Satan (1929): Sheldon Lewis (right foreground) threatens Thelma Todd.

A midget, a gorilla and a demon in the guise of Satan, who is operating a secret society, comprise some of the terrors. ... All hokum." – *Variety,* April 24, 1929.

1125 *The Silent House* (Butchers, 1929). Great Britain. 95 minutes.
Alternate title: The House of Silence.
Producer: Archibald Nettlefold.
Director: Walter Forde.
Cast: Frank Perfitt, Arthur Pusey, Mabel Poulton, Gibb McLaughlin, Arthur Stratton.
Notes: Hypnotism, clutching hands, and a haunted house with a secret panel for concealing corpses and a snake pit are featured in this grand-guignol horror tale.

1126 *Tarzan the Tiger* (Universal, 1929). 15 chapter serial.
Director: Henry MacRae.
Screenplay: Ian Heath (based on the novel *Tarzan and the Jewels of Opar* by Edgar Rice Burroughs).
Photography: Wilfred Cline.
Cast: Frank Merrill (Tarzan, Lord Greystoke), Natalie Kingston (Jane).
Notes: A hidden city populated by beastmen was featured in this excellent adaptation of Edgar Rice Burrough's character.

1127 *The Unholy Night* (M-G-M, 1929).
Director: Lionel Barrymore.
Screenplay: Dorothy Farnum, Edwin Justus Mayer (story by Ben Hecht).

Where East Is East (1929): Estelle Taylor and Lon Chaney.

Photography: Ira Morgan.
Cast: Ernest Torrence, Dorothy Sebastian, Roland Young, Natalie Moorhead, Polly Moran, Sojin, Sidney Jarvis, George Cooper, John Miljan, Boris Karloff, John Loder, Lionel Belmore, John Roche, Richard Tucker, Philip Strange, Claude Fleming, Gerard Barry, Clarence Geldert.

The Woman in the Moon (1929): A rocket ship blasts off from the moon.

Notes: This melodramatic but rather tame detective mystery relied almost entirely on dialogue to advance its plot; Boris Karloff, who would rise to fame two years later in *Frankenstein,* is among the supporting players.

1128 *Where East Is East*

(M-G-M, 1929). 7 reels.
Director: Tod Browning.
Screenplay: Richard Schayer, Waldemar Young (based on a story by Henry Sinclair Drago and Tod Browning).
Titles: Joe Farnham.
Photography: Henry Sharp.
Film Editor: Harry Reynolds.
Art Direction: Cedric Gibbons.
Costumes: David Cox.
Cast: Lon Chaney (Tiger Haynes), Lupe Velez (Toyo), Estelle Taylor (Mme. deSylva), Lloyd Hughes (Bobby Bailey), Louis Stern (Father Angelo), Mrs. Wong Wing (Ming), Duke Kahanamoku (wild animal trainer), Richard R. Neil.

Notes: Yet another Chaney-Browning excursion into unrelenting morbidity, *Where East Is East* starred Chaney as Tiger Haynes, a wild animal trapper hideously scarred by his jungle exploits. When Chaney's wife (Estelle Taylor) callously seduces the fiancé (Lloyd Hughes) of their daugher (Lupe Velez), Chaney vengefully sics a wild gorilla on her as punishment, but, after he relents and tries to save her from the ape, Chaney is mauled instead.

Review: "Lon Chaney pictures might be described as romantic adventure yarns written and directed by Tod Browning with the hero scarred, crippled, or at least horribly embittered, and the background as exotic as a diligent search of the Atlas can discover. Most of the Chaneys make money, some, of course, being better than others. *Where East Is East* is one of the better efforts. Chaney himself is rather subordinated, with the picture belonging to Estelle Taylor and Lupe Velez as mother and daughter, respectively. Theme, rather than any twist of plot, holds the attention. From the instant a close-up and caption calls attention to a captive gorilla, the smart pupils will easily and correctly surmise that it is the plot function of this gorilla to remove the evil woman at the critical moment. Locale is Indo-China. ... There are elephants, coolies, rickshaws, jungle, river boats, and Lupe Velez in form-revealing costumes." — *Variety,* May 29, 1929.

1129 *The Witching Eyes*

(Ernest Stern, 1929). Feature-length assumed but unverified.

Screenplay: Ernest Stern.

Notes: A Haitian voodoo witch doctor, lusting after the daughter of a recently deceased Negro leader, puts a curse on a poet she is in love with in order to claim her for himself.

1130 *The Woman in the Moon* (UFA, 1929). [*Die Frau im Mond*]. Germany. 120 minutes.

Alternate titles: Girl in the Moon; By Rocket to the Moon.

Director: Fritz Lang.

Screenplay: Fritz Lang, Thea von Harbou.

Photography: Kurt Courant, Oskar Fischinger, Otto Kanturek.

Art Direction: Otto Hunte, Emil Hasler, Karl Volbrecht.

Special Effects: Konstantin Tschetwerikoff.

Technical Consultants: Hermann Oberth, Willy Ley.

Cast: Gerda Maurus, Willy Fritsch, Gustav von Wangenheim, Klaus Pohl, Margaret Kuper.

Notes: Fritz Lang directed the German film *Woman in the Moon* (*Die Frau im Mond*) for release by UFA. Lang co-wrote the screenplay with wife Thea von Harbou; the story relates the construction of a spaceship and the subsequent lunar voyage, which takes on overtones of *Treasure of the Sierra Madre* when gold is discovered on the moon. In this film, Lang predicted the 10-9-8-7, etc. launch countdown later used for actual spaceflights, which he confessed years afterward was merely an attempt to be melodramatic rather than scientific.

Review: "Many models are used and are skillfully photographed. ... Unfortunately the human beings concerned in these exploits can't compete with the machines." — *Variety,* November 13, 1929.

EPILOGUE

Although silent movies continued to be made on into 1929, sound came to the horror film with *The Terror,* released by Warner Bros. in 1928. Warners had revolutionized the motion picture industry and ushered in the sound era with *The Jazz Singer,* starring Al Jolson, in 1927. Although largely a *silent* film with a synchronized music score and only a few scenes containing actual speech, the dialogue portions of *The Jazz Singer* electrified audiences, and the proverbial handwriting was on the wall — silent movies were on their way out. Warners made the first all-talking film, *The Lights of New York,* in 1928, followed by *The Terror* the same year.

Adapted from a derivative mystery play by Edgar Wallace, *The Terror* dealt with a *Phantom of the Opera*-type maniac who terrorizes guests in an isolated English mansion. The film was stiff and crude, even in its day, with plenty of redundant dialogue, arch overacting, static camerawork and (for a story that took place in England) unintentionally hilarious Brooklyn accents. Nevertheless, this film was the first synchronized sound movie of its type, and remains significant, if only for this historical fact.

BIBLIOGRAPHY

The American Film Institute Catalog of Motion Pictures. Feature Films (1911-1920); Univ. of California Press, 1988.
The American Film Institute Catalog of Motion Pictures. Feature Films (1921-1930); R. R. Bowker Company, 1971.
Cinema of the Fatastic by Chris Steinbrunner and Burt Goldblatt. Saturday Review Press, NY, 1972.
Classics of the Horror Film by William K. Everson. Citadel Press, Secaucus, N.J., 1974.
The Dead That Walk by Leslie Halliwell. Continuum, N.Y., 1988.
The Encyclopedia of Horror Movies, edited by Phil Hardy; Harper & Row, 1986.
Films of Science Fiction and Fantasy by Baird Searles. AFI Press/Harry F. Abrams, Inc., N.Y., 1988.
Horror and Science Fiction Films: A Checklist by Donald C. Willis. Scarecrow Press, 1972.
Horror and Science Fiction Films II by Donald C. Willis. Scarecrow Press, 1982.
Horror and Science Fiction Films III by Donald C. Willis. Scarecrow Press, 1984.
The Hunchback of Notre Dame, edited by Phillip J. Reilly. Magicimage Filmbooks, Hollywood/Atlantic City, 1988.
An Illustrated History of the Horror Film by Carlos Clarens. G. P. Putnam, N.Y., 1967.
The Library of Congress. Motion Picture Copyright Listings.
More Classics of the Horror Film by William K. Everson. Citadel Press, Secaucus, N.J., 1986.
The Motion Picture Guide. Volume X: Silent Films by Robert Connelly. Cinebooks, Inc., 1986.

TITLE INDEX

References are to entry numbers except those in italics which refer to pages with photographs.

À la Conquête du Pôle *see* The Conquest of the North Pole
Aaron's Rod 953
The Accursed Cavern 10
Adventures of Pimple Trilby 531
The Adventures of Three Nights 437
Aelita 996
After Death 438
After the Welsh Rarebit 439
The Agony of Fear 616
The Airman's Enemy 440
The Alchemist 441
The Alchemist's Hallucination 4
Algol 852
Alice's Spooky Adventure 997
Alladin and the Wonderful Lamp (1906) 77
Alladin and the Wonderful Lamp (1917) 775
Alone with the Devil 532
Along the Moonbeam Trail 853
Alraune (1918 Neutral) 816
Alraune (1918 Phoenix) 817
Alraune (1928) 1094
American Suicide Club 229
An Ancestor's Legacy 533
The Ancient Roman 162
Andalusian Superstition 365
Das Ander Ich *see* The Other Self (1918)
Der Andere *see* The Other
Anita 854
Another's Ghost 230
The Ape 1095
An Apish Trick 163
The Apparition 44

The Arrow Maiden 712
The Astronomer's Dream 11
At the Sign of the Jack o' Lantern 924
At the Sign of the Three Socks 618
Atlantis 442
Au Secours! 954
L'Auberge Ensorcelée *see* The Bewitched Inn
Die Augen der Mumie Ma *see* The Eyes of the Mummy
Aunt Eliza Recovers Her Pet 109
Avarice 776
The Avenging Conscience 534; *page 61*
The Avenging Hand *see* The Wraith of the Tomb
The Avenging Specter 535

Babes in the Woods (1907) 87
Babes in the Woods (1913) 443
Babes in the Woods (1917) 777
Babes in the Woods (1925) 1025
The Baby's Ghost 305
Bachelor Brides 1047
Back to Life After 2,000 Years 231
Balaoo 444
Balaoo; ou, Des Pas au Plafond *see* Balaoo
Balaoo, the Demon Baboon *see* Balaoo
The Ballad of a Witch 164
La Ballata di una Strega *see* The Ballad of a Witch
Baron Munchausen 306

Title Index

Baron Munchausen's Dream 307
The Barton Mystery 855
The Basilisk 536
The Bat 1048; *page 184*
Beauty and the Beast (1899) 18
Beauty and the Beast (1905) 66
Beauty and the Beast (1908) 110
Beauty and the Beast (1913) 445
Beauty and the Beast (1916) 713
The Beauty of the Sleeping Woods 111
Bebe and Spiritualism 366
Bébé Fait du Spiritisme *see* Bebe and Spiritualism
The Bee and the Rose 112
The Beechwood Ghost 232
Beelzebub's Daughters 45
The Beetle 830
Behind the Curtain 998
Le Belle au Bois Dormant *see* Sleeping Beauty (1902)
Le Belle au Bois Dormant *see* The Beauty of the Sleeping Woods
The Bells (1913) 446
The Bells (1914 Gaumont) 537
The Bells (1914 Sawyers) 538
The Bells (1918) 818
The Bells (1926) 1049; *page 185*
Beneath the Tower Ruins 308
Bertie's Book of Magic 367
Between Worlds *see* The Weary Death
The Bewildering Cabinet 88
The Bewitched Inn 5
The Bewitched Manor House 165
The Bewitched Matches 447
The Bewitched Messenger 233
The Bewitched Traveller 59
The Bewitched Window 309
Beyond the Wall *see* The Weary Death
Das Bildnis des Dorian Gray *see* The Picture of Dorian Gray (1917 German)
Bill Bumper's Bargain 310
Bill Taken for a Ghost 311
Billy Gets Married *see* The Haunted Honeymoon
Billy's Séance 368
The Bishop of the Ozarks 955
The Black Box 618

The Black Crook 619
The Black Imp 67
Black Magic 714
The Black Opal 448
Black Orchids 715
Black Oxen 956
The Black Pear 1096
Black Shadows 856
Blade am Satan's Bog *see* Leaves from Satan's Book
A Blind Bargain 925; *page 130*
The Blood Seedling 620
Blood Vengeance 312
The Bloodstone 113
Bloomer as a Ghost 449
Bobby, "Some" Spiritualist 369
The Bogey Woman 166
The Bogus Ghost 716
Boîte à Malice *see* The Trick Box
Un Bon Lit *see* A Midnight Episode
Bonzolino 999
Le Bourreau Turc *see* The Terrible Turkish Executioner
Brand of Evil 450
Brand of Satan 778
The Bribe 621
The Bride of Mystery 539
The Bride of the Haunted Castle 234
The Bridge of Time 622
The Brute 371
Der Bucklige und der Tänzerin *see* The Hunchback and the Dancer
The Budda's Curse 235
Die Büchse der Pandora *see* Pandora's Box
Buster's Spooks 1116
The Butcher's Dream 167
By Rocket to the Moon *see* The Woman in the Moon
By the House That Jack Built 313

The Cabinet of Dr. Caligari 831; *pages 98, 99, 100, 102*
The Cafe l'Egypte 1000
Cagliostro (1910) 236
Cagliostro (1920) 857
Cagliostro (1928) 1097
Cagliostro (1929) 1117
Les Cake-Walk Infernal *see* The Infernal Cake Walk

Title Index

Call from the Dead 623
The Call of Siva 957
Capturing the North Pole 168
The Cardboard Box 958
The Case of Becky 624
The Castle Ghost 237
The Castle Ghosts 114
The Cat and the Canary 1072; *pages 200, 201*
The Cat That Was Changed into a Woman 169
The Cat's Revenge 115
Le Cauchemar du Fantoche *see* Fantoche's Nightmare
The Cavalier's Dream 12
The Cave Dweller's Romance 451
La Caverne Maudite *see* The Accursed Cavern
Chamber of Horrors 717
The Chamber of Horrors *see* Conscience (1912)
Les Chauldron Infernal *see* The Infernal Cauldron and the Phantasmal Vapors
La Chatte Métamorphosée en Femme *see* The Cat That Changed into a Woman
The Cheval Mystery 625
Le Chien des Baskerville *see* The Hound of the Baskervilles (1914 French)
The Chimes 540
Chinese Magic 26
The Chinese Parrot 1073
A Christmas Carol (1908) 116
A Christmas Carol (1910) 238
A Christmas Carol (1914) 541
The Chronicle of the Gray House 959
Chronicles of Bloom Center 626
Chronik von Grieshuus *see* The Chronicle of the Gray House
La Chute de la Maison Usher *see* The Fall of the House of Usher
The Circular Staircase 627
Cléopâtra 19
Cleopatra's Tomb *see* Cleopatra
Cleopatre *see* Cleopatra
The Clock-Maker's Secret 89
The Clown and the Alchemist 27
The Clown Hero 452

The Club Pest 628
The Clue of the Pigtail 960
The Coffin Maker 1098
Col. Heeza Liar and the Ghost 961
Col. Heeza Liar, Ghost Breaker 629
Col. Heeza Liar in the Haunted House 630
Colonne de Feu *see* The Column of Fire
The Column of Fire 20
Conjuring a Lady at Robert Houdin's 1
The Conquering Power 893
The Conquest of the North Pole 372
Conscience (1912) 373
Conscience (1917) 779
The Conscience 68
The Convict Guardian's Nightmare 78
Convicted by Hypnotism 374
The Cook in Trouble 60
The Corsican Brothers 13
The Coughing Horror 1001
Countess Ankarstrom 239
Cragmire Tower 1002
Crime and Penalty 718
Le Crime de Lord Arthur Savile *see* Lord Arthur Savile's Crime
The Crimson Moth 542
The Crimson Stain Mystery 719; *page 81*
A Cry in the Night 631
The Cry of the Night Hawk 962
The Curse of the Crimson Idol 543
The Curse of the Hindoo Pearl 375
Curse of the Lake 376
The Curse of the Scarabee Ruby 544
The Curse of the Wandering Minstrel 314

La Dama di Picche *see* Queen of Spades
The Damnation of Faust 46
Dance of Death 832
The Dance of Fire 170
Dandy Dick of Bishopgate 315

Title Index

Danse Macabre 926
Dante's Inferno (1909) 171
Dante's Inferno (1924) 1003; *pages 160, 161*
Dante's Purgatorio 453
The Dark Mirror 858
The Darling of Paris 780; *page 90*
Davy Jones' Locker 47
The Dawn of Freedom 720
The Dead Alive 721
The Dead Man Who Killed 454
The Dead Secret 465
A Deal in Real Estate 545
A Deal with the Devil (1914) 546
A Deal with the Devil (1916) 722
Death (1911) 316
Death (1921) 894
The Death Kiss 723
The Death Stone of India 456
La Défaite de Satan *see* The Defeat of Satan
The Defeat of Satan 172
The Demon 317
The Demon of Dunkirque 240
D'Épouvante *see* Island of Terror
Desire 859
Destiny *see* The Weary Death
Destiny's Skein 632
The Detachable Man 241
The Devil (1908) 117
The Devil (1909) 173
The Devil (1910) 242
The Devil (1915) 633
The Devil (1921) 895
The Devil and the Gambler 118
The Devil and Tom Walker 457
The Devil as a Lawyer 318
The Devil in a Convent 21
The Devil-Stone 781
The Devil's Assistant 782
The Devil's Locksmith 833
The Devil's Manor *see* The Haunted Castle (1896)
The Devil's Mother-in-Law 243
The Devil's Profession 634
The Devil's Sonata 319
The Devil's Three Songs 119
The Devil's Toy 724
La Diable au Convent *see* The Devil in a Convent
The Diabolical Box 377

The Diabolical Lodger *see* The Diabolical Tenant
The Diabolical Tenant 174
Diamond of Disaster 547
The Dinosaur and the Missing Link 783
Distilled Spirits 635
Do the Dead Talk? 834
Docteur Goudron et le Professeur Plume *see* The System of Dr. Tarr and Professor Fether
Docteur Tube; Story of a Madman *see* The Madness of Dr. Tube
Dr. Charlie Is a Great Surgeon 320
Doctor Goudron's Secret *see* The System of Dr. Tarr and Professor Fether
Dr. Hallin 896
Dr. Jekyll and Mr. Hyde (1908) 120
Dr. Jekyll and Mr. Hyde (1909) 175
Dr. Jekyll and Mr. Hyde (1911) 321
Dr. Jekyll and Mr. Hyde (1913, Imp) 458
Dr. Jekyll and Mr. Hyde (1913, Kineto-Kinemacolor) 459
Dr. Jekyll and Mr. Hyde (1920, Arrow) 860
Dr. Jekyll and Mr. Hyde (1920, Paramount) 861; *pages 110, 111*
Dr. Jekyll and Mr. Hyde (1920, Pioneer) 862
Dr. Jekyll and Mr. Hyde (1925) 1026
Dr. Jekyll and Mr. Hyde Done to a Frazzle 548
Doctor Mabuse 927
Dr. Messner's Fatal Prescription 244
Dr. Nicola in Tibet *see* The Mystery of the Lama Convent
Doctor Polly 549
Dr. Pyckle and Mr. Pryde 1027
Dr. Trimball's Verdict 460
The Doctor's Experiment 121
Doctor's Secret 176
The Dollar-a-Year Man 897
The Doll's Revenge 90
Don Juan and Faust 928
Don Juan's Compact 461
Doomed 177
Dopo la Morte *see* After Death

Title Index

Der Dorfgolem *see* The Golem's Last Adventure
Double Duds 725
Drama au Château d'Acre; ou, Les Morts Reviennet-Ils *see* A Drama of the Castle; or, Do the Dead Return?
A Drama of the Castle; or, Do the Dead Return 378
The Dream Cheater 863
The Dream Dance 636
The Dream of an Opium Fiend 122
The Dream of Old Scrooge 245
Drums of Jeopardy 963
D.T.s or the Effects of Drink 69
The Duality of Man 246
The Duel in the Dark 637
The Dust of Egypt 638

The Egyptian Mummy (1913) 462
The Egyptian Mummy (1914) 550
The Egyptian Mystery 178
Ein Seltsamer Fall 551
The Electric Goose 70
Electric Transformations 179
The Electric Villa 322
The Electric Vitalizer 247
Az Elet Kiralya, Dorian Gray *see* The Picture of Dorian Gray
The Eleventh Dimension 639
Elixir of Life 726
Ella Lola, à la Trilby 14
The Enchanted Cup 37
The Enchanted Kiss 784
The Enchanted Wreath 248
Escamotage d'une Dame Chez Robert Houdin *see* Conjuring a Lady at Robert Houdin's
Esmeralda (1906) 79
Esmeralda (1922) 929
Esther Redeemed 641
The Evil Philter 180
An Evil Power 323
The Evil Power 463
Évocation Spirite *see* Raising Spirits
Evolution 1028
The Experiment 642
The Exploits of Elaine 552
Eyes in the Dark 785

Eyes of Satan 464
The Eyes of the Mummy 819

The Fairy Bookseller 249
The Fairy Jewel 250
The Fairy of the Black Rocks 71
The Fairy's Sword 123
A Faithless Friend 124
The Faker 1118
The Fakir's Spell 553
The Fall of the House of Usher (1928, Epstein) 1099
The Fall of the House of Usher (1928, Webber) 1100
Fantoche's Nightmare 125
Le Fantôme du Moulin Rouge *see* The Phantom of the Moulin Rouge
The Fatal Pact 379
Faust (1904) 61
Faust (1907) 91
Faust (1909) 181
Faust (1910, Cines) 253
Faust (1910, Éclair) 251
Faust (1910, Pathé) 252
Faust (1911) 324, 898
Faust (1921) 898
Faust (1922) 930
Faust (1923) 964
Faust (1926) 1050; *page 187*
Faust (1927) 1075
Faust and Marguerite (1900) 28
Faust and Marguerite (1904) 62
Faust and Marguerite (1911) 325
Faust and Mephistopheles 15
Faust and the Lily 465
Faust aux Enfers *see* Faust in Hell
Faust in Hell 48
Feathertop (1912) 380
Feathertop (1913) 466
La Fée Carabosse; ou, Le Poignard Fatal *see* The Witch
Felix Switches Witches 1075
The Ferryman's Sweetheart 182
The Fiendish Tenant 254
The Fiery Hand 965
The Fighting Gringo 786
The Fire Detective 1119
The Fisherman's Nightmare 326

240 Title Index

Five Sinister Stories *see* Tales of the Uncanny
Flames 820
Flower of Youth 92
The Flying Dutchman 966
La Foile du Docteur Tube *see* The Madness of Docteur Tube
Foiled 643
Fools in the Dark 1004
The Forbidden Fruit 183
The Forbidden Room 554
The Forces of Evil; or, The Dominant Will 555
The Foreman's Treachery 467
Fortune Favors the Brave 184
The Fox Woman 644
Frankenstein 255; *page 37*
Frankenstein's Monster *see* The Monster of Frankenstein
Die Frau im Mond *see* The Woman in the Moon
The Freak Barber 72
The Freak of Ferndale Forest 256
Freaks 645
Frilby Frilled 727
From Death to Life 327
From Life to Death; or, Flight to the Sun *see* The Student of Prague; or, A Bargain with Satan
From the Beyond 568
Fun with the Bridal Party 126
The Fungi Cellars 967
Funnicus and the Ghost 469

Gavroche and the Ghosts 381
Gavroche et les Esprits *see* Gavroche and the Ghosts
Genuine 864
Gertie on Tour 787
Gertie the Dinosaur 185
Gevatter Tod *see* Death (1921)
The Ghost Breaker (1914) 556; *page 64*
The Ghost Breaker (1922) 931; *page 133*
The Ghost Club 557
The Ghost Fakirs 646
The Ghost Holiday 93
Ghost Hounds 788
The Ghost House 789

The Ghost in the Garret 899
The Ghost of Mudtown 257
The Ghost of Old Morro 790
The Ghost of Rosie Taylor 791
The Ghost of Seaview Manor 470
The Ghost of Self 471
The Ghost of Slumber Mountain 835
The Ghost of Sulphur Mountain 382
Ghost of the Hacienda 472
The Ghost of the Mine 558
Ghost of the Rancho 821
Ghost of the Twisted Oaks 647
The Ghost of the White Lady 473
The Ghost of Tolston's Manor 968
The Ghost Story 94
A Ghostly Affair 559
Ghosts (1912, Essanay) 383
Ghosts (1912, Hepworth) 384
Ghosts (1914, Ivy Close) 560
Ghosts; or, Who's Afraid? *see* The Ghosts (1914, Vitagraph)
The Ghosts (1914, Danish) 561
The Ghosts (1914, Vitagraph) 562
Ghosts and Flypaper 648
The Ghost's Warning 328
The Girl in the Moon *see* The Woman in the Moon
Go and Get It 865
God of Vengeance 563
The Goddess 649
Goddess of the Sea 186
The Golden Beetle (1907) 95
The Golden Beetle (1911) 329
The Golden Pomegranates 1005
The Golden Supper 258
The Golem (1914) 564
The Golem (1916) 728
The Golem (1920) 866; *pages 115, 117*
Der Golem: Wie Er in de Welt Kam *see* The Golem (1920)
The Golem and the Dancer 792
Der Golem und der Tänzerin *see* The Golem and the Dancer
Golem und Wie auf de Welt Kam *see* The Golem (1914)
The Golem's Last Adventure 900
Der Golem's Letzte Abenteuer *see* The Golem's Last Adventure

Title Index

Goofy Ghosts 1101
The Gorilla 1076
Den Graa Dame *see* The Grey Lady
Graf von Cagliostro *see* Cagliostro
The Grasping Hand 650
Grave Digger's Ambitions 474
The Gray Horror 651
The Great Ganton Mystery 475
The Great London Mystery 867
The Great Physician 476
The Greater Will 652
The Green Archer 1029
The Green Eye of the Yellow God 477
Green-Eyed Monster 729
The Grey Dame *see* The Grey Lady
The Grey Lady 187
Greywater Park 1006
Das Grinsende Gesicht *see* The Man Who Laughs (1921)
Guarding Britain's Secrets 565

Habeas Corpus 1102
L'Hallucination de l'Alchimiste *see* The Alchemist's Hallucination
Les Hallucinations du Baron de Munchausen *see* Baron Munchausen's Dream
The Hand of the Skeleton 653
Hands Invisible 566
The Hands of Orlac 1007
The Hanging Lamp 127
Hansel and Gretel (1909) 188
Hansel and Gretel (1923) 969
Hansel and Gretel (1924) 1008
Happy Hooligan in Dr. Jekyll and Mr. Zip 868
Haunted (1915) 654
Haunted (1916) 730
The Haunted Attic 567
The Haunted Bedroom (1907) 96
The Haunted Bedroom (1913) 478
The Haunted Bedroom (1919) 836
The Haunted Bell 731
Haunted by Conscience 259
Haunted Cafe 330
The Haunted Castle (1896) 2

The Haunted Castle (1897) 6
The Haunted Castle (1908) 128
The Haunted Castle (1909) 189
The Haunted Castle (1921) 901
The Haunted Castle (1922) 932
The Haunted Chamber 479
The Haunted Curiosity Shop 31
The Haunted Hills 1009
The Haunted Honeymoon 1030
The Haunted Hotel (1907) 97
The Haunted Hotel (1913) 480
The Haunted Hotel (1918) 822
The Haunted House (1899) 22
The Haunted House (1907) 98
The Haunted House (1911, Gaumont) 331
The Haunted House (1911, Imp) 332
The Haunted House (1912) 385
The Haunted House (1913, Kalem) 481
The Haunted House (1913, Mutual) 482
The Haunted House (1913, Pathéplay) 483
The Haunted House (1917) 793
The Haunted House (1918) 823
The Haunted House (1921) 902
The Haunted House (1922) 933
The Haunted House (1925) 1031
The Haunted House (1926) 1051
The Haunted House (1928) 1103; *page 214*
The Haunted Man 190
Haunted Spooks 869
The Haunting of Silas P. Gould 655
Haunting Winds 656
Haunts for Hire *see* Haunts for Rent
Haunts for Rent 732
Das Haus Ohne Turen und Fenster *see* The House Without Doors or Windows
The Hawk's Trail 870
Häxan *see* Witchcraft Through the Ages
The Head of Janus *see* Der Januskopf
The Headless Horseman 934
Heba the Snake Woman 657
The Heir of the Ages 794

Help! *see* Au Secours!
Henpeck's Nightmare 568
Her Dolly's Revenge 191
Her Father's Gold 733
Her Invisible Husband 734
Her Temptation 795
The Herncrake Witch 386
Hidden Death 569
High Spirits 1077
Hilde Warren and Death 796
Hilde Warren und der Tod *see* Hilde Warren and Death
The Hindoo's Charm 387
The Hindu Tombstone *see* The Indian Tomb
His Brother's Keeper 872
His Egyptian Affinity 658
The Hole in the Wall 903
L'Homme aux Figures de Cire *see* The Man of the Wax Figures
L'Homme Qui Vendit Son Âme au Diable *see* The Man Who Sold His Soul to the Devil
L'Homme Qui Rit *see* The Man Who Laughs (1909)
Homunculus 735
Hop Frog 260
Hop Frog, the Jester *see* Hop Frog
Hop O'My Thumb 388
Horrible Hyde 659
Hot Water 1010
The Hound of the Baskervilles (1914, Pathé) 570
The Hound of the Baskervilles (1914, Vitascope) 571
The Hound of the Baskervilles (1915) 660
The Hound of the Baskervilles (1920) 873
The Hound of the Baskervilles (1921) 904
The Hound of the Baskervilles (1926) 1052
The House of a Thousand Candles 661
The House of Fear 572
The House of Hate 824
The House of Horror 1120
House of Silence 825
The House of Silence *see* The Silent House
The House of the Lost Court 662
House of the Seven Gables 261
House of the Tolling Bell 874
The House of Whispers 875
The House with Nobody in It 663
The House Without Doors or Windows (1914) 573
The House Without Doors or Windows (1921) 905
Hugo the Hunchback 262
The Hunchback 192
The Hunchback and the Dancer 876
The Hunchback of Cedar Lodge 574
The Hunchback of Notre Dame *see* Esmeralda (1922)
The Hunchback of Notre Dame 970; *pages 147, 148, 150, 151, 152*
Der Hund von Baskerville *see* The Hound of the Baskervilles (1914, German)
Der Hund von Baskerville *see* The Hound of the Baskervilles (1920)
Der Hund von Baskerville *see* The Hound of the Baskervilles (1926)
Hydrothérapie Fantastique *see* The Doctor's Secret
The Hypnotic Monkey 664
The Hypnotic Violinist 575
The Hypnotic Wife 193
Hypnotism 263
The Hypnotist at Work 7

I Accuse 826
I Believe 797
If One Could See into the Future 333
The Imaginary Voyage 1032
The Imp Abroad 576
The Imp of the Bottle 194
An Impossible Voyage 63
In the Bogey Man's Cave 129
In the Grip of a Charlatan 484
In the Grip of the Vampire 389
In the Long Ago 485
In the Power of the Hypnotist 486
In the Toils of the Devil 487
In Zululand 665
Incident from Don Quixote 130

Title Index

An Indian Legend 390
The Indian Tomb 906
Das Indische Grabmal *see* The Indian Tomb
The Infernal Cake-Walk 49
The Infernal Cauldron and the Phantasmal Vapor 50
L'Inferno *see* Dante's Inferno
L'Inhumaine *see* The Living Dead Man
The Inner Brute 666
The Inner Mind 334
An Innocent Sinner 667
Die Insul der Seligen *see* The Island of Bliss
Interplanetary Revolution 1011
Inventing Trouble 668
Invisible Power 577
The Invisible Thief 195
The Island of Bliss 488
Island of Terror 489
The Isle of the Dead 490
Itching Palms 971

J'Accuse *see* I Accuse
Jack and the Beanstalk (1902) 38
Jack and the Beanstalk (1903) 51
Jack and the Beanstalk (1912) 391
Jack and the Beanstalk (1917) 798
Janus-Faced *see* Der Januskopf
Der Januskopf 871
The Japanese Mask 669
A Japanese Peach Boy 264
The Jealous Professors 265
Jewell of Death 736
Jim Hood's Ghost 1053
Jones' Nightmare; or, The Lobster Still Pursued Him 335
Jorinde and Joringle 877
Just Spooks 1033

Das Kabinett des Dr. Caligari *see* The Cabinet of Dr. Caligari
The Key of Life 266
The Kidnapped Stockbroker 670
Kitty in Dreamland 336
A Knight Errant 99
The Knight of the Snows 392
Kökarlen *see* The Phantom Chariot
Koko Sees Spooks 1034
Kyoren no Onna Shisho *see* Passion of a Woman Teacher

The Laboratory of Mephistopheles 8
The Lady of Shallot 393
A Lady of Spirits 578
The Last Look 972; *page 153*
The Last Performance 1121
Leaves from Satan's Book 907
Lebende Buddahs *see* Living Buddahs
Legally Dead 973
Legend of a Ghost 100
The Legend of Cagliostro 394
The Legend of Sleepy Hollow (1908) 131
The Legend of Sleepy Hollow (1912) 395
The Legend of the Lake 337
The Legend of the Lone Tree 671
Legend of the Phantom Tribe 579
The Legend of the Undines 267
La Légende des Ondines *see* The Legend of the Undines
Légende du Fantôme *see* Legend of a Ghost
The Leopard Lady 1104; *page 215*
The Leprechaun 132
Life Without Soul 672
The Light Within *see* The Weary Death
Lilith and Ly 837
The Lion Tonic 396
Little Red Riding Hood (1901) 32
Little Red Riding Hood (1907) 101
Little Red Riding Hood (1911, C&M) 338
Little Red Riding Hood (1911, Essanay) 339
Little Red Riding Hood (1911, Majestic) 340
Little Red Riding Hood (1917) 799
Little Red Riding Hood (1921) 908
Little Red Riding Hood (1922, Hepworth) 935
Little Red Riding Hood (1922, Selznick) 936
Little Red Riding Hood (1925) 1035

Title Index

Little Red Riding Hood (1929) 1122
The Little Red Schoolhouse 974
Little Snow White 268
Little Snowdrop *see* Little Snow White
Live Man's Tomb 397
The Live Mummy 673
A Lively Skeleton 269
Living Buddahs 1012
The Living Dead 341
The Living Dead Man 975
The Lobster Nightmare 270
Le Locataire Diabolique *see* The Diabolical Tenant
The Lodger 1054
Lola 737
London After Midnight 1078; *page 205*
Lord Arthur Savile's Crime 909
Lord Feathertop 133
The Lost Shadow 910
The Lost Soul; or, The Dangers of Hypnosis 976
The Lost Whirl 1105
The Lost World 1036; *page 170*
Lotta Coin's Ghost 76
Le Loup-Garou *see* The Werewolf
Love from Out of the Grave 491
The Love of a Hunchback 271
The Love of a Siren 342
Love Without Question 878
Love's Mockery *see* Der Januskopf
Luke's Double 738
Lunatics in Power 197
Lured by a Phantom 272

Die Macht der Finsternis *see* The Power of Darkness
Maciste in Hell 1037
Madness 838
The Madness of Dr. Tube 675
The Magic Garden 134
The Magic Mirror 135
The Magic Skin (1913) 492
The Magic Skin (1915) 676
The Magic Skin *see* Desire
The Magic Sword 33
Magical Matches 398
The Magician 1055; *page 190*
A Magnetic Influence 399

La Main du Squelette *see* The Hand of the Skeletin
La Main Qui Étreint *see* The Grasping Hand
La Maison Hantée *see* The Haunted House (1907)
The Man and His Bottle 136
The Man from Beyond 911
The Man in the White Cloak 493
The Man Monkey 198
The Man-Monkey 343
The Man of Mystery 800
The Man of the Wax Figures 494
The Man Who Cheated Life *see* The Student of Prague
The Man Who Laughs (1909) 199
The Man Who Laughs (1921) 912
The Man Who Laughs (1928) 1106; *pages 218, 219*
The Man Who Sold His Soul to the Devil 879
The Man Without a Soul 739
Manoir du Diable *see* The Haunted Castle (1896)
The Manor of the Devil *see* The Haunted Castle (1896)
Man's Genesis 400
The Marriage of Psyche and Cupid 580
The Marvelous Pearl 200
The Master Mind 880
The Master Mystery 839
Max and the Clutching Hand *see* The Grasping Hand
Max et la Main Qui Étrient *see* The Grasping Hand
Max Hypnotized 273
The Medium's Nemesis 495
Mephisto and the Maiden 201
Mephisto's Son 80
The Merry Frolics of Satan 81
A Message from Mars 913
Metropolis 1056; *page 191*
Mezhplanetnaya Revolutsiya *see* Interplanetary Revolution
Midnight 740
A Midnight Bell 914
A Midnight Episode 23
A Midnight Scare 581
The Midnight Specter 677
Mingling Spirits 741

Title Index

The Minotaur 274
The Miracle 977
The Mirror of Life 202
The Miser's Convention 582
The Miser's Doom 24
Miss Faust 203
Miss Jekyll and Madame Hyde 678
Miss Trillie's Big Feet 679
The Missing Link 1079
The Missing Mummy 680
Mr. Tvardovski 742
Mr. Wu 1080; *page 206*
The Mistletoe Bough 64
Mockery 1081; *page 207*
The Modern Dr. Jekyll *see* Dr. Jekyll and Mr. Hyde (1908)
The Modern Sphinx 743
A Modern Yarn 344
Le Momie du Roi *see* The Mummy of the King Ramses
Money to Burn 937
A Monkey Bite 345
The Monkey Man 137
The Monkey Talks 1082
Monkey's Paw (1915) 681
Monkey's Paw (1923) 978
The Monster (1903) 52
The Monster (1925) 1038; *page 172*
The Monster Dog *see* The Pet
The Montser of Fate *see* The Golem (1914)
The Monster of Frankenstein 881
The Moonstone 204
The Moonstone 346
Moonstruck 205
Mortmain 682
Il Mostro di Frankenstein *see* The Monster of Frankenstein
Mother Goose 206
Der Müde Tod *see* The Weary Death
Die Mumie Ma *see* The Eyes of the Mummy
The Mummy 347, 348, 349
Mummy Love 1057
The Mummy of the King Ramses 207
Murders in the Rue Morgue 583
Museum Spooks; or, Dreams in a Picture Gallery 275
My Friend the Devil 938

The Mysteries of Myra 744
The Mysterious Mrs. M 745
The Mysterious Retort 82
The Mysterious Stranger (1911) 350
The Mysterious Stranger (1913) 496
The Mystery Mind 882
The Mystery of Grayson Hall 584
The Mystery of Souls 351
The Mystery of Temple Court 276
Mystery of the Death Head 585
The Mystery of the Fatal Pearl 586
Mystery of the Glass Coffin 401
The Mystery of the Hidden House 587
Mystery of the Lama Convent 208
The Mystery of the Sleeping Death 588
The Mystic 1039
The Mystic Hour 801
The Mystic Mirror 1107
The Mystic Swing 28a
The Mystical Maid of Jamasha Pass 402
The Myth of Jamasha Pass *see* The Mystical Maid of Jamasha Pass

Nachte des Grauens *see* Night of Terror
Nachtgestalten 883
Naidra, the Dream Worker 589
Nan in Fairyland 403
Nature Fakirs 102
Neal of the Navy 683
Necklace of the Dead 277
The New Jonah 209
The Newsboy's Christmas Dream 498
A Night in the Chamber of Horrors 590
A Night of Horror *see* Night of Terror
A Night of Horror in the Menagerie *see* Night of Terror
Night of Terror 746
A Night of Thrills 591
Nosferatu 939; *pages 135, 137*
Nosferatu eine Symphonie de Grauens *see* Nosferatu

Title Index

Notre Dame 499
Notre Dame de Paris 352
A Novice at X-rays 16
Une Nuit Terrible *see* A Terrible Night
The Nursemaid's Dream 138
Nursie and Night 404
The Nymph's Bath 210

The Occult 500
The Ocean Waif 747
Oh That Molar! 103
Oh, You Skeleton 278
Old Scrooge 279
The Old Shoemaker 211
An Old-Time Nightmare 353
On Time 1013
One Exciting Night 940; *page 139*
One Hour Before Dawn 884
One Glorious Night 941
One Million Dollars 684
The 1,000,000 Spook 104
One Spooky Night 979
One Too Exciting Night 405
One Way Street 1040
Onesime et la Maison Hantée *see* Simple Simon and the Haunted House
Only a Room-er 748
L'Oracle de Delphes *see* The Oracle of Delphi
The Oracle of Delphi 53
Oriental Black Art 139
The Oriental Mystic 212
Orlac's Hände *see* The Hands of Orlac
The Other 501
The Other Person 915
The Other Self (1915) 685
The Other Self (1918) 827
Owana, the Devil Woman 502

The Palace of the Arabian Nights 73
Les Palais des Mille et un Nuits *see* The Palace of the Arabian Nights
Pan Tvardovski *see* Mr. Tvardovski

Pandora's Box 1108
Papa Gaspard; or, The Ghost of the Rocks 213
Parsifal 406
Passion of a Woman Teacher 1958
The Pearl Fisher 105
The Penalty 885; *page 121*
The Perils of Paul 886
Die Pest in Florenz *see* The Plague in Florence
The Pet 916
Pete's Haunted House 1059
Peter's Evil Spirit 592
Le Petit Chaperon Rouge *see* Little Red Riding Hood (1901); Little Red Riding Hood (1929)
Phaedra 214
The Phantom 280
The Phantom Carriage *see* The Phantom Chariot
The Phantom Chariot 840
Phantom City 1109
The Phantom Foe 887
Phantom Honeymoon 841
The Phantom Light 593
Phantom Melody 888
The Phantom of the Moulin Rouge 1041
The Phantom of the Opera 1042; *pages 174, 176*
The Phantom Signal 503
The Phantom Sirens 215
The Phantom Violin 594
The Phantom Witness 686
Photographing a Ghost 17
The Picture of Dorian Gray (1913) 504
The Picture of Dorian Gray (1915, Russian) 687
The Picture of Dorian Gray (1915, Thanhouser) 688
The Picture of Dorian Gray (1916) 749
The Picture of Dorian Gray (1917, German) 803
The Picture of Dorian Gray (1917, Hungarian) 802
The Pied Piper 106
The Pied Piper of Hamlin (1911, Pathé) 354

The Pied Piper of Hamlin (1911, Thanhouser) 355
The Pied Piper of Hamlin (1913) 505
The Pied Piper of Hamlin (1917) 804
The Pit and the Pendulum (1910) 281
The Pit and the Pendulum (1913) 506
The Plague in Florence 842
The Plot 595
The Poison Pen 843
Poisoned Waters 507
Polidor, a Member of the Death Club see Polidor at the Death Club
Polidor Al Club Della Morte see Polidor at the Death Club
Polidor at the Death Club 407
La Portrait Spirite see A Spiritualist Photographer
Portrét Doriana Greja see The Picture of Dorian Gray
The Power God 1043
The Power of Darkness 942
Prehistoric Man 140
Prehistoric Poultry 805
Prelude 1083
The Price of Silence 917
The Primrose Ring 806
The Prince of Darkness 39
The Prince of Tempters 1060
The Princess and the Fisherman 216
The Princess in the Vase 141
The Princess of Darkness 596
The Professor and His Waxworks 107
The Professor's Secret 142
Le Puits et le Pendule see The Pit and the Pendulum
The Puppet's Nightmare see Fantoche's Nightmare
Puritan Passions 980; *page 154*

Le Quatre Cents Farces du Diable see The Merry Frolics of Satan
The Queen of Hearts 981
The Queen of Spades (1910, German) 282
The Queen of Spades (1910, Russian) 283
The Queen of Spades (1912) 408
The Queen of Spades (1913, Celio/Kleine) 508
The Queen of Spades (1913, Fidelity) 509
The Queen of Spades (1916) 750
The Queen of Spades (1921) 917
The Queen of Spades (1927) 1084
Queen of the North Woods 1123
Queen of the Sea 828

Die Rache des Homonculus see Homunculus
Rah, Rah, Rah 751
Raising Spirits 25
The Rajah's Casket 83
Randin and Co. 510
Der Rattenfänger von Hamlin see The Pied Piper of Hamlin
The Raven (1912) 409
The Raven (1915) 689
La Rayons Roentgen see A Novice at X-Rays
The Real Thing at Last 752
The Reincarnation of a Soul 511
The Reincarnation of Karma 410
The Resident Patient 919
The Return of Richard Neal 690
Rêve d'un Astronome see The Astronomer's Dream
Le Revenant see The Apparition
The Revenge of the Ghosts 217
Revolt of the Robots see Aelita
The Reward of the Faithless 807
Rhapsodia Satanica see Satanic Rhapsody
The Right to Be Happy 753
Rival de Satan see A Rival to Satan
A Rival to Satan 284
The Roadside Inn 512
Robert, the Devil; or, Freed from Satan's Power 285
Roi de Thule see Lured by a Phantom
Romance of the Mummy 286
Rosalie and Spiritualism 356

Title Index

Rosalie Fait du Spiritualism *see* Rosalie and Spiritualism
Rubezahl's Hochzeit *see* Rubezahl's Marriage
Rubezahl's Marriage 754
The Ruling Passion 755
Ruslan i Ljudmila 597

The Sacred Order 982
St. George and the Dragon (1910) 287
St. George and the Dragon (1912) 411
The Saloon-Keeper's Nightmare 143
Satan 412
Satan Defeated 357
Satana 358
Satanas 844
Satanic Rhapsody 691
Satan's Castle 513
Satan's Smithy 144
Satan's Treasure 40
The Savage 1061
The Saving of Faust 359
Scared Silly 1085
Scared Stiff 1062
The Scarlet Crystal 808
The Scented Envelopes 983
Schatten *see* Warning Shadows
Der Schatten des Meeres *see* The Sea's Shadow
Schlöss Vogelod *see* The Haunted Castle (1921)
The Scorpion's Sting 756
Scream in the Night 845
Scrooge (1901) 34
Scrooge (1913) 514
Séance de Spiritisme *see* A Spiritualistic Séance
The Sea's Shadow 413
The Secret of the Hand 288
Secret of the King 757
The Secret Room 692
The Secrets of House No. 5 414
Les Sept Châteaux du Diable *see* The 7 Castles of the Devil
The Serpent Man *see* The Snake Man
The Serpents 415
The 7 Castles of the Devil 35

Seven Footprints to Satan 1124; *page 227*
The Seven Swans 809
The Shadow of the East 1014
A Shadowed Shadow 758
She (1908) 145
She (1911) 360
She (1916) 759
She (1917) 810
She (1926) 1063
Sherlock Holmes 943
Sherlock Holmes Baffled 54
Sherlock Holmes in the Great Murder Mystery 146
The Shielding Shadow 760
Shivering Spooks 1064
Shooting in the Haunted Wood 218
The Show 1086; *page 209*
The Shrine of the Seven Lamps 984
Siegfried 1015; *page 164*
The Silent Castle 416
The Silent Command 693
The Silent House 1125
The Silent Mystery 829
The Silent Stranger 761
The Silver Buddah 985
Simple Simon and the Devil 417
Simple Simon and the Haunted House 515
Simple Simon and the Suicide Club 516
Sinews of the Dead 598
Singed Wings 944
The Skeleton 289
Skelley's Skeleton 762
The Skivvy's Ghost 418
Slave of Desire 986
Sleeping Beauty (1902) 41
Sleeping Beauty (1912) 419
Sleeping Beauty (1913) 517
Slumberland 147
The Snake Man 290
Snow White (1903) 55
Snow White (1913) 518
Snow White (1916, Educational) 763
Snow White (1916, Paramount) 764
Snow White (1917) 811
The Snowman 148
The Soap Bubbles of Truth 291

Socellerie Culinaire *see* The Cook in Trouble
Sold to Satan 765
A Son of Satan 1016
Sorceress of the Strand 292
Le Sorcier *see* The Witch's Revenge
Sorrows of Satan (1917) 812
Sorrows of Satan (1926) 1065; *page 194*
The Soul of Pydra 694
Souls Before Birth *see* One Glorious Night
The Soul's Circle 766
The Speckled Band 420
Sparrows 1066; *page 195*
The Specter 149
The Specter of the Vault 695
The Spectre 293
A Spectre Haunts Europe 920
The Spectre of Jago 421
The Spell (1913, Powers) 519
The Spell (1913, Vitagraph) 520
Spell of the Hypnotist 422
Lo Spettro del Sotterrano *see* The Spectre of the Vault
Lo Spettro di Jago *see* The Spectre of Jago
Lo Spettro di Mezzanotte *see* The Midnight Spectre
Lo Spettro Vendicatore *see* The Avenging Spectre
A Spider in the Brain 423
The Spiders 846
Spiffkins Eats Frogs 424
Die Spinnen *see* The Spiders
Spionne 1087
The Spirit 219
The Spirit of the Lake 220
The Spirit of the Sword 294
The Spirit of '23 945
A Spirited Elopment 696
Spiritism 889
Spiritismo *see* Spiritism
Spiritisten *see* The Ghosts
Spirits Free of Duty 697
A Spiritualist Photographer 56
A Spiritualist Meeting 84
A Spiritualistic Convert 425
A Spiritualistic Séance (1908) 150
A Spiritualistic Séance (1910) 295

A Spiritualistic Séance (1911) 361
The Spook Raiser 698
Spook Ranch 1044
Spook Spoofing 1088
Spooks (1922) 946
Spooks (1927) 1089
Spooks and Spasms 813
Spooks Do the Moving 151
A Spooky Romance 987
Star of India 521
The Star Rover 890
Der Steinerne Reiter *see* The Stone Rider
The Stone Rider 988
The Story of Hansel and Gretel 1017
The Strange Unknown 699
La Strega de Siviglia *see* The Witch of Seville
The Stroke of Midnight *see* The Phantom Chariot
The Stronger Mind 427
The Student of Prague; or, A Bargain with Satan 522
The Student of Prague 1067; *page 197*
Der Student von Prague *see* The Student of Prague; or, A Bargain with Satan
The Suicide Club (1909) 221
The Suicide Club (1914) 599
Sumurun 891
Supernatural Power 428
Svengali (1914) 600
Svengali (1927) 1090
Sweeney Todd 1110
The Sword and the King 222
The System of Dr. Tarr and Professor Fether 429
Le Système du Docteur Goudron et du Professeur Plume *see* The System of Dr. Tarr and Professor Fether

Tales of Horror *see* Tales of the Uncanny
Tales of the Uncanny 847
Talked to Death 223
Tarzan the Tiger 1126
The Tell-Tale Heart 1111

Title Index

The Temptations of Joseph 601
The Temptations of Satan 602
The Tenderfoot's Ghost 523
A Terrible Night 3
The Terrible People 1112
The Terrible Turkish Executioner 65
The Terrible Two in Luck 603
Terror 1113
Testing a Soldier's Courage 296
Der Teufelsschlosser *see* The Devil's Locksmith
That's the Spirit 1018
The Thief and the Porter's Head 430
The Thief in the Dark 1114
The Thief of Bagdad 1019
The Thieving Hand 152
Thinnen Stout 767
The Thirteen Club 74
The Thirteenth Chair 848
The Thirteenth Hour 1091
Those Who Dare 1020
Thou Shalt Not Kill *see* The Avenging Conscience
The Three Lights *see* The Weary Death
Three Wax Men *see* Waxworks
The Three Wishes 700
Through the Centuries 604
Thy Soul Shall Bear Witness *see* The Phantom Chariot
Tin Hats 1068
'Tis Now the Very Witching Time of Night 224
To Let 849
Too Much Champagne 153
Torgus, the Coffin Maker 892
Tötentanz *see* Dance of Death
Toula's Dream 154
The Tragedies of the Crystal Globe 701
Trail of the Octopus 850
Trance *see* Anita
The Treasure of Cibola 768
The Trembling Hour 851
Trésor de Satan *see* Satan's Treasure
The Trick Box 57
Trick Film/Title Unknown 155
Trifling Women 947

Trilby (1908) 156
Trilby (1912, Austrian/Hungarian) 431
Trilby (1912, Standard) 432
Trilby (1913) 524
Trilby (1914) 605
Trilby (1915) 702
Trilby (1922) 948
Trilby (1923) 989
A Trip to Davy Jones' Locker 297
A Trip to Mars 298
A Trip to the Center of the Moon 75
A Trip to the Moon 42
The Troublesome Fly 43
Tut-Tut and His Terrible Tomb 990
20,000 Leagues Under the Sea 769

The Ugliest Queen on Earth 225
Ulysse et la Géant Polyphème *see* Ulysses and the Giant Polyphemus
Ulysses and the Giant Polyphemus 76
Uncle Josh in a Spooky Hotel 29
Uncle Josh's Nightmare 30
Unconquered 814
Undine 525
Undressing Extraordinary 36
The Unfaithful Wife 703
Unheimliche Geschichten *see* Tales of the Uncanny
The Unholy Night 1127
The Unholy Three (1925) 1045
The Unholy Three (1930) *page 180*
The Unknown 1092; *page 210*
The Unknown Country 606
The Unknown Purple 991; *page 156*
Unknown Treasures 1069
Unseen Hands 1021
The Untameable 992

The Vampire (1913, Kalem) 526
The Vampire (1913, Searchlight) 527
The Vampire (1914) 607
The Vampire of the Desert 528
Le Vampires *see* The Vampires, the Arch Criminals of Paris
The Vampires, the Arch Criminals of Paris 770

Title Index

Vanity's Price 1022
Der Velorene Schatten *see* The Lost Shadow
Vendetta (1914) 608
Vendetta (1922) 949
Une Vengeance d'Edgar Poe *see* The Vengeance of Edgar Poe
The Vengeance of Edgar Poe 433
The Vengeance of Egypt 434
Vengeance of the Dead 299
Ich Verlorene; or, Das Gefahren der Hypnose *see* The Lost Soul; or, The Dangers of Hypnosis
Der Verlorene Schatten *see* The Lost Shadow
Viaggo al Centro della Luna *see* Trip to the Center of the Moon
The Vij 609
The Voice on the Wire 815
Le Voyage Dans la Lune *see* A Trip to the Moon
Le Voyage Imaginaire *see* The Imaginary Voyage

Wachsfigurenkabinett *see* Waxworks
Wages of Sin 157
Wahnsinn *see* Madness
Wanted—A Mummy 300
The Warning 704
Warning Shadows 993
Wave of Spooks 158
Waxworks 1023; *page 168*
The Weary Death 921
Wedded Beneath the Waves 301
Wedding Feast and Ghosts 159
Weird Bemesis 705
The Werewolf (1913) 529
The Werewolf (1923) 994
West of Zanzibar 1115; *pages 222, 223*
What an Eye 1024
What the Gods Decree 530
When Soul Meets Soul 435
When Spirits Walk 610
When the Mummy Cried for Help 706
When the Spirits Moved 707
Where East Is East 1128; *page 228*
Which Is Witch? 708
Whiffle's Nightmare 611

While John Bolt Slept 612
While London Sleeps 1070
While Paris Sleeps 995; *page 158*
Whispering Shadows 950
Whispering Wires 1071
The White Ghost *see* The Ghost of the White Lady
The White Pearl 709
The White Spectre 613
The White Wolf 614
The Wild Ass's Skin 226
Willy Fantôme *see* Willy the Ghost
Willy the Ghost 362
The Witch (1906) 85
The Witch (1909) 227
The Witch Kiss 108
The Witch of Abruzzi 363
The Witch of Seville 364
Witch of the Dark House 771
The Witch of the Glen 302
The Witch of the Mountains 772
The Witch of the Ruins 303
Witchcraft Through the Ages 951; *page 142*
The Witching Eyes 1129
The Witching Hour 922
The Witching House 773
The Witch's Ballad *see* The Ballad of a Witch
The Witch's Cave 88
The Witch's Cavern 228
The Witch's Donkey 160
The Witch's Revenge 58
The Witch's Spell 304
The Wizard 1093
Wolf Blood 1046
The Woman in the Moon 1130; *page 229*
The Woman in White 436
Woman of Mystery 615
The Wonderful Charm 161
The Wraith of Haddon Towers 710
The Wraith of the Tomb 711

The X-Ray Fiend 9
X-Rays *see* The X-Ray Fiend

The Yellow Face 923
Der Yoghi *see* The Yogi
The Yogi 774
The Young Diana 952; *page 143*

NAME INDEX

References are to entry numbers except those in italics, which refer to pages with photographs.

Aas, Olaf 840
Abel, Alfred 927, 1056, 1117
Abel, David 937
Adalbert, Max 921, 927
Adams, Claire 885, 973
Adams, Dora Mills 862
Adams, Kathryn 686
Adamson, Ewart 944
Adolfi, John G. 974
Adoree, Renee 1080, 1086; *page 209*
Agnew, Robert 1069
Aitken, Spottiswoode 534, 1020
Alberni, Luis 911
Albert, Elsie 445
Alberti, Fritz 1015, 1056, 1067
Albertini, Luciano 881
Alby, Rina 412
Alcorn, Olive Ann 1042
Alden, Mary 922
Aldor, Bernd 803
Alexander, Dick 1104
Alexander, J. Grubb 731, 808, 850, 1073, 1106
Alexander, Lois 769
Alexandre, Rene 352
Allan, Hugh 1119
Allen, Harry 972
Alma, Marian 1067
Alstrup, Oda 175
Alvarado, Don 1082
Andersen, Johs 951
Anderson, Ida 1016
Andra, Fern 864
Andre, Victor 42
Andreiev, Andrei 1108

Andriot, Josette 530
Andriot, Lucien 1047
Androschin, Hans 894, 1007
Ankerstjerne, Joan 951
Anthony, Walter 1072, 1073, 1106, 1121
Apfel, Oscar C. 446, 556
Arbuckle, Maclyn 952
Arbuckle, Roscoe "Fatty" 897
Archainbaud, George 778, 1014
Ardell, Alice 1057
Arden, Edwin 552
Arehn, Nils 840
Arliss, George 895
Arliss, Mrs. 895
Armstrong, Robert 1104
Arnaud, Yvonne 859
Arno, Siegfried 1108
Arnold, C. Wilfred 1054
Arnold, Gertrud 959, 1015
Arnold, John 1080, 1086
Arnyai, Karoly 817
Arthur, Johnny 991, 1038, 1085
Ash, Gordon 913
Asher, Max 644
Asher, Will 822
Ashton, Charles 1110
Ashton, Sylvia 1104
Asian, Raoul 827
Askonas, Paul 431, 1007
Astor, Gertrude 1072; *page 200*
Astor, Mary 980
Atkinson, George 893
Aubrey, James 751
August, Edwin 258, 511, 843

Name Index

August, Joseph 1003
Ault, Marie 1054
Austin, George 1038
Austin, Leslie 862
Auzinger, Max 816
Ayme, Jean 770
Ayres, Sydney 656

Backus, George 661
Baclanova, Olga 1106
Badet, Regina 608
Badger, Clarence 644
Baggot, King 458, 731, 761, 870
Bailey, William N. 887
Baker, C. Graham 1114
Baker, Friend 769
Baker, George D. 638, 986
Baker, Graham 751
Baker, Sam 1019, 1079
Balcon, Michael 1054
Ball, Eustace Hale 815
Ballieuzek, V. 750
Bannerman, Margaret 820
Bantock, Leedham 514
Bara, Theda 780; *page 90*
Barclay, Eric 1050
Baringer, A. B. 941
Barker, Bradley 663, 880, 1095
Barlatier, Andra 966
Barnett, Chester 702
Barras, Charles M. 619
Barrat, Robert 950
Barrett, Dorothy 699
Barrie, James M. 752
Barriscale, Bessie 633
Barry, Gerard 1127
Barry, Leon 760
Barry, Wesley 865
Barrymore, John 861, 943; *pages 110, 111*
Barrymore, Lionel 880, 949, 1049, 1086, 1091, 1115, 1127
Barter, H. H. 769
Barthelmess, Richard 809
Bartlett, Lanter 485
Barton, Ralph 893
Basserman, Albert 501
Bataille, M. 444
Batalov, Nikolai 996
Bately, Ernest G. 631

Bates, Les 1070
Bates, Louise 733
Bates, Thomas 620
Bauman, W. J. 562
Baumbach 894
Baxter, Warner 1115; *page 223*
Beal, Frank 622
Beaudine, Harold 1101
Beaudine, William 1066
Beaumont, Tom 958
Beck, Elga 837
Becker, Denise 79
Becker, Theodor 842
Bedford, Barbara 1081, 1103
Bee, Richard 1103, 1120, 1124
Beebe, Marjorie 1114
Beery, Noah 865
Beery, Wallace 963, 1021, 1036
Beggs, Lee 550
Belcher, Charles 1004, 1019
Bell, Karina 907
Bell, Little Enid 855
Bellamy, George 541, 756
Bellew, Dorothy 711
Belmont, Baldy 1096
Belmore, Lionel 1127
Bemis, Jim 1009
Benedict, Brooks 1076
Benham, Harry 321
Bennet, Spencer Gordon 1029, 1112, 1119, 1123
Bennett, Alma 1036
Bennett, Charles 743
Bennett, Enid 836
Bennett, Mickey 972
Bennison, Andrew 1093, 1114
Benoit, George 989
Bentley, Thomas 540
Benton, Curtis 769
Beranger, Clara S. 861
Berber, Anita 847, 857, 883, 927
Beresford, Frank 1020
Berger, Greta 522, 927, 1015, 1056, 1087
Berger, Hans 894
Bergman, Henry 684
Berkeley, Claude 1104
Berliet, Jimmy 1032, 1041
Bern, Paul 1022, 1060
Bernard, Sylvia 1066
Bernhard, Karl 842

Name Index

Bernon, Bluette 42
Berranger, George A. 534
Bertina, Francesca 889
Bertollini, F. 171
Bertram, Arthur 640
Besserer, Eugenie 627
Betz, Harry 1045
Bevani, Alexander 1042
Biensfeldt, Paul 927, 988
Biggers, Earl Derr 1073
Bildt, Paul 901
Bingham, Edfrid A. 944
Bird, Betty 1052
Birkett, Viva 605
Biro, Lajos 1103
Bishop, Andrew 1016
Biswanger, Erwin 1015, 1056
Bitzer, Billy 400, 534
Bizuel, Jacques 950
Blache, Herbert 602, 992
Blackton, J. Stuart 944, 874
Blackwell, Carlyle 624, 747, 1052, 1063
Blake, Tom 899
Blanche, Alice Guy 79, 506, 615
Bland, Sidney 749, 759
Blinn, Genevieve 779
Blom, August 175
Blood, Adele 724
Blythe, Betty 1063
Blythe, Sidney 1063
Boardman, Virginia True 925
Boasberg, Al 1076
Boese, Carl 866
Boheim, Olly 1056
Bolder, Robert 1022
Bolm, Adolph 926
Bonn, Ferdinand 600
Bonnard, Mario 358
Booth, Walter R. 24, 26, 31, 34, 36, 37, 104, 247
Borden, Olive 1082
Borelli, Lyda 691
Borgstrom, Hilda 840
Boring, Edward 755
Borke, Hilde 660
Borlin, Jean 1032
Bosetti, Romeo 356, 381
Bosworth, Hobart 781, 814, 1073
Boteler, Ward 924
Botz, Gustav 871, 939

Bourgeois, Gerard 207, 284, 433
Bouwmeester, Theo 315
Boylan, Malcolm Stuart 1093
Boyle, Jack 972
Bow, Clara 956
Bowers, John 1020
Brabin, Charles 467, 662
Bracken, Bertram 779
Bracy, Sidney 582, 1103
Bradbury, James 1104
Brady, Ed 683
Brandes, Werner 571
Brandon, William 640
Brandt, Julietta 842
Brawn, Jack 638
Breamer, Sylvia 895, 937
Breese, Edmund 1103
Brenert, Hans 852
Brenon, Herbert 458, 755
Brent, Evelyn 1014
Bretherton, Howard P. 1070
Brian, Mary 1060
Briant, R. 971
Bridenbecker, Milton 1042
Brignone, Guido 1037
Britton, Edna 839
Brockwell, Gladys 779, 795, 970
Brodin, Norbert 925, 956
Broening, H. L. 764
Brooklyn, Mary 1043
Brooks, Louise 1108
Brough, Mary 541
Brower, Robert 505, 641
Brown, Charles 638
Brown, Clarence L. 702
Brown, Harry J. 1109
Brown, Karl 534, 897, 941
Browne, Earl 1066
Browne-Faire, Virginia 1036
Browning, Tod 1039, 1045, 1078, 1086, 1092, 1115, 1128
Brownlee, Frank 903
Bruneau, Helen 970
Brunette, Fritzi 875
Bruun, Axel 907
Bryson, Winifred 970, 998
Buckland, Wilfred 781
Buckley, Floyd 552, 839
Budd, Ruth 845
Buel, Kenean 810

Name Index

Buffington, Adele 1109
Bunny, George 843, 1036
Burger, G. 904
Burgess, Gelette 992
Burke, Joe 679
Burnham, Beatrice 795
Burns, Binnie 602
Burns, Edmund 1071
Burns, Edward 1073
Burns, Fred 1051
Burns, Jack 839
Burns, Vinnie 615
Burrough, Tom 810
Burroughs, Edgar Rice 1126
Burt, Katharine 944
Burt, William 733, 1104
Burton, J. W. 556
Busch, Mae 1045
Bushman, Francis X. 310, 690
Butler, Alexander 812, 830
Butt, Lawson 966, 1003
Butts, Billy 1066
Byrne, Jack 758
Byron-Webber, R. 855

Cahn, Edward 1106, 1121
Cain, Robert 922
Caine, Sylvia 930
Calder, Joseph 903
Caldwell, A. A. 845
Calhern, Louis 972
Calvert, Charles 565, 711
Calvert, E. H. 1093
Camp, C. Wadsworth 878
Campbell, Alan 638
Campbell, Betty 904
Campbell, Colin 485
Campbell, Margaret 973
Campeau, Frank 1071
Canham, Frank 1001, 1002, 1005
Cannon, Maurice 989
Cannon, Pomeroy 947
Cannon, William 1070
Capellani, Albert 352, 952
Carewe, Arthur Edmund 931, 989, 1042, 1072
Carey, Harry D. 649, 786
Carleton, Lloyd B. 966
Carlisle, Robert 1121
Carlsen, Traute 896

Carlysle, Jack 890
Carmen, Jewell 1048; *page 184*
Carminati, Tulio 1048
Caron, Pierre 879
Carpenter, Edward Childs 1104
Carpenter, Francis 798
Carpenter, Horace B. 556, 781
Carr, C. 806
Carr, Percy 940
Carrer, Ben 702
Carson, Willie May 1104
Cartellieri, Carmen 1007
Carter, Harry 693
Carlyle, Montgomery 885
Caserini, Mario 75
Catelain, Jacques 975
Cavalcanti, Alberto 975, 1122
Cavanaugh, William H. 719
Cavendish, Kitty 739
Cecil, Edward 779, 1042
Cecil, Nora 1124
Cemesnova, Mme. 317
Chadwick, I. E. 1049
Chair, Louis 1041
Chalmers, Thomas 980
Chandlee, Harry 940
Chaney, Lon 591, 885, 925, 970, 995, 1038, 1042, 1045, 1078, 1080, 1081, 1092, 1115, 1128; *pages 120, 130, 147, 148, 150, 152, 172, 174, 176, 178, 180, 205, 206, 207, 210, 222, 223, 228*
Chapelson, Mary 520
Chapin, Frederick 747
Chaplin, Syd 1079
Charell, Erik 883
Chase, Colin 779
Chaston, Fred 899
Chatrian, Alexander 818, 1049
Chatham, C. Pitt 919
Chatterton, Tom 917
Chautard, Emile 950, 1120
Chesebro, George 1046
Chesney, Arthur 1054
Childers, Naomi 638
Christensen, Benjamin 951, 1081, 1103, 1120, 1124
Christie, A. E. 658
Christie, Al 707, 741
Christy, Ivan 1124
Christy, Nan 743

Name Index

Clair, Ethlyne 1123
Clair, Rene 1032, 1041
Clark, Betty Ross 924
Clark, Bridgetta 893
Clark, Frank Howard 1046, 1051, 1113
Clark, Gilbert 1081
Clark, Harvey 937
Clark, Marguerite 764, 809
Clark, Violet 878
Clark, Wallace 769
Clarke, Downing 899
Clarkson, Joan 962, 965, 967, 977, 981, 982, 984, 985
Clary, Charles 885, 998, 1013, 1071
Clawson, E. J. 740, 753, 1042, 1115
Clayton, Gilbert 989
Clayton, Marguerite 1046
Clerget, Paul 824
Clifford, William 736
Clifton, Elmer 643
Cline, Wilfred 1126
Close, Ivy 393, 419, 655
Clovelly, Cecil 861
Cobb, Clifford 820
Cody, Albert 818
Cogley, Nick 1079
Cohen, Alfred A. 1076
Cohill, William A. 672
Cohl, Emile 125, 217
Cohn, Alfred A. 991, 1013, 1072
Colbert, Suzanne 848
Colby, A. E. 953, 962, 965, 967, 977, 981, 982, 984, 985
Collins, Alf 70
Collins, Edward (aka Edwin) J. 708, 929
Collins, H. J. 503
Collins, Monte 924
Collins, Wilkie 204, 346, 455
Collot, Otto 501
Commerford, Thomas 450
Comont, Mathilde 1019
Compson, Betty 741
Conan Doyle, Sir Arthur 54, 146, 420, 571, 904, 919, 923, 943, 958, 1036, 1052
Conklin, Charles 1071
Conklin, Chester 1042, 1103, 1120
Conklin, William 683
Conley, Lige 946

Connelly, Edward 893, 947, 1045, 1086
Conness, Robert 701, 790
Constant, Max 989
Conti, Albert 1073
Conway, Booth 929
Cook, Clyde 1062
Cook, John 753, 937, 1038
Coombs, Guy 667
Coombs, Jackie 1109
Cooper, Arthur 103
Cooper, Bigelow 701
Cooper, D. P. 962, 965, 967, 977, 981, 982, 984, 985
Cooper, George 998, 1068, 1127
Cooper, Gladys 752, 812
Cooper, Toby 748
Corbin, Virginia 775
Corcoran, Ethel 638
Cordova, Leander 1063
Corelli, Marie 608, 812, 907, 949, 952, 1065
Corey, Jim 1021
Cornwall, Blanche 506
Cortez, Ricardo 1065, 1081
Cossar, John 970
Costello, Carmen 1106
Costello, Helene 1070
Costello, Maurice 373, 595, 719
Cotner, Frank 1051
Cotton, Lucy 672, 895, 950
Coulter, Lucia 1078, 1086, 1092
Counselman, William 1071
Courant, Kurt 796, 1130
Courtleigh, William, Jr. 683
Courtot, Marguerite 692
Covington, Bruce 1042
Cowles, Ed 1044
Cowles, Jules 1036, 1078
Cox, David 1106, 1128
Cox, Douglas 749
Coxen, Edward 537, 743, 818, 966
Craig, Neil 690
Crampton, Howard 458, 715, 769, 850
Crane, Frank H. 785
Crane, Ward 1042
Crawford, Joan 1092; *page 210*
Crawley, Constance 710
Creelman, James Ashmore 980, 1121

Name Index

Crisp, Donald 825
Crittendon, T. D. 776, 786
Crocker-King, C. H. 940
Crossland, Alan 949
Crossley, Syd 1076
Crowell, Josephine 534, 1010, 1106
Cruze, James 321, 360, 795, 897, 941
Cumming, Dorothy 1040
Cunningham, Jack 818, 821, 875, 931
Curley, Pauline 672
Curran, Thomas 1096
Currier, Frank 913
Curtis, Allen 644, 726
Curtiz, Michael *see* Kertesz, Mihaly

Dagover, Lil 831, 846, 921, 959; *pages 98, 99, 102*
Dale, Margaret 940
Dalton, Dorothy 858
Daly, Arnold 552
Daly, Jane 1115
Dane, Viola 662, 696
Danforth, William 809
Dangerfield, E. 748
Daniels, Bebe 944
Dantan, Andre A. 879
Dante 1003
D'Aragon, Lionel 812
Darbyshire, Iris 1110
Darmond, Grace 661, 760, 870
Darro, Frankie 1113
Darvas 1111
Davenport, Edgar 481
Davert, Jose 1041
Davidson, Lawford 930
Davies, Marion 952; *page 143*
Davis, Dolly 1032
Davis, Harry 1069
Davis, Mildred 869
Davis, Owen 737
Davis, Ulysses 647, 671, 766
Davis, William 882
Daw, Marjorie 779, 1040
Dawley, Herbert M. 835, 852
Dawley, J. Searle 255, 764, 779, 809, 841
Dawson, Ivo 878, 915

Day, Alice 1076
Day, Joel 550
Day, Marceline 1078
Day, Richard 1086, 1092
Dayton, James 736
Dean, Louis 780
Dean, Raye 913
de Balzac, Honoré 226, 492, 676, 859, 863, 893, 986
de Beranger, Andre 1048
de Biccari, Violet 672
DeBrey, Claire 903
De Brulier, Nigel 970
Debucourt, Jean 1099
De Carlton, George 672
de Casseres, Ben 939
de Chomon, Segundo 98, 111, 1037
de Cordoba, Pedro 858, 952
De Cordova, Leander 845
Deesy, Alfred 802
De Forrest, Patsy 727, 751
de Grasse, Joseph 591
De Grasse, Sam 1106, 1121
de Kigoure, Rina 1107
Delacroix, Lucienne 912
De la Motte, Marguerite 1020
Delaney, Charles 1091, 1118
Del Colle, Ubaldo Maria 695
de Leon, Walter 931
de Liane, Lola 867
de Liguoro, Giuseppe 171
de Liguoro, Rina 1097
de Lord, Andre 429
Delpierre 42
Delva, Yvonne 848
Delysia, Alice 759
Demaurey, Edna 893
DeMille, Beatrice C. 781
DeMille, Cecil B. 556, 781, 1047
deMille, William C. 789
Dempster, Carol 940, 943, 1065
Deneubourg, George 848
Denny, Reginald 943
Denton, Jack 759
DePew, Hap 1096
de Putti, Lya 906, 1060, 1065
de Rosselli, Rex 786
De Ruiz, Nick 148, 1092, 1106
Desfontaines, Henri 260, 281
Deslys, Kay 1104
D'Esterre, Mme. 904, 919

258 Name Index

DeTitta, Arthur 1065
Deutsch, Ernest 866
Devant, David 867
De Vere, Harry 970
De Vilbiss, Robert 989
De Vogt, Carl 846
De Vonde, Chester 1115
Deyers, Lien 1087
Dexter, Elliott 922
Dickens, Charles 116, 238, 245, 279, 514, 541, 753
Diegelmann, Wilhelm 488, 804, 921
Diessi, Gustav 1108
Dieterle, Wilhelm (later William) 1023, 1050
Dietrich, Robert A. 522, 564, 735
Dietze, Max 1056
Dieudonne, Albert 675
Dillon, Edward 963
Dillon, John F. 1040
Dillon, John Webb 780, 824
Dione, Rose 989
Dix, Beulah Marie 789, 1104
Doeblin, Hugo 847
Don, David 727
Donlin, Mike 991
d'Ora, Daisy 1108
Doro, Marie 709
Dorris, Anita 1090
D'Orsay, Lawrence 1065
Douglas, L. 830
Dove, Billie 1013
Dowling, Joseph 537, 818, 875, 1020, 1021
Dowling, William 1036
Doxat-Pratt, B. E. 915
Drago, Henry Sinclair 1128
Dresser, Louise 1080
Drew, Anne 872
Drews, Karl 959
Drivetti, Giovanni 881
Drumier, Jack 542
Dryer, Carl Theodor 907
Du Bray, Claire 786, 807
Du Crow, Tote 1019, 1044
Du Maurier, George 14, 156, 431, 432, 524, 531, 600, 605, 679, 702, 727, 948, 989, 1090
Dumont, J. M. 897
Du Montel, Helene 236
Dunaew, Nicholas 638, 807

Duncan, Bud 664, 674, 680
Dunham, Maudie 830
Dunmyre, L. 911
Dunn, J. Malcolm 861
Dunn, Josephine 1065
Dunn, Winifred 1066
Durand, Jean 325, 417, 515
Durant, Fred W. 749
Dwiggins, Jay 638
Dyer, William J. 715, 850

Earles, Harry 1045; *page 180*
Ebert, Carl 564
Eddy, Helen 699, 851
Edeson, Arthur 1019, 1036, 1040, 1048, 1076, 1114
Edeson, Robert 682
Edwards, J. Gordon 703, 729, 780
Edwards, John 665
Edwards, Mattie 665
Edwards, Neely 1057
Edwards, Snitz 931, 1019, 1042
Egan, George 727
Eggert, Konstantin 996
Eis, Alice 526
Ekman, Gosta 1050; *page 187*
Elkas, Edward 638
Elliot, William J. 711, 904, 923
Ellis, Robert 692
Elvey, Maurice 599, 820, 904, 919
Elvidge, June 843
Elmer, Billy 556
Engle, Billy 1072
English, John W. 1081
Epstein, Jean 1099
Erb, Ludwig G. B. 719
Erckmann, Emile 818, 1049
Erdelyi, Geza 817
Erickson, Knute 1038
Escherich, Ernst 837
Esmelton, Fred 1073
Estabrook, Howard 744
Esterhazy, Agnes 1067
Evans, Bertram 1054
Evans, Cecile 1071
Evans, Estella 856
Evans, Fred 531
Evans, Joe 531, 603
Evans, Madge 724
Everest, Barbara 739

Name Index

Ewers, Hanns Heinz 522, 817, 1067, 1094
Exeter, Alexandra 996
Eycke, Leon 1004

Fabian, Maxmillian 1091
Fadovan, A. 171
Fahrney, M. J. 736
Fair, Elinor 1047
Fairbanks, Douglas 1019
Fairfax, Marion 806, 865, 943, 1036
Falk, Richard 817
Falkenstein, Julius 927, 1087
Falko, Alexei 996
Fame, Park 1093
Fane, Dorothy 749
Farley, Dot 1022
Farnham, Dorothy 1127
Farnham, Joe 1078, 1081, 1086, 1092, 1115, 1128
Farrar, Geraldine 781
Farrington, Adele 794
Fassbender, Max 803
Faversham, William 684
Fazenda, Louise 1048, 1120
Feher, Friedrich 831, 905
Fejos, Paul 918, 1121
Fellner, Hermann 838
Felton, William 536
Fenton, Leslie 1121
Fenton, Mark 893
Ferdinand, Franz 833
Ferguson, Al 1113
Ferguson, Helen 991, 1044
Ferris, Miriam 749
Feuillade, Louis 169, 366, 770
Fichtner, Erwin 571, 660, 873
Field, George 743
Field, Gladys 862
Finch, Flora 1072, 1103, 1118
Finlayson, James 1030
Fischinger, Oskar 1130
Fischbeck, Harry 895, 911, 1065
Fisher, Margarita 782
Fitzgerald, Cissy 638, 1022, 1124
Fitzhamon, Lewin 123, 124, 136, 138
Fitzroy, Emily 1048, 1081
Fleck, Jakob 431, 600, 854

Fleming, Carroll 547
Fleming, Claude 1127
Fletcher, Cecil 640
Fleisler, Joseph R. 1108
Florey, Robert 1098
Flugrath, Edna 541
Flynn, William J. 998
Fons, Olaf 442, 735, 906
Foote, Courtenay 890
Ford, Francis 594, 829
Ford, Harrison 745
Ford, James 1120
Ford, Starret 947
Ford, Victoria 658, 707
Forde, Eugenie 779
Forde, Walter 1125
Forest, Emil 998
Forrest, Alan 693, 705, 903
Forshay, Harold 862
Forster, Rudolph 959
Forsythe, Blanche 759
Fort, Garret 1013, 1047
Foster, Morris 637
Fouche, Miriam 810
Fox, Finis 955
Fox, John 941
Fox, Virginia 971
Fox, William 1082
Fort, Garrett 1047
Framer, Otto 988
Francis, Alec 737
Francis, Eve 975
Franey, William 644, 726
Frank, J. Herbert 638
Franklin, Chester M. 775, 777, 798, 998, 1091
Franklin, S. A. 775, 777, 798
Franklin, Martha 989
Frauchois, Rene 1082
Fraunholz, Fraunie 506, 615, 747
Frazee, Edwin A. 823
Frazer, Robert 938
Freisler, Fritz 827
French, Bert 526
French, George 1096
Freska, F. 891
Freund, Karl 571, 844, 846, 866, 871, 892, 910, 1056
Frey, Ellen 1056

Name Index

Friedlander, Louis (aka Lew Landers) 1106
Fries, Otto 1079
Fritsch, Willy 1087, 1130
Froehlich, Carl 413
Frolich, Gustav 1056
Fryer, Richard 973
Fuerth, Jaro 871
Fuglsang, Frederik 1052
Fuller, Dale 1120
Fuller, Mary 255, 621
Fulton, Helen 688
Furber, Douglas 1091
Furtham, Charles 973
Futrelle, Jacques 731

Gad, Urban 728
Gaddis, Pearl 646
Gadsdon, Jacqueline 1091, 1115
Gail, Jane 458, 769
Gaillord, Robert 595
Gal, Guyla 817
Gale, Alice 780
Galeen, Henryk 564, 804, 866, 939, 1023, 1067, 1094
Gallery, Tom 971
Gance, Abel 378, 433, 675, 826, 954
Gance, Marguerite Abel 1099
Gard, Lester 867
Gardin, Vladimir R. 920
Gardner, Helen 415, 678
Garga, Beatrice 1056
Garrick, Richard 663
Garry, Charles 948
Garry, Claude 352
Gaskill, Charles L. 678
Gasnier, Louis 552, 650, 760, 824
Gaston, Mae 829
Gates, Harvey 973, 998
Gathoney, Richard 913
Gaudio, Eugene 769
Gauntier, Gene 486
Gautier, Theophile 286
Gaye, Howard 1003
Gebuhr, Otto 866
Geier, Firmin 1055
Geldert, Clarence 1127
Genath, Otto 1015
Georg, Heinrich 1056
George, John 715, 947, 1092

Gerard, Douglas 1013
Gerber, Neva 815, 850, 1043
Gerrard, Douglas 779, 888
Gerstad, Merritt B. 1078, 1081, 1092
Gert, Valeska 1094
Gibbons, Cedric 1039, 1045, 1068, 1078, 1081, 1086, 1092, 1115, 1128
Giblyn, Charles 858
Gibson, Hoot 1044
Gibson, Margaret 766
Gilbert, C. Allan 732
Gilbert, Eugenia 1109
Gilbert, John (aka Jack) 995, 1086; *page 209*
Gilbert, Lewis 904
Gilbert, Yvette 1050
Gillespie, Arnold 1078
Gillette, William 943
Gillingwater, Claude 1076
Gillmer, Reuben 668, 849
Gilmour, J. H. 824
Gilroy, Barbara 733
Girard, Joseph W. 769, 815, 973
Gish, Dorothy 899
Gittens, Wyndham 1113
Glackens, L. M. 732
Glass, Gaston 1076, 1118
Glass, Max 1090
Gliese, Rochus 564, 754, 804, 866, 910
Gluckstadt, Wilhelm 490
Goddard, Charles L. 552
Goethe, Johann Wolfgang von 46, 62, 251, 252, 253, 465, 1050
Goetzke, Bernhard 906, 921, 927, 1015
Gogh, John 1076
Goldberg, Jesse J. 672
Gontcharov 283
Gonzalez, Myrtle 671
Good, Frank 1093
Goodrich, Jack 1106
Gooden, Arthur 821
Gordon, Bruce 874
Gordon, Harris 688, 733
Gordon, Huntley 858
Gordon, Kilbourne 1115
Gordon, Maude Turner 1093
Gotho, Heinrich 1056
Gottowt, John 522, 852, 864, 939, 1023

Name Index

Gotz, Carl 857, 1108
Gouget, Henri 429, 444
Gough, John 767, 1076, 1103
Goulding, Alf 869
Goulding, Edmund 895, 1003
Gounod 310, 930, 1074
Gowland, Gibson 1042
Graatkjar, Axel 852
Graham, Charles 684, 839
Granach, Alexander 939, 993, 1090
Grandin, Ethel 719
Grange, Maud 786
Grant, Valentine 646
Granville, F. L. 917
Grassby, Bertram 779, 795, 1004
Grattan, Stephen 755
Grau, Albin 939
Grauer, Ben 938
Graves, Walker Coleman, Jr. 1021
Gravina, Cesare 970, 1042, 1106
Gray, Daniel J. 1045
Gray, Jamie 1021
Gray, Lisa 1056
Gray, Tommy 1010
Green, Alfred 931
Green, Howard J. 1118
Green, Judd 1110
Green, Tom 9, 632
Greenbaum, Josef 571, 660
Greenbaum, Julius 873
Greenwood, Winifred 743, 897
Gregg, Helen 1113
Grey, Gloria 1003
Grey, John 1004, 1010
Green, Alfred 931
Gregor, Nora 912
Gribbon, Eddie 1047, 1048
Griffith, Corinne 956
Griffith, D. W. 141, 400, 534, 940, 1065
Griffith, Raymond 1065
Gripp, Harry 578
Grisanti, Antonio 358, 412
Griswold, Grace 940
Grodon, Dorothy 917
Gronau, Ernst 864
Grove, Sybil 1096
Grund, H. 1090
Guarracino, Umberto 881
Gudenan, Paul Gerd 1015

Guelstoff, Max 993
Guiol, Fred 1030
Guissart, Rene 995
Guitty, Madeleine 994
Gullan, Campbell 917
Gunning, Wid 1103, 1124
Gunther, L. 894
Gura, Sascha 832, 876
Gurtler, Danny 871
Guyon, Cecile 374
Gwenn, Edmund 752
Gys, Leda 508
Gys, Robert 1032, 1041

Haack, Kathe 852
Hackett, Walter 950
Haddock, William 839
Haggard, H. Rider 360, 759, 810, 1063
Hale, Alan 941, 956, 1104
Hale, Creighton 552, 764, 848, 989, 1072, 1124
Hall, Charles D. 1042, 1072, 1106
Hall, Donald 682, 972
Hall, Ella 693
Hall, George Edwardes 859
Hall, Willard Lee 893
Hall, Winter 825, 922
Haller, Ernest 1060, 1120
Hallett, Al 1051
Halliday, Jack 724
Hallor, Ray 1096
Halsey, Forrest 1065
Hameister, Willy 831, 832, 837, 842, 864
Hamer, Gladys 1055
Hamilton, J. S. 974
Hamilton, Lloyd 664, 674
Hamilton, Mark 1066
Hamilton, Dr. Nikola 565
Hamilton, William 1118
Hammerstein, Elaine 963
Hamper, Genevieve 703, 729
Hamrick, Burwell 781
Hancock, H. E. 713
Hanford, Ray 1046
Hanlon, Alma 801
Hanlon, Dan 769
Hansen, Alfred 819
Hansen, Juanita 887

Hanus, Emmerich 501
Hanus, Heinz 894
Hansson, Erling 907
Harbaugh, Carl 1066
Harding, Lyn 855
Hardy, Oliver 1102
Hardy, Sam 1060
Hare, Lumsden 943, 1040
Harlan, Kenneth 851, 885
Harrington, J. S. 1096
Harris, Dr. Clarence J. 663
Harris, Joseph 782
Harris, Marcia 1065
Harris, Thurston 136
Harrison, E. Harvey 855
Harrison, Irma 940
Harrison, Mona K. 640
Harron, Johnny 998
Harron, Robert 400, 534
Hartmann, Paul 901, 959
Hartmann, Sadakichi 1019
Harvey, W. M. 683
Hasler, Emil 1130
Hasselquist, Jenny 891
Hastings, Wells 899
Hatch, William Riley 552
Hathaway, Henry 1047
Hatton, Mrs. Raymond 924
Hatton, Raymond 781, 970
Haven, Harry 1043
Hauptmann, Gerhardt 442
Hawks, J. G. 925
Hawks, Kenneth 1114
Hawley, Ormi 632
Hawthorne, Nathaniel 133, 466
Hayden, Charles J. 862
Hayden, N. 915
Hayes, Danny 972
Hayes, Herbert 780
Hayes, J. Milton 477
Haynes, Manning 978
Hayward, Duke 715
Hayward, Lydia 978
Hazelton, George C. 689
Hazelton, Robert 972
Hearn, Mary 893
Heath, Ian 1126
Heatherley, Clifford 923
Hecht, Ben 1127
Heffron, T. N. 661
Hegesa, Grit 838

Heinrich, Hubert 1015
Heinz, Wolfgang 939
Hellbronner, Max 1094
Helm, Brigitte 1056, 1094; *page 191*
Hely, Annesley 929
Henderson, Lucius 321
Henley, Robert 649
Henry, Gale 644, 726
Hepworth, Cecil 59, 324, 536
Herbert, Holmes 1080
Herbert, Lucas Y. 1099
Herbert, Nora 854
Herder, Lilli 993
Heriat, Philippe 928
Heribel, Renee 1097
Herlth, Robert 921, 959, 1050
Herman, Al 987
Herring, Aggie 925, 1076
Herterich, Franz 896
Hervil, Renee 909
Herzfeld, Guido 939
Herzig, Sig 1101
Herzinger, Charles 1048
Herzka, Julius 912
Hesch, Gottlieb 1108
Hesperia 508
Hessling, Catherine 1122
Heuser, Heinrich 988
Hevener, Jerold 659
Hewitt, Earl R. 656
Heywood, W. L. 971
Hiatt, Ruth 1079
Hichens, Robert 820
Hicks, Sir Seymour 514
Hiers, Walter 931
Hilburn, Percy 1115
Hill, C. A. 1046
Hill, Doris 1114
Hill, Maude 980
Hill, Robert F. 1072
Hintze, Anny 1056
Hirsch, Walter 1106
Hitchcock, Alfred 1054
Hitchcock, Raymond 1082
Hobling, Franz 912
Hoerl, Arthur 963, 1096
Hoff, Halvard 907
Hoffman, Carl (aka Karl) 735, 838, 847, 857, 871, 883, 927, 988, 1015, 1050, 1107
Hoffman, Hugh 992

Hoffman, Otto 836
Hoger, J. C. 896
Hole, Gussy 838
Holger-Madsen, Forest 187
Holland, Cecil 955
Hollander, V. 891
Holm, Astrid 840, 951
Holmes, Stuart 703, 729, 991, 1013, 1022, 1062, 1106
Holtz, Tenen 1120
Holubar, Allan 769
Homans, Robert 973
Hope, F. 1068
Hopkins, Jack 672
Hopper, Hedda 943
Horbiger, Paul 1087
Horn, Camilla 1050
Hornbostel, Eugene 1091
Horne, James W. 714, 971, 1062
Horsetzky, George C. 1108
Hosch, Eduard 894, 912
Houdini, Harry 839, 911
Hough, Horace 1071
Hough, R. Lee 1082
Houseman, Arthur 1048, 1071
Howard, A. 688
Howard, George B. 714
Howard, Helen 791
Howard, Milford W. 955
Howard, Norman 565
Howard, Wanda 689
Howard, William K. 1042
Howland, Olin 926
Hoyer, Edgar 907
Hoyt, Arthur 1036
Hoyt, Harry O. 1036, 1093
Hubermann, Frau Galafres O. 431
Hubert, Ali 891
Hudson, Earl 1036, 1040
Huebsch, Erner 842
Hughes, Dorothy 1065
Hughes, Lloyd 836, 1036, 1128
Hugo, Victor 199, 780, 912, 929, 970, 1106
Hulcup, Jack 324
Hulette, Gladys 1069
Hull, George 1065
Hull, Henry 940, 972; *page 153*
Humes, Fergus 915
Hummel, Wilson 885

Humphrey, Orral 767
Humphrey, William 670
Humphreys, Cecil 812
Humphreys, William 1045
Hungerford, J. Edward 782
Hunt, Irene 761
Hunt, Jay 970
Hunte, Otto 846, 927, 1015, 1056, 1087, 1130
Hunter, Edna 731
Hunter, Glen 980
Hunter, T. Hayes 719
Hurlbut, William J. 720
Hurst, Brandon 861, 970, 973, 1019, 1106; *page 150*
Hurst, Paul 1051
Huszar, Karl 927
Hutchinson, Charles 801
Hutchinson, William 626
Hyams, Leila 1093
Hyland, Peggy 856, 917
Hyman, B. 947

Illes, Eugen 816
Illinsky, Igor 996
Imeson, A. B. 749, 1074
Ince, Ralph 415, 648
Ince, Thomas H. 633, 836
Ingleton, E. Magnus 776, 807
Ingleton, I. M. 702
Ingraham, Lloyd 924
Ingram, Rex 715, 807, 893, 947, 1055
Inslee, Charles 680
Irish, William 1103, 1120, 1124
Irrah, Tatjana 660
Irving, George 1121
Irving, H. B. 537
Irving, I. W. 1020
Irving, Washington 131, 395, 457, 934
Ishlington 1054
Ivers, Julia 922
Ives, Charlotte 800

Jaans, Robert 1121
Jaccard, Jacques 705, 1021
Jackson, Adrian 780
Jackson, Charles Tenny 1086
Jackson, Fred 903

Name Index

Jackson, Horace 991
Jacobs, W. W. 681, 978
Jacoby, Hans 1090
Jacques, Norbert 927
Jaenzon, Julius 840
Jakidawdra 386
James, B. 915
James, G. S. W. 634
James, Gladden 872
James, Walter 1038
Jamison, Bud 1003
Jannings, Emil 746, 819, 852, 1023, 1050; *pages 186, 187*
Janowitz, Hans 831, 871
Jansen, Ole 769
Janssen, Walter 921
Jarman, Jack 748
Jarvis, Sidney 1127
Jasset, Victorin 79, 444
Jeayes, Allen 904
Jenkins, William 874
Jenks, G. E. 656
Jennings, Devereaux 1079
Jennings, DeWitt 1039, 1070, 1124
Jensen, Eugen 833, 912
Jensen, Eulalie 970, 1047
John, Georg 796, 846, 847, 921, 927, 988, 1015, 1023, 1056, 1087, 1094
Johnson, Adrian 779
Johnson, Betty 556
Johnson, Cammilla 1066
Johnson, Edith 627
Johnson, J. W. 556
Johnson, Julian 1065
Johnson, Nobel 1019
Johnson, Richard 772
Johnson, Seesel Ann 1066
Johnston, Gladys 970
Johnston, Julianne 1019
Johnston, Lorimer 1003, 1049
Jones, Billy "Red" 1066
Jones, F. Richard 899
Jones, Fred C. 875
Jones, Leviticus 769
Jones, Morgan 547
Jordan, Jack 749
Joy, Ernest 781, 825
Juergens, Lu 873
Julian, Rupert 753, 1042, 1104
June 1054

Junkermann, Hans J. 927
Jurowski, Georg 1015
Juttke, Herbert 1052

Kahanamoku, Duke 1128
Kahane, Arthur 488
Kallina, Anna 912
Kammauf, Franz 837
Kampers, Fritz 988
Kanturek, Otto 1130
Kardos, Andor 817
Karger, Maxwell 903, 913
Karloff, Boris 1049, 1127; *page 185*
Karr, Darwin 506
Kastner, Bruno 796
Kayser-Heyl, Willy 871
Kayser-Titz, Willy 873
Keaton, Buster 902
Keefe, William 886
Keen, Malcolm 1054
Keenan, Frank 537, 818
Kefer, Pierre 1099
Keith, Ian 1060
Kellard, Ralph 760, 845, 880
Kellerman, Annette 828
Kellino, W. P. 668
Kelm-Brunnet, Farjaux 42
Kelsey, Fred 786, 955, 1076, 1091, 1118
Kelso, Mayme 1071
Kennedy, Ed 1073
Kent, Crauford 1079
Kent, Larry 1103
Kent, Leon D. 685
Kenton, Erle C. 933
Kenton, William 955
Kenton, Albert 1038
Kenyon, Charles 885
Kenyon, Doris 747, 972; *page 153*
Kernell, William 1114
Kerr, Robert 946
Kerrigan, J. Warren 402, 492, 863, 875
Kerry, Norman 970, 1014, 1042, 1092
Kertesz, Mihaly (aka Michael Curtiz) 817
Kesson, David 1045
Kesson, Frank 1070
Kettlehut, Eric (aka Erich) 1015, 1056

Name Index

Kierska, Marga 842
Kilgour, Joseph 720
Kimball, Edward 989
King, Bradley 1081
King, Burton 839, 845, 911
King, Claude 1078
King, Henry 884
King, Louis 1113
Kingsley, Arthur 929
Kingston, Natalie 1126
Kinoshita, Keisuke 968
Kirby, Fred 1013
Kirk, Charles M. 940, 1065
Kirkby, Ollie 714
Kirkham, Kathleen 782
Kirkland, David 924
Kirkland, Hardee 457, 995
Kirmse, Carl 846
Kirsch, Richard 832
Klaren, Georg C. 1052
Klein, Cesar 864
Klein, Charles 1111
Klein, Robert 743, 1003
Klein-Rogge, Rudolph (aka Rudolf) 831, 921, 927, 988, 1015, 1056, 1087
Kline, Ben 992, 1073
Kline, Eddie 902
Klitsch, Wilhelm 854
Klopfer, Eugen 892
Klopstock, Fredrich 412
Knaak, Franz 842
Knight, Castleton 1083
Kobe, Hans 892
Kober, Erick 837, 1067
Koch, Georg August 1015
Kohner, Paul 1106
Kolker, Henry 704
Kolm, Anton 431
Kolm, Luise 431, 600, 854
Komissarenko, E. 1011
Korff, Arnold 901
Kormendy, Kalman 817
Korner, Lother 522
Kornman, Tony 970
Kortner, Fritz 827, 993, 1007, 1108
Kotsonaros, George 1070, 1093
Kozlovsky, Sergei 996
Kraft, Tenna 907
Kraly, Hans 819, 891
Krampf, Gunther 1007, 1067, 1108

Kraszevski, I. J. 742
Krauss, Charles 374, 530
Krauss, Henri 352
Krauss, Werner 746, 831, 832, 1023, 1067; *pages 98, 99, 100*
Kraussneck, Arthur 959
Kricheldorff, H. 852
Kronegg, Paul 896, 976
Kronert, Max 866
Krueger, Lizzy 413
Kuehne, Friedrich 571, 660, 816
Kugler, Frank G. 810
Kuhle, Walter 1056
Kuinzhi, Valentina 996
Kuper, Margaret 1130
Kupfer, Margarete 871
Kuter, Leo E. 947
Kuwa, George 1073
Kyser, Hans 1050

LaBadie, Flo 637
Lachman, Harry 1055
Lackaye, Wilton 702
Lackteen, Frank 1029, 1119
Lacombe, G. 1041
Laemmle, Carl 458, 970, 1042, 1072, 1073, 1106, 1121
Laemmle, Carl, Jr. 1121
Laemmle, Carla 1042
Laemmle, Edward 1044
Lafayette, Andree 989
Laidlaw, Roy 970
Lake, Alice 903, 991
La Marr, Barbara 947
Lambert, Glen 1105
Lamothe, J. L. 685
Lampel, Alfred 896
Lamyn, Charles 1099
Lancaster, Leland 917
Landau, Mrs. David 899
Landers, Lew *see* Friedlander, Louis
Landis, Winifred 1003
Landshoff, Ruth 939
Lane, Charles 861
Lane, Lupino 822
Lang, Fritz 796, 831, 832, 837, 842, 846, 906, 927, 1015, 1056, 1087, 1130; *page 132*
Lang, Phil 619

Langley, Herbert 1074
Lanner, Margarete 1056
Lanning, Frank 1092
La Plante, Laura 1072; *page 200*
La Porte, Elizza 1067
Lara, Lea 803
La Reno, Richard 715
Larinaga, Forster 927
Laroque, Rod 1047
Larsen, Viggo 187
La Rue, Fontaine 925, 1021
La Saint, Edward J. 627
La Salle, Katherine 667
Lasky, Jesse L. 556, 781, 931
La Strange, Dick 556
Laurel, Stan 1027, 1102
Lavine, Jack 1066
Law, Bert 818
Law, Walter 780, 848
Lawrence, Edmund 704
Lawrence, Max 819
Lawson, Jack 681
Lazarus, Sidney 1076
Learn, Bessie 641
Lebedeff, Ivan 1065
Leblanc, Georgette 975
Lederer, Franz 1108
Lederer, Otto 647, 1049
Lee, Miss Carey 780
Lee, Donald W. 1068
Lee, Etta 992, 1019, 1073
Lee, Frankie 991
Lee, Gwen 1114
Lee, Lila 897, 931, 941, 1096
Lee, Marion 791
Lee, Rowland V. 937
Lee, Virginia 798
Lees, Margot 1074
Legar, Fernand 975
Lehrman, Henry 1013
Leighton, Lillian 730, 781
Leiko, Maria 892
Leisen, Mitchell 1019
Leni, Paul 1023, 1072, 1073, 1106
Leon, Alesia 634, 718
Leonard, Robert 693, 806
Lermontof 317
Lerner, Jacques 1082
Leroux, Gaston 444, 1042, 1093
Lerski, Helmar 1023

Leslie, Lily 704
Lessey, George 503, 505
Lester, Kate 956, 970
Lester, William 1053
Lettinger, Bruno 846
Lettinger, Rudolph 831
Leubas, Louis 770
Levesque, Marcel 770
Le Viness, Carl M. 656
Le Vino, A. S. 890
Lewin, Albert 1068
Lewis, Eva 970
Lewis, Ida 537, 818
Lewis, Jane 638
Lewis, Leopold 538, 818
Lewis, Mitchell 1039
Lewis, Ralph 534, 795, 893, 1003
Lewis, Sheldon 552, 862, 1020, 1124; *page 227*
Ley, Willy 1130
L'Herbier, Marcel 928, 975
Libbert, H. 1039
Lictenstein, Rose 1056
Liebmann, Robert 847, 857, 873
Liedtke, Harry 819, 891
Lilzer, Wolfgang 1094
Lincoln, Elmo 775
Lind, Jens G. 907
Lindau, Paul 501
Lindau-Schulz, Margaret 838
Linder, Max 273, 650, 954
Linson, Harry 478
Lipton, Lew 1068
Little, Anna 618, 825
Littlefield, L. D. 911
Littlefield, Lucien 556, 1047, 1072
Lloyd, Frank 618, 956
Lloyd, Harold 869, 1010
Loane Tucker, George 797
Loder, John 1094, 1127
Loeb, William B. 950
Logan, Jacqueline 925, 1104, 1118; *page 215*
Logue, Charles A. 839, 845, 1069
Lohner-Beda, Fritz 854
Lolli, Alberto Carlo 421
London, Jack 890
Lonergan, Philip 547, 686, 885
Long, John Luther 643
Lonsdale, Harry 457, 779
Looney, J. F. 778

Name Index

Loos, Theodor 735, 883, 1015, 1056
Lorenz, Howard 1096
Loring, Hope 867
Lorraine, Lillian 683
Loryea, Milton 769
Lovatt, Jack 718
Love, Bessie 986, 1036
Love, Montagu 724, 778, 1103
Lovering, Joseph 602
Lowe, Edmund 895, 1093
Lowe, Edward T. 450, 970
Lowe, Edward T., Jr. 1091
Lowndes, Mrs. Belloc 1054
Lubitsch, Ernest 819, 891
Lucas, Wilfred 400, 989
Lucoque, Lisle 759
Lucoque, Nellie 759
Luddy, Edward L. 1024
Ludwig, Ernst 803
Lugosi, Bela 871
Lund, Gustav 187
Lundholm, Lisa 840
Lundin, Walter 1010
Lux, Margit 817
Luxford, Lola 966
Lyon, Ben 1040, 1060, 1061
Lyons, Eddie 658, 707, 741
Lyons, Harry Agar 953, 962, 965, 967, 977, 981, 982, 984, 985, 1001, 1002, 1005
Lytell, Bert 913

McAllister, Paul 702
McAvoy, May 874, 1061
MacBean, L. C. 752
McCarey, Leo 1102
McCarthy, Henry 1076
McCauley, David 672
McComas, Ralph 730
McConnell, Gladys 1119
McConville, Bernard 775, 777
McCormac, Muriel 1066
McCoy, Gertrude 662
McCullough, Philo 989
MacDermott, Marc 467, 848
MacDonald, Donald 914
McDonald, Francis 715, 815, 989
McDonald, J. Farrell 931, 995
McDonald, Jack 995, 1109

McDowell, Claire 753, 776, 1020
MacDowell, Nelson 1036
McGowan, Robert 741
McGrane, Thomas J. 719
McGrath, Harold 963
McGregor, Malcolm 992
McGuire, George 1036
McGuire, Tom 1079
McIntosh, Burr 1029
Mack, Charles E. 940
Mack, Hughie 638, 751, 947
Mack, Max 501, 551
Mack, Willard 1038
MacKay, Charles 878
MacKay, Joseph 755
McKay, Winsor 185, 787, 916
MacKaye, Fred 1121
Mackaye, Percy 980
McKee, Raymond 925
MacKenzie, Donald 760
McKim, Edwin 727
McKim, Robert 1044, 1048
McLaglen, Victor 1045
McLane, Mary 1066
McLaren, Mary 745
McLaughlin, Gibb 1125
MacLean, Kenneth 1019
McLean, May 1106
MacLennan, Andy 1078, 1086
McNamara, Ted 1082
McNamara, Tom 1066
McNeill, Thelma 1124
MacPherson, Jeanie 556, 781
MacQuame, George 970
McRea, Duncan 662
MacRae, Henry 529, 1126
McWade, Edward 457, 1038
McWade, Margaret 1036
Madden, Edward 724
Madison, Cleo 715, 1021
Madison, Virginia 925
Madsen, Holger 561
Maggi, Luigi 358, 412
Magnusson, Carl 840
Mahoney, Elizabeth 791
Mailes, Charles 400, 1118
Malatinszky, Boske 817
Malcolm, C. H. 1047
Malina, J. 976
Mallet-Stevens, R. 975

Malten, Felicitas 1107
Manichoux 770
Mann, Frankie 1013
Mann, Hank 860
Mann, Ned 1048
Mannheim, Lucie 988
Manning, Mildred 995
Mannstedt, Otto 842
Mansfield, Martha 861; *page 111*
Mantell, Robert B. 703, 729
Marau, Jean 994
Mardo, Estelle 595
Marion, Frances 949
Marion, George, Jr. 1048, 1066
Marjaroni, Mario 878
Marks, Maurice 724
Marks, Willie 745
Marlowe, Christopher 1050
Marriott, Moore 1110
Marschall, Hans 837
Marsh, Mae 400, 534
Marsh, Marguerite 839
Marsh, Oliver T. 991
Marshall, Perle 1093
Marshall, Tully 781, 814, 970, 1072, 1076
Marshall, William 931, 1013
Martin, Irvin J. 1019
Martin, J. H. 72, 99
Martin, Joe 715, 947
Martinelli, Arthur 913
Marvin, Grace 1042
Mason, Dan 1073
Mason, James 885, 1109
Mathews, Dorcas 836
Mathews, H. C. 445
Mathis, June 893, 903
Matieson, Otto 1070, 1071, 1111
Matray, Ernst 796
Matsutaro, Kawaguchi 1058
Matthews, A. E. 752
Mattison, Ernest 951
Mattoni, Andre 1090
Mattox, Martha 1072
Mattraw, Scotty 1019
Maude, Arthur 633, 710, 911, 913
Maude, Cyril 652
Maugham, Somerset 1055
Maupin, Ernest 690
Maurus, Gerda 1087, 1130
Maxmillian, Max 1067
May, Alice 938
May, Joe 796, 906
Mayer, Carl 831, 864, 876, 892
Mayer, Edwin Justus 1127
Mayer, Louis B. 862, 1045
Mayer, R. 976
Maynard, Ken 1051, 1109
Mayne, Eric 893
Mayo, Archie 1069
Mayo, Christine 704, 848
Mayo, Frank 1014
Mayo, Melvin 699
Meeker, George 1114
Mehaffy, Blanche 1030
Meinert, Rudolph 571
Melford, Mark 386
Méliès, George 1, 2, 3, 4, 5, 6, 7, 8, 10, 11, 16, 19, 20, 21, 23, 25, 40, 42, 44, 45, 46, 48, 49, 50, 52, 53, 56, 57, 58, 60, 61, 62, 63, 65, 67, 73, 76, 81, 82, 84, 85, 122, 126, 129, 130, 139, 161, 174, 176, 184, 306, 372
Menasco, Milton 1036
Mendes, Lothar 1060
Menessier, Henri 1055
Menjou, Adolphe 944, 1065
Menzies, William Cameron 1019, 1048
Merchant, Jay 1106
Mereanton, Louis 608
Meredith, Louis 652
Merivale, Philip 605, 950
Merkyl, John 1045
Merrill, Frank 1126
Merrill, Walter 1070
Merritt, Abraham 1124
Merwin, B. 476
Mescall, John 1104
Messinger, Buddy 775, 1024
Messter, Oscar 413
Mestayer, Harry 661
Metcalfe, Earle 843
Methley, A. A. 550
Metzner, Erno 891
Meuthel, Lothar 866
Meyer, Carl 901
Meyer, Torbin 1106
Meyerhold, Vsevolod 687
Meyers, Amos 893
Meyers, Carmel 896

Name Index

Meyers, W. Ray 970
Meyrink, Gustav 866
Mierendorff, Hans 796
Migliar, A. 915
Milburn, James 769
Miljan, John 1042, 1069, 1127
Millarde, Harry 938
Miller, Frank 929, 930, 964, 990
Miller, J. Clarkson 843, 972
Miller, Mary Louise 1066
Miller, Patsy Ruth 970, 1004; *pages 148, 151*
Miller, Virgil 1042
Miller, Walter 1029, 1112, 1123
Miller, William Chrystie 400
Millhauser, Bertram 824, 887, 1004, 1104
Milowanoff, Sandra 1041
Milta, A. 171
Milton, John 412, 719
Milton, Maude 913
Mineau, Charlotte 1066
Minter, Mary Miles 791
Miranda, Tom 1120
Mitchell, George 1046
Mitchell, Howard M. 856
Mitchell, Rhea 821, 870
Mizoguchi, Kenji 1058
Mohr, Hal 1022, 1038, 1066, 1121
Molnar, Ferenc 895
Molnar, Franz 633
Molnar, Julius, Jr. 1106
Mong, William V. 1103, 1120, 1124
Montagu, Ivor 1054
Montague, Fred 556
Montana, Bull 865, 1036
Moody, Harry 1051
Moon, Lorna 1080
Moore, Matt 734, 769, 1004, 1045
Moore, Tom 588, 692, 806
Moorhead, Natalie 1127
Moran, Lee 707, 741
Moran, Lois 1060
Moran, Polly 1073, 1091, 1127
Morante, Milburn 1046
Morena, Erna 883
Moreno, Antonio 638, 824
Morgan, Ira 1039, 1127
Morgan, Jeanne 1065
Morgan, Kewpie 1079
Morgan, Paul 846, 847

Morgan, Sidney 640
Morin, A. 1032
Morosco, Walter 1070
Morris, Governeur 885
Morrison, James W. 720, 878, 991
Morse, N. Brewster 872
Morton, Cyril 536
Mosjoukine, Ivan 597, 609
Mower, Jack 782
Moyse, Mr. 420
Mudie, Leonard 913
Muenzer, Kurt 838
Mulhall, Jack 963
Mullally, Jode 556
Mullen, Gordon 989
Muller, Hans Carl 1015
Murfin, Jane 1061
Murillo, Mary (aka Marie) 703, 729, 810
Murname, Allen 744
Murnau, F. W. 844, 871, 876, 891, 901, 939, 1050
Murphy, Joe 1072
Murphy, Martin 769
Murray, Charlie 1076
Murray, J. S. 547
Murray, Mae 806
Murski, Alexander 1052
Murton, Walter W. 904, 958, 965, 1001, 1002, 1005
Musidora 770
Musuraca, Nicholas 1113
Myers, Harry 625

Nagel, Conrad 944, 1068, 1078
Nakano, Eiji 1058
Naldi, Nita 861, 911
Nally, William 972
Nambu, K. 1019
Nanten, Louis 718
Napierkowska, Stacia 352
Nares, Owen 752, 812, 819, 1065
Navatzi, M. 317
Neame, Elwin 393, 419, 560, 655
Negri, Pola 819, 891
Negri-Pouget, Fernanda 253
Neil, Richard R. 1128
Neilan, Marshall 865
Neill, James 624, 781
Neill, Roy William 1022

Neilson-Terry, Dennis 859
Nelson, Jack 836
Nelson-Terry, Phyllis 948
Nemetz, Max 939
Neppach, Robert 876, 892
Nero, Curtis 1115
Nerz, Louis 912, 1007
Nerz, Louise 894
Nesbitt, Miriam 467
Nettleford, Archibald 1125
Neumann, Harry 1044
Neumann, Lotte 551
Neuss, Alwin 175, 551, 571, 660
Neuss, Robert 735
Newfield, Sam 1116
Newhard, Robert 970
Newlands, R. H. 1106
Newman, Frank 553
Newman, I. 553
Newmeyer, Fred 1010, 1061
Newton, Charles 743, 1022
Niblo, Fred 836
Nichols, George 1047
Nichols, Marguerite 772
Nicholson, Meredith 661
Nielsen, A. R. 156
Niemeyer, Marianne 754
Nigh, William 1080
Nilsson, Anna Q. 1022, 1040
Nissen, Aud Egede 735, 891, 927
Nissen, Helge 907
Nitzchmann, Erich 921, 959, 1067
Nixon, Marian 1073
Noble, John W. 684
Nolan, Mary 1115
Nolan, William 868, 1019
Nording, Frl. 600
North, Wilfred 872, 1112
Norton, Barry 1093
Norton, Edgar 1106
Norwood, Ellie 904, 923, 958
Nourse, Dorothy 1065
Novarro, Ramon 947
Novello, Ivor 1054
Nowell, Wedgewood 715, 807

Oakman, Wheeler 485
Ober, Robert 1039
Oberth, Hermann 1130
Obolenskaya, Olga 609

O'Brien, Gypsy 880, 952
O'Brien, John B. 1020, 1053
O'Brien, Willis H. 783, 805, 835, 1036
O'Connell, William 1049, 1082
Odon, Fritz 817
O'Donahue, James T. 1076
O'Donnel, Spike 1066
O'Fredericks, Alice 951
Ogle, Charles 255, 477, 503, 621; page 37
O'Grady, Monty 1066
Ohnet, Georges 938
Okada, Yoshiko 1058
Oland, Warner 703, 887, 1118
Olcott, Sidney 486, 646
Oliver, Guy 409, 627
Oliver, Harry 1066
Oliver, Paul 1041
Olmstead, Gertrude 989, 1038
Olonova, Olga 719
Olsen, Ole 156, 187, 442
O'Malley, Pat 749, 865
O'Neal, Edward 855
O'Neill, Edward 739, 820
O'Neill, James 602
O'Neill, Thomas P. 1106
Oppenheim, E. Phillips 1060
Oppenheim, James 790
Orla, Ressel 846
Orlamond, William 1120
Orlova, V. 996
Ormston, Frank D. 769
Osborne, Bud 736
Osmun, Leighton 781
Oswald, H. 992
Oswald, Richard 551, 571, 660, 803, 847, 883, 1052, 1117
Otsep, F. 750
Otto, Henry 731, 1003
Otzep, Fydor 996
Overbaugh, Roy 861
Owen, Harold 1080
Owens, Raymond 552

Pabst, G. W. 1108
Paetzold, Dore 866
Pagano, Bartolomeo 1037
Pain, Barry 925
Palerme, Gina 954

Pallette, Eugene 794
Palm, A. Carle 1038
Palmer, Zoe 915, 1110
Pankau, Mia 1094
Panzer, Paul 882
Papa, Salvatore 171
Parke, William, Jr. 899
Parke, William, Sr. 970, 973
Parker, Albert 943
Parker, Max 1047
Parkinson, H. B. 1074
Parks, Frances 784
Partos, Gustav 1121
Pasha, Kalia 1115, 1124
Paton, Stuart 769, 785, 815
Patrick, John 1070
Paul, Fred 953, 962, 977, 981, 982, 984, 985, 1001, 1002, 1005
Pauline, J. Robert 882
Paulsen, Harald 864
Pavanelli, Livio 1052
Pawn, Doris 656, 885
Payne, Douglas 565, 711
Peacock, Lilian 644, 726
Peake, Marion 822
Pearson, Leo 776
Pearson, Virginia 1042
Pebal, H. 976
Pederson, Maren 951
Peggy, Baby 1035
Pembroke, Scott 1096
Pendleton, Edna 769
Penrod, A. G. 910
Percy, Eileen 1062
Percy, Thelma 890
Percyval, Wigney 810
Perdue, Derelys 955
Perfitt, Frank 1125
Perkins, Osgood 980
Perrault, Charles 111, 388, 419, 517
Perret, Leonce 389, 848
Perry, Paul 789
Peters, House 794
Peterson, Jerry 972
Petrovich, Ivan 1055, 1094; *page 190*
Phelps, Lee 885
Philbin, Mary 1042, 1106, 1121; *pages 174, 176, 218*
Philips, Augustus 255
Philips, H. W. 786

Phillips, Bertram 964, 990
Phillips, Edward 1049
Pick, Lupu 735, 746, 803, 1087
Pickford, Jack 1048; *page 184*
Pickford, Mary 340, 1065; *page 195*
Pidgeon, Walter 1076
Pierson, Leo 620
Pike, William 839
Pio, Elith 187, 907, 951
Pittaschau, Ernst 803
Pivar, Maurice 1042, 1106
Planer, Franz 1094
Platen, Karl 921, 927, 993
Plumb, Hay 324
Pluto, Mr. 638
Poe, Edgar Allan 146, 197, 260, 281, 409, 429, 506, 522, 534, 583, 689, 847, 920, 1067, 1083, 1099, 1100, 1111
Poelzig, Hans 866, 959
Poff, Lon 1003, 1106
Pohl, Klaus 1130
Polito, Sol 955, 1103, 1120, 1124
Pollack, Lew 1106
Pollard, Harry 782
Pollock, Channing 1056
Pommer, Erich 831, 842, 921, 1015
Pontoppidan, Clara 906, 951
Porten, Henny 413
Porter, Edwin S. 12, 28, 28a, 38
Potechina, Lydia 927
Poten, Victor 924, 971
Potter, Gertie 138
Poulton, Mabel 1125
Pouyet, Eugene (aka Gene) 893, 947
Powell, Michael 1055
Powell, William H. 943
Powers, Tom 536
Prager, W. 488
Prasch-Grevenberg, Auguste 927
Prejean, Albert 1032, 1041
Pretty, Arline 720
Price, Kate 791
Pridella, Claire 324
Pringle, Aileen 1039
Prior, Herbert 505
Proncarolo, Emilio 171
Protazanov, Jacob 996
Prout, Eva 339

Prouty, Jed 1069
Puffy, Charles 1081, 1106
Puglia, Frank 1106
Pusey, Arthur 855, 915, 1125
Pushkin 282, 283, 509, 597, 918

Quirk, Billy 550

Rabinovitch, Isaac 996
Radcliffe, Violet 775
Rains, Fred 822
Rale, M. W. 552, 744
Ralph, Hanna 852, 1015, 1050
Ralph, Louis 1087, 1094
Ralston, Jobyna 1010
Rameau, Emil 819
Rand, Sally 1047
Randoe, Anders 1121
Rankin, Arthur 1022
Ranzenhofer, Artur 894
Rapee, Erno 1106
Rashig, Kraft 1108
Rasp, Fritz 993, 1052, 1056, 1087, 1107
Raspe, Rudolph E. 307
Ratterman, William H. 699
Rawlinson, Herbert 618, 808
Ray, Ailene 1029, 1112
Ray, Albert 914, 1071, 1114
Ray, Charles 914
Rayford, Alma 1051
Raymond, Charles 867
Razeto, Stella 627
Read, J. Parker, Jr. 972
Read, James 603
Reagan, Martin 810
Reardon, James 849
Reed, Langford 99, 106
Reed, Luther 952
Reed, Tom 1042, 1121
Reeve, Arthur B. 552, 839
Rehnkopf, Paul 1087
Reich, Hans Leo 1056
Reicher, Frank 624
Reicher, Hedwig 1104
Reid, Hal 974
Reid, Jane 1113
Reid, Marguerite 647
Reid, Wallace 504, 781, 825, 931

Reimann, Walter 831, 852, 1094
Reinhard, Arthur 1056
Reinhardt, Max 488
Reinhart, William 845
Reisner, Charles F. 1079
Renick, Ruth 922
Rennspiles, Ernst 816
Renoir, Jean 1122
Retzlag, Fran 413
Reumert, Poul 951
Reuter, Marga 871
Rex, Eugen 993
Rex, Ludwig 873
Reynolds, Art 1096
Reynolds, Harry 1078, 1092, 1115, 1128
Rice, Frank 1044
Richard, Frieda 1015, 1050
Richman, Charles 720, 938
Richtell, Rose 534
Richter, Heinrich 1063
Richter, Kurt 522, 819, 891, 910
Richter, Paul 927, 1015; *page 164*
Rickson, Lucille 998, 1022
Ridgely, Richard 477, 676, 701, 790, 801
Ridon, Reilly 501
Rifenborich, R. P., Jr. 765
Rigby, L. G. 1071, 1082
Righelli, Gennaro 1090
Rinehart, Mary Roberts 627, 1048
Rippert, Otto 735, 832, 842
Risdon, Elizabeth 599
Rittau, Gunther 1015, 1056
Rittner, Rudolph 1015
Roach, Bert 1018, 1068
Roach, J. Anthony 856
Robbins, Clarence Aaron 1045
Roberts, Alice 1108
Roberts, Theodore 556, 781
Roberts, Harry 855
Roberts, Iris 1015
Robertson, John S. 861
Robinson, W. C. 400
Robison, Arthur 746, 993
Roche, John 1127
Rock, Charles 541, 739
Rock, Joe 1027, 1057
Roemer, Joseph 832
Rogan, Florence 1066
Rogell, Albert 1109

Name Index

Rogers, Ed 882
Rogers, Will 934, 941
Rohmer, Sax 953, 962, 965, 967, 977, 981, 982, 984, 985, 1001, 1002, 1005
Rohrig, Walter 831, 921, 959, 1050
Rolfe, Benjamin A. 839, 878
Rollins, Jack 1021
Roop, J. L. 1105
Roscoe, Albert 856
Rose, Jackson 890, 998
Rose, Louis B. 647
Rosen, Phil 780, 1118
Rosher, Charles 1066
Rositto, Alonzo (Angelo) 1124
Rosmer, Milton 739, 797
Rosner, Erwin 832
Ross, Milton 885
Ross, Phil 965
Rosson, Richard 1093
Roth, Sandy 1079
Roussell, Henri 429
Routh, George 699
Rowe, George 1030
Rowland, Richard A. 1120
Royce, Julian 640
Rubens, Alma 949
Ruby, Irving B. 911, 940
Rudolph, Lansa 871
Ruibar, Herr 833
Rule, B. C. 1095
Russell, James 631
Russell, John 1065
Russell, William 937
Ruttenberg, Joseph 938
Ruttman, Walther 1015
Ryan, Chet 784
Rye, Stellan 522, 573

Sacchetto, Rita 473
Sackville, Gordon 772
Sainpolis, John 801, 992, 1042
Sais, Maria 674, 714
Sakai, Yoneko 1058
Salfrank, Herman 921
Salisbury, Monroe 782, 888
Salmonova, Lyda 522, 564, 754, 804, 866, 910
Saltikoff, N. 742
Salzburg, Janet 436

Sampson, Teddy 643
Sanderson, Challis 930
Sandrock, Adele 927
Santell, Alfred 664, 1004, 1074
Santschi, Thomas 485, 620
Sargent, E. 659
Sartov, Hendrick 940
Sascha, Alexander 1094
Saunders, Mrs. Celestine 950
Saunders, Willy 362
Savage, Nellie 1065
Sawyer, Ruth 806
Scardon, Paul 648, 678, 720
Schade, Betty 776, 807, 808
Schaefer, Anne 647
Schaeffer, A. L. 1066
Schayer, Richard 1128
Schenk, Earl 924
Schlegel, Margarete 871
Schmidt, Kai 1081
Schneevoight, George 653, 907
Schneider, Rudolf 993
Schneiderman, George 1071
Schnell, G. H. 939
Schoenfeld, Emmy 951
Schofield, Paul 991
Scholl, Edward 940
Schon, Margaret 1015
Schonemann, E. 996
Schopfer, Karl 896
Schreck, Max 939; *pages 135, 137*
Schreiber, Helmut 1094
Schrock, Raymond 1042, 1044
Schroeder, Greta 866, 939
Schroth, Heinrich 1094
Schunemann, Emile 842, 846
Schuenzel, Reinhold 838, 847, 857, 883
Schutz, Maurice S. 1032, 1041
Scott, Mansfield 884
Scott, William 1003
Scully, Mary 1040
Seastrom, Victor 723, 840
Sebastian, Dorothy 1127
Sedgwick, Edward 1042, 1044, 1068
Sedgwick, Eileen 1068
Seeber, Guido 522, 564
Seesel, Charles O. 895
Seitz, George B. 552, 760, 824
Seitz, John F. 893, 947, 1055
Sekely, Dr. Bela 1106

Name Index

Selander, Concordia 840
Sellon, Charles A. 1038, 1071
Semler, Gustav Adolph 816
Semmels, Harry 887
Semon, Larry 751, 813
Seroff, George 1042
Seydelmann, Armin 833, 894, 912
Shamroy, Leon 1111
Shannon, Alexander 862
Shannon, Norris 795
Shanor, Peggy 824, 882
Sharits, Dan 1091
Sharp, Henry 1128
Shaw, Brinsley 991
Shaw, Harold 541, 605
Shea, William 638
Sheehan, Perley Poore 970
Shelderfer, Joe 638
Sheldon, E. Lloyd 779
Shelley, Mary W. 255, 672, 735, 881
Sheridan, Frank 940
Sherman, Evelyn 989
Sherman, Jane 970
Sherry, Craighall 1087
Sherry, J. Barney 1060
Short, Don 885
Short, Gertrude 1086
Short, Lew 1096
Shotwell, Marie 773, 848
Shrock, Raymond L. 639, 1042, 1045
Shuftan, Eugene 1056
Shulter, Edward 890
Shumway, L. C. (aka Lee) 699, 765, 1048
Siegel, Bernard 1042
Siegmann, George 534, 851, 1013, 1072, 1106
Sills, Milton 973
Silvers, Louis 1120
Simov, Victor 996
Sinclair, Irene (pseudonym for D. W. Griffith) 940
Sittenham, Fred 882
Slavinsky, Y. 750
Sloane, Paul H. 938
Sloman, Edward 765, 791, 890
Small, Edward 1076
Smalley, Phillips 504
Smiles, Finch 1036

Smiley, John W. 672
Smiley, Joseph 731, 843
Smith, Albert E. 373
Smith, C. Aubrey 773
Smith, Frank 761
Smith, George Albert 6
Smith, James 534
Smith, Oscar 1093
Smith, Sidney 626
Sneeze, Mr. 638
Snow, Marguerite 321, 360
Snyder, Matt 458
Sojin, K. (aka Kamiyama) 1019, 1048, 1073, 1124, 1127
Solntseva, Yulia 996
Sonja, Magda 827
Sorelle, William 458
Sorensen, Axel 187
Sorina, Alexandra 1007
Sothern, E. H. 800
Sothern, Jean 744
Southern, Eve 779, 1103
Sparkuhl, Theodor 891
Specht, Georges 954
Spence, Ralph 1013, 1068, 1076
Stahl-Urach 927
Standing, Percy Darrell 672
Standing, Wyndham 1022
Stanlaws, Penrhyn 944
Stanley, Forrest 952, 1072
Stanmore, Frank 964, 990
Stannard, Eliot 820, 1054
Stanwood, Rita 556
Stanton, Richard 649, 795
Stapleton, Lady Doris 867
Starevich, Ladislas 597, 609, 742
Stark, Curt A. 413
Starke, Pauline 1003
Stassny, Fritz 1007
Statler, Marjorie 1063
Statter, Arthur 1040
Stegler, Allan 903
Steinbruck, Albert 866
Steinsleck, Anne Marie 976
Stem, Herbert 1100
Stern, Ernst 1023, 1129
Stern, Louis 1128
Sternberg, Hans 921
Stevens, Charles 1019
Stevens, Edwin 724

Name Index

Stevens, George 638, 861, 878
Stevenson, Charles 950, 1010
Stevenson, Robert Louis 120, 321, 548, 551, 659, 738, 847, 860, 861, 868, 870, 1026
Stewart, Anita 648, 1071
Stewart, Roy 1066
Stifter, Manus 871
Stockdale, Carl (aka Carlton) 818, 1070, 1096
Stone, Lewis 947, 1036
Stonehouse, Ruth 839, 1095
Storey, Edith 415, 638
Storey, Thomas L. 1119, 1123
Storm, Olaf 1056
Storm, Theodor 959
Stow, Percy 64, 66, 106, 179
Stowell, William 457
Stowitz 1055
Strabny, Fritz 894, 912
Strandin, Ebon 907
Strange, Philip 1127
Stratton, Arthur 1125
Stratz, Rudolf 901
Streeter, Coolidge 911
Stribolt, Oscar 951
Strickland, Helen 790
Strobl, Julius 854
Strobl, Karl Hans 883
Strong, Eugene 719
Strong, Jack 478
Strong, Porter 899, 940
Strumwasser, Jack 937
Struss, Karl 1066
Sturgis, Edwin 973
Sturm, Hans (aka Hannes) 866, 910, 1012
Sullivan, C. Gardner 836, 1038, 1047, 1066
Sullivan, E. P. 619
Sullivan, Frank 1039
Sullivan, Jack 970
Summers, Walter 1063
Summerville, Slim 1073
Suratt, Valeska 810
Sutch, Herbert 940
Sutherland, Edward 897, 922
Svennberg, Tore 840
Swain, Mack 1071, 1081
Sweet, Blanche 534, 624
Swickard, Charles 633

Swickard, Josef (aka Joseph) 1003, 1014
Sylvaire, Renee 429
Sylvester, Charles 1019
Symonds, Henry 865
Szlatenyl, Violette 817
Szollosi, Rozsi 817
Szomogyl, Julius 900

Taggart, Ben L. 810
Taggart, Errol 1086, 1092
Tainguy, Lucien 42
Talbot, Rowland 749
Talmadge, Constance 550
Talmadge, Richard 1013
Tanaka, Kinuyo 968
Tapely, Rose 373
Tarlarina, Mary Cleo 412
Tate, Cullen 781
Taylor, Alma 536, 1053
Taylor, Estelle 1128; *page 228*
Taylor, J. O. 972
Taylor, Rex 1043
Taylor, Sam 1010
Taylor, William Desmond 922
Tchapelski, S. 742
Teare, Ethel 642, 680, 698
Tearle, Conway 956, 1039
Tearle, Godfrey 752
Teje, Tora 951
Tell, Olive 878, 1060
Temple, Fay 756
Temple, Olive 481
Tenbrooke, Harry 1124
Tennyson, Alfred 393
Terhune, Albert Payson 719
Terry, Alice 893, 1055
Terry, Ethel Grey 885, 991
Terry, Frank 1105
Terry, Paul 1031
Terry, Phyllis Neilsson 702
Terwilliger, George 632
Testa, Eugenio 881
Tetzlaff, Ted 1118
Texiere, Jacob 907
Thalberg, Irving 970
Theby, Rosemary 625, 829
Thesiger, Ernest 752
Thomas, Augustus 922

Thomas, Elton (pseudonym for Douglas Fairbanks) 1019
Thomas, L. 976
Thomas, Queenie 964, 990
Thompson, Frederick A. 800
Thompson, Hugh 828
Thompson, N. J. 719
Thorndike, Sybil 929
Thornton, Edith 679
Tichenor, Edna 1078, 1086
Tiedtke, Jakob 804, 891
Timayo, Mineta 713
Todd, Arthur L. 875
Todd, Frederick A. 898
Todd, Lola 1049
Todd, Thelma 1103, 1120, 1124; *page 227*
Tollaire, August 1082
Tolstoy, Alexei 996
Tolstoy, Leo 942
Toluboff, Alexander 1081
Tooker, William 938
Torf, Sylvia 1067
Torrence, David 943, 963, 1039
Torrence, Ernest 944, 970, 1127
Torzs, Jeno 817
Totman, Wellyn 1091
Toulot, Jean 954
Tourneur, Andree 893
Tourneur, Maurice 429, 494, 702, 995
Towney, Robin 552
Trautner, Hans 1094
Travers, Madelaine 885
Trebaal, Edouard 885
Tree, Sir Herbert 605
Trent, Jack 1073
Treville, Georges 420
Trevor, Norman 1093
Troutman, Ivy 663
Trunelle, Mabel 478, 701, 790
Tryoler, William 1042
Tryon, Glenn 1030
Tschechowa, Olga 901
Tschetwerikoff, Konstantin 1130
Tseretelly, Nikolai 996
Tucker, George Loane 739, 797
Tucker, Richard 1127
Tudor, F. C. S. 634
Tully, Richard Walton 989
Tupper, Edith S. 874

Tupper, Pearl 970
Turnbull, Margaret 825
Turner, Florence 1073
Turner, Otis 618
Turner, William H. 1121
Turzhansky, V. 609
Tuszinsky, Ladislaus 827, 912
Tuttle, Frank 980
Tweed, Frank 980
Tyler, Tom 1113

Urban-Kneidinger, Lola 854
Urban, Joseph 952
Uehara, Ken 968

Vajda, Ladislaus 1108
Vale, Louise 542
Valentin, Herman 1087
Valentino, Rudolph 893
Van, Beatrice 710
Van Buren, Mabel 556, 781, 814
Van Dyke, W. S. 870
Van Enger, Charles J. 1042
Van Horn, Andreas 660, 803
Van Meter, Harry 970
Van Neame, Elsie 829
Van Trees, James 922
Varesi, Vilda 800
Vassilieva, S. 597
Vater, Erwin 1056
Vaultier, George 1041
Vautier, Sydney 711
Vaverka, Anton 1042
Veidt, Conrad 831, 838, 844, 847, 857, 871, 883, 906, 1007, 1023, 1067, 1106, 1121; *pages 99, 102, 168, 197, 216, 218, 219*
Veiller, Bayard 848
Velez, Lupe 1128
Veltee, Claudius 431
Venohr, Albert 939
Ventigmilla, Baron Giovanni 1054
Venturini, Edward 934
Verne, Jules 769
Vernon, Charles 467
Vernon, Maurice 1080
Victor, Henry 749, 759
Viertel, Berthold 901
Vignola, Robert G. 952

Name Index

Vigus, Mary Spain 1069
Vincent, James 646
Visaroff, Michael 1120
Vitrotti, Giovanni 164
Volante, Guido 358, 412
Volbrecht, Karl 1015, 1087, 1130
Von Alten, Ferdinand 993, 1067
Von Belajeff, Olga 1023
Von Francois, Hardy 939, 1015
Von Gerlach, Arthur 959
Von Harbou, Thea 906, 927, 959, 988, 1015, 1056, 1087, 1130
Von Horn, Andreas 571
Von Munchofen, Helen 1056
Von Newlinsky, Michael 1108
Von Schlettow, Hans Adalbert 927, 1015
Von Seyffertitz, Gustav 781, 943, 1049, 1066, 1069, 1093; *page 195*
Von Sternberg, Joseph 1022
Von Twardowski, Hans Heinz 831, 864
Von Walther, Hertha 1087
Von Wangenheim, Gustav 939, 988, 993, 1130
Von Winterstein, Edward 921
Vorins, Henri 79
Vosburgh, Alfred D. 671
Voshell, John M. 1106

Wadsworth, William 439, 578, 696
Wagner, Blake 1004
Wagner, Erika 894
Wagner, Fritz Arno 901, 921, 939, 959, 993, 1087
Wagner, Richard 966
Waite, Malcolm 1082
Wales, Ethel 1038
Walker, H. M. 869
Wallace, Edgar 1029
Wallace, Morgan 940
Waller, Fred, Jr. 980
Wallock, Edwin 970
Walsh, George 986
Walsh, Raoul 1019, 1082
Walter, Hans 842
Walthall, Henry B. 534, 689, 991, 1078

Walton, Gladys 992, 1095
Ward, Fannie 814
Ward, Lucille 767
Ward, Marion 1106
Ward, Roscoe 1115
Warde, Ernest C. 547, 818, 863, 875
Ware, Frank 1103, 1120, 1124
Warm, Hermann 831, 921, 1067
Warner, H. B. 556, 884
Warren, A. E. 1045
Warren, Fred 1049
Warren, Giles R. 616
Warrenton, Gilbert 1072, 1106
Washburn, Bryant 690, 821
Watson, Adele 1096
Watson, Hildegarde 1100
Watson, James Sibley 1100
Watson, Roy 766, 1046
Wayne, Richard 991
Webb, Dick 930
Webb, George 786
Webb, Kenneth 880
Webber, George F. 974
Webber, Melville 1100
Weber, Lois 504
Webster, H. 450
Wedekind, Frank 1108
Wegener, Paul 522, 564, 754, 774, 792, 804, 866, 883, 891, 910, 1012, 1055, 1090, 1094; *pages 115, 117, 190*
Weigel, Helene 1056
Weijden, Tor 840
Weisse, Hanni 551, 571
Welch, William 769
Welcker, Gertrud 927, 959
Weldon, Jess 947
Wellesley, Charles 1036, 1045
Wells, H. G. 195, 489
Welsh, Scott 1071
Wendhausen, Fritz 988
Wenstrom, Harold 952
Wentzel 675
Werckmeister, Hans 852
Werndorff, O. F. 857
Werner-Kahle, Hugo 976
West, Charles H. 258
West, Dorothy 258
West, Fred 1079
West, R. H. 718

Name Index

West, Roland 991, 1038, 1048
West, Vera 1106
West, Walter 1110
Weyher, Ruth 993
Wharton, Bessie 744
Wharton, Leopold V. 552, 744
Wharton, Theodore W. 552, 744
Whelan, Tim 1010
White, Chrissie 536
White, Glen 780
White, Jack 946
White, Pearl 552, 824
Whitlock, Lloyd 1066
Whitney, Claire 755
Whitson, Frank 663
Whittaker, Charles E. 1061, 1106
Whytock, Grant 1055
Wiene, Robert 831, 864, 942, 1007
Wikman, Anders 842
Wilbur, Crane 1038
Wilcox, Robert B. 1089
Wilde, Oscar 504, 688, 749, 803
Wiley, Harrison 1118
Wilkinson, J. 971
Willard, John 1072
Willets, Gilson 661, 818
Williams, Earle 648
Williams, George B. 1042
Williams, Percy 1078
Williamson, Bob 1051
Williamson, Mrs. C. M. 662
Willis, Hubert 739, 904, 919, 923, 958
Willkom, Anne 1015, 1056
Wilson, Basil 1095
Wilson, Ben 815, 850, 1043
Wilson, Frank 722, 962, 965, 967, 977, 981, 982, 984, 985
Wilson, Henry 1055
Wilson, Lois 818
Wilson, Stacey Gaunt 977
Wilson, Tom 971, 1004, 1013
Wiman, Dwight 980
Windsor, Claire 1068
Wing, Ward 893
Wing, William E. 616

Wing, Mrs. Wong 1128
Winter-Blossom 1019
Winters, Laska 1124
Winther, Karen 951
Winton, Jane 1082
Witman, P. H. 1019
Woitscheff, Hilde 1056
Wolcott, Florence 646
Wolfe, Jane 814
Wolheim, Louis 861, 943, 972
Wolter, Hilde 816
Wong, Anna May 1019, 1073
Wood, Cyrus 1003
Woods, Frank 400
Woods, Lotta 1019
Woods, Walter 897, 941
Worne, Duke 850
Worsley, Wallace 885, 924, 970
Worthington, William 618, 821
Wright, Humbertson 962, 967, 977, 981, 982, 984, 985, 1001, 1002, 1005
Wright, Joseph 1045, 1106
Wright, Nanine 649
Wulze, Harry 726
Wunerlee, Frank 940
Wyckoff, Alvin 781
Wyler, William 970

Yokota, Tatsuyuki 1058
Yorke, Edith 1042
Young, Clara Kimball 702, 737
Young, James 702, 737, 895, 989, 1049
Young, Roland 943, 1127
Young, Waldemar 1039, 1045, 1078, 1086, 1092, 1115, 1128

Zanuck, Darryl F. 1079
Zecca, Ferdinand 35, 41, 135, 195
Zehn, Willy 873
Zellner, Arthur 913
Zhelyabuzhky, Yuri 996
Zucker, Frank 911